# SINSATIABLE

*Also by Shelia E. Lipsey*

Into Each Life

# SINSATIABLE

# SHELIA E. LIPSEY

*www.urbanchristianonline.net*

Urban Christian books are published by:

URBAN BOOKS
10 Brennan Place
Deer Park, NY 11729

ISBN-13: 978-1-893196-98-8
ISBN-10: 1-893196-98-4

First Printing August 2007
Printed in the United States of America

10  9  8  7  6  5  4  3  2  1

*This is a work of fiction. Any references or similarities to actual events, real people, living, or dead, or to real locales are intended to give the novel a sense of reality. Any similarity in other names, characters, places, and incidents is entirely coincidental.*

Submit Wholesale Orders to:
Kensington Publishing Corp.
C/O Penguin Group (USA) Inc.
Attention: Order Processing
405 Murray Hill Parkway
East Rutherford, NJ 07073-2316
Phone: 1-800-526-0275
Fax: 1-800-227-9604

# From the Author

*Sinsatiable (as defined by author)*—An insatiable craving for the worldly things in life which feel good, look good, taste good and bring momentary pleasure, yet in the end yield no lasting satisfaction.

Our lives are but for a fleeting moment, yet so many of us live on the verge of desperation—hoping and clinging to things, people and stuff. We become lost and caught up in what we think we can gain from this world. The pleasures of sin often take hold of many of us because of its innate ability to entice us in the areas where we are the weakest. Don't be mistaken my readers, sin *is* captivating. Sin *does* feel good. Sin *does* look good. Sin can dress well and it can go around raggedy. Sin *is* articulate. Sin takes on any form it so chooses in order to do what it chooses to do to you and to me. Sin is clever but it is only clever long enough for it to pull you into its deadly grasp. Sin, however, cannot maintain a form of goodliness or Godliness because it is made up of neither. It eventually has to rear its ugly, vile, deceitful head and reveal what it really is—death. Not physical death because we each must die, but eternal death. Do not be fooled into thinking, not even for one moment, that you can fight the many forms of sin, and win, under your own strength. If you think that, you have already been deceived and defeated by it. The only sure way to fight sin, to conquer sin, and to defeat sin, is to go to the One who has the power to destroy sin—that one true sovereign one is *God*. Without Him, we are nothing. In Him, we are more than conquerors. In Him all things are eternal.

## *Dedication*

In Memory of Gerald K. English
July 29, 1972–September 20, 2006

No More Pain

# Acknowledgments

God, I love you because you first loved me. Knowing this, I must acknowledge you first—not just list your *name* first, but I must acknowledge you first in every endeavor I undertake. I must acknowledge you first as long as I am living and breathing because you, God, are the One who shakes me every morning, who causes me to rise up. I acknowledge you for your majestic gifts, for every good and perfect gift does come from you, and so I thank you for that. For the talent to put my thoughts and emotions (the good, bad and the ugly) on paper, I thank you. For giving people the mindset to *want* to read what I have to say, Lord, I truly thank you. I acknowledge you for all that you have done, all that you do, and all that you will do. I give you praise, honor and glory, my Father, for believing in me to do what you have assigned me to do, even when I doubt myself.

Father, I pray that I be content and eternally grateful for whatever *you* choose to do with the books you place on my heart to write. If I touch one million people, Father let me remain humble. If I touch but one, Father let me say glory to your name. You have said that if one sheep goes astray, that the Good Shepherd will leave the ninety-nine and search for that one which is lost and bring it home. It is so amazing to know that the words that you have given me to write do touch the lives of as few as one and so many, I cannot fathom.

God has placed people along my path to help me with this dream I am living. My *mommy*, Cora Ann Bell, I must always acknowledge you. I will always be thankful for you for your love, for the way you raised me, for your faith, for your footsteps that have gone with me along every path I travel. Thank you for teaching me by example what it means to love and to be loved. To Carl Weber, the one who God used to breathe life into *Urban Books* and who through you, birthed *Urban Christian*, I must always extend my gratitude to you for your belief in my dreams. God is using you to help so many people and so, again, I pray that you will continue to have God's favor over your life and the life of your family. To my editor, Joylynn Jossel, thank you for your editorial assistance, and for your sweet spirit. Thank you, Audrey, for being a friend through the years, for reading my rough drafts, for supporting me and telling me the truth and not what I *wanted* to hear. You have been committed to helping me become successful by doing whatever I have asked you to do, and so I pray, Audrey, that you will always know that you are appreciated and loved by me. To my goddaughter, LaDetria K. Titus, thank you for loving me the way that you do, for helping to provide and take care of me. You are my blessing from God, and I love you. To my goddaughter, Tiffany Davis, thank you for looking out for me in so many ways, for driving me around, and for just being you. To Toya Garth, thank you for your printing assistance. You came to my aid, not only on this book, but with *Into Each Life* and I appreciate you and may God Bless you. Cheryl and Bolden, thank you for your constant friendship and love. To my sons, grandchildren, family, friends, and loved ones, thank you for everything you do to support me. To each and *every* person, those that I know and those I don't know, you are the glue that binds all of this together. You make it possible for me to keep doing what I do by your commitment to read and purchase my novels. Lastly, I pray that we all will see you more clearly, God, and love You more dearly.

# 1

"How much did you say? Girl, now that's some graduation gift! I wonder how much dough you'll get if you earn a Master's degree—a million?"

"Tameria, you're as crazy as they come. My grandparents put this money in a trust for me when I was sixteen years old and the only stipulation to receiving the money was that I had to earn my college degree," Aisha explained.

"I sure wish I had a set of grandparents who left me a little change," Tameria said.

"I just wish they were still alive to see me fulfill my dreams." Aisha Carlisle became teary-eyed at the thought of her grandparents' generosity. The only child in her household, Aisha was far from spoiled but she was also blessed beyond measure. With the money from her trust fund she planned on fulfilling her dreams of opening a dance studio. Memphis presented limited opportunities to perfect her gift of dancing. Most of the dance studios in the south catered to country line-dancing, ballet or tap. But she was into more than that. She wanted to incorporate her natural soulful rhythm into her dancing by choreographing her very own dance style. Her dream was to teach young girls how to be both refined and hip in their dancing all at the same time.

She was barely fourteen when she first saw a youth group from a visiting church perform a liturgical dance to the soulful tune, *Open Your Heart* by Yolanda Adams. Their grace and perfect rhythm left her breathless. It wasn't long after that she formed a dance group of her own. Now here she was, seven years later with an undergraduate degree in dance and ready to step out into her future. With God on her side, she knew she could do nothing but soar like an eagle because He had shown favor and blessings upon her life.

Aisha still shivered at the thought of how much God loved her. She was a little bushy head preteen when she came to accept Him as her personal Lord and Savior. Aisha was twelve years old when she first told her mom and dad that she wanted to be saved. They said that she should wait until she was a little older. But Aisha refused to wait until her parents thought the time was more appropriate. She had a strong desire to belong to God and no one and nothing was going to stop her. So on a beautiful Sunday morning in June 1994, she boldly walked to the front of the meager-sized sanctuary of Stone Chapel and accepted Jesus Christ as her personal Lord and Savior. Not once had she ever looked back with regret, even when she faced tragedy in her small, close-knit family.

Her first meeting with tragedy occurred two days after her sixteenth birthday when her maternal grandparents, whom Aisha lovingly called Oma and Opa, were killed in a car accident. Aisha recalled the events leading up to their untimely death. Her family and friends had celebrated by surprising her with a lavish sweet sixteen birthday bash. While she was busy opening her gifts, Oma and Opa told her to save their gift and open it last. She did as she was told and after all the other gifts had been *oohed* and *aahhed* over, she nervously unwrapped the pink ribbon from around the pink oblong box, expecting to find a trinket or necklace inside. Her guess was right. There was a white gold locket tucked neatly inside the soft salmon-colored tissue paper. The locket had her initials set in tiny diamonds on the back and the words Jeremiah 29:11 engraved on the front. Inside were pictures of her grandparents holding an infant Aisha on the day of her christening.

"Aisha, always remember that God's plan for you is to prosper. He wants you to have a bright future and an eternal hope." Oma beamed with love as she spoke to her granddaughter.

"Aisha, always put God first in your life and whenever life begins to get you down, and the trials and tribulations begin to come—and they will," Opa added, "cling to that passage of scripture in Jeremiah. It'll remind you of God's will for your life. You hear me, young lady?" Her grandfather spoke with such conviction and wisdom. She loved both of them so much.

"Come on, open the other part of your gift," her grandmother urged before Aisha could respond. Aisha pulled out the small envelope tucked neatly inside the box. When she opened it, her eyes grew as big as diamonds. "I can't believe this is for me."

"What is it, Aisha? Tell us what it is," several of her friends and family squealed.

"It's a bank account that's been set aside for me, but it doesn't say how much is in it." Aisha turned toward her grandparents. "How much, Oma? How much is it for, Opa?"

"We aren't disclosing that to you just yet, young lady," her grandfather smiled slyly. "But we've been putting a little aside for you ever since you were born. You won't know how much until you graduate from college. "

"Graduate from college?" But Maaaaa," she whined. "Look how long that'll be."

"Now Aisha, Oma and Opa know exactly what they're doing," her mother said with a look of irritation and impatience. Sandra Carlisle thought her daughter was much too whiny and spoiled. Of course, her husband and his parents were to blame and she had resented it. They seemed to forget that Benjamin Carlisle had another daughter up north in Michigan. Sandra loved Aisha, her only child, but another part of her felt as if she was in constant competition with Aisha for Benjamin's affection and his attention. It was Sandra's belief that Aisha managed to be the winner of both every single time. The resentment settled in her heart and whether she chose to admit it or not, Sandra had a difficult time hiding her feelings toward Aisha.

"Aisha, your mother's right," her dad added. "Your grandparents know just like I do, that if they give you a substantial amount of money now, you're just going to blow it all on clothes or junk. Your current allowance is enough to provide spending money for your binge-buying, so this is a great present for you. You can let it sit in a money market account and draw interest. That way, by the time you graduate from college, you would have accumulated a nice bit of interest on your principal. And besides, when you graduate from college you should be more mature and level-headed and in a better position to make decisions about how to use your money. Honey, you will have had more time to think about what you *really* want to do with it.

"Oh, okay," Aisha said with a half-way poked-out lip. She leaned over to hug her grandparents, and with more enthusiasm said, "Thank you, Oma. Thank you, Opa. I love you both so much." She planted an affectionate kiss on each of their cheeks.

After Aisha's sweet sixteen affair, Oma and Opa went to

spend a few weeks at a timeshare they'd purchased years ago in Miami. Having lived in Memphis all of their lives, they loved southern living. They enjoyed their retirement years and as often as they could they traveled wherever their hearts desired. It was in Miami that disaster struck while they were on their way to play bridge with some other retirees. Somehow Opa lost control of the vehicle he was driving and crashed into a tree. Both of them were pronounced dead at the scene of the terrible crash.

During this difficult time in her life, Aisha still tried to remain focused on God. She bravely spoke at her grandparents' funeral, sharing with everyone her deep love and devotion for them. She spoke like the wonderful young woman she was as she told of her grandparents' love and devotion for God and family. She also performed a touching and emotional dance while fighting back her tears of grief.

The grief at times was unbearable for Aisha because her grandparents had been such a vital part of her life and she missed them terribly. But she was determined to make Oma and Opa proud of her. Envisioning them in heaven, Aisha worked hard at her studies and with her dancing. By the time she was ready to enter college, she was at the top of her graduating class. She had also started a small liturgical dance ministry at church that she called *The Jeremiah Troupe*, in memory of Oma and Opa. Each time she thought of them, she twirled the locket they'd given her between her fingers, then brought it up to her lips and lightly kissed it. Somehow it made her feel like they were right by her side and that all was right in her world. The future was hers. All she needed to do was grab hold of it!

# 2

When Aisha graduated from college she not only had a degree in Fine Arts, but an unshakeable faith and trust in God, and a huge world that she was ready to conquer. The money her grandparents left her had grown substantially since placing it in a money market account. With her father's help, she researched property after property searching for the perfect location for a studio. Thanks to her father's savvy financial wisdom, she should have enough for a substantial down payment on a place. She was on her way to the life she had always dreamed about. A life filled with dancing.

Aisha set out to find the perfect place to open a dance studio. It couldn't be just any old place. It had to be centrally located and close to the public transportation line because the young girls she had identified to be her future students would be mostly from the inner city neighborhoods and transportation for those girls would be practically non-existent if she didn't choose the right area.

"Miss Carlisle, I believe you'll love this piece of property. It's ideal for what you're trying to accomplish." The leasing agent, Thaddeus, used his most convincing voice to sell Aisha on the 3,600 square foot space.

Aisha's excitement grew by the minute. She felt a mixture of exhaustion and exhilaration at the thought of her dream coming to fruition. *A. Carlisle Studio of Dance and Choreography.* What a nice ring the name had to her.

"Right this way, Miss Carlisle," leasing agent, Thaddeus Phelps said, as he pointed to the vacant building. "I believe you'll agree with me when I say this property simply exudes an upscale style and quality. As you can see, the decor of mahogany, marble and bronze sets it apart from the ordinary business space."

"I like it so far. This just might have potential."

"Ma'am, it's ideally located at the focal point of the city."

Aisha followed the realtor into the mammoth open space. This was it. She felt it. She had seen over two dozen properties in the past three weeks. This free-standing building was the first place that had sparked her interest. The agent continued to make his sales pitch.

"As you can see, there's a full service business center next to this property that's available for you to use as well."

"Will the business center be accessible at any time?" she asked.

"Yes, you'll have access to the property twenty four hours a day, seven days a week. There are full utility and janitorial services, free parking in the garage, and a reception and conference area."

"That's great. When was this building constructed?"

"It's only ten years old, Miss Carlisle, which is an added plus."

Aisha immediately fell in love with it.

"Let's walk over to the window," Thaddeus continued. "This view provides a relaxing atmosphere and helps to remove claustrophobic tendencies. The atrium and courtyard gardens are beautifully landscaped, as you can see. You'll have full access to the courtyards as well. So, what do you think so far?"

"I'd like to know what they're asking for it. I mean, I like what I have seen so far and it does seem like it could be the ideal place."

"For $2,600 a month you can lease this prestigious business address without the inconvenience of downtown traffic and parking." When he finally took a moment to rest from his spiel, Aisha was already sold.

"I love it. I absolutely love it!" She couldn't hold back her emotions much longer. She knew within her spirit that this was the place for her studio.

In Aisha's twenty-four years she had learned how to discern the will of God and what was coming from Satan and his schemes. It wasn't that she was self-righteous, but she was brought up in the church and in some form of Bible study since she was a toddler, so scriptures and the teachings of God were almost second nature to her. She couldn't imagine making any major decision without prayer and sometimes fasting. Now she was at another milestone— owning her own studio. She couldn't begin to thank God enough for all of His blessings.

"I really believe this is the place I'm supposed to have," she explained to Thaddeus. "It's everything I'm looking for and then some. This is what I'd like to do."

"What is that, Miss Carlisle?"

"By the way, call me Aisha. I'm going to sleep on it and then give you a call tomorrow. If the Holy Spirit is still pushing me in this direction, then you might have yourself a tenant. How does that sound?"

"No problem at all, Miss Carlisle . . . Aisha."

"Well, tomorrow it is." Aisha extended her long, slender hands to meet his.

"I'll look forward to hearing from you tomorrow. In the

meantime, if you have any questions or concerns, please just give me a call."

Aisha couldn't wait to tell her parents about the building. Instead of going home to her one-bedroom apartment, she headed to her parents home to share the exciting news. During her senior year of college she'd secured a job as a dance instructor for a small privately run dance academy. After graduating, she had continued working at the academy. The pay wasn't grand but it was enough for her to take care of herself. Along with her father's financial generosity toward her, she was making it okay. But she yearned for her own place in life. She didn't want to work for someone else. She didn't want to run to her father every time she needed some extra money. She wanted to live and walk in her own dream.

When she made it to her parents' Whitehaven home, she rang the doorbell over and over again, barely able to contain her happiness. Her father opened the door and a big welcoming smile appeared on his face.

"What is it?" he asked her when he saw how excited she looked. "You look like you just won the lottery or something," he teased.

"I feel like it," was Aisha's response as she walked with him inside the spacious house.

Sandra appeared at virtually the same time Aisha and her father entered the family room.

"Hello, Aisha," her mother said in an irritated voice. "I should have known that it was you ringing that doorbell like you're crazy or something."

Aisha ignored her mother's discontent and instead began sharing the news with them about the property she'd just seen.

"Mom, Dad. I think I've found the perfect place for my dance studio! You have to see it." Aisha couldn't contain her excitement. She paced the room, bursting with joy as she told them everything the realtor had told her about the property. "Mom, why don't you go with me tomorrow to take a look at it?"

"Aisha, I'd love to, but tomorrow's not a good time," Sandra replied.

"Dad," Aisha walked over to where her father was seated in his recliner. "Can you go with me?"

"Princess, I sure wish I could." Benjamin had started calling Aisha 'Princess' when she was a little girl. "But I have an important meeting to attend tomorrow. It's scheduled to last most of the day," he said apologetically. He hated to disappoint his daughter, especially when it was something that pertained to her dancing. Aisha centered everything around her love of dance and he supported her fully. He made another suggestion that he hoped would work out for her. "Your half-sister called earlier today. She's supposed to be here tomorrow. Maybe you could ask her to go with you."

"I don't know, Daddy. I'll think about it. But I'm sure Selena isn't coming all the way to Memphis to spend her time looking at vacant buildings with me. I'll try to call Tameria. Maybe she can go with me. If not, I'm a big girl. I can go by myself." Aisha turned and walked toward the kitchen before Benjamin could respond.

Benjamin sighed then picked up the sports section of the Commercial Appeal and began reading about the Grizzlies' losing streak.

Aisha opened the door to the stainless steel refrigerator. Grabbing a bottle of water, she turned, almost bumping into her mother. She didn't know that Sandra had followed her into the kitchen.

"Aisha, you shouldn't be so quick to throw a tantrum when you can't have your way."

"What? What on earth are you talking about, Mommie

Dearest?" Aisha said with sarcasm mixed with anger. Her mother could be such a nit picky person at times. It infuriated Aisha.

"I'm talking about the way you dismiss what your father says whenever it doesn't suit your fancy. I don't understand for the life of me why you can't reach out to Selena. She's your half sister, for Christ's sake." Sandra stood with her arms folded and a furrowed brow, obviously waiting on a response from Aisha.

Selena was the love child born to Benjamin Carlisle and his high school sweetheart, Yvette. The two of them rushed to get married when Yvette had discovered that she was pregnant. When Selena was three and a half years old, Benjamin met Sandra at a Minority Marketplace Expo. She was perusing the aisles with a couple of co-workers when she stopped at Benjamin's company's booth. She eyed the array of African American history books and literature he had set up before her eyes lingered on the tall, handsome, dark haired man with hypnotizing eyes standing behind the booth. Though it was completely out of character for Sandra, she openly flirted with him. Needless to say, Benjamin reveled in the much needed attention she showered on him. He certainly wasn't getting any attention at home.

Sandra purchased *The Souls of Black Folk* and along with the money for the book, she gave him her business card. Ignoring the gold wedding band on his ring finger, Sandra consciously set out to make him hers. And within two years, she'd gotten what she wanted—Benjamin. Mesmerized by Sandra's beguiling charm, Benjamin filed for divorce from Yvette.

Rejected, hurt and destroyed, Yvette took Selena and moved from Memphis to Detroit to be close to her family and far away from Benjamin. While growing up, Yvette allowed Selena to visit Benjamin periodically during the summer, but only when it was convenient for her.

Selena and Benjamin had an on-again off-again father-daughter relationship. Growing up being poisoned by her mother's constant belittling of Benjamin, it wasn't until Selena was a young adult that she began to see that most of what her mother had told her about her father had been untrue. However, the distance between them made it difficult for them to ever establish a close bond like he had with Aisha.

It was entirely different when Aisha was born. The day Sandra discovered she was pregnant with Aisha, Benjamin ran through the house yelling and screaming for joy. Benjamin pampered and petted Sandra's tummy; doing everything he could to make sure she had an easy pregnancy. He cried so hard when seven pound eight ounces Aisha Carlisle entered the world, the nurses and doctor thought they were going to have to give him a sedative. Benjamin cut her umbilical cord and since then the cord of love he had for Aisha was never broken.

Sandra soon took second place to her husband's love and attention. It was like Benjamin was trying to make up for all the years he'd missed out on with Selena. Over time, jealousy slowly crept up on Sandra. Benjamin still handled everything and he tried to be a good husband, but it was no secret that Aisha was his treasure, his *princess* as he'd come to call her. As a result, Sandra began pouring herself into her work as a social worker at the Department of Human Services. If she didn't make it home from work until late, she wasn't missed. If she stayed out all day on Saturday, Benjamin didn't mind. As long as Aisha was around he was happy and content. There was nothing too good for his little princess.

As for Aisha and Selena's relationship, whenever the sisters saw each other, their times together were pleasant enough though uneventful. Aisha often thought about how it would have been if she'd grown up with her older sister in the same household. Part of her longed for such a relationship but the other part of her didn't want anything or anyone to interfere with her and her father's relationship. There was only room for one princess in her father's life and Aisha was determined to remain that princess.

Aisha had to admit that she was disappointed when her father told her he couldn't go with her to see the building. As for Sandra, Aisha was used to her mother's *anything to keep me from spending time with my daughter* excuses.

"How long is Selena going to be here?" Aisha asked her mother.

"She's coming to visit some of her cousins on her mother's side. If I'm not mistaken, I believe your father said she's going to be here for at least four or five days. Maybe the two of you can catch up on what's going on in each of your lives, since you never really talk to each other."

"Mom, you know Selena and I have never been close. She was raised in Michigan and we've lived in Memphis all of our lives. Selena and I are both adults now, plus she's so much older than I am."

"Honey, she's still your father's child, which means she's your sister and the two of you ought to be closer than you are."

"It's not my fault that we live hundreds of miles apart, Mom." Aisha felt herself becoming defensive again. Her mother always managed to somehow twist things around when she wanted to avoid talking about something. This time she managed to cleverly switch the conversation from talking about Aisha's dance studio to the distant relationship she had with Selena.

"Mom, please. I was really hoping you could come and see the building."

"I have a full work load this week, Aisha." Sandra became silent and looked like she was in deep thought. "I tell you what, maybe I can squeeze in a half an hour or so sometime around the lunch hour. But I'm telling you, I can't spend a lot of time from the office tomorrow. I have a huge case file of clients to finish certifying and then I have to have all of them entered into the computer system by the end of the week."

"Okay, lunch time would be great," Aisha said excitedly. "I had already planned to check out some dance equipment and office furniture first thing in the morning anyway, so I can meet you after that. Oh, Mom, I can't believe this is happening. I'm going to have my own dance studio with my very own students."

By this time, her father had come into the kitchen. "So, you feeling better now?" he asked Aisha, after hearing Sandra say she would meet up with her after all.

"Yes, Daddy. And, Daddy, I'm sorry if I came off like a spoiled brat. Forgive me?" she asked, walking over to the kitchen bay window where he stood, and planting a kiss on his cheek.

Benjamin smiled. Aisha could melt his heart like butter on a stove. "There's nothing to forgive. You're my princess. I just want you to be happy."

Aisha quickly jerked around, slamming the palm of her hand against her forehead. "Oh, there is something else I have to do."

"Slow down, child. What do you have to do?" he asked.

I have to follow-up with some of the people who left messages about the newspaper ad I ran," Aisha said nervously.

"What newspaper ad?" her father asked.

"I ran an ad about dance lessons for teenage girls. So far the response has been great. I've talked to several parents about their kids. But I missed some calls too, so I need to start calling them back and see what kind of interest they really have in dance. Once I secure my building, I'm going to host an open house for potential students, family, friends and everybody!"

"Sounds like you have everything worked out, Princess," her daddy said smiling at his princess. "I'm proud of you." He walked over to her and kissed her on the forehead. "I think I'm going to leave you and your mother to yourselves. I'm going to go in my office for a couple of hours. I have some paperwork to review for my meeting tomorrow."

Benjamin adored Aisha and there was nothing he wouldn't do for her. Unlike Selena, he had seen Aisha grow up from a little girl to a beautiful young woman. He was aware that Sandra had her moments of jealousy, but Aisha was his little girl.

The pride and joy of his life, he didn't want Aisha to grow up questioning his love for her like Selena had done. However, he didn't blame Selena, he blamed himself. As her father, he should have made more of an effort to see her and communicate with her, even though her crazy momma did everything she could to make it impossible for him to have a relationship with her. Yvette had no problem cashing his child support checks every month, but whenever he tried to see Selena, it had to be on her terms and her terms alone. Those terms turned out to be a week every now and then in the summer. He and Selena had a decent relationship now that she was an adult because she finally understood that her father wasn't entirely to blame for their fragile relationship. But Selena still harbored her share of envy at the exceptionally close relationship he had with Aisha. Still, their relationship was strained to say the least. Selena's understanding of the dice life had thrown her way was one thing, but could understanding keep her from truly begrudging her sister's fairy tale life? That was yet to be seen.

When she saw it the next day, Sandra barely was able to contain her amazement over the proposed property for Aisha's studio. It was everything Aisha had described and more.

Later that evening, Aisha came over to her parents' home and went over the details of the property with her father. They discussed the proposed terms of the lease and determined that the money Aisha's grandparents left her would be enough for Aisha to invest in her dream including purchasing and renting the equipment required. Her father talked to her about the importance of managing her money carefully so she would be able to pay the monthly note on the two-year lease agreement.

The following morning, along with her father, Aisha went to the family lawyer to make sure everything was on the up and up concerning the lease. After assuring them that it was, Aisha contacted the leasing agent and told him that she wanted to lease the building.

It didn't take long for Aisha to open the doors of her very own dance studio. With the help of Tameria and church friends, Aisha turned the vacant space into a first class studio. Glassless mirrors lined the walls. Gym mats, dance barres, and portable dance equipment filled each of the rooms that Aisha had designated for specific dancing lessons and age groups.

# 3

Aisha and Tameria had been best friends since kinder-garten and nothing had changed over the years. In kindergarten, when they laid down side by side to take an afternoon nap, they often whispered and giggled until they both fell asleep. They had simply been inseparable ever since. They practically spent their entire childhood at each other's homes—eating meals, having sleepovers and even helping to clean each others' bedrooms. The two of them accepted Christ almost at the same time and like Aisha, Tameria was also baptized at Stone Chapel. Since then, Aisha had taken her Christian upbringing seriously by being a hard-working, faithful church girl.

Shortly thereafter, the pastor retired from Stone Chapel and her parents decided it was time to make a change. They moved their membership to a church north of Whitehaven called Faithside Temple. Aisha followed but still main-tained her commitment to serving in her new church home and keeping in contact with friends she'd made at Stone Chapel.

Aisha's new studio had seen its share of success. Some of

the girls who attended Stone Chapel and Faithside Temple were now her formal students. At times it was hard for her to grasp the fact that she actually owned her own studio. Sometimes she'd walk through the studio's beveled double glass doors and actually pinch herself to make sure she wasn't dreaming.

"Aisha, I can't believe how much the studio has grown in just two years' time. Girl, it's like you've been doing this all of your life. How many children do you have enrolled in your classes now?" Tameria's voice rang with enthusiasm and vigor. She often found herself amazed at the favor of God radiating in her best friend's life.

"Between the three classes—Lyrical, Hip Hop and Dance Team—I have a total of seventy-seven students plus an ever expanding waiting list," Aisha answered. "The studio is growing so fast that I'm going to have to hire another instructor. I can't do it all by myself any longer. Of course, that's a good thing, so don't think for one minute that I'm complaining."

"I don't see how you do it."

"Tameria, I wish you loved dancing as much as I do. We'd make a good team."

"I'm sorry to say, but you know dance just isn't my thing. My passion is in the health-related field. That's my calling. Hey, just think, once I enter into my Residency, I can offer medical assistance to some of your students. God knows you work them hard enough—with all of that bending, twisting, stretching, shaking and jumping, they're going to need a good physician from time to time." The two of them laughed and gave each other a high five.

"You're right about that, girl. But you know for yourself that perfection only comes from commitment, dedication and practice, practice and more practice. These girls know that I will not accept mediocrity. They will need to either give it their all or shut it down. It's all or nothing. Even my younger students have memorized my favorite phrase. I will dance, I will dance, I will dance unto the Lord."

"Yeah, I know, but right now can you dance on out of here this evening? It's after six o'clock and we're supposed to be going to that play tonight, remember? And it starts at exactly eight o'clock," Tameria reminded her.

"Come on, help me straighten up around here and then we can leave. You know, I have no idea what I'm going to wear.

"Aisha, we've had plans for almost a month to attend this premiere, and you mean to tell me that you haven't decided what you're going to wear? I should have known to check up on you more closely."

"Don't worry. I'll find something in that closet of mine."

It had been a couple of years since the two of them had been to the legendary Orpheum Theatre on Main Street. They had forgotten about the grandeur and elegance it seemed to exude from just walking inside the massive doors.

The teal sleeveless evening dress Aisha had settled on was perfect for the event. The form-fitting dress accentuated her curvaceous body. Her stomach was flat as a pancake and her lean, shapely legs were undoubtedly the legs of a dancer as they made the teal Stuart Weitzman pumps she wore stand out with each sure and certain step she made. She had splurged on the shoes even though she knew they were way out of her price range. She walked like a graceful dancer. She didn't notice the eyes of several gentlemen following her every move. Her auburn colored natural twists hung to her shoulders. She was glad she had finally let go of the permed look. She couldn't imagine relaxing her hair ever again.

"Ladies, please allow me to show you to your seats," the well-groomed usher said, extending his white gloved hand.

"Thank you," was Aisha's response.

She and Tameria took their lower level seats and sat back to enjoy the play. At the end of the production, when the little girl in the play was taken from her parents, Aisha found herself crying. Even though it was just a play, she couldn't help but feel the emotions of losing someone. She thought about the tragic death of her grandparents.

"Isn't this touching?" Tameria whispered, reaching inside her small beaded purse to pull out a Kleenex. "This play is *soooo* good. Look at the two of us crying like babies." They both let out a soft snicker, being careful not to disturb anyone with their chatter.

"Girl, you know we have to do better. I didn't go through all of that trouble putting on make-up just to have it smeared all over my face. We look like raccoons," Tameria said as they prepared to exit the theatre.

"I know that's right. But I just couldn't help it. It was so moving and so surreal. Now what are we going to do to lift our spirits after this tear jerker?" Aisha asked.

"How about having a drink with me?" The gentleman standing next to them spoke. Aisha turned swiftly in his direction.

"Excuse me?" Aisha said, not hesitating to show her annoyance at the gentleman for listening in on their conversation.

"I didn't mean to eavesdrop," he said. "But I couldn't help but overhear you. I saw the two of you during the intermission but I couldn't get through the crowd to say anything. Let me introduce myself. I'm Chandler, Chandler Larson. And may I ask your names?" he said, extending his hand and focusing his baby browns on Aisha.

Totally ignoring his outstretched hand, Aisha retorted, "No, I don't think so. I'm not in the habit of just giving my name out to strange men." Her voice reflected her anger and caution. She had no idea where this man had come from. *What does he mean, he couldn't get to us during intermis-*

*sion? How long has this fool been watching us?* She felt quite uncomfortable. Grabbing hold of Tameria's elbow, she said, "Excuse us. Come on, Tameria. Let's get out of here."

Tameria followed her best friend with a tad bit of reservation. This Chandler Larson was quite a looker. His black tuxedoed suit clung to his tall frame flawlessly. His coal black dreads rested neatly against his scalp and tapered off at the nape of his neck. His eyebrows were thick and when he spoke they seemed to carry on a conversation of their own. Every word he spoke revealed glistening white teeth which had to have been bleached. His muscular physique could easily make a girl feel secure and protected.

"Tameria, come on." Aisha moved her hand to Tameria's wrist pulling her toward the door. "Let's get out of here before another crazed maniac walks up. I can't believe the nerve of that guy."

"Aisha, get over it. He was only flirting with you. Stop getting so uptight. Just because a man approaches you like that doesn't mean he's some serial killer or rapist. That was just his pick up line to get a conversation going with us."

"Well, he obviously needs to get a new one because that one surely won't work with me. You might fall for some jacked up line like that, but as for me, I think he must be nuts. You know good and well that you just don't walk up to somebody that you don't know and eavesdrop on their conversation."

"Aisha, ease up. Come on, before you go berserk."

"Now you're talking," was Aisha's response.

The two ladies chatted about the play on their way to the secured parking garage. After paying the $10 parking fee and exiting the garage, Tameria steered her champagne colored Mazda onto MLK Boulevard.

"Aisha you need to ease up some."

"What are you talking about now?" Aisha looked over at Tameria with a confused look.

"I'm talking about what just happened back there. What I'm saying is, don't be on the defensive so much. You can't possibly expect to find a potential mate if you keep brushing off every man that tries to get next to you."

"For one thing, you know me, right?"

"Uh huh."

"Then you ought to know that I am not out searching for a mate. I'm leaving that all up to God. He's going to handle that. "

"How do you know that God didn't send what's his name? Chandler. And look what you did. You all but told the poor guy to get out of your face. You're a trip." Tameria smiled pulling up into the crowded parking lot of Logan's Steakhouse.

"Enough of that conversation, Tameria. I see we're eating steak tonight. I'm glad. I've only eaten a blueberry muffin today and I'm absolutely famished."

They went into the restaurant and within seconds were escorted to a booth. It didn't take long for the two of them to decide on what they were having. Tameria enjoyed the thickly sliced T-bone, prepared medium well with a Caesar salad and steamed vegetables. Aisha ordered a tender sirloin tip, well done with a green salad and a loaded baked potato. They laughed and talked, enjoying each other's company like they always did.

"Tell me, how's it going with your new beau?" Aisha asked.

"Chase is quite a guy," Tameria answered. "I really like him. He's attentive, he loves the outdoors like I do and he adores his mother. That's a huge plus right there. I've heard that if a man treats his momma right, then he surely will treat his lady with some real respect and admiration. And the fact that we're both in the medical field is great because he understands that my schedule is hectic and our time together is quite limited. He's already doing his Residency in Neurosurgery. To tell you the truth, I can't find a single thing wrong with the man."

"A neurosurgeon? Wow, that's fantastic. You never told me that. But uh, what about his beliefs, Tameria? Is he a Christian? You know you shouldn't date someone who doesn't share the same Christian beliefs as you."

"Didn't I tell you that I can't find anything wrong with the man? He's a Christian and has been since he was thirteen years old. He's active in his church and works with the youth ministry when he isn't on call at the hospital. I'm telling you, girl, God has his hand in this relationship."

"Well, I'm happy for you. That one time I met him, even though it wasn't for long, he appeared to be a nice guy. He was all over you. Quite affectionate, you know."

"Yeah, he's like that. I have to admit that I'm crazy about him. I think I'm actually falling in love with him."

" Really? Oh, Tameria, that's good. Do you think he feels the same about you?"

"Yep, he even told me as much the other night."

"He told you that he loved you and you didn't tell me?"

"I've been busy, Aisha. You know how medical school is and you know how busy you always are. By the time we make it home, it's too late to talk on the phone and we're both wiped out."

"You're right about that. Our schedules are hectic as all get out. This is the first time we've had a chance to chill out and talk in quite a while. Just be prayerful and take it slow. And please don't give up the booty. Make him wait, girl."

Tameria stopped eating. A look of guilt spread across her face.

Aisha knew her friend too well. She was holding something back. She hoped it wasn't what she was thinking. Surely Tameria hadn't given up her virginity to Chase. She didn't care how great he was. She wanted Tameria to honor the commitment they first made, not only to each other, but to God, to remain pure until their wedding day.

"Tameria, please tell me you haven't? Please," Aisha pleaded

"No, I haven't done anything. But things are really getting hot and heavy. I've never felt like this before. Even Kevin Dixon didn't arouse the kind of feelings in me that I have when I'm with Chase. And you know how crazy I was about him in high school."

Aisha remembered all too well. Kevin Dixon had been Tameria's first and only boyfriend in high school. The three of them attended Christ the King Academy. Kevin was the star quarterback of the varsity football team and he was crazy about Tameria Matthews—the prettiest girl on the varsity cheerleading squad. During their junior year of high school, they were inseparable. Tameria believed he was going to be the man she would marry one day until his daddy's job transferred him up North. Tameria was devastated. She barely ate for almost two weeks and lost about ten pounds.

In the beginning, Tameria and Kevin emailed each other every day and talked on the phone just about every weekend, but after a couple of months the phone calls and emails tapered off. By the end of their senior year, the couple hadn't spoken to each other in almost three months. In the end, the distance proved to be too much for the young high school sweethearts to sustain a relationship. Since that time, Tameria hadn't been seriously involved with anyone, until she met Chase at University of Tennessee Medical School. They hit if off like they had known each other all their lives.

Aisha was delighted to see Tameria happy once again. And Chase did seem like quite a catch. He had that special charisma that drew people to him like a magnet. Yet Aisha was still cautious and she wanted her friend to be even more cautious. She didn't want to see Tameria's heart broken.

"Tameria, you have to be careful. I told you not to put yourself in a position where you would be tempted. What ever happened to hanging out with other friends instead of just the two of you being alone? You don't need to be alone with him."

"I know and you're right. But it's hard."

Aisha didn't let up. "Everything will go much better for you in a group setting. Any time you find yourself alone with Chase, you know your hormones and *his* are going to start raging. Just be more careful. If he really is the one, remember that everything will work out. He'll respect the fact that you are celibate and a virgin, and he won't try to push you to do anything rash."

"I know that, Aisha. And like I said, you're right. Our last few dates have been just the two of us in his apartment. And I have to put a stop to it. I don't plan on giving it up until I'm standing before a minister and saying those two little words, *I do*."

"I know that's right," Aisha grinned. "Now that's what I'm talking about. She took a bite of her steak. "Girl, this is the best sirloin I've tasted in a long time. How is your t-bone?"

"Great, but the food here is always good. Now, I want you to admit something."

"Admit what?"

"That the man at the theater tonight was definitely fine," Tameria laughed. "Come on, admit it."

"Girl, when I turned around and looked up at him, I could feel my face turning ten shades of red," Aisha laughed. "He was so good looking I could barely stand to look at him."

"I knew it," Tameria squealed. "Boy, am I glad to hear that."

"Glad about what?"

"Glad that you still got some feelings inside of you, some yearnings for a man. You stay too uptight."

"You're so silly. You know dancing is what matters to me. It's the only relationship I have time for right now, and of course, putting my all into being the woman God wants me to be."

"Aisha, all I'm saying is, just give somebody a chance. At least go on a date from time to time."

"I do. Remember when I went to dinner and a gospel concert with Gaston from church?"

"That was almost six months ago."

"Naw, it wasn't that long ago," Aisha paused. "Was it?"

Tameria eyed Aisha, raising one eyebrow and then nodding her head.

"I can't help it, Tameria. I just can't see myself allowing a man to get too close to me. I believe when that time comes along, God will awaken those special feelings inside of me and that's when I'll know it's time. But He hasn't done that yet, which is absolutely fine with me."

"Then I'm going to start praying a little bit harder for you. You haven't had a real boyfriend—not ever. You're waaay overdue for one. We're both twenty-four years old. And you, my dear, have never even been kissed."

"Yes I have!" Aisha laughed loudly. "I can't believe you said that."

"When then? Tell me. And I'm not talking about the time Gaston kissed you on your hand either." Both ladies laughed so loud that heads turned in their direction.

The ladies finished their dinner and then went to Tameria's apartment. Like they did when they were teenagers, they undressed down to their undies and put on flannel pajama pants and white t-shirts.

"Come on. Let's say our prayers before we start watching TV. Remember how we used to do that just in case we fell asleep while watching the TV?" Aisha reminded Tameria.

"We did do that when we were little, didn't we? I had forgotten all about that," Tameria said while chuckling as she knelt down beside the bed.

Aisha followed suit. They both clasped their hands together and closed their eyes. After they each finished praying their silent prayers, they curled up in Tameria's queen size bed with a bowl of buttered popcorn. They talked while flipping the remote between BET, MTV and Discovery Health. Aisha soon nodded off. After a while, Tameria fell asleep too.

Tameria's light snore woke Aisha and she got up to go into the other bedroom.

"I'm out of here," she mumbled to Tameria as she exited the room.

"Um, huh," Tameria sleepily responded while she turned on her side and pulled the quilt over her head, returning to her dream-filled sleep.

# 4

Aisha's voice was stern, but gentle, as she instructed the students on their routine. "Girls, how many times do I have to tell you? We have to get this routine right. We have a recital in three and a half weeks and most of you are still making the same mistakes. Now let's start again. One . . . two . . . three . . . turn.    One . . . two . . . three . . . bend. . . . One . . . two, three . . . left. . . . One . . . two, three . . . right. Great. Now, let's do it again. This time we're going to dance to the music. Remember, count in your mind. Don't look at the person next to you. Concentrate, relax and allow the steps to flow naturally. Remember, you're angels, graceful, light on your feet. Now let's take it from the top."

"Aisha, you have a call on line two," the receptionist's pleasant voice rang over the intercom.

"Keep it up, girls. I'll be right back." She turned and walked hurriedly to her office to answer the call. "Hello, this is Aisha."

"Aisha. Good afternoon. Thaddeus here," he said through the phone receiver.

"Oh, hi, Thaddeus. What's up?"

"I'm calling about the lease on your building. As you know, it expires in three months.

"Yes, I'm aware of that. But like I told you last month, I am planning on renewing before the lease expires. I can't find another location as perfect as this one, and I'm totally pleased with it."

"That's great to hear, Miss Carlisle."

"Miss Carlisle?" Aisha began to feel somewhat uneasy. "Where's the formality coming from, Mr. Thaddeus Phelps," she mocked.

The other end of the receiver was silent.

"Thaddeus, is something wrong?" she asked. "You're sounding different. Tell me. What is it?"

"Well, I have some good news and some bad news."

"Just tell me."

"I'll start with the good news first. The good news is that the owner believes your dance studio is a great outlet for the young girls you're teaching. You've been a great tenant. The owner of this building couldn't ask for anyone better."

"Okay, Thaddeus, what's going on? You're scaring me."

"Look, the bottom line is that the owner has decided to sell. He's run into some financial hardships and has to liquidate several of his properties. This property happens to be one of them."

"What? Are you telling me that he's selling this property? But he can't do that, Thaddeus. I've put too much into this building. There's no way I can find a place like this with the space, the perks and all at a price I can afford. Doesn't he have some other property he can sell?"

"I'm sorry, Aisha. He's made up his mind. He's going to get rid of it. The good news is that we're giving you a heads up on this so if you want to, you can purchase the building. All you need is a down payment of $35,000."

"$35,000," Aisha screamed into the receiver. "Are you

out of your mind? I don't have that kind of money. I've already invested every bit of my inheritance into leasing and remodeling this studio, Thaddeus. You, of all people, know that. Over half of my students are inner city youths, which means they're paying according to their income levels. I barely have enough to cover the rent every month, now you expect me to come up with $35,000?"

Aisha couldn't believe what she was hearing. All she could see was her dream going down the drain. Maybe she could relocate. Maybe she could find somewhere else to make a home for her studio. But with what? She had no funds and she was already using her small savings account to pay the rent on her apartment and her car note. What could she do?

"Look, Thaddeus, just give me six months or so and maybe I can find a way to come up with the money. Or maybe, with a little prayer and fasting I can get the owner to change his mind about selling this building."

"I can't give you six months. The most you have is ninety days. By then, your lease will be up. After that, if you don't have the money, you've got to move. As you know, this is a prime location. There are plenty of people who would pay top dollar for this building."

Thaddeus hated to be the bearer of such bad news. Aisha was such a wonderful girl but there was nothing he could do. "Look, maybe I can help you find another place," Thaddeus suggested. "I mean, surely there has to be another ideal location. This isn't the only property that makes a good studio."

So that Angie, her receptionist, couldn't hear any more than she had probably already over heard, Aisha walked over to the door of her office and slammed it shut. Then she yelled uncontrollably into the phone again. "What is it that you don't understand, Thaddeus? There *is* no other perfect place. This is it. I won't move. I can't," she began to cry and yell. "It would be the end of the road for many of my girls. I've put too much time and effort into this building."

"I'm sorry, Aisha. But if it makes you feel any better, I do understand. Really I do. But on the other hand, I have a job to do and unfortunately, it's out of my control. I'll be in touch."

Without saying goodbye, Aisha slammed the cordless phone down on its base, knocking it over on the floor. A feeling of hopelessness began to consume her. "Lord, what can I do? I can't give up this place. I just can't," she prayed out loud. "You know that my credit isn't the best since opening the studio. I've maxed out all of my credit cards to buy equipment and operating supplies. I'm up to my head in debt already trying to keep this place going. The girls depend on the studio. It's a refuge, a safe haven for many of them, Lord. You know that. Please, don't allow this to happen," she pleaded out loud. "I can't afford to start over somewhere else. I need you to intervene in this situation, and I need you to do it in a hurry," she pleaded to God.

Tameria couldn't believe it when Aisha called her and told her she needed to see her right away. Tameria agreed to meet her for a few minutes at the hospital.

When Aisha pulled up at the hospital entrance, she called Tameria on her cell phone to let her know that she was downstairs. Tameria told one of the nurses that she would be back in fifteen minutes, and then took the ten flight of stairs until she arrived in the lobby. She saw Aisha pacing back and forth near the entrance.

"Hey, girl, what's wrong?" Tameria asked as she walked up and touched Aisha on her shoulder. Aisha was visibly upset.

"Where did you park?" Tameria asked her.

"Over there," Aisha responded, pointing to the nearby parking area.

"Let's go sit in your car for a few minutes and you can tell me what's going on."

While sitting inside of Aisha's midnight blue Acura, Aisha told Tameria all about her conversation with Thaddeus earlier.

"What are you going to do, Aisha? That's money we can only dream about having. I wish I could do something to help you. Shoot, I only have about $1,500 that I can loan you. You already know that I'm up to my neck in student loans just to stay in med school."

"Thanks, Tameria. But I can't accept your money anyway. You're trying to make it just like me. God will make a way. He has to."

"Have you talked to your parents?" Tameria asked with a frown etched across her forehead.

"No, I didn't ask Mom and Dad. You know the both of them just recently retired, so they're still getting used to living off their pensions. I can't do that to them. And even if they did have it to loan to me, I have no idea when or if I could even pay it back. I know it wouldn't be any time soon. The studio is barely turning a profit." Aisha looked shaken.

"You should move, Aisha. Maybe see about renting a space at church or a gym or something," Tameria said, throwing both hands up in the air.

"What is it that you people don't seem to understand?" she vented at Tameria. "I can't do that," she screamed again. "I have no money. No m-o-n-e-y. You of, all people should understand where I'm coming from. That building is mine, Tameria. God gave it to me. And I won't move. I refuse to move."

Tameria had never seen Aisha behave like this. It was almost frightening. "Okay, look if you can't afford to move then what are you going to do? I mean I would think trying to temporarily relocate to a church or a gym would be better than possibly losing the studio altogether," Tameria said, almost crouching in submission as she spoke.

Giving her a somewhat evil stare, Aisha said between tears and anger, "I have an appointment at the bank tomorrow morning. I'm going to see if I can possibly get a small business loan again. Something will work out. It just has too."

Aisha tried hard to make herself believe the words she was saying to Tameria. She couldn't fathom the idea of giving up the studio. It was her life. Surely God wouldn't allow her to lose it.

# 5

Early the next morning, Aisha got up, bathed and dressed. After choosing a conservative navy blue two piece suit with a white high collared cotton shirt, Aisha dabbed on a small bit of makeup and off she went to convince the bank that she had to have a loan. On the way she prayed again while in the car quoting scriptures, "Believe and ye shall receive, you have not because you ask not . . ." When she arrived at the bank, she parked and before getting out, she asked God to let the loan officer be sensitive to her request.

A half hour later, after explaining to the loan officer her dilemma, Aisha was still in the outer waiting area. The loan officer told her she would call her when she completed reviewing her request. After an additional fifteen minutes of waiting, Aisha heard her name being called.

"Come in and have a seat again, Miss Carlisle," the woman instructed.

"Thank you," Aisha replied and sat down in the brown leather chair in front of the loan officer's desk.

"Well, I've reviewed your loan history with us," the female loan officer spoke in a cold detached voice. "Though your payment history has been fair, I have noticed that there have been a few times you've been more than ten days late."

"Yes, that's correct," Aisha replied. "But it's just like you said, only a few times. Most of my students are from the inner city and pay on a sliding income scale. Many are on government assistance which means at times, I have to wait until I secure their payments and I might run a few days late in paying you. But I always call and let you know and I've never missed a payment," Aisha said almost pleadingly. "I really need this loan. If I don't get it, I can lose my studio altogether and I just can't let that happen."

The loan officer paused, not once looking at Aisha. She continued to peruse the file before her, shaking her head from side to side a few times.

Aisha's hands were sweating. She prayed underneath her breath. "Please help me Lord."

Finally, after what seemed like an eternity, the woman looked up. "To be truthful, Miss Carlisle, I don't see much that we can do to help you. With what you already owe us, and the $35,000 you're asking for, I just don't see how you could possibly repay them both."

"Ma'am, please. I need this loan. There has to be something you can do." Aisha pleaded.

"Let me go over some figures here again for just a minute." The woman entered number after number into her desktop computer. When she finished this time she looked up at Aisha and said, "Miss Carlisle."

"Yes," Aisha answered with anticipation. She felt like a breakthrough had just occurred.

"We might be able to pay off your existing loan and refinance it as one new loan. If we do that, the most we could loan you will be $14,500. And, of course, your payment will increase substantially, by about thirty-five percent."

Aisha's face turned sour upon hearing the amount. What

was she going to do? She knew one thing was for sure, she couldn't turn this down. She would just have to accept it and then figure out some other way to get the remainder of the money. But how?

"I'll accept that," Aisha answered.

"Okay, but let me remind you again, Miss Carlisle, that your monthly payments will increase considerably. Right now your debt ratio is hovering on the edge. You can't afford to get another loan anytime soon and you won't be able to get anything from us until you have at least paid this loan down by more than half of your recomputed balance."

"I understand, and thank you. Just write up the papers. God and I will have to deal with the rest. Thank you," she repeated.

After spending over two and a half hours at the bank, Aisha left with a sigh of relief. Walking out of the bank, she looked up toward the sky and said, "Thank you. I knew you wouldn't let me down." As for the remaining funds, she would have to get creative in a heart beat to find a way to come up with the additional $20,500. She had a little less than three months to get the money to Thaddeus.

She buttoned her black leather bomber jacket, protecting herself against the onslaught of cold weather moving in on the city, pulled her matching leather cap down over her head and raced to the coffee shop a couple of blocks from her studio. She'd soothe herself with a tall cappuccino with loads of whipped cream on top. Usually she stayed away from the caffeine but today she felt like she could use an extra boost of energy. She would go to the studio and work it off later.

Once inside the coffee shop, Aisha sat down at the small round table, sipping on her cappuccino and reading over her loan papers. She then decided to make a list of possible things she could do to get the rest of the money. She was in deep thought, in her own world, when she heard the captivating, distinct voice hovering above her head.

"Hi there. Looks like we have something in common," he said.

Aisha quickly raised her head toward the voice. It was the guy from the theatre. She couldn't believe she recognized him after all this time. What was he doing here? Had he been following her? Surely not. It had been over two months since they were at the theatre.

"And what exactly do we have in common?" she responded tersely while stuffing her loan papers inside her purse.

"Cappuccino, of course." He flashed a boyish smile at her.

"Is that right? So what does this warrant?" Aisha asked him. "Since we have *soooo* much in common, do I owe you a gold ribbon or something?"

"My, my. Aren't we the feisty one?" he answered with a smile plastered across his handsome face. "Look, let's start over again. I'm Chandler Larson." He extended his hand out toward Aisha while talking.

Aisha allowed his outstretched hand to embrace hers.

When he let go of her hand, he said, "I'm not trying to come on to you. But I'd be lying if I said that I don't find you attractive. I'd like to sit here and share a cappuccino with you. That's all."

She didn't know what to think. She began to really look at him. He seemed harmless and she was in a public place. She didn't have to tell him anything she didn't want to, so maybe it was okay to let him sit down and drink his cappuccino.

"Okay. Have a seat. But I'm very busy and I don't have a lot of time," Aisha griped.

"That's fine. I promise not to wear out my welcome." Chandler placed his cup on the round table, pulled out the

chair and sat down. Sitting comfortably in the chair, he took
a sip of the steaming cup of cappuccino.

"So, Chandler, what type of work do you do?" Aisha's
curiosity had gotten the best of her. "Are you a private eye
or something?" she asked sarcastically. "I mean, you ap-
pear at the most unlikely times."

Chandler flashed a broad grin. Aisha couldn't help but
think to herself how handsome he was. She quickly dispelled the thought and concentrated on his answer.

"You're quite the humorous one aren't you? By the way,
funny lady, do you have a name? I've told you mine, so the
least you can do is tell me yours. Can't you?" His eyes
pleaded innocently.

"Aisha. I believe that's all you need to know."

"Ahhh, Aisha. What a pretty name. But of course it goes
with such a pretty face." His infectious smile captivated her
and she knew that a blush had surely spread over her face.

She quickly changed the subject. "Now, like I asked,
what's your line of work?"

"I'm a land developer. Far from a private eye, huh?"

"You're right about that," Aisha muttered underneath
her breath. She took another sip of cappuccino.

"Come again?" he asked.

"Oh nothing. I was just thinking out loud."

"What about you?" Chandler asked.

"What about me what?" Aisha replied, appearing confused.

"What do you do for a living?"

"I own a dance studio."

"A dancer," he repeated slowly before taking another
drink of his cappuccino. "Why am I not surprised?" His
voice was sure, and she didn't know why this man in-
trigued her so.

"Why are you not surprised?"

"Because you have a graceful and poised look. And that

teal evening dress you had on at the theatre revealed that you do some serious working out," he flirted.

That uneasy feeling began to rise in Aisha. She just wasn't used to having some guy come on so strong. She was used to being in control of situations and making the other person feel uneasy. Now the tables were turned.

"Look, it's been nice talking to you, but I have to leave now," Aisha replied while hurriedly gathering her coat, hat and purse. Standing up, she continued to say, "I have some business to take care of."

"Sure, I understand. I certainly didn't mean to detain you, Aisha. But look, will you give me a call sometime?" Chandler reached inside his jacket and pulled out his business card.

"Why on earth would I want to do that?" she asked. "Now, if you'll excuse me. Good day, Mr. Larson."

Before he could respond to her cold remark, she grabbed her Nine West purse and dashed for the door. When Chandler moved from the table, he spotted a thin, burgundy, leather wallet lying on the floor next to the chair where she had been sitting. Chandler assumed that when she stood up abruptly she must have forced the wallet out of her purse. He bent over and picked it up and immediately raced through the door after her.

He looked up and down the street but she was nowhere in sight. How could she have vanished so quickly? Leafing through the wallet, he saw the beautiful face of the mysterious woman on her driver's license. He read the address on the license while thinking, *looks like I'm going to have the chance to see you again after all, Aisha Carlisle.*

Tucking the wallet safely away in his inside jacket pocket, he smiled as he walked casually to his car.

# 6

Aisha waltzed into the studio, spoke to Angie, then went into one of the dressing rooms to change into her work out clothes. Her afternoon class would be arriving in less than fifteen minutes. While waiting on them, Aisha decided to do some stretches and warm up exercises. Like she had told Chandler, she would work off the cappuccino. She had to admit that Chandler Larson was pleasantly polite. Smiling slightly, she began doing her stretches.

As soon as all of her students arrived, Aisha gathered them together in a circle on the dance mats.

"Listen to me, young ladies. We only have three weeks before your dance presentation. Everything has to be flawless. I will accept nothing less. From the beat and rhythm, to the musical forms, everything must be perfect. Performing at the Mayor's charity gala is a once in a lifetime opportunity for us and I won't blow it. So expect to be here an extra half hour every day until the day of the gala."

By the end of the practice session, the girls were exhausted and so was Aisha. She gathered her gym bag and her coat and cap. She was just as eager as the girls were to get home.

Before Aisha left for the evening, Angie told her that she needed to talk to her about something. They went into Aisha's office.

"What is it, Angie? Is everything okay?"

"Aisha, look I'm not trying to butt into your business, but I can tell that something is wrong," Angie said.

"I don't know what you mean, Angie. Why would you think something's wrong?" Aisha asked her.

"Because, I've noticed you've been, well you've been giving the girls a pretty rough time lately. It's so unlike you."

"Angie, you know how important it is for us to do well at the gala. This could bring in corporate sponsors. It could be beneficial for the studio in so many ways," Aisha explained.

"I know. But you just seem different. I mean, I've never known you to get this stressed out before a performance or an event, especially with the girls. Do you want to talk about it?"

"No, not right now, Angie. I've got too many things to do. Anyway, it's nothing. Like I said, I'm just trying to get things in order for the charity gala. This is going to be a fantastic opportunity. I just don't want to blow it."

Angie knew better. Ever since her boss had received the phone call from Thaddeus last week, she had been a different person. She was usually quite even-tempered and patient with her students, but now she often heard Aisha raising her voice at them and making them do their routines repeatedly without resting. Something was wrong, but Angie didn't know what.

"Thanks for being concerned. Look, I'm going to get out of here and go home. I'm pooped."

"Sure, I'm going to be right behind you," Angie replied.

As Aisha walked to the parking garage, she couldn't hold back the fact that she was on edge about the future of the studio. It wasn't just having to come up with the rest of the money to buy the building that was stressing her out, she was also behind on practically all of her personal bills. She had to do something, but what? Aisha opened her purse and began piddling through it in search of her car keys. She pulled them out and just as she was about to close the snap she noticed that her wallet wasn't inside. She looked through the scarce contents before turning around and heading back toward the studio.

"Angie," Aisha said as she walked back inside the studio.

Angie spun around in her chair and asked, "What are you doing back here?"

"Have you seen my wallet? I can't find it. You know how bad I am about misplacing stuff."

"No, I haven't seen it. Do you remember the last place you had it?"

"I had to have it when I stopped by the coffee shop. But I put it back inside my purse after paying for my cappuccino."

"Maybe it fell out inside your car. Did you look in there?"

"No, that's a good idea. But I'm going to check in here since I came all the way back. Maybe it's in my office."

"Okay," Angie responded and resumed shutting down the computer for the day.

Aisha turned and went into her office in search of the wallet but it wasn't on her desk, the floor or inside any of the drawers. Next she went and checked the locker where she kept her gym bag and the room where she'd done her stretches earlier. After being unsuccessful in finding it she gave up and proceeded back out the door. Taking Angie's advice she looked around inside the car. But again, she was out of luck. She was glad that she had deposited the loan check into her business account. Thank God for small miracles. If it hadn't been for her distraction by that Chandler guy, maybe she wouldn't have been thrown off track. She quickly dismissed any thought of him. On her way home, she stopped by the coffee shop and searched around the area where she had been sitting. She asked the manager if any one had perhaps turned in a wallet but he told her that no one had. Too tired to worry about it anymore, Aisha left the coffee shop, climbed back inside her car and headed for her apartment.

The next day Tameria decided to stop by and check on Aisha while she had a little time off from her hospital rotation. She wasn't scheduled to report until later on in the evening and since she hadn't seen or talked to Aisha in days, she thought she'd surprise her with a visit.

When Tameria came, Aisha was glad to see her. Their time spent together was sparse since both of them had such busy schedules. Aisha stopped what she had been doing and devoted her attention to Tameria.

"Aisha, have you decided what you're going to do about getting the rest of the money for the building?" Tameria inquired.

"Nope. And I don't have much time left to figure it out, so I've got to do something. I'm going to have to meet with my students' parents. I can't put it off much longer. I guess I'm going to have to increase my fees. I know that might mean losing a few students, actually I might lose more than a few but I have no choice. Then I'm going to call some of the kids on the waiting list and hold an audition for more students."

"More students!" Tameria was upset at hearing this. She knew that Aisha couldn't take on any more students right now. She was already pushing herself over the top. "How in the world are you going to pull that off? I know you can't be talking about enrolling any more kids. Girl, you must be crazy."

"No, I am not crazy, Tameria. It's just that I have to do what I have to do. Don't you know how important this is to me?" It was obvious that Aisha was about to break. Tameria hated to see her dearest friend come apart like this.

"Oh, I'm sorry. I didn't mean to interrupt. I didn't see the receptionist so I just took the liberty to come on back."

Tameria and Aisha both looked up at the same time. The tall, dark-haired lady stood in the doorway. Elisa Santana was the mother of one of her more talented students, Gabby.

"Oh, no, you're not interrupting, Miss Santana. This is my best friend, Tameria," Aisha looked at Tameria. Tameria, this is Elisa Santana. Her daughter is a student here."

"Nice to meet you, Miss Santana," Tameria replied.

"We were just talking," Aisha tried to wipe the tear away from her eye that was about to find its way down her red cheeks. "Please come on in."

Tameria stood up from the chair she was sitting in, "Look, you two go on and talk. I'm going to go in the practice area for a minute and watch the girls go over their routine. I know they're going to do great at the gala," Tameria replied. "Nice meeting you, Miss Santana."

"And you as well, Tameria," Elisa Santana responded kindly.

"Tameria, we'll talk later," Aisha said as Tameria exited the office. Diverting her attention to, Elisa, Aisha asked, "Now, how can I help you, Miss Santana?"

"Gabby told me that you planned on meeting with the parents some time this week. If it's in the afternoon, I won't be able to attend. I have to go in to work early the remainder of the week. So do you think you could let me know why you want to meet with us?"

Elisa Santana was pencil thin, tall and quite attractive with olive skin. Her daughter, Gabby, had some of the same features as her mother and was just as pretty. Elisa's toned legs were supported by three-inch violet heels. The sleek fitting grape mini dress she wore hugged every curve on her body and the hem of the dress almost met up with the thick auburn tresses flowing down her back.

"Of course, Miss Santana. Have a seat."

Without giving her the intimate details of her dilemma, Aisha proceeded to tell Elisa Santana about her fee increase.

"Miss Santana, my expenses are increasing, and unfortunately, I have to pass some of that cost on to my students. If I don't raise my rates then I'm afraid I'll have to make some serious cuts in other areas in order to keep the studio running. I know you're a single mother trying to raise a teenage daughter, but I hope you understand." Aisha tried to break it to Miss Santana as easily as she could.

Much to Aisha's surprise, Miss Santana replied, "I understand. And really, it's no problem. Just tell me when the new rate goes into effect and I'll take care of it."

Aisha was amazed. Elisa Santana hadn't bothered to even ask her how much of an increase. She didn't seem the least bit upset or bothered by the notice of an increase.

"Don't you want to know how much the increase is going to be?" Aisha asked, trying not to sound too astonished.

"Why, of course," Elisa said, slinging her tresses over her shoulder. "But it really won't make any difference because Gabby isn't going anywhere else. She loves you and I love the way you teach and that's that. The increase is no problem."

*Wow*, Aisha said to herself. *Does she have a rich boyfriend somewhere lurking in the background or what?* Aisha grinned slightly.

Sure enough, when Aisha told Miss Santana that the tuition was going up by twenty five percent, Elisa answered with an "Okay," and nothing else was said.

"If only the other parents would be so easy," Aisha told Tameria after Elisa Santana and Gabby left.

"Girl, what is she doing? Every time you see her, she looks like she just stepped out of a fashion magazine."

"I know that's right," Aisha responded. "And she drives a BMW, plus she has a nice house. Must be nice."

"Maybe I'm in the wrong field," Tameria laughed. "How do you know about her house?"

"One day she needed someone to take Gabby home because she had to work late, so I told her I would do it. She lives in Twinkle Town subdivision in a multi-level house with this perfectly landscaped lawn."

It wasn't that Aisha was surprised that some of her students were not from the inner city. However it was somewhat surprising that Elisa Santana lived in an upscale neighborhood on a single parent income.

"Whatever line of work she's in must be paying her a pretty hefty salary, then," Tameria said as she stood in the door of Aisha's office.

"Yeah, maybe I need to hook up with her and find out what she's doing so I can do it too. Then maybe I won't have this huge worry hanging over my shoulders," Aisha remarked. "Anyway, enough of envying someone else's good fortune. Come on, let's go. I have to run some errands before I go to Bible study tonight. Since I can't find my wallet, I guess I'll have to go ahead and replace my drivers license and social security card. I'm glad I had my small purse. If I had been carrying my other purse I would have had the wallet with all my credit cards and pictures and other stuff inside. Girl, God is good. He looks out for me." Aisha let out a long sigh. "Come on, let's get out of here."

Aisha told Angie goodnight and she and Tameria left for the afternoon.

"Tameria, I can't believe I forgot to tell you," Aisha said as she whirled around as soon as they walked through the glass double doors exiting from the building.

"What? What is it?" Tameria asked.

"You remember that guy we saw at the Orpheum a couple of months ago? You know the one who walked up on us while we were talking, and you said he was only trying to throw us a line?"

"Yeah, I remember that fine hunk of flesh, but I said he was trying to throw *you* a line, not me. Anyway, what about him?" she countered, her curiosity piqued.

"I ran into him when I was leaving the bank today. I was at the coffee shop having a cappuccino when I heard this heavy, charming voice say hello. And when I looked up, it was none other than Chandler Larson. That's his name."

"Chandler Larson? What happened? What did he say? I want to know everything," Tameria rambled while they raced down the busy Memphis expressway.

Aisha really didn't have much to tell her . . . for now anyway.

# 7

"We're going to continue our study on peace. The Hebrew meaning of peace is shalom, which means complete, whole, nothing missing." Pastor Shipley was an excellent Bible scholar. He had a way of making the word of God plain enough for everyone to understand. Since becoming Pastor of Faithside Temple four years ago, the membership had almost tripled and was continuing to grow. It definitely was getting closer to fitting the description of a mega church. He drew in a great deal of young people as well as adults.

"Now if you want some of this peace, you have to stay focused on God," he continued. "God wants his children whole. How can you be whole if you're consumed with worry, if you're troubled by financial woes and sickness and heartache? God doesn't want that for his children. He stands ready to deliver you and make you complete. But you have to be willing to obey His word. You have to be willing to praise Him even in the midst of troubled times. The word of God says that many are the afflictions of the righteous, but the Lord delivereth them out of them all!

God's word is true and his promises are real," Pastor Shipley emphasized to the Bible study class.

Aisha understood that everything Pastor Shipley taught
was true. And if she just remained faithful and obedient,
then things would work out fine.

After leaving church, she stopped off at the corner store
before heading to her apartment. When she drove her car
into the circular drive, she mouthed a prayer of thanksgiving to God. She pulled out her keys, grabbed the bag of
groceries, and raced up the marble walkway leading to her
humble abode. She placed the key in the lock and the lights
inside the living room automatically came on. She walked
into the silence of the apartment, stepping out of each shoe
as she walked along the Oriental rug covering her darkly
stained hardwood floors. She placed the groceries on the
kitchen island and began carefully pulling out the head of
lettuce, shaved turkey breast and sourdough bread. Standing in front of the fridge, she yanked it open and checked to
see if she had mustard and a piece of red onion for the
sandwich she planned to make for her dinner.

"Oh, yes," she said, breathing a sigh of relief when she
found the items. She then went into her bedroom and pulled
off her capris and blouse. She couldn't wait to climb into a
hot steamy shower, and then prepare her sandwich in time
for the new episode of *American Idol*.

The water pounding against her body felt like tiny electric currents that energized her, yet made her feel relaxed at
the same time. She held her head back with her eyes closed
and allowed the warm water to bathe her ebony skin. She
carefully took the bath sponge and moved it up and down
the length of her perfectly sculptured body and muscular
legs.

After twenty minutes, she felt the water cooling down
and stepped carefully out of the shower stall on to the soft
white bath rug. When the cool air kissed her body, a shiver

raced up and down her spine. She quickly grabbed her towel and wrapped it around her upper body. After drying off, she ambled into her bedroom. She picked up the fuchsia cotton robe off of her bed and placed it over her body in place of the towel, stepped into her cloth slippers and walked into the kitchen to prepare her turkey sandwich.

While preparing her dinner she checked her voice mail messages. *You have six new messages. To listen to your messages, press one now,"* the automated voice said.

"Aisha, it's your daddy. I'm just checking on you." *Press two to save, press three to erase, or press four to go to the next message*, the voice instructed. Aisha continued to listen to all six of her messages. Surprisingly there was a message from her sister, Selena, and another call was from a church member about the upcoming Greeters' banquet. Aisha was part of the Greeters' Committee and had volunteered to help make the arrangements for the quarterly banquet. Her last message was from one of the parents from the studio.

"Hi, Aisha, I'm sorry to bother you, but I'm calling about Cherise. She won't be at rehearsal tomorrow. She has strep throat. I sure hope none of the other girls come down with it. Call me if you have any questions. We'll see you next week. Bye."

*Shucks*, Aisha thought. *That's all I need is for my girls to come down with strep. Oh well, I'm not going to worry about anything tonight.* She erased the message and continued to fix her sandwich before settling down in her bed to watch *American Idol.*

The blare of the alarm clock jarred Aisha from her sleep. She turned over sleepily, rubbing her eyes and glancing over at the clock. She turned the alarm off, eased out of the bed and walked into the bathroom. She washed her face and brushed her teeth and then cleaned up the mess she'd left on her nightstand the night before. She must have really been tired. She couldn't remember what happened after *American Idol* went off. She had even fallen asleep without saying her prayers.

"Lord, forgive me," she mouthed out loud. Dragging her feet along, she went into the kitchen, poured herself a glass of V8 and released another slow yawn as she retrieved her morning paper from her doorstep. The sound of the phone interrupted her routine.

"Good morning, princess. How are you?" .

"Good morning, Daddy. I'm fine. I'm sorry I didn't call you back last night. I fell asleep."

"Oh that's okay. I just wanted to check on you and make sure everything was going all right. You doing okay?"

"Sure, Dad. I told you I'm fine. I've been working on the routine for the Mayor's charity gala so I'm pretty wiped out. I want everything to be sensational. This is a once in a lifetime opportunity for my dance studio."

"I know, princess. But you still have to take care of yourself. Okay? Your mom and I are proud of you. I hope you know that. Let us know if we can help you in any way. Now, have a good day. Call me later if you get a chance."

"I will. Bye, Daddy," Aisha said and then blew a kiss into the receiver.

"Bye, princess."

After ending the call with her father, Aisha dialed Tameria's phone number but then stopped abruptly when she realized that Tameria was doing a thirty-six hour med rotation at the hospital. She was going to miss talking to her. But she knew she might as well get used to it. Becoming a doctor was challenging and revamping her social and personal life was the sacrifice Tameria had to make in order to succeed. If anyone understood, it was Aisha. She had to do the same thing to make her dance studio successful. Now she faced a whole new dilemma—holding on to it. With the morning came the fresh onslaught of her problem. Perhaps today would be the day things would turn around for her. She remembered that she still hadn't located her wallet. She leafed through her purse and her dance duffel bag for the umpteenth time, but still, her wallet was nowhere to be found.

*Oh, well, forget it,* she thought. "If it turns up, fine, and if it doesn't, then so be it. It certainly won't be the first time I've misplaced something of importance," she said out loud.

She took a quick shower before putting on a thigh-length jean skirt over her dance leotards and body suit, then packed her duffel bag with a change of clothes, a couple of energy bars and a can of V8 Splash before heading out the door.

On the other side of town, Chandler Larson's early morning thoughts quickly zeroed in on the mysterious Aisha Carlisle. For weeks after he first laid eyes on Aisha at the Orpheum Theatre, he had thought about her. Lately, he'd been thinking about how it would be to have a nice, sophisticated woman by his side. Not a trickster like the last serious relationship he had been involved in that ended unpleasantly, to say the least. As for the hit and run kind of females, they were beginning to be a bore to him.

Chandler was tired of going home to an empty apartment but unfortunately his job didn't allow him the time he needed to really find that special someone. That's why he was thrilled when he ran into Aisha at the coffee shop. He picked up her wallet from his small breakfast table and kneaded the soft leather in his hands while sipping his coffee. He didn't like the fact that he had to lie to her about being a land developer, but it was all he could think of at the time. There was no way he could confide in her right off the bat about his real career. At thirty-one the playa in him had just about played out and he was ready to settle down. But it would have to be with someone who could deal with his true profession. Maybe, just maybe, that someone could be Aisha Carlisle.

# 8

Lead Detective Chandler Larson's job in the Memphis Police Department's Undercover Division was one he'd dreamed about all of his life. Ever since he was a little boy, he often daydreamed of being a cop and an undercover agent. He lived for the excitement and danger he encountered on an almost daily basis. Imagine scrawny Chandler Larson had grown up to be a big, bad, police detective, saving the world from the evil guy. Chandler snickered at the thought of how far he'd come from a skinny, pimple-faced little country boy living in Montgomery, Alabama.

He glanced over at one of his partners. "Hey, Jay, did I tell you about this dime piece I ran into the other day?" Chandler's face was beet red as he thought about the mysterious bombshell.

"You're always meeting some so called 'dime piece'," his co-worker teased. "Tell me just how hot this one is. I'll believe anything just as long as it gives me a minute to take a break from this computer. Man, my eyes are beginning to cross. I've been staring at this screen so long. I can't run a trace on this suspected carjacker yet. I've run addresses, aliases and tats and still I'm coming up empty. So tell me. What's she like?" Jay leaned back in his chair, crossed his legs and put both hands behind his neck. His beer belly peaked from under his celery green polo.

"This one might just be it, Jay. This isn't the first time I've seen her either. I spotted her at the Orpheum a couple of months ago but she got away from me before I could make my move. I thought I'd never see her again and so I told myself that it just wasn't meant to be and left it at that. Then here I am at the coffee shop, right?"

"Yeah, and?"

"And I look over and see her sitting at the table alone. Man, this girl has got it going on. Her hair was laid back, man, flowing down her back, natural and all. I'm talking about silky black thick twists. Oooh, wee. Mercy!" Chandler squealed.

Jay laughed. "Come on, tell me more."

"Well, like I said, her hair was pretty as silk, man. She had on a salmon-colored pant set and I can tell that the lady was all about the business." Chandler sat on the edge of his paper-filled desk and continued talking to Jay while sipping on another cup of coffee.

"So what'd you do? Did you say anything to her?"

"What? Are you crazy?" Chandler asked as he almost bounced up from off of the desk with excitement. "You know I wasn't about to let her walk out of my life a second time. So, tell you what I did," he said, gesturing with his hands.

"What?" A look of utter enjoyment was plastered across Jay's round plump face.

I took my smooth, charming self over to her table." Chandler made a *humph* sound and continued with his story.

Jay stopped fumbling with the file on his desk and looked up and gave Chandler his full attention.

"Man, I was determined to use my best line on her. You know, the one I reserve for the special little honeys." Chandler spoke with total confidence as he flashed a wide toothy grin at Jay.

"Let's hear what you said, man."

"First, I walked up to her and introduced myself. I reminded her that I'd seen her at the Orpheum."

"And what'd she say?"

"What do you mean what'd she say? She let me sit down beside her. I said to myself, 'Yea, yea, yea.'"

"She let you sit down? Man, how do you do it?"

"I just do it, because I got it like that." Chandler spoke with a bit of cockiness. "Anyway, we talked a few minutes. I could tell she liked me even though she was playing hard to get. Girl got it all going on. She has great conversation and a mean streak to boot. Yea, I'd like to really get to know her."

"The thing is, does she want to get to know you?" Jay laughed hard, almost causing the chair to tilt over from the weight of his chunky body.

"Not to worry about that. I know how to handle that situation. Anyway, when she left, I saw this wallet lying on the floor by the chair where she had been sitting. I picked it up, opened it and found out it belonged to her. I ran outside and tried to catch her but I couldn't find her. Lucky me."

"Lucky you? You said she got away didn't you?"

"Yeah, but now I know where she lives."

"Are you going over to her house?"

"*Naw*, I'm not going to be that bold. I'm going to run a check on her and see if I can find a phone number. Once I do that, I'll give her a ring, let her know I found her wallet and offer to bring it over. Boing . . . then I make my move."

"Your move? What kind of move, man?"

"Nope, can't tell. I can't let you in on all my playa secrets, not just yet, Jay." Chandler let out a laugh. "Now, let me run this check and get some work done around here for a minute."

"Yeah, me too. I've got to get some leads on this fool before I leave here today. I'm sick of this punk going around carjacking innocent folks like he's somebody or something." Jay's face showed the obvious anger he had over the suspected carjacker that had continued to elude them.

Before leaving the police station that evening, Chandler decided to contact Aisha so he could get her wallet back to her. *Maybe I should put it in the mail and leave well enough alone.* He paused in his thoughts. *Naw, then I would definitely blow my chance of seeing her again. I'm going to call her.*

Chandler listened as the phone rang once, twice, three, four times. *Does she have an answering machine,* he thought to himself.

"Hi, you've reached 555.8976. I can't take your call at the moment, but please leave a message or stay on the line and your call will be forwarded to me," the recording said. Chandler decided to hang on and see if the call would reach her. Within a few seconds he heard the soft, sexy voice on the other end.

It had been a long day for Aisha. Just as she was exiting the studio, her cell phone rang as she tried locking the door. Fumbling to answer it, she dropped her keys on the floor. She simultaneously picked them up and answered the phone. "Hello," Aisha said while turning the door lock to the studio.

"Uh, hello," Chandler stammered. "May I speak to uh . . . Aisha Carlisle please?" Chandler didn't know why he was nervous. He just knew that he was.

"This is she. Who's calling please?" Aisha didn't recognize the voice on the other end. But whoever it was sure did sound good. His deep baritone voice sent a tiny shiver up and down her spine.

"This is Chandler. Chandler Larson."

Aisha couldn't believe this guy. How did he get her number? Was he some kind of fatal attraction or what? She was disturbed by this invasion of privacy. "Look, I don't appreciate you stalking me. I told you at the coffee shop that I had no reason to call you. What's up with you?" she asked angrily.

"Listen, Miss Carlisle, it's not at all like you think. I'm not a stalker so don't worry about anything like that. He wasn't about to tell her that he ran a criminal background check on her by using her driver's license.

Aisha, still agitated at his call asked, "Well, how can I help you?"

"I think it's how I can help you. You see, the other day at the coffee shop you left in such a hurry that you dropped your wallet. I saw it on the floor and picked it up. I tried to catch up to you but you disappeared without a trace. I was calling now to see how we might arrange for you to get it. I didn't want to just show up on your doorstep unexpectedly, you see."

Aisha felt stupid for being so short with Chandler. She didn't know why this man made her stay in a defensive mode. "Oh, thanks, Mr. Larson. I can come and pick it up if you'll just tell me where. I've been trying to figure out where I lost it. I went back to the coffee shop but no luck."

"Look, no need to come to me. I tell you what I can do. Do you work in the area of the coffee shop? If so, we could meet up there or I could drop it off by your place of work. Whatever you say; I'm at your beck and call," he laughed.

Aisha couldn't help but smile. Her defenses began to drop and she started to hear the kindness in Chandler's voice. She felt like he was truly being sincere and just trying to help her out. But she was used to keeping up her guard when it came to men. She'd dated a few guys here and there but none seriously. Her dance studio took up so much of her time and when she wasn't at the studio, she was at church or trying to get in a little R&R between down times. A serious relationship was the farthest thing from her mind.

"My dance studio is about two blocks from that coffee shop. You can bring it to me there, if you don't mind."

"That sounds great. How about tomorrow around eleven?" he asked.

"Eleven will be fine. The name of the studio is *A. Carlisle Studio of Dance and Choreography*. The address is 457 East Bellevue. If things change, you can call me and we can make some other arrangements."

"Okay, I've got it."

"Goodnight and thanks again, Mr. Larson," she said in a kind voice.

"Goodnight, Miss Carlisle. Look, before I hang up can we cut the formalities? Just call me Chandler, okay?"

"Okay, and you may call me Aisha. Goodnight, Chandler."

"Goodnight, Aisha."

A pleasant feeling took the place of her previous frustration.

After closing his flip phone, Chandler double checked to make sure he had his badge, his Glock pistol and the case file detailing his next undercover assignment. He nodded at several of his fellow officers as he left the office. Like a kid on Christmas Eve, Chandler couldn't wait for tomorrow to arrive.

# 9

Chandler expertly guided the black Infiniti into the parking space. His black trousers swayed with the wind as he maneuvered his long muscular legs down the parking lot corridor. The melon silk shirt outlined his massive chest. The black leather jacket hit his hips as the soft material protected him against the brisk winter day. Snow was forecasted over the next couple of days and Chandler felt that a leather jacket wasn't going to cut it much longer. He pushed the elevator button for the second floor. When he stepped out of the parking garage, a few feet ahead of him was a sign that read, *A. Carlisle Studio of Dance and Choreography,* followed by an arrow. He followed the sign and arrow until he came to the studio. He felt nervous at the thought of seeing her again.

"Good morning, how may I help you?" Angie asked.

"Chandler Larson, I'm here to see Aisha Carlisle," he replied. Angie thought to herself how fine this Chandler Larson was. When Aisha told her he would be coming by to bring her wallet, Angie had no idea he would be such a knockout. That was the one thing Aisha failed to tell her.

"Ummph," Angie moaned under her breath. *If fineness was against the law, this brother would be locked up for life.* "Let me get her for you, Mr. Larson. Have a seat please."

"Thanks. And call me Chandler."

"Oh, all right, Chandler. Aisha will be right with you."

Angie walked into Aisha's office. Aisha was on the phone and it was obvious she was upset and pleading with someone. About what, Angie had no idea. She hated to see her boss in apparent distress.

"Excuse me, just a minute please," Aisha told whoever was on the other end. "What is it Angie?" she asked rather curtly.

"I'm sorry for barging in, Aisha. But a Mr. Chandler Larson is in the lobby," Angie said apologetically.

"Is it eleven o'clock already? Just get my wallet from him. No, on second thought, I'll be out in a minute."

"Sure, I'll tell him," Angie said.

"Angie, will you close the door behind you?"

"Of course," Angie responded.

Aisha waited until Angie left before she resumed her phone conversation.

"Look, just give me a little more time. I'm doing all I can to come up with the money. I can't lose this place. I just can't. Talk to the owner and see if I can get an extension. Please, Thaddeus. Do it for me," she begged.

"Look, I told you, Aisha. There's no extension," Thaddeus explained over the phone. "This guy has to sell and he wants his money now. I know you said you had part of it and I'll come by later this evening and get that but you don't have much time to come up with the rest. I'm sorry, Aisha. I really am. I hate that it has to be this way. I'll see you later."

Thaddeus hung up the phone and Aisha fell back into the cloth-covered swivel office chair. She had to get herself together. No time for tears. She mouthed a quick prayer.

"Lord, I need you to come through for me on this. I can't do this without your help. You know how important this studio is to me." She stood up, pressed her hands against her red leotards, smoothed out her matching red knit top and proceeded to welcome the stranger on the other side of the door.

Aisha approached Chandler in the reception area.

"Chandler, good morning," she said politely.

"Good morning, Aisha."

"Thanks for coming by to bring my wallet," Aisha said to him. "I really appreciate it." She extended her hand to meet his and flashed a fake smile his way. He looked more handsome than she had remembered from the coffee shop and the Orpheum. It was as if she was seeing him for the first time. He stood towering over her, appearing to be almost six feet. She knew that he worked out from the way his clothes hung so perfectly over his chiseled body. His broad shoulders oozed manliness. His goatee and well-trimmed mustache accentuated his smile and his pearly whites. *Be still my heart.*

"It's all my pleasure. I believe this has to be fate, don't you?" Chandler asked exchanging nervousness for boldness.

"I don't know if I agree with that statement or not. And what makes you say that anyway?"

"Because three times I've had the pleasure of running into you. Now here's your wallet, and if you should ever lose it again, may I be so lucky again as to find it." His smile spread even further as he handed Aisha her wallet.

Aisha felt a shiver run up and down the course of her spine. "How can I repay you?"

"I have the perfect answer to that question, Aisha."

"And what is the perfect answer?"

"May I have the pleasure of your company at dinner this evening?" He thought he might as well go for it. After all, she asked how he could be repaid.

"Well . . ." she hesitated.

"Uh, uh, let's not even go there. You asked what you could do to repay me. I just want to enjoy getting to know you a little better, that's all. Nothing more, nothing less."

"Okay. Dinner will be fine. How does six thirty sound?"

"Six thirty sounds great. Do you like Italian?" Chandler asked happily.

"As a matter of fact, I do."

"Good, I know a nice little Italian place in midtown. Where do you want me to pick you up?"

"Since you already know where I live, why not come to my place?"

"That sounds even better. So six-thirty it is. Before I leave, do you have time to give me a quick tour of your studio? From what I've seen already it's truly state of the art. I'm quite impressed."

"Why, thank you, Mr. Larson."

"Why do you insist on being so formal? I asked you to call me Chandler, remember?"

"Yes, of course, I remember. Since I have a few minutes before my next class, I'd love to show you around—Chandler," she said emphatically. "Come on. Follow me."

Angie glanced up from her computer at her boss and Chandler. *They would make a cute couple,* she surmised to herself before resuming her work.

Aisha was excited that Chandler wanted to tour the studio. She loved it when others took an interest in what she did. For the moment, she pushed back the memories of the problems she faced and instead concentrated her efforts on giving Chandler a full-scale tour.

"Right around this corner and down the corridor is another practice room. I use it for my hip-hop class," Aisha told him.

"Hip-hop? I see," he grinned while clasping his hands

behind his back and leaning forward to view the inside of the classroom.

"This next room holds from ten to twenty students," Aisha said stepping inside the room. "I use this room for my lyrical dance class. Here is where my girls learn to incorporate ballet, which is the reason for the barres, blended with jazz and a touch of modern dance. Together they make up the lyrical dance style. It's definitely one of the more complicated dance techniques to learn and teach," Angie explained as they walked slowly around the mirrored room.

"I'm definitely impressed. I've never been inside a dance studio before," Chandler said strolling next to her.

"Well, there's more to see. Follow me. As they walked along the narrow hall, Aisha felt comfortable next to him. Their conversation was smooth and easy.

"What is this room used for?" Chandler asked as they approached a room somewhat smaller than the previous two he'd seen.

"Step inside and I'll show you," Aisha eagerly said. "This is the girls' dressing room. "Here," she said opening a door on the far side of the room. "See the various costumes and dance accessories? From ballet to funky hip-hop, we have a costume for the occasion. There's another wardrobe area right across the hall too," she said, pointing again.

Pausing in the dressing room, Chandler said, "Wow, you have a fantastic setup here. I had no idea this place was as large as it is. You can't tell when you first walk in."

"Yeah, I know. It's deceiving isn't it?" she replied.

"You have it going on."

Aisha smiled. "Do you dance?"

"Me? I don't think you could call doing the electric slide dancing."

She released a giggle. "Come on, I know you have to know how to step don't you? And what about slow dancing?"

"Sure, in that case, the answer to your question is yes." Before they both realized it, forty-five minutes had gone by. Chandler glanced at the clock hanging on the soft mint green painted wall. "My, the time is slipping by. I'd better go and let you get back to doing your thing."

"It was no problem showing you around. I enjoyed it," Aisha remarked. "But I do have a lot to do and I'm sure you do too."

"Yes, I do," he replied as they simultaneously walked out of the dressing room and up the hall toward the reception area.

Chandler stopped once they reached the front of the studio and turned toward Aisha. "Thanks again for the tour."

"You're most welcome. I'll see you at six-thirty."

"Okay. And you did say Italian would be fine, didn't you?" he reiterated.

"Yes, I love Italian," she said.

"Goodbye, Aisha," he said and reached for the door.

Pausing and turning around he said, "Oh and goodbye, Angie."

"Goodbye, Mr. Larson," Angie answered and smiled.

Chandler strolled out of the door feeling exhilarated.

Aisha stood at the door for a moment as if waiting to see if Chandler would return.

*Something's starting to brew between those two. Maybe this Chandler guy will be the one to penetrate Aisha's shell. Whatever went on in that office prior to him coming was definitely forgotten about when he walked in. That's a good sign. A real good sign,* Angie thought as she watched Aisha happily retreat to her office.

# 10

"This *lasagna classico* tastes superb," Aisha complimented as she finished off the last of the entrée.

"I'm glad you like my choice. It's one of my favorites. Actually when I was growing up, I remember my grandmother used to make lasagna that tasted just like this. That's one of the reasons I like this place."

"I haven't been here before," Aisha said looking around the quaint Italian bistro. "But it's really nice. I will have to come back some time."

"Good, maybe you'll allow me to escort you here again," Chandler cautiously flirted.

"Maybe," Aisha answered softly without looking at Chandler.

"Tell me a little about yourself, Aisha." Chandler stared directly into her eyes, making her feel somewhat captivated by his magnetism. She had to admit, she was really enjoying his company. It had been such a long time since she'd entertained a man and it felt good being with him.

"I think I should be asking you that question," she responded.

"Oh, why is that?" Chandler's eyebrows raised in curiosity.

"Because you know more about me than I do about you. Remember, you found my wallet which means that you know where I live. You know how to reach me. You know what I do for a living and where I do it. And you know I like Italian food." Aisha managed to laugh.

"I can't argue with that, pretty lady," Chandler replied.

"So, I'm waiting," Aisha said. "Spill your guts," she said while laughing.

"I see that you are not going to let me off the hook are you?" Chandler said while throwing his head back and chuckling.

Pausing, he took a sip of the red wine he'd ordered with dinner. Aisha followed suit.

"Before I start telling you my life's story, are you ready for dessert?" Chandler asked.

"No, I'm stuffed. If I have dessert I'll have to return to the studio tonight and work off the calories," she said jokingly.

"Well, we don't want you to have to do that," Chandler answered.

For the next hour, Aisha and Chandler laughed and talked. Aisha found herself telling Chandler how she started the studio, about the death of her grandparents, and all about her students. The one thing she didn't mention was the financial trouble she was facing with the studio.

In return, Chandler told her about his so-called job as a land developer, purposely failing to divulge that he was actually a detective in the Memphis Undercover Special Units division.

"Tell me, do you really like doing what you do? You know, building things?" she asked him

"Yeah, I do. I've never thought of being anything else. My father was a land developer. He taught me everything about it." Chandler didn't really consider himself to be lying, not totally anyway. His father might be considered as a land developer to some degree. It didn't matter that anyone else would have merely stated that his dad was a landscaper.

"Wow, that's interesting, but I know how you feel. I've dreamed of being a dancer since I was a little girl. My mother said I used to dance around the house as soon as I took my first step," Aisha giggled.

"It's good to be able to live your dream, don't you think?"

"Yes. I thank God every day that I'm living mine." Aisha paused before asking him, "Do you mind if I get a little more personal with you?"

"No, what is it?"

"Do you have someone special in your life?" She didn't want to come off too brash, but she had to know. A man as fine as Chandler had to be involved with someone. It wasn't that she wanted to be involved with him, she was simply curious.

"No, I don't. I was serious about a girl back home at one time."

"Where is back home?" she asked him.

"Montgomery, Alabama."

"I have a couple of cousins who live in Alabama."

"Is that right?"

"Yeah.

"See, we have quite a few things in common, Aisha." He flashed his hypnotizing smile.

"Come on. Finish telling me about this girl."

"We met in college and became serious. I thought she was the one I would spend my life with."

"What happened?"

"It's a long story, but to sum it up, I caught her, and I mean literally caught her and a good buddy of mine in the act."

"Oh, that's terrible, Chandler."

"Tell me about it. After that, I decided to move to Memphis to get a fresh start on things, you know?"

"I'm really sorry that happened to you," Aisha remarked, with genuine sympathy for Chandler resonating in her voice.

"I lost a lot of trust when that happened," Chandler admitted to Aisha. A tinge of sadness began to overcome him as he reminisced about the break up.

"It happens sometimes," Aisha told him. "I don't know what your religious beliefs are, but I know that whenever I'm facing a difficulty or trial in life, I turn to God. Without my faith, I know I wouldn't have made it through a lot of situations in my life."

"Yea, I know what you mean and I feel you on that. I don't attend church as often as I should with my work schedule and all, but I do believe in the man upstairs, no doubt, no doubt." Chandler emphasized.

"I'm glad to know that."

Finally, Chandler decided to call it a night. He didn't want to wear out his welcome. He wanted the chance to see Aisha again. "Hey, it's getting late," he told her.

"Yeah, you're right," Aisha responded looking at her watch. "I can't believe we've been in here for two hours!" she exclaimed.

"That means you enjoyed my company. You see, I told you that I wasn't so bad," Chandler laughed reaching over and gently grabbing her hand.

Aisha flinched for just a second but didn't remove her hand from his.

"I have an early day tomorrow," he told her.

"So do I."

Chandler asked the waiter for the check. After paying the bill, he stood up and reached out his hand toward Aisha to help her get up out of her chair.

"Thank you, Chandler."

Chandler and Aisha chatted and listened to the radio as he drove her back to her apartment. When he pulled up to her complex, he turned the engine off and looked over at the beautiful woman sitting next to him.

"I guess I'm going to get out of your hair," he said wanting to kiss her badly. "I can't thank you enough for the wonderful dinner and the lovely conversation."

"The pleasure was all mine. You saved me from going through a lot of changes when you found my wallet and returned it. Plus, I really enjoyed your company this evening, Chandler," she admitted.

"You see?"

"See what?" she responded.

"If you had been receptive to me from the get go, then we would be good friends by now, little lady. But no, at the Orpheum and at the coffee shop you had to diss a brother like he had the plague or something." Again a grin stretched across Chandler's chiseled face.

"Okay, you're right. I'm a big enough girl to admit when I'm wrong. But you also know that in this day and age, a girl has to be careful, real careful. And men do, too, for that matter."

"Okay I'll let you off the hook with that. But I do want to see you again. Can I see you again?" he asked as he moved in closer to her space. She felt her breath becoming somewhat heavy and her heart began to race as he moved within a hair of her body.

"What do you say, Aisha? Can I see you again?"

"I, I'd like that. But I want to warn you," Aisha said in a rather serious tone, "I'm not interested in a relationship. Friendship, yes, but if you have anything else on your mind, look elsewhere."

"I understand. And I only had friendship in mind myself. I don't believe in moving too fast either. But I also want to be honest. I am attracted to you. You're a beautiful, sexy woman." Chandler didn't want to come on too strong. And part of what he said was actually true. He was definitely attracted to Aisha. But he did want more than friendship. He wanted to take things a step further. But only in time. Only in time.

Aisha couldn't allow herself to become romantically involved right now, no matter how attracted she was to Chandler. She had to concentrate all her efforts on getting the money for the dance studio. Maybe after she crossed that hurdle and if she and Chandler were still friends, then perhaps she could entertain the notion.

"Will you call me?" Chandler asked her.

"Sure, I'll call you," Aisha answered, looking him straight in the eyes. "And Chandler."

"Yes?"

"Thanks again for returning my wallet," Aisha told him before reaching for the car door.

"Wait, let me," Chandler said, opening his door, climbing out and walking over to the passenger's side. He proceeded to open Aisha's door for her.

He walked her to the door of her apartment. After pulling out her keys, she unlocked the door and opened it slightly. Turning to face him, she stood on tiptoe and planted a soft kiss on his left cheek. He was taken aback but tried not to show it. He felt that the best way for him to respond was not to respond at all. Instead, he wrapped his long thick fingers around the pewter doorknob and carefully opened it wider so she could walk inside.

"Goodnight. We'll talk soon," he said, turning and walking back to his car.

Closing the door behind her, Aisha rested against it and smiled. This time she definitely had something to tell Tameria.

Aisha performed her nightly ritual of showering, exercising, saying her prayers and then off to bed. Almost as soon as her head hit the pillow she began to drift off to sleep. The wine had relaxed her and Chandler's company had taken her mind off her problems. For now, everything was good . . . if only for one night.

# 11

The day had finally arrived for the Mayor's Charity gala and Aisha had been running around like a chicken with its head cut off all day. She searched until she found her cell phone to call her Daddy and Mom to make sure they were on schedule.

When her father answered the phone, Aisha didn't hesitate to ask, "Daddy, are you and Mom getting ready?"

"Not yet, princess. We have plenty of time."

He could here Aisha's heavy breathing. "Princess, I already know what you're thinking, but there's no need to get worried. I may be a little slow but your mother and I will be on time. I know how important tonight is to you. It's not every day you get to show off in front of the Mayor and his guests."

"You're right about that, Daddy. Look, I'm going to hang up now. I need to get a shower and start getting ready," Aisha said in a rushed tone. "I told the girls to meet me two hours before the gala starts. We've already practiced a couple of times at the Cannon Center, but I want to do a last minute run through," she hurriedly explained.

"Girl, you know you work those girls hard. But anyway, okay, Aisha. We'll see you later on tonight."

"Bye, Daddy."

Aisha hung up the phone and dashed into the oversized all-white bathroom. She reached through the shower stall and grabbed the brass knob and turned on the shower while stepping out of her clothes. The warm steaming water kissed every inch of her body. Aisha began to relax and let go of all her anxiety over the gala. Without giving her any warning, her mind quickly turned to Chandler Larson.

*It's been well over a week since he returned my wallet. I can't believe he hasn't bothered to call. But then again, I haven't put forth an effort to call him either. I can't help it if I'm not an aggressive girl. I like to be pursued.*

Suddenly, the script was flipped and Aisha's thoughts of Chandler were replaced by her present dilemma with the building. She still had no idea where she was going to get the rest of the money to keep her studio. She'd looked at other prospective sites but none suited her. Plus, there wasn't a bank or mortgage company out there that would give her the time of day with the kind of debt ratio she had. Her only hope of keeping the studio alive was to hold on to the building she was in.

"Lord," she cried out while the beads of water continued to pound her milk ebony flesh. "You say that if I believe in you and your word that I can ask what I may and it will be done. Well, Lord, I'm asking you to open a window and pour me out a huge blessing. I can't lose this studio. I just can't."

The water began to turn cool and Aisha jumped out of the shower, grabbed her plush tangerine bath towel and dashed off into her room, drying off with every step she made. She slipped on a midnight blue jacquard corset-back dress. Her blue satin heels bore a crossover front strap and knotted gold metal ornament encrusted in crystals. She sprayed on a splash of Adore before she styled her hair into a single curl twist traveling down the course of her back. She reached along the side of the oak sleigh bed and retrieved her duffel bag, checking inside to make sure her dance clothes were all in place. Stealing one last glance in front of the full length mirror she said out loud, "Aisha Carlisle, you don't look too bad there, girl. Knock 'em dead tonight!"

Crystal chandeliers extended from the high beam ceilings of the Cannon Center ballroom. A separate cocktail area was host to a bevy of drinks from hard liquor to teas to diet sodas. The balcony offered a serene panoramic view for people watching. Each table was draped in crisp white cotton table cloths with an elegant centerpiece of fresh cut flowers in a glass vase. Cloth napkins and silverware were arranged ever so perfectly next to fresh caeser salad, ice tea and water. Some of the guests had already taken their seats while others walked around chatting with one another. Some huddled in cliques and others made their way around the massive ballroom alone.

The pedestal stage offered an abundance of room for Aisha and her dance troupe. The crowd stopped to focus on the group of girls standing in perfect pose when the blue velvet curtains on the stage swung open. The girls, dressed in lavender puffed sleeve leotards and matching georgette skirts, were another crowd pleaser. The guests began to applaud when the girls began to move to the beat of the music. When Aisha graced the stage, moving in perfect rhythm with her dance team, her energetic charge seemed to ignite the audience and louder applause reverberated off of the walls. The upbeat music Aisha chose showed off the skillful maneuvers of the young girls before they ended some ten minutes later with a high-twist and boogie step.

The dance team performed perfectly. Aisha felt a lump rising up from the pit of her stomach to her throat as she surveyed the crowd. The applause sounded heavenly to her ears. She signaled for the girls to take another bow before they pranced off the stage. Aisha remained for a final bow and one last look at all the faces. *Thank you Lord*, she said to herself.

While waiting on each of the girls' parents to pick them up from backstage, Aisha complimented her students for their outstanding performance. When the last girl departed, Aisha changed back into her evening clothes and set out to locate her parents. She didn't have to look far as she eyed the sophisticated couple heading her way.

"Princess, you were great. I know you must be very proud of the girls," her father spoke with obvious pride. He hugged Aisha before continuing. "I don't think they made one awkward step during the entire routine."

Her mom responded before Aisha could say anything. "If they did, we couldn't tell anyway. Just like your father said, we're proud of you."

'Thanks, Momma. Thanks, Daddy," she said proudly. "I'm glad the two of you are here. When I looked out in the crowd and I didn't see you, I thought you got held up or something."

"Excuse me." The voice behind her sounded somewhat familiar to her. She hesitated slightly before turning around. There stood the towering Chandler Larson. His black on black Sean John tuxedo suit was tailored perfectly, fitting him to a tee. The handsome features of this man mesmerized her. She breathed in the heavenly aroma of his cologne while peering into his mysteriously dark, sexy eyes.

"Chandler," she mumbled. "How are you?"

"I'm good," he replied. "Look, I'm sorry to interrupt, but I wanted to tell you how much I enjoyed the performance. I had no idea you'd be attending this evening's event, and I certainly had no idea you and your girls would be the star attraction," he said.

"I must say, I'm equally surprised to see you here," she responded with a smile.

Looking over in the direction of her parents, she said, "By the way, these are my parents, Mr. and Mrs. Benjamin Carlisle. Mom, Dad this is the man I told you about. You know, the one who found my wallet. Chandler Larson."

"Nice to meet you both," Chandler said as he extended his hand out to each of them. He quickly saw features of Aisha in both parents. She had her father's high cheekbones and her mother's thick mane and tantalizingly sexy almond-shaped eyes.

"It's good to know there are still honest people around," Mr. Carlisle said, staring Chandler straight in the eyes.

"Thank you, sir," he replied. "I think honesty is always the best policy. My mother taught me that it's better to suffer the consequences from telling the truth than to suffer the consequences from telling a lie. I try to remember that in everything I do. It's carried me a long way, sir."

"Your mother is a wise woman, Chandler. A wise woman indeed," Benjamin commented.

Mrs. Carlisle slightly nodded in agreement with her husband of forty-two years.

"Daddy, Mother, if you don't mind I'm going to do a little socializing," Aisha said.

"Go on, princess, do your thing," her father urged proudly. Your mother and I are going back to our table. Join us when you finish.

"I will," Aisha answered.

Aisha felt Chandler's hand cup the small of her back. An unexpected warm sensation came over her when she felt the gentleness of his touch. She turned and glanced up at him. His smile fascinated her as he extended his free hand in front of him, directing her steps. Like a partner leading her to the dance floor, she allowed him to maneuver her through the bevy of guests that filled the Cannon Center.

"You're quite a gentleman, Chandler. But really, there's no need for you to chaperone me. I'm quite comfortable mingling on my own."

"So, you're trying to get rid of me, huh?"

"No. Of course not. I'm only saying that I'm used to these types of functions, but I'm not used to having someone following my every move, if you know what I mean."

"Yes, I do know what you mean and I understand. So that being said, I'll leave you to do your thing." He tried to hide his obvious disappointment. He hadn't meant to come on too strong, but Aisha was hypnotic.

"Maybe I'll catch up to you before the evening is over."

"Sure," he responded. "I see a couple of familiar faces myself, so I guess I'll go mingle as well."

"Thanks for understanding," Aisha told him.

"No problem, no problem at all," Chandler responded then reluctantly walked in the opposite direction.

Aisha chatted with several of her students' parents, as well as some influential constituents she hoped would become corporate sponsors for the studio. She even had a chance to converse with the mayor who raved about the performance.

Satisfied that she had done her share of socializing, Aisha began to look for her parents again. When she saw them sitting at their table, she went over and sat down next to them. Other guests soon began to locate their tables when they saw the waiters preparing for the sit down dinner. Aisha scanned the room and saw Chandler sitting at a table near the middle section of the vast room. He seemed totally absorbed in the conversation he was having with, of all people, the Chief of Police. Her attention was quickly averted from Chandler to someone tapping her on her shoulder. It was Gabby's mother, Elisa Santana.

"Hi, Miss Santana," Aisha said, offering her hand.

Elisa shook her hand lightly.

"Has anyone claimed this seat?" Miss Santana asked, pointing to the vacant chair next to Aisha.

"No, as far as I know, it's yours," Aisha said while looking at the other guests to see if they were saving the seat for someone. After being assured that it was okay, Elisa sat down. Moments later, the servers began serving the main course.

Aisha introduced her parents to Elisa and the other guests at the table introduced themselves.

"Aisha, the girls were fantastic this evening."

"Thank you, Miss Santana."

Elisa Santana's daughter, Gabby, was one of Aisha's star students. The compliment from Miss Santana excited Aisha. From what Aisha had heard, Elisa Santana was quite a dancer herself. Gabby had told many of the girls that her mother used to dance for a living. Aisha didn't know if what Gabby said was true. Since Elisa had never said anything about the kind of work she did, Aisha didn't bother to ask. Some things Aisha felt just weren't her business when it came to her students and their parents. But what she did know was that Elisa Santana was quite sophisticated. Aisha noticed from the times Elisa hung around the studio to watch the girls practice, that compliments didn't come easy for her, not even when it came to her own daughter.

"Their routine was original. Did you choreograph the entire dance routine?"

"Yes, ma'am."

"Please, I've told you, don't say ma'am to me. Call me *Elisa*. I insist."

"Okay, Elisa. How did you like Gabby's solo? I think she's a natural."

"Well, of course you might think I'm partial to her because she's my daughter, but actually I'm not. She was exceptionally good tonight. Sometimes I tend to be a little tough on her I know, but it's really paying off. She loves your class too."

Conversation was soon silenced by the clacking of eating utensils as guests dined on rosemary-seasoned chicken breasts sautéed with fresh broccoli and garlic cream. As usual, Aisha pushed away from the table when the servers brought dessert.

"Princess, aren't you going to eat your dessert?" Benjamin asked her, knowing full well what his daughter's response would be.

"Daddy, I can't." Aisha glanced at the raspberry-swirled white chocolate cheesecake topped with slivers of white chocolate as if she was having second thoughts about eating it. "You eat it, Daddy. I know that cheesecake is your favorite," she said instead.

"Right you are, so if you insist, then I'll take it. No use letting it go to waste," he chuckled, winking his eye at Aisha while reaching over his wife and taking the dessert dish that Aisha had picked up and held in her hand.

Aisha saw the less-than-pleased expression on her mother's face when her father accepted the dessert, but she pretended not to notice.

"Well, if you'll excuse me again. I'm going to walk off some of that delicious meal. I'll return later, Daddy," Aisha said, walking over to him and kissing him on the top of his head.

"Do you mind if I tag along?" Elisa asked her, scooting away from the table.

"No, certainly not," Aisha responded.

Walking slowly around the ballroom, the two ladies talked about the success of the gala before a woman walked up and complimented Aisha again.

"She's right, you know," Elisa said in response to the woman's comment about Aisha's studio being one of the best.

"Yes, it's great to hear that people love what I'm doing with the girls and the studio. But to be honest, I don't know how much longer I'm going to have it." The moment the words came out of her mouth, Aisha regretted having said them.

"You can't be serious. You heard what that woman just said. You run one of the best studios in the city. Where are you going?"

"Never mind. I shouldn't have said that. I'm sorry." Aisha quickly apologized, hoping that Elisa wouldn't push her to explain what she'd meant.

"No, I can't let it slide. Something's going on. Tell me. What is it, Aisha? Maybe I can help," Elisa replied, sincerity mixed with curiosity in her voice.

"Really, it's nothing, Elisa," Aisha commented, hoping she'd convinced Elisa there was nothing wrong. *The last person I need to confide in is one of my students' parents. That is simply bad business,* Aisha thought, as the two of them continued strolling through the steady maze of chattering people. Yet, somehow, for reasons unknown, Aisha felt drawn to Gabby's enigmatic mother.

"Oh, there's something going on alright," Elisa insisted. "And you're not going to get rid of me until you tell me what that something is. Come on. Let's go out on the terrace where we can talk privately. I want all the details."

Elisa lightly took hold of Aisha's fingertips and led her to the terrace. Turning her head around, Aisha thought she saw Chandler walking toward the open bar, but she couldn't be sure as someone immediately blocked her view and Elisa tugged her again.

"Now, let's hear it," Elisa told her.

One of the servers came out on the terrace balancing a

tray of red and white wine. Elisa grabbed a glass for her and one for Aisha. Without asking her if she drank, Elisa practically pushed the red wine in Aisha's direction.

Aisha took a sip of the bittersweet wine and exhaled.

"I'm listening," Elisa said, continuing to pressure Aisha to talk.

"I really should wait and tell all of my students' parents at once."

"Tell us what? Girl, will you please just tell me what's going on?" Elisa said, almost sounding a little frustrated with Aisha.

Aisha stammered as she began to speak. Part of her *wanted* to tell Elisa what was going on and the other part of her was saying that this was no time to confess her problems to someone she barely even knew. So with added caution, Aisha told Elisa about her plans to meet collectively with the parents in a couple of days, and let them know that the studio may have to go on sabbatical, at least temporarily, is how she put it.

"Sabbatical? That's a bunch of crock, and you know it," Elisa hissed. "Why would you even consider closing the studio? I don't care if you say it's a sabbatical or whatever, I still don't understand your reasoning." Elisa began to throw out question after question to Aisha.

"Do you need more students? Is it cash flow? Are you sick? What? What is it?" Elisa asked, with both of her hands suddenly spreading out in the air.

Drained with Elisa's constant insistence that she divulge what was going on with the studio, along with the glass of mind-relaxing wine, Aisha proceeded to tell Elisa about her money problems. The thing is, once Aisha started talking she couldn't seem to stop. A half hour later, they were still out on the terrace and she had basically confided in Elisa about everything pertaining to the studio.

82 *Shelia E. Lipsey*

"Aisha, you can't give up the studio and that's that," Elisa responded adamantly after listening to Aisha pour out the seriousness of her situation.

"Elisa, didn't you hear anything I just said? I don't have the money. I don't exactly have a choice," Aisha retorted. Didn't Elisa understand anything she'd just told her? Apparently, Elisa somehow must not believe the gravity of her situation, or so Aisha thought.

"Aisha, I have an idea. Let me check on something first and I'll give you a call tomorrow afternoon."

"Are you sure? What do you have in mind?"

"Just wait, let me look into some things first. I don't want to give you false hope. But I'm almost sure something can be done to save your dance studio. Tomorrow, okay?"

"I didn't tell you all of this for you to make this your problem, Elisa. I hate the fact that I told you, period. I shouldn't be sobbing on your shoulder," Aisha commented.

"Tomorrow, Aisha," Elisa said again, using her hand to wave Aisha off.

Hesitating, Aisha answered, "Tomorrow it is. Thanks, Elisa." Aisha reached over and hugged the alluring woman.

"Don't thank me yet. I'm going to find Gabby and then I'm out of here. I have to work tonight."

"Tonight? It's almost ten o'clock."

"I know, but try telling that to my boss. Gotta go, we'll talk tomorrow." Elisa Santana whirled around. Her rhinestone t-strapped black stilettos clicked in perfect rhythm with the sashay of the draping ruffles on her black three-tiered halter dress as she proceeded to exit the terrace to locate her daughter.

Elisa found her standing in a corner with some of her friends. "Gabby, come on. We have to leave. I cannot be late for work."

"But, Mom," the fourteen year old whined. "I wanted to stay a little longer. There's no one else leaving this early."

"Not tonight, Gabby. I have to work and you know it."

"Can't I go home with Cherise and her mom? She already said it was okay."

"What have I told you about going behind my back and making plans and then telling me at the last minute?" Elisa said, slightly raising her voice to let Gabby know she was displeased with what she'd done.

"I didn't go behind your back. Cherise asked her mom if I could spend the night and I said I would have to check with you first. Please Mom. Tomorrow's Saturday and I don't want to be at home by myself tonight."

"Don't start, Gabby. I don't have time for this." Elisa was quickly becoming frustrated with her only child. Actually it would save her a considerable amount of time if Gabby could spend the night with her friend, Cherise.

She was glad Gabby made friends so easily. When she first met Cherise at the dance studio, Gabby and her hit if off immediately. Cherise's mom, Stacey, didn't work and she often volunteered to chauffeur the girls to and from their dance recitals and rehearsals.

"Let me check with Stacey. Where are they?" Elisa asked, scanning the room.

"Right over there by the refreshment table," Gabby answered, pointing a few feet away.

Elisa Santana's long sculpted legs strolled across the room and walked up to Stacey just as she was about to pop a hors d'oeuvre in her mouth.

"Hi, Stacey."

"Hi, Elisa. And yes, I said Gabby could spend the night. You don't even have to ask and you know it. I love having her over," Stacey said then popped the hors d'oeuvre in her mouth.

"I just don't want her to wear out her welcome, Stacey. You know that."

"Girl, please, you should know better than that by now. Anyway, Gabby's an angel."

"No, you're the angel. I don't know what I'd do without you."

"Elisa, really, it's nothing."

"Well, I have to go. I don't want to be late."

Elisa kissed Gabby on the forehead, said her goodbyes to Cherise and Stacey and rushed toward the escalators of the Cannon Center. Within minutes she had reached her car and maneuvered the baby blue Z4 Roadster on to the open stretch of Highway 205. She turned up the volume on the surround sound system and listened to Destiny's Child, *I Need A Soldier*. Moving to the beat, she sang along with the group as they sang, *"I need a soldier; someone who can take care of me. One who carries big things, if you know what I mean."*

# 12

Elisa Santana keyed in her secret code and the massive wrought iron gates of the private parking garage swung open. She sped inside and drove her car into the space that read *Diamond's Spot*, her professional name.

When she swung open the door to The Lynx Association, she stepped on to the thick plush carpet in the main entry-way. The forty-foot limestone fireplace revealed the obvious, that the members of the Lynx were no ordinary people. The grandeur of the lobby with its granite countertops, marble floors and solid gold hardware gave off an aura of warmth and wealth.

"Good evening, Miss Santana," the tuxedo-clad bellman spoke.

"Evenin', Thomas," Elisa replied but never stopped walking. She continued along the winding mahogany pan-eled corridor until she reached the private elevator for em-ployees. The elevator doors quickly opened. She smiled at her reflection through the mirrored doors, leaned in closer and pouted her lips before reaching in her bag and pulling out an oversized silver and black key. After placing it inside the matching keyhole and turning it, the elevator doors closed just as quickly as they had opened. Elisa leaned against the cold elevator wall then breathed a sigh of welcome relief.

*My God it's been a long day and I still have four hours to go.* "Wake up, girl," she said out loud while continuing to glare at her flawless reflection. She fumbled through her purse again and pulled out a thumb-sized glass vial. Opening it, she used her middle fingernail to remove some of the white powder. Raising her finger up to her nose, she snorted it and then took another dab of it and placed it on the tip of her tongue. *Now, that should do it . . . who ever said diamonds are a girl's best friend was definitely wrong.*

The elevator doors swung open to deafening music, but she had grown accustomed to it. She swayed her hips to the beat of a rapper singing about some *Candy Shop*.

"What's up, Diamond?" one of the bartenders yelled out over the music.

"If you have to ask, you don't need to know," she quickly answered and smiled. "Gotta go." She rushed past him and the staring eyes of the well-dressed men sitting at the tables. Several young ladies danced erotically on an elevated platform, keeping up with every beat booming from the sexually explicit lyrics.

"Diamond, where have you been? I thought you were off tonight," a rather young-looking, scantily-clad Puerto Rican girl said as she walked up to her.

"No, Gabby had to perform tonight at the Mayor's charity gala. Don't you remember me telling you that?"

"Oh yeah; I forgot that's all. It's been wild around here. How'd she do?"

"Great, as usual," Elisa answered, without breaking stride. The girl followed her and they kept talking until they reached Elisa's dressing room. Elisa stepped out of her stilettos and eased her dress down over her firm round hips. "So things have been jumping tonight, huh?"

"Yes indeed. So you know I'm not complaining. It's a gold mine in here tonight and I got the cheddar to prove it." The girl pulled out a fat wad of one hundred dollar bills from between her size triple D breasts.

"Sookie, sookie now," Elisa responded. "Let me take a shower and get ready so I can earn my fair share. I'll check you later. Oh, is Jason here tonight? I need to talk to him about something."

"Yeah, the boss man is somewhere around here."

"Thanks. I'll catch him after my set ends. I think I might have a proposition for him that he won't want to refuse," Elisa said with a smirk.

"I hear you. You know he seems to just about drool over your propositions. I can't wait to see what you're going to wave under his greedy little nose this time around," the girl said, walking away and laughing as she exited Elisa's dressing room.

"You know it's only the best for me," Elisa managed to remark just as the girl closed the dressing room door. Elisa stripped down to nothing. On her way into the meager-sized bathroom to take a shower, she mumbled, "Miss Aisha Carlisle, I'm about to show you what the real world is all about. You're going to go from zero to ninety in no time flat if you stick with me. Oh yes, indeed," Elisa said, stepping into the shower and allowing the jet spring of water to saturate her body.

# 13

Tameria sat in Aisha's office with her legs propped up on the chair next to her. She told Aisha about a woman who was brought into the emergency room with a knife embedded in her shoulder as she munched on a bag of hot Cheetos that she had gotten out of the vending machine. Aisha liked hearing about Tameria's hospital experiences. The fact that Tameria had the ability to help the sick and injured was a tremendous thrill to Aisha.

"Tameria, you never have a dull moment at that hospital. It must work on you though, seeing the worst of the worst injuries and even death coming through those emergency room doors," Aisha remarked.

"True, but I have to learn how to leave it behind when I walk out those hospital doors. Sometimes it's easier said than done," Tameria replied.

"I can only imagine." Changing the subject Aisha asked, "Where's that man of yours? The great resident neurosurgeon, Dr. Chase Gray?"

"He has four days off, which is a rarity for him, so he decided to go home to St. Louis and visit his family. He hasn't seen them in about six or seven months," Tameria answered her friend.

"No wonder you're here keeping me company. Maybe Chase needs to leave town more often. That way I can get to have my best friend to myself."

"Yeah, yeah." Tameria waved her hand toward Aisha and laughed. "Tell me the latest on your dilemma. Have you figured out what you're going to do?"

"Not really. I'm still seeking God's direction," Aisha lied. "But one of the parents did offer to help me."

"One of *whose* parents? Yours?"

"No, not mine. You know that my parents don't have the kind of money I need."

"Well, who in the world is it? And just how did they offer to help you?"

Aisha looked around to see if she saw anyone in earshot of her office then continued talking. "You know. With the studio."

Using both hands to make a quote sign, Tameria asked sarcastically, "And like I said, how is this *parent* supposed to do that?"

"Look, Tameria, I don't know just yet. She's supposed to call me. She has to check on some things first."

"She? Who exactly is this person, Aisha? I hope you're not talking about any of these girls' parents." Tameria said, wrinkling her brow.

"Actually it is one of the parents here. Her name is Elisa Santana. I think I've mentioned her to you before. Her daughter's name is Gabby, one of my lead dancers."

"I vaguely remember seeing her. But how did she know about the studio?"

"We were talking at the Mayor's gala the other night."

"What? Why would you tell her your business? You don't know that woman like that." Tameria scolded.

"It wasn't like I *meant* to tell her. It just came out. Anyway, who knows? She may or may not be able to help me. I know that wherever she works, she must be doing pretty well for herself financially."

Tameria stared at her best friend with obvious concern. "And how do you know that?"

Aisha moved around anxiously in her chair. " 'Cause she has a nice ride and the woman is always dressed like a runway model. The lady's got style and plenty of it too."

"Just be careful about telling folks your business. You know how that can backfire."

"Sure, I know. I'm thinking that maybe she knows the owner of this building or something. Why else would she offer to help? Unless she's sitting on a gold mine," Aisha joked. "Seriously, though, whoever the owner is, he won't reveal himself to me. I went online and did a property search but it pulled up some company name. When I looked for the company online, it came up blank too. But whoever he is he always has Thaddeus contact me. What do you think about that?"

"I guess I'm not surprised. The man probably has a lot of properties. Why would he want to meet his tenants anyway? That's what leasing agents like Thaddeus are paid to do."

"I know. But enough of this conversation. Let's get out of here and go get something to eat," Aisha suggested, then leaned back in her chair and yawned.

"That's right on time because I'm on call tonight. That means no real food for me for at least the next twenty something hours."

Aisha and Tameria drove down on Beale Street to the Hard Rock Cafe for lunch. Afterwards the two friends walked up and down the famous street and did a little window shopping. Aisha confided in Tameria about her spark of interest in Chandler. She told her that Chandler didn't call often but when he did, she enjoyed their conversation. Chandler was an easy-going kind of man, something Aisha liked. She didn't want to feel pressured into anything with anyone.

Admitting to Tameria that she was attracted to him was a big step for her. Tameria reminded Aisha that she was young and beautiful with feelings and emotions and that there was nothing wrong with liking Chandler. Aisha swung her arms back and forth while they peeped inside some of the quaint shops lining the busy street. At the end of their stroll, they stopped off at *A Schwab*, the store that has everything imaginable, and purchased a bag of old fashioned, soft peppermint candy sticks. Two hours after leaving, Tameria drove Aisha back to the studio in time for her afternoon dance class.

Elisa made her entrance into the dance studio and as usual, all eyes fell on her sleek cat-like moves. Dressed in fashionable flared black athletic pants, a bright yellow sports bra, and crisp white Saucony running shoes, she walked to the receptionist desk and, as if in slow motion, approached the counter.

Angie immediately greeted her. "Good afternoon, Miss Santana."

"Hello, Angie. Is Aisha here or has she already left for the afternoon?"

"No, she's still here. She's in her office on the phone. As soon as I see her phone light go off, I'll let her know you're here. You can have a seat if you'd like."

"No, thanks. Just tell her I'll be in the back in one of the classrooms. I might as well do a few stretches while I wait. That is all right, isn't it?"

"Sure, I know she won't mind. I'll tell her where you are when she finishes her call. Check Classroom 4. It should be empty."

*Shelia E. Lipsey*

"Thanks, Angie," Elisa answered while walking toward the classrooms.

Aisha relaxed in her office chair and listened to Chandler over the phone trying to convince her to spend some time with him.

"Chandler, I don't know if I can make it tonight. I'm beat and I still have errands to run after I leave the studio."

Chandler held on to the other end of the phone and exhaled. He was not going to give up on trying to persuade her to see him again. Her reserved demeanor only made him want her more. Whatever it took to get Aisha Carlisle, he had resolved to do. He wasn't used to women turning him down. Aisha was different too. She piqued the playa in him. He refused to respond to her answer of *no*. Instead, he remained silent and waited for her to say something.

"Are you still there?" she asked him.

"Yes, of course. I was just thinking." He used his special voice that was a mixture of sadness and sexiness.

"Thinking about what?"

"About how I can get you to share just a small fraction of your time with me. I'll tell you what. Why don't I come by the studio in say, an hour?"

"I . . ."

He cut her off before she could continue. "Stop right there. I won't take no for an answer. I want to see you, Aisha. Won't you at least have dinner with me, nothing else? I promise not to keep you out past your bedtime. I'll even run your errands for you while you rest," he agreed.

She found him particularly amusing. Whenever she talked to him, he always managed to make her laugh about something before they hung up. But she still reminded herself to tread lightly with Chandler. She didn't want to get too involved too quickly.

Chandler's persistence soon paid off when he heard Aisha tell him, "Oh, okay. You've twisted my arm. I'll see you in an hour."

"An hour it is."

Aisha barely had time to hang up the phone when Angie buzzed in.

"Yes, Angie?"

"Gabby's mother is here to see you. She's in Classroom 4 doing stretches," Angie spoke through the intercom.

"Thanks. I'll go find her." Aisha glanced at the clock sitting on the window ledge. "Remember to lock up before you leave, Angie. And have a good evening."

"Thanks. I'll holler at you when I'm walking out."

Aisha proceeded down the hallway, anxious to find out what the mysterious Elisa Santana had to say. As she approached Classroom 4, Aisha stopped at the doorway and watched Elisa glide across the dance floor with the delicate grace of a gazelle. *Maybe Gabby was telling the truth about her mother having been a dancer*, Aisha reasoned as she continued to silently watch Elisa.

Elisa danced toward the balance barre. When she spotted Aisha standing in the doorway, she signaled with her hand for Aisha to join her. Moving in behind Elisa, Aisha grabbed hold of the dance barre and began to sway to the sound of the music being pumped in through the surround sound speakers. The two of them moved simultaneously away from the barre and began performing their individual dance moves. Elisa gyrated her hips in a circular rhythm, taking steps back, forward and to the side. Her arms took on moves of their own as she effortlessly shimmied across the floor.

Aisha was oblivious to Elisa as she became lost in the music herself. Aisha's body moved along the dance floor and her fingers snapped to the beat of the song. The two of them continued their free style dancing until the song ended.

"You're good, Elisa," Aisha complimented.

"Thank you. That means a lot coming from a professional like yourself."

"Looks like you could probably teach me a thing or two. How long have you been dancing?" Aisha asked, curious to know why Elisa never mentioned that she was such a great dancer. "And don't try to tell me anything otherwise, because you most definitely know the art."

"Like Gabby, I took dance lessons, mostly during my pre-teen years. It's always been a great outlet for me. I wish I could have gone to college and pursued it even further, but life has a way of taking you in its own direction, you know?" Elisa said with a somber look clouding her face.

"Yes, as a matter of fact, I do," Aisha answered.

"But I don't know if I could have ever been as good as you are," Elisa responded.

"I think you already are."

"I don't think so," Elisa added.

"Well I do. Anyway, when the truth is the truth, tell it, is what I always say." Aisha proceeded to walk over to the towel cabinet and grabbed a couple of towels, tossing one to Elisa.

"Thanks." Elisa wiped beads of sweat from her brow. "Do you want to talk in here?"

"Angie will be leaving in a few minutes so I'd prefer to go up front. I'm expecting a friend to drop by in about an hour and that way I can hear him when he sounds the buzzer."

"No problem." They proceeded to the front of the dance studio and Aisha led her into the break room."

"Would you like some coffee, soda, water?"

"Water will do just fine unless you have a PowerAde or something."

"Sure, PowerAde it is." Aisha opened the door to the refrigerator and pulled out two ice-cold PowerAdes. "Hope you like strawberry."

"Love it. Thanks," Elisa responded and reached for the beverage. After taking a couple of gulps, Elisa started talking. "First of all, let me start by telling you that I think I have a solution to your problem. That is if you'll listen with an open mind."

Red flags went off in Aisha's head when Elisa advised her to listen with an open mind. *Must be something illegal or too far-fetched.* "Sure, let's hear it."

Angie appeared at the door. "I'm leaving, Aisha. I'll see you tomorrow. Goodnight, Miss Santana," Angie said, flipping her hand back and forth.

"Goodnight, Angie."

"Have a good evening, Angie," Elisa told her.

Elisa took Aisha off guard when she told her, "I have a confession to make."

"A confession? What kind of confession?" Aisha twitched. What was Elisa about to confess? Aisha's nervous feeling escalated.

'I'm a dancer too, Aisha. I hadn't mentioned it before because until now it wasn't necessary."

With her mouth gaping open, Aisha nodded her head, unsure as to where this surprisingly strange conversation was leading.

"Close your mouth. You don't have to look so shocked," Elisa told her while snickering softly. "You just told me that I was a good dancer."

"Yes, I . . . I know. It's just that. Well, what can I say?" Aisha continued to stutter. "I mean, uh, who do you work for? And what kind of dancer are you?" Aisha asked with reservation, afraid of the answer that was already brewing in her mind. *I know she's not about to tell me that she's a stripper*, Aisha thought to herself. *No, way.*

"I work for a private association.

"What kind of association?" Aisha's eyebrows furrowed together. She was curious as to what Elisa meant.

"I'm employed at The Lynx Association. You have heard of it, haven't you?"

*Another red flag.*

"Yes, I've heard of it, but I don't know what it entails. I only know it's supposed to be some sort of upscale country club."

"Basically you're right."

"You don't have another job?"

"Nope, The Lynx is it. I have clients there who pay me quite well, to say the least."

Aisha asked her, "You mean they pay you to, you know, dance like me?"

Elisa's hair swayed as she tossed her head back in laughter at Aisha's obvious naiveté.

"You really don't have any idea what I'm talking about, do you?"

Aisha couldn't answer. She knew that Elisa wasn't being paid to do some lyrical dance move. How stupid of her, but she didn't know if she wanted to hear the rest of Elisa's so-called confession.

"Look, Elisa. There's no need for you to tell me your personal business. Whatever you do, then that's your thing."

"I know but what I do can play an important part in saving this studio," Elisa said with an outstretched hand while looking around the break room.

"And how is that?" Aisha asked.

"I'm what my clients call, 'a private dancer.' In addition, the Lynx pays me a base salary of $1,000 a week."

Aisha swallowed hard before saying, "Did you just say one thousand dollars a week?" Aisha spoke in an exasperated voice saying, "That's simply unbelievable."

"Believe me, it's true. Most weeks I go home with as much as $3,500 to $5,000. That's chump change considering the money these men have and they're not stingy with it either. Especially when they're getting what they want out of the deal."

"What you're really telling me is that you're a stripper."

"Call it what you may, it pays the bills, sweetheart," Elisa said in a perturbed tone for the first time during their conversation.

"And exactly what are they getting for their money, Elisa? For that kind of money it sounds like it requires more than just dancing," Aisha told her with a look of disgust at the thought of what Elisa Santana could really be doing.

"If a client wants it to be more than that, then I'm sure some girls will oblige, but as for me, I'm strictly a private dancer. Whatever they want me to do during the time they're paying me, then I do it."

"I see. What does that include, Elisa?" Aisha was hesitant about asking her, afraid of what her answer would be.

"I know what you're hinting at. And the answer is I draw the line when it comes to certain things and other things I don't disclose to anyone. But I will say this much, if they want me to take off my clothes, I do it. If they want me to drop it like it's hot, I do it. If they want me to put it in their face, then I put it in their face. I'm making a living and a doggone good living for me and Gabby, don't you think?"

"I can't deny that. But why are you telling me this? How can what you do help my situation? Do you think one of these gentlemen will invest in the studio or do they own a bank or what?"

"Honey, they own banks, car dealerships, sports teams, radio stations. You name it and I betcha there's someone there who owns it. They're doctors, lawyers, executives too."

"I hear you. But I still don't understand what all this has to do with me," Aisha remarked.

"Here's how you play into the deal. A couple of weeks ago one of the girls had to leave town because of an illness in her family. One of her parents is really sick. She won't be coming back for a few months, if she comes back at all."

"Stop right there," Aisha insisted. "I know where you're going with this. I could never do such a thing as strip. That's what this adds up to. I'm a Christian and you know it. I can't do it. I appreciate the fact that you're concerned about me and the dance studio, but . . . stripping? Taking my clothes off and God knows what else, for money?" Aisha snapped.

Elisa stood up and cut Aisha off by showing the palm of her hand. "Look, I'm not going to sit here and beg you, nor am I going to try to convince you to do something that goes against your beliefs. So suit yourself. But I'm telling you this, the Lynx Association is a classy, discreet and well respected gentleman's organization. Contrary to what you might think, it is not one of those sleazy strip joints lined up and down Brooks Road. You've got it all wrong. I tell you what. Before you make up your mind, why don't you come and be my guest tomorrow night?"

"I, I, don't think that's a good idea. There's no way I'm going to such a place."

"Didn't I tell you that it's nothing like what you think? It's really top of the line. It's like going to a private party, except there are more men than women attending."

Rubbing her hands together, Aisha stood up now. *What on earth could have ever possessed me to tell Elisa about my problem in the first place? I must have been on the brink of insanity to tell her my business*, Aisha chastised herself.

Elisa wouldn't let up. If she could convince Aisha to go with her to the Lynx, she was pretty sure she could convince her that if she wanted to get out of the hole she'd dug for herself then the Lynx would be her shovel.

"Like I said, thanks but no thanks," Aisha told her.

"I'm not asking you to do anything but come and have a glass of wine or a *diet soda* if you prefer," she said jokingly. "You can check out the atmosphere and meet a couple of the other ladies who work there. Come on, I promise no one will get out of line or make you uncomfortable. And if you find out that it's something you wouldn't feel right about doing, then so be it. You just up and leave. No harm done." Elisa raised her eyebrows and placed one hand on her waist.

Aisha thought about it a few seconds and then answered, "Let me think about it, but I already know that my answer is still going to be no." The buzzer on the front door sounded. "That must be my friend and I'm not even close to being ready."

"Go, scoot. We can talk later. I'll go out the back entrance."

"That's not necessary, really."

"No, it's all right. My car is parked on the back side of the parking garage anyway. Not many people park back there so I don't have to worry about anybody scratching up my little baby," Elisa said as she started walking toward the back exit leading to the garage.

"Suit yourself," Aisha told her. "Hey, Elisa."

"What?"

"For what it's worth, thanks for trying to help. But I know God has a ram in the bush for me."

"Sure he does, honey. And believe me you can have your pick of *rams* at the Lynx," Elisa remarked, then sashayed around and strutted away. Just as she reached the exit door, she said, "I'll call you tomorrow and let you know what time I'm picking you up."

Elisa smiled and walked out the back door, leaving Aisha dumbfounded. The buzzer sounded again. Aisha jumped. She waved both hands in the air in frustration then went to unlock the door.

"I'm coming," she yelled.

The tension Elisa had managed to raise in Aisha quickly deflated when she saw Chandler with a sexy grin on his handsome face and a single red rose in his hand.

"Hello, there," he said. He handed the single rose to her. "This is for you."

"Thank you, how thoughtful," she answered, while inhaling the sweet fragrance of the rose. "Let me put this in some water. I think I have a vase in my office."

"Okay," he said as he stepped inside the studio.

"Have a seat and I'll be right back," she said and disappeared before he could answer.

She told him again from her office, "This was really nice of you, Chandler."

"You're welcome. A pretty lady like yourself deserves a bouquet of flowers but I was afraid I might run you off."

She walked back from the studio. "Now why would you think something like that?"

Smiling again, he answered, "Let's not even go there."

She laughed. "Will you give me a about fifteen minutes, Chandler. I had a visitor before you so I haven't had a chance to change. I'm sorry."

"No need to apologize. I'll sit right here like a good little boy until you're ready," he teased.

While he waited, he marveled over the fact that he had begun to develop a tender spot for Aisha. Over the years, especially since his heart had been crushed, he'd become cold, hard and callous when it came to women. There was no way he was going to let another woman get as close to him as he had allowed his ex-fiancée, Tracye, to get. At times, he could swear he felt the remnants of heartbreak that she'd left stamped indelibly on his heart. After the initial shock of seeing her naked body underneath one of his friends, he turned and walked out of the apartment they had shared for over two years. Each time she called and pleaded for his forgiveness, he attacked her with the most derogatory words he could think of. He just couldn't forgive her infidelity.

He made a 360 after that and changed from being kind, thoughtful, loving Chandler to a misogynistic brute full of unleashed anger. Despite his angry actions towards her, Tracye had refused to back off and continued to beg him to take her back. Several weeks after their breakup, Chandler gave in to her persistence and agreed to meet her at the apartment.

Using his key, he walked in and saw her standing near the living room door. Chandler didn't bother to say a word. He briskly walked over to her, yanked her shoulder length hair so hard that it snapped her neck back. Tracye tried to break free from his grasp, but the hold he had on her was too powerful. With each blow to Tracye, Chandler hoped she felt his pain, pain that she had caused. When he was done, he spit at her. "You want forgiveness," he asked her. "Look in the mirror. That's how I forgive!" he screamed before storming out the door.

Tracye never reported Chandler's assault to any one. She was far too ashamed and afraid. She didn't know if any one would believe that the normally mild-mannered Chandler Larson would do something so violently vindictive.

Shortly after his retaliation against Tracye, Chandler packed his bags, left Montgomery and moved to Memphis. Not once had he regretted his attack on Tracye, someone he once loved. When he applied for the position as a police officer with the Memphis Police Department, he found that he enjoyed his job more than he had anticipated. There were times when he thought of how he exacted his revenge on Tracye and in a weird way, he believed his ability to assault her without feeling remorse was actually a good trait because on the streets of Memphis there was no time to feel anything for anyone who was breaking the law. As for Aisha, he was drawn to her coyness and the innocence she exuded. He planned on using her attributes to reel her in. And getting her to have dinner with him was his first conquest in breaking her down.

Aisha wanted to go back to the quaint little Italian bistro. Chandler was happy to oblige. This time they dined on shrimp primavera and sipped white Zinfandel. Though Aisha was not a drinker, she indulged in a glass of wine on special occasions. Dining with Chandler was on that list of special occasions. Chandler used his playa expertise to make her feel at ease by talking about things that interested her, such as Aisha's fascination with dancing. The sparkle in her eyes told him that she liked him. Maybe Aisha Carlisle would be the one to help him regain a small bit of trust in women again—just maybe.

Tameria had been right. It felt good to be out with someone of the opposite sex. The conversation, the ambiance of the romantic setting of the restaurant, wine, good food, all of it made her feel exceptionally special. For a moment, she was able to forget her troubles and enjoy herself.

After dinner and on the way home, the two of them continued chatting. In between conversation, they listened to the radio. After arriving at her apartment, Aisha invited Chandler in for a cup of coffee and a slice of her mother's homemade butter pound cake.

She offered him a seat on her multi colored sofa, then took the time to express her gratitude. "Thanks for dinner, Chandler, and for running my errands too," she laughed. "Just for that, you deserve an extra big slice of my momma's cake," Aisha said, laughing lightly.

"No problem. I told you, I'd do anything to see you and

spend some time with you. Now where's that cake?" he asked, rubbing his hand in a circular motion over his flat abs.

"If you'll hold your horses, I'll go in the kitchen and cut you a slice. I have instant coffee, if that's okay with you."

"Instant is good," he answered.

"How do you take your coffee?"

"Black will be fine."

She smiled at the thought of how at ease she had begun to feel around him. When she brought him the cake and coffee, she stood in front of him with her arms folded.

"What are you doing?" he asked with a pleasant but weird look.

"Waiting to see your reaction when you taste a forkful of cake," she said, tapping her foot.

"Okay, let's see what you have here, Miss Carlisle," he said.

He closed his eyes as the moist, buttery cake all but melted in his mouth.

"Ummmm, this is fantastic," Chandler remarked, while taking another bite of the cake.

"I'm glad you like it." Satisfied that he was satisfied, Aisha sat down at the other end of the sofa and rested her head against the plush thickness of the sofa and sighed.

He sipped the coffee while looking at her. "Is something wrong?"

"No, I'm just tired and I have a lot on my mind, that's all."

"Anything you want to talk about?" he asked.

She wished it was that easy. *Talk about your problems and they'll go away. Ha, what a laugh,* she thought to herself. "No, I'll be fine. And I hate to end the evening so early, but I really am ready to call it a night. I have another long day tomorrow."

"So this is how you treat the fellas, huh? Get them to feed

you, run your errands, hold conversation with you then you throw them out," he teased.

"I thought that's what men liked," she teased back.

"I guess some of us do." He took the final bite of cake. "Before you throw me out, may I use your bathroom?"

"Of course, it's down the hall and to the left."

"Thanks, I'll be right back."

*What's he doing in there? He's been in there an awfully long time.* Just when she decided to call his name to make sure he was okay, he came walking down the hall. She smelled the aroma of the incense sticks she had in the bathroom for those not so pleasant bathroom stops. She giggled slightly as she thought about what he must have done in the bathroom.

"You okay?" she asked him.

"Sure, I'm fine. But I think I made a mess in your bathroom."

"What do you mean?" she looked confused.

"I better show you. Come here for a minute." She hesitated before getting up.

"I'm sure it's nothing that can't be fixed."

"I hope you're right. But you still better take a look." She ambled down the hallway to the bathroom. She stopped at the doorway and gasped.

"Oh my God," she said and placed both hands over her mouth in total surprise.

"Chandler, I don't believe this." The tub was filled with bubbles and the scent of jasmine incense wafted to her nostrils. "Thank you *soooo* much."

"No problem. I'd do anything to see that look you have on your face again and again. He grabbed her hand. "Come on so you can lock the door behind me. Then I want you to go and relax in your bubble bath."

She walked him to the door. He looked down at her radiant beauty and wanted her.

"Chandler, thanks for everything," she said.

"I'll call you tomorrow, if that's all right with you."

"Sure, I'd like that."

He kissed her on the forehead and left. She watched as he walked down the stairway. A smile covered her face—and his.

# 14

Time was passing swiftly for Aisha, which was definitely not a good thing. It wouldn't be long before Thaddeus would be calling to see what her final plans were. Each day she went to the studio was a reminder of her circumstances. Talking to Chandler helped her to forget her problems, but only for that moment. Outside of that momentary reprieve, there was hardly a time that she wasn't searching for some way to come up with the money she needed.

Aisha sat in her office and allowed her mind to drift to Elisa's offer to visit the Lynx. The more she tried not to think about it, the more she did think about it. No matter how much she tried to pray her way to a solution, nothing seemed to change, so later on in the afternoon when she happened to see Elisa bringing Gabby to dance class, she convinced herself that seeing Elisa was a sign.

Aisha stopped Elisa at the door just as she was leaving.

"Elisa, hold up," Aisha called out and began to walk toward her.

Elisa returned Aisha's greeting with one of her own.

"Oh, hi, Aisha. How are you?" Elisa asked.

Aisha softly said, "Fine. Do you have a minute? I want to talk to you about something."

Elisa looked at the jeweled watch on her wrist. "Aisha, I'm sorry but I can't right now. I just ran in here to pay Gabby's tuition and drop her off. Maybe we can talk later tonight or perhaps tomorrow."

"Look it will only take a minute. Let me walk you to your car," Aisha insisted.

Elisa pursed her lips then answered, "Well, okay."

While they walked to the parking garage, Aisha explained to Elisa that she had changed her mind and wanted to know if the offer still stood to check out The Lynx.

Looking less than shocked, Elisa nonchalantly replied, "No problem. Is Friday night, oh say, around 10:30 good for you?" Elisa asked her.

Not expecting such a quick answer, Aisha fidgeted then said, "Ten thirty, Friday? Uh, I guess so. Yeah . . . that's good." Aisha, somewhat uneasy, looked around the parking garage like she thought the angel Gabriel was eavesdropping.

"Okay, we'll talk later. But right now, I have to go, Aisha."

Elisa flicked the switch on her key chain to unlock her car door, opened it with ease, then slid inside. While Aisha stood like a frozen block of ice, Elisa started the engine.

"You won't be sorry," Elisa said, placing the car in reverse then driving off.

Aisha couldn't believe she'd given in to Elisa's offer to visit The Lynx. All of her instincts had told her not to go, yet, here she was standing in what she'd classified as none other than a high class strip joint. If her pastor could see her now, he would probably stroke out; not to mention her father and mother. And Tameria? What would she think of her holy roller best friend now?

Aisha's thoughts were put on hold as she walked with

Elisa through the doors and into a magnificently luxurious foyer.

"Elisa, this place is like wow. It reeks of money."

"Honey, this place *is* money. Come on, let me show you around. Elisa started walking and Aisha cautiously followed along.

"The Lynx is designed like a five star hotel with private suites," Elisa explained. "An individual suite can cost as much as seven or eight grand."

"Whaaat? That's unbelievable. Why so much?"

"Because the men here mean business. Some of them live in the city and own their suites and come and go at their leisure. Others live out of town and fly here for a few days or a weekend. They want to guarantee their exclusivity."

"Okay, I understand that much. But what's there to hide?"

Elisa stopped walking and stared at Aisha for a second or two before speaking. "Most of these men have families. There's no way they want to jeopardize their families in any way, so they lead two very separate and secretive lives. The Lynx provides them with a means to freely do whatever it is they want to do within the confines of these walls. Remember when I told you that some of the girls are private entertainers?"

"Yeah."

"Well, take me for instance. I have two clients here that I entertain exclusively in the privacy of their suites. One comes the fourth weekend of every month and the other gentleman is here a few times a month. Then on my free nights, I might dance in the open area for some of the regulars and make sometimes a thousand or more a night."

"What's the open area?"

"It's where the bar and the dance stage are located. I'll show you. We have to catch the elevator to get to it, unless you want to do the stairs," Elisa offered.

"No, I'd rather take the elevator," Aisha told her.

They got on the elevator and Aisha noticed the number pad next to the fourth floor button. "Hey, what's on the fourth floor that requires a keypad?"

"The owner's private space. Only a select few have been up there and I do mean a few," Elisa emphasized.

"Are you?" Aisha leaned against the elevator wall and waited on Elisa's response.

"Am I what?"

"Are you one of the select few?"

"Nope, and I don't think any of the other ladies who work here have been there either. Plus, I don't even know the owner. None of the girls here do."

"That's unbelievable. Why is everything so secretive? I don't understand."

Elisa sniffed and wiped her nose. "Aisha, like I already told you, this is no run of the mill kind of place. I meant what I said; these men live totally different lives outside of these walls," she explained to Aisha with less patience. "They pay for their privacy and they pay handsomely. I really don't know who owns this place and I really don't care, as long as my money is right."

The elevator doors opened and the two ladies stepped out into a carpeted corridor.

"Now, come on, let's go to the open area. I want to see what you can do."

"What are you talking about?"

"I'm talking about dancing."

Aisha stood still with a stunned, frightened look on her face. "No, Elisa. That wasn't part of the agreement. Anyway, I can't dance in a place like this."

Ignoring Aisha's disenchantment, Elisa continued, "Yes, you can." Elisa started walking, leaving Aisha behind, but not for long. Aisha quickly chose to follow Elisa rather than be left standing at the elevator alone.

"Well, how do you like it?" Elisa turned and watched Aisha's face brighten like a kid with a brand new toy.

"It's absolutely gorgeous in here."

Elisa grinned. "You're going to learn to listen to me yet."

Aisha tried not to look directly at the men inside of the open area but her eyes apparently had a mind of there own. Some of the men were dressed in fine Italian suits and others in more leisurely attire. Her eyes grew big as she watched two ladies dancing seductively on a raised stage. They caressed the pole like it was a man. Their breasts bobbled up and down slowly, and Aisha saw that they had the full attention of the gentlemen seated around the tables.

"Here's my dressing room." Elisa ushered her into a well designed, expensively furnished room that reminded her of a hotel suite. She walked over to the mini-bar and mixed herself a martini. "What can I get you?"

"Nothing, I don't drink. I mean, I drink wine occasionally," Aisha tried to explain. "But that's only if I'm at a formal dinner or something like that."

"No need to explain to me. Plus, there's a first time for everything. I'll make you an apple martini. You'll love it. And I promise that you won't even taste the alcohol. It'll help ease some of your jitters."

Aisha paused before she nodded her head. "Okay," she said, thinking about a scripture she had to memorize when she was part of her church youth group. *For that which I do, I allow not; for what I would, that do I not; but what I hate, that do I.*

Being at an establishment like The Lynx, Aisha realized that she was definitely not the Aisha people were used to seeing. Everything was evolving so quickly for her. She'd gone from surrounding herself with do right, God-fearing Christian people to being with a bunch of sinners and hypocrites in a place that was nothing more than an upscale strip joint. It wasn't that she looked down on Elisa or any of the other people at The Lynx, but no one could ever have told her that she would be in the midst of them contemplating becoming one of them.

She sipped on the slightly bitter but tasty apple martini. Elisa told her she only put less than a shot of liquor in the martini but Aisha's head felt lighter by the time she finished the drink. *Strike two*, she thought, gluing her eyes on the empty glass. Not only am I sitting among these people, I'm drinking among them. Maybe she *was* looking down on them. Her mind reflected on a story she heard at church several years ago. There was a man who said he found himself standing around some sinners looking at and listening to what they were saying and doing. Before long he was sitting among them. Soon he found himself not only sitting among them, but he was actually doing what they were doing.

In a way, Aisha felt the same way that man felt. Here she was, sitting in Elisa's dressing room contemplating her next move. Was she on her way to doing the same thing that she once criticized people like Elisa for doing? How had she arrived at this point in her life? Now was the time for her to get up and get as far away as she could from The Lynx and all that it represented. But she didn't budge from her chair. Instead, she watched as Elisa changed into a skimpy one piece outfit that reminded Aisha of Frederick's of Hollywood lingerie. She couldn't move. It wasn't until she felt Elisa touching her on her shoulder when she focused in on her surroundings again and came out of her daydream.

"Aisha, you look like you're in a trance or something. Don't tell me you're high after one itty bitty apple martini?" Elisa laughed.

"No, no, it's nothing like that. Look, Elisa. Thanks for showing me around. But really, I don't think this is for me. I want to get out of here," Aisha declared and proceeded to stand up.

"Okay, okay. Tell you what. Can you just hold on for a

minute? I have to at least do a few dances before I can leave. Remember, this is my job. You can stay here in my dressing room or you can come along with me and sit in the open area. I'll tell one of the other girls to keep you company. How's that?" Elisa offered with sincerity.

"I guess that'll be all right. And Elisa?"

"What?"

"I'm sorry you brought me all the way out here for nothing. I really am."

"Hey, don't worry about it. Now come on. Let me introduce you to Kim. She's been working here for about three years. She'll be glad to sit with you while I do my thing. And you'll see for yourself how easy this job is. Now come on. There's nothing to be afraid of."

Elisa opened the dressing room door and walked out with Aisha behind her. As they made it back into the open area, Elisa scanned the room for Kim. When she saw her, she pointed to a table and instructed Aisha to sit down until she went over to talk to Kim.

Aisha, feeling like the men were all staring at her, shamefully refused to look up. She sat quietly, hoping and praying that this night would soon come to an end.

Elisa brought Kim over to the table and introduced her to Aisha. Kim sat down next to Aisha while Elisa excused herself to prepare for her set.

"Do you want to hang out here and watch Elisa do her thing? Or would you prefer to go to her dressing room and wait on her there?" Kim asked politely.

"I really want to see Elisa dance but I feel so weird being out here and all," Aisha told Kim.

"It's your call, but I can tell you this, Elisa is good, real good," Kim added. "She might be the oldest girl here, but she's also the best. Everybody looks up to her," Kim told her.

Aisha took a good look at Kim closely for the first time and thought to herself, *that's because you look like you're not much older than some of my students.*

"I guess I'll watch for a while."

"Once her set starts, if you change your mind and want to leave, then we'll go back to the dressing room."

Aisha watched as Elisa confidently came out on the stage moving sensuously and without any inhibitions. With each step she took, she captivated her audience. The beat of the music and the lustful stares from the men drew Elisa into a world that was void of anything else that might have been going on. Her seductive moves across the dance stage oozed sexuality. Aisha realized how talented Elisa really was. If only she'd chosen to use her skills in another environment she would be the envy of many in the art of dance, including Aisha.

While sneaking looks at the men scattered around the open area, Aisha could tell they were mesmerized by Elisa's performance. Elisa swayed her hips with each beat of the song. Several poles were on the stage. Elisa danced her way over to one of them. Her long dancer's legs caressed the pole, while she moved her hands and butt in a sexually explicit manner. Yet, Elisa didn't look vulgar at all. Aisha studied her expert moves and choreography and felt herself fascinated by Elisa and her talent. She was actually an excellent performer.

Taking another sneak peek at some of the men, Aisha noticed there were note pads of some sort in front of each man. From time to time, Aisha would see them write something on the pads.

Leaning over toward Kim, Aisha whispered, "What are those men writing down?"

"If a man wants to show his pleasure for the dancer, he keeps something like a running tab. Those note pads have each dancer's name on it and whatever amount he wants to tip her he writes it down and turns the pad and the money over to Jason, the manager," Kim explained.

"I see," Aisha replied and then focused back on Elisa's performance.

Kim kept talking while Aisha watched Elisa. "Jason is over there at the bar. He's the one with the black suit on and smoking a cigar."

Aisha twisted around slightly in her chair and made eye contact with the gentleman Kim had described. She quickly shifted back around, embarrassed that he'd seen her looking at him.

Curious, Aisha asked, "What does he do?"

Glad to oblige Aisha with an answer, Kim replied, "First of all, he's a very wealthy banker. He's also on the board of directors here. And he's the owner's overseer."

"Overseer? What do you mean? What does he oversee?" Aisha looked at Kim while using her peripheral vision to watch Elisa.

"After he collects all of the money at the end of the night, he deducts 15% commission for The Lynx. The rest goes to the dancer. He also hires and recruits new girls and anything else the owner tells him to do. You know, a glorified gopher," Kim laughed and surprisingly, so did Aisha.

Elisa finished her dance to a round of cat calls, as well as applause and screams for an encore. Willing to please, she gave them what they wanted. Watching her, Aisha no longer had reservations about why Elisa was considered the *top dog* among the other dancers.

When Aisha and Elisa finally left The Lynx, Elisa had made a cool $2,300. And that was for less than two hours of dancing. Aisha was astonished. *Could this possibly be my way out? Could it? Maybe God could use a den of ill repute to bless me. He did say that the wealth of the wicked would be laid up for the righteous,* Aisha told herself. *Maybe this is the way. Why else would it come so easy for me?*

Remaining quiet on the way home, Aisha contemplated her next move. Crunching numbers in her mind, she soon figured that if she could rake in at least a third of what Elisa brought home every week, she'd have enough money for the down payment on the building before the deadline. It was also possible that she could make enough to pay off some, if not all, of her delinquent credit card bills. Of course, unlike Elisa, she'd probably have to dance her butt off almost every night to make that kind of money, but for Aisha, it would be well worth her time and effort.

Elisa pulled up in front of Aisha's apartment. "I'll talk to you later," Elisa told her. "I'm going home and hit the sack. I'm beat."

"Drive safe," Aisha responded, climbing out of the car. Before completely closing the door, she leaned over slightly and stuck her head back inside. "Elisa, how soon can I start?"

# 15

Aisha and Chandler laughed in unison with the rest of the movie goers when Big Mama waddled across the screen in a bright yellow bathing suit.

Holding her hand as they exited the movie theatre, Chandler asked her, "You having a good time?"

"Yes. I haven't enjoyed myself like this in a long time, Chandler. That Martin Lawrence knows he's a fool," Aisha laughed and moved in closer to Chandler. "You know, usually if I'm not at some church function, I'm at my dance studio."

"Well, I say it's time you start taking some time to relax and enjoy life. Don't get me wrong, I know you're driven to succeed and that's great. But you need to cool out every now and then. You know what I'm saying?"

"Yea, I know. My best friend, Tameria, you know the one you saw at the Orpheum?"

"Yea, I remember her."

"Both she and her boyfriend are in med school. He's a third or fourth year neurosurgery resident. But even though they're always working, most of the time their rotations are the same so they still get a chance to spend time with each other. So you see, they share a lot in common. But as for me, there aren't many guys who understand my passion for dance. I live and breathe dancing."

"I beg to differ," was Chandler's response. He brought her in closer to him as they walked along Tom Lee Park. "I like to watch you dance. I like to see how you work with your students. You're good at what you do, Aisha. That was evident when I saw the performance at the Mayor's Gala. And earlier today, when I came by the studio, I could tell you were born to dance."

"That's nice of you to say, Chandler. My father is the only other man who understands how seriously I take my dancing. He always pushes me to follow my dreams and never stop even when I reach that pot of gold at the end of the rainbow. I love him for that." Aisha's eyes gleamed when she spoke about her father.

"You a daddy's girl?" Chandler teased.

"Sure am. Always have been too."

"Do you have sisters and brothers?"

"I have a half-sister who lives in Detroit. I don't see her or talk to her that often. Her name is Selena."

"Selena," he said the name slowly. "That's a pretty name too. But I'm partial to Aisha." He laughed, stopped and pointed her in the direction of a bench. The two of them sat down. He wrapped his arm around her shoulders; she snuggled in against his chest.

"Aisha?"

"Yes?"

"I really do like you. You know that?"

Her response was to giggle like a school girl.

"Hey," he pulled her face around to meet his. When his lips caressed hers, her heart raced and her pulse beat wildly. The chemistry they felt for one another was intense. Aisha returned his kiss and wrapped both of her arms around his neck.

Chandler thought of how Aisha's lips tasted like sweet honey nectar. She was not only pretty, smart and intelligent but she had begun to stir inside of him feelings he had kept under wraps for so long. He liked this girl a lot and his intention was to make her feel the same way about him.

They sat underneath the twinkling stars at Tom Lee Park until the breeze picked up. "Come on. I'll take you home," Chandler said to her.

Aisha agreed. "I'd like that. It's gotten a little chilly out here."

When they arrived at her apartment, Aisha invited him inside and he eagerly accepted. She made each of them a cup of spiced tea.

Chandler complimented her. "This tastes good." He sipped the warm tea again before setting it down on the table.

"I'm glad you like it. I'm a lover of tea. Hot, cold, regular, green, spiced. It makes no difference. Just as long as it's tea," she grinned.

"Ahhh, now I know the way to your heart," he teased.

She threw her head back and laughed. "You think so?"

"Yeah, I do." He gently moved back the twist of hair that had fallen in her face. Leaning in, he lightly kissed her on the neck.

"Hi, come on in," Tameria told Chase. Kissing her on the cheek he walked inside her apartment. She reached for his rain-soaked jacket and umbrella. "Let me get that."

"Thanks, baby. It's really coming down out there. No sign of it letting up either."

"It's a good thing we don't have to report to the hospital tonight."

"I know that's right." Chase walked up behind Tameria

and surprised her by grabbing her around the waist and twirling her around to face him.

Chase was a jokester. His cheerful, love-of-life personality was one of the things that had attracted Tameria to him in the first place. Plus the fact that they both were medical students helped too. Like Tameria, Chase understood the stress and commitment of being in med school. The two of them often pulled thirty-six hour shifts, sometimes not seeing each other but for a few minutes in passing. But after dating for almost seven months, Tameria knew he was the man of her dreams.

Chase teased, "Umh, you smell good. Just like fried chicken with red beans and rice."

She thumped him lightly on the head and said, "Boy please, you're so silly. Just for that I'm not feeding you."

"You mean you cooked for me? You must really love me." Rocking her back and forth in his arms, he squeezed her tightly.

"Ummm, you think so?" She rubbed the right side of her face across the smoothness of his right cheek. They laughed at each other before exchanging another kiss. She loved the way she fit perfectly inside his arms. She nestled in closer and returned his fervor, skillfully manipulating her tongue with flickering motions in between his moist lips. In turn he lightly sucked on hers. She didn't flinch when his hands caressed her large yet well-proportioned butt. Her sounds of satisfaction echoed off the thin walls of the apartment.

"Hey, what about dinner?" she whispered and pulled away. "I fixed your favorite."

In a husky voice he answered, "You're my favorite." He didn't stop kissing her as he moved in closer to his destination. He eased her back on the sofa with one hand and used his fingers to gently massage her private places like a skilled surgeon. As if on cue, she opened her gate to allow him easy access to her most intimate spots.

*What would Aisha think if she saw me now?* She hated when thoughts of Aisha invaded her moments. But just as quickly as she thought of Aisha, those same thoughts vanished and she arched her back to meet his every stroke. The thunderous roar of the storm raging outside deafened their sounds of passion. She gave in to his every desire and he fueled her burning flame with his torch of love.

Tameria and Chase had been sexually intimate for almost two months. The flames of guilt over committing fornication had basically died out. Her concentration was centered on the relationship she shared with Chase and so was his. She'd sought God's forgiveness numerous times in the beginning when she gave her virginity to Chase. But now, Tameria felt no shame. The only reason she hadn't confided in Aisha was because she didn't want to get into a confrontation with her. She cared about her friendship with Aisha and respected her beliefs because Aisha's beliefs used to be her beliefs as well. But love had changed all that. Chase was the man she planned to spend the rest of her life with and Tameria concluded that that was enough justification for her.

There was a time she thought she would be shy about being intimate with Chase, or any man for that matter. Her short stature, combined with her M'onique-shaped body, used to make her uncomfortable at times. But thanks to Chase loving her just the way she was, Tameria had learned to love every inch of her 198 pounds of voluptuous frame.

As for Aisha . . . well there was no time to think about her right now. The pleasure she was experiencing with Chase captured her mind, body and soul, and for now, there was no room for anything or anyone else.

# 16

Chandler turned over in his bed, raised his head and looked lazily at the clock sitting on top of his chest of drawers. He yawned and stretched while thinking about his undercover assignment in Nashville. Normally, he would have no more than a three hour drive to Nashville but it had been snowing most of the day and it was still coming down hard so he was in for an even longer drive. But he had a job to do, rain, sleet or snow.

Being an undercover cop kept his adrenaline pumping. He couldn't see himself being anything else in law enforcement. It was a dangerous job and he basically had to act much like some of the lowlives he helped put away. Not knowing when or if someone would shout *five-o*, hiding his true identity and always having to look over his shoulder during an assignment was part of it.

His uncle had worked undercover in Toledo, Ohio for almost twenty years before he died from lung cancer. Smoking three packs of menthol cigarettes a day until the day he died, his uncle had been a true man of the law. He lived and breathed law enforcement, forsaking his family for long, dangerous assignments. The one thing that was different for Chandler was that he didn't have anyone to report to but himself.

After his volatile break up with Tracye, Chandler soon arrived at the conclusion that the best thing for him to do would be to leave Montgomery and start a new life before he found himself in deep trouble, which is why he didn't think twice about relocating when he found out the MPD was recruiting for new officers.

He had completed the MPD online application, and within weeks he'd been contacted and scheduled for his first round interview. His Associates Degree in Criminal Justice helped him tremendously. It was a dream come true when he was accepted into the Memphis Police Academy. The training had been rigorous but he had persevered. When graduation day arrived, he had stood proudly to receive his badge and uniform. There were no words to describe the amount of satisfaction he felt being a cop.

Chandler stretched his arms out and released one last yawn before raising his towering frame from underneath the quilt his great grandmother had made many years ago. He didn't bother grabbing his robe. He was already fully dressed in the same outfit he'd worn when he made his entrance into the world thirty-one years ago. He loved being naked. It made him feel free, unbound by any and everything. He turned on the shower, walked over to the linen closet, grabbed a couple of towels and then stepped underneath the water, allowing the beads of warm water to massage his skin.

*Ring. Ring.* He stopped soaping himself and listened. *Every time I get in the freaking shower, the phone rings. Well, whoever it is this time will just have to wait,* he thought.

He moved his head swiftly from side to side to shake the water off his face before starting his ritual. He made a frothy lather by rubbing the soap briskly between his hands. He reached down and grabbed his best friend and gently massaged it, being thorough in cleaning it. He followed the same method for his taut buttocks and well defined calves. He finished rinsing himself off and stepped out of the shower to welcome the coolness that embraced him.

Chandler and his unsuspecting partner, known as Smooth, climbed in the black on black H3. Chandler's job gave him a high that no drug could. Chandler had worked this undercover assignment for almost a year under the alias Nash, as a member of a notorious drug ring. Finally it was all about to come to an end. He'd gained the total trust of his associates, and they thought of him as one of their 'to the death' brothers. But in a few hours he would put away several members of the drug ring for a long time, including, Smooth, who was clueless about the true identity of his so called partner, Nash.

"Hey, Smooth, let's roll man," Chandler told him. "That shipment will be coming in about half an hour. Get up and let's move it," he ordered Smooth. "If I miss out on this deal, you can put your concrete suit on, cause you'll be heading for your new home—the river."

"Look Nash, don't talk that trash to me. You think I'm about to blow this. No way. We got millions riding on this one and I plan to get my fair share," Smooth barked back.

When the shipment of cocaine arrived as scheduled, Chandler's back-up was already strategically planted in inconspicuous places along the drop off area. He strolled along the boardwalk, confident that he was about to bust a major gang and get several million dollars worth of drugs off the street along with the top suppliers.

Everything had gone as planned. Chandler could see a piercing set of blue eyes change colors when the supplier made the exchange and Chandler flashed his badge.

"You're five-o," the gang banger yelled. If looks could have killed him, Chandler would have been dead on the spot. Several of the gang members reached for their weapons, but the back-up police officers were too quick for them and the bust ended nonviolently with a number of major arrests.

The next evening, Chandler slowly opened the door to his apartment. He had left Nashville the moment he finished writing his report. Hanging around the city after such a major bust was not a good idea. He was glad to get home. He had a few days to relax before starting a new assignment. Before plopping down on the cushiony sofa, he ambled over to his bar and poured himself a shot of vodka with a spot of cranberry juice. Then he lay down on the sofa and pushed play on his answering machine.

When he woke up, it was the next morning. "I must have been more tired than I realized," he said out loud. He eased up from the couch and looked around in a state of confusion. Whenever he had a long term assignment, it took him a while to adjust to being at home in familiar surroundings. He focused on the view in front of him displayed through the large picture window. He thought of Aisha and their last time together. *Man, I'd like to see her. I will make her my priority for today.*

# 17

On her way to her first night at The Lynx, Aisha felt a jittery feeling in her stomach. Convinced that God had a hand in her decision to accept Elisa's job offer, Aisha tried to justify what she was about to do by praying. *Lord, I don't always understand your way of working things out. I only hope that I can do this and get through it so I can keep the studio.*

Elisa had assured Aisha, more than once, that she could make the money she needed and then some; and Aisha didn't have a problem accepting what Elisa said as the truth. She'd seen for herself the money Elisa made the night she went with her to The Lynx.

Aisha nervously walked inside and asked the doorman to page Elisa.

Ten minutes passed before she saw Elisa coming in her direction.

Elisa witnessed the uneasy look on Aisha's face as she approached her. Elisa reached out and gave her a hug of support and reassurance.

"I'm scared. I shouldn't be doing this, Elisa," Aisha fretted. "Suppose I make a fool of myself?"

"That's hardly possible. You're a great dancer, choreographer and you're beautiful too. Now let's go get you dressed," Elisa instructed.

Elisa escorted Aisha to a dressing room two doors away from hers. Aisha looked around the room with a sinking feeling. Elisa walked over to a small armoire and searched through several outfits before pulling out one.

"You want me to put that on?" she asked, turning her nose up at Elisa.

"This is not the time for cold feet, Aisha. That is, if you really are serious about saving your studio," Elisa chided.

Aisha hesitated momentarily, looked over at Elisa then reached for the outfit.

She slowly replaced her clothes with the skimpy front buttoned micro mini dress with a wide vinyl belt that rested on her narrow but shapely hips. The matching thong and spiked bracelet accessories caused her to shiver. How could she have resorted to doing something like this? But when she thought of the financial dilemma she was in she knew something had to be done. *It's only for a few weeks, then I'll have enough cash to make the down payment on the building*, she managed to convince herself.

"You're going to make a bank load tonight with that outfit. When I saw it, I knew it was you. Here, take a sniff of this." Elisa passed her a vial with a white powdery substance inside. There was a tiny spoon attached to the side of the vial.

"What is this?" Aisha stared questionably at the vial.

"Just a little something to make you more relaxed, that's all. Don't worry. It's not habit forming. It's just crushed Valium. My doctor prescribes it for me. I crush it up so it'll get into my system faster. Believe me. It's safe. Plus I know you've heard of Valium.

"Yes I've heard of it, but I'm not into doing drugs." Aisha had never done any kind of drug. She'd never been drawn into that world. The only thing she'd ever taken close to strong drugs was when her orthopedist prescribed Tylenol with codeine after she sprained her ankle dancing a couple of years ago.

"Look, take a hit. Don't be such a prude, girl."

"No, I don't think so."

A knock came on the door. "Who is it?" Elisa asked harshly.

"It's me, Kim. I wanted to check on Aisha," she explained.

"Come in," Elisa ordered.

Kim complimented her on the outfit she had on.

"Girl, you are going to be a hit with the clients tonight," Kim told her.

"Thanks, Kim," Aisha responded timidly

"You need to lighten up though," Kim told her. "You're standing there like a piece of wood."

"See, I told you. You need something to help you relax," Elisa commented. Reaching for the vial and taking it out of Aisha's trembling hand, Elisa said, "Kim, will you tell this shaky woman that this stuff is just a mild relaxer?"

"That's what it is, Aisha. It's just Valium. All of us take a snort of it from time to time. I mean we all get uptight every now and then." Pointing to the vial in Elisa's hand, Kim continued. "Does it look like we're dope fiends or something?" she stretched her arms out by her side and eyed Aisha.

"No, I'm not calling you dope fiends. I just don't think sniffing or snorting—whatever you call it—Valium, is right for me. It's still drugs, no matter how you look at it."

"Okay, suit yourself," Kim told her and shrugged her shoulders and stole a glance in Elisa's direction.

"Aisha, we're not trying to pressure you into something you don't want to do. So I'm going to say this and then I'm going to leave it alone. Just like you know what it takes to motivate your students or to be a success in your line of work, we know what it takes for ours. When you go on that stage for the first time, girls have been known to become physically ill, faint, fall, or whatever."

Aisha looked at Elisa and then at Kim. "Really?" she commented.

"Really," Kim added.

"Which is why we suggest that the first time you take the stage you should reduce the chances of bumming by being prepared. But if you think that you're going to go on that stage for the first time and perform in front of a room full of men like a pro, then have it your way. We were just trying to help you through this first performance, that's all."

Aisha didn't say a word. She had barely moved a muscle the entire time the two women had been talking to her.

Another knock came at the door. "Who is it now?" Elisa asked.

"Your friendly neighborhood banker," Jason's voice answered from the other side of the door. Without waiting on them to invite him in, he turned the knob, opened the door and walked into the room.

Aisha turned and looked at the same man she'd seen that night at the bar. She felt even more terrified at what she was about to do.

Jason stared at her from head to toe. "My, my, my, Elisa you were absolutely right, she is divine, simply divine."

Aisha clumsily took a step backward from Jason as he walked close enough for her to smell his liquor-laced breath.

"No need, sweetheart. I don't bite," he said wickedly. "Your set will be starting in twenty minutes," he told her, then walked out of the room, leaving the door wide open.

Kim walked over and closed the door.

Removing the vial from Elisa's hand again, Kim opened it and placed some of the powder on the tiny spoon, then sniffed it up each of her nostrils.

Aisha sat down in the leather chair and pretended not to be bothered by Elisa or Kim's constant prodding. While the two of them joked about some of the men at The Lynx, Aisha sat in silence until she heard Elisa announce, "Show time."

The blaring rap music pumped into The Lynx. Unsure at first, Aisha almost stumbled on to the stage. Seeing the men was so terrifying that Aisha turned and ran back off the stage. Elisa and Kim had been right after all. Aisha could hear the men yell their dissatisfaction at her abrupt departure.

Aisha ran to meet Elisa as she walked toward her. Tears were starting to crest in the corners of her eyes.

"What are you doing?" Elisa scolded.

"I can't do it. I just can't do it," Aisha cried.

Elisa hugged her. "It's alright," she said, suddenly changing her harsh tone to a more sympathetic one. "But I tried to warn you that it wasn't going to be easy the first time, didn't I?"

Aisha nodded.

Elisa reached inside the pocket of her skirt and pulled out the vial again. This time when she pushed it toward Aisha, she didn't *just say no*. Instead, with Elisa's help, she began to imitate what she'd seen Kim do minutes earlier. The yellowish-white substance felt strange going up her nose but Elisa insisted that she take several snorts of the drug, and Aisha did. Within minutes, she began to feel relaxed and her anxiety soon passed.

With less apprehension and fear, Aisha walked back out on the stage and started dancing to the deafening music. She closed her eyes and allowed herself to imagine she was on stage at the Orpheum dancing for dignitaries and high society people who'd come just to watch her perform. Her rhythm picked up and the wild beat of another artist rapping carried her into the world she loved best, the world of dance. Before long, Aisha was working the stage like she'd been performing at The Lynx for years. Wrapping her slender legs around the pole, she held on with one hand and threw her head back while moving seductively, keeping up with each beat of the song. She swayed her hips, closed her eyes and allowed the drugs and music to take her into another world. The men showed their satisfaction by egging her on. One man in the audience started calling her Luscious until another man joined in and did the same. Others were seen scribbling in their special note pads. Jason grinned a sheepish grin of satisfaction.

Aisha slowly slid to the floor in a Chinese split oblivious to the approval of the gentlemen gathered in the lounge. When she stepped off the stage some ten minutes later to thunderous applause, her shyness and apprehension had disappeared. She had become one with the music. She jumped up and down in front of Elisa. The exhilaration she felt was overpowering.

"Hey, you really knocked them off their feet tonight," Elisa commented.

Kim came over and congratulated her too. "You did it," Kim screamed and then hugged Aisha. "I'll see you after your next set ends."

"Where are you going?" Aisha asked Kim.

"I have to go behind you now. You're going to be hard to beat, girlfriend," Kim teased and sashayed off.

"I'm proud of you, Aisha."

"Thanks to you, Elisa. When I went back on stage, I closed my eyes, listened to the music and then I pretended I was a famous dancer on Broadway. It worked. It really worked."

"I could tell. See that taste of Valium helped because after you got that edge off of you, I didn't see a shy or scared bone in your body, Luscious."

"Luscious? Where did that come from?" Aisha asked curiously.

"Everyone has to have a stage name. You got yours tonight. Didn't you hear the men calling you, Luscious?"

"No, all I heard was the music. Were they really calling me Luscious?" Aisha couldn't believe it.

"They sure were. So from now on, you're Luscious."

Aisha laughed. "Luscious, that's me," she said in a sexy cat-like voice.

"See, I told you it wasn't going to be so bad, didn't I? Before you know it, you're going to be able to buy that building, and you're going to have enough cash left over to buy anything else you might want." Elisa hooked her arm inside of Aisha's and both women laughed as Aisha went to change for her next set.

It was three thirty in the morning when Aisha returned to her apartment. She thought she would be exhausted, but much to her surprise, she wasn't sleepy at all. She walked over to her sofa, threw her duffel bag on the floor and her cell phone on the table, and sat down. Tonight had been better than she could ever have imagined and her feelings of guilt at what she was doing quickly dissipated. Her first night at her new part-time job had netted her over sixteen hundred dollars. Throwing the money up in the air, she looked up and said, "Thank you, thank you, God," then prepared for bed.

The next morning Aisha was awakened by the sound of thunder and lightening. Rain pounded against her bedroom window. Yawning and stretching she sat up in the bed, reliving the previous night's events. Several minutes passed before she climbed out of bed and took a hot shower. Afterwards, she called Angie and told her to cancel today's classes after listening to the news saying that severe thunderstorms and tornado warnings were expected throughout the day. When she made a cup of spiced tea, she remembered what Elisa had told her before she left.

"I left you a little something inside your purse. After tonight, you're going to need something to pick you up."

Aisha hadn't bothered to look in her purse to see what Elisa meant and had soon forgotten that she'd even told her. But her memory was beginning to take focus and she searched inside her purse until she saw a vial like the one Elisa had. Aisha's first instinct told her to throw the vial away but the loud ringing of the phone stopped her and she placed it in her nightstand drawer.

"Hello," Aisha answered. Elisa was on the other end.

"Good morning. You up yet?" she asked.

"Yeah, this storm woke me up. So I called in and cancelled lessons for today."

"Yeah, I know. Angie just called and told me. By the way, did you find the present I left you?"

"Yes, I did. But, Elisa, please don't do that again. I told you, I'm not into drugs. I know I did it last night, but I'm not going to do that again."

"Like I said, it's up to you. But if you change your mind, you'll have it. I know you're beat and sometimes you need something to get you started, that's all. If you do decide you want to try a hit every now and then, there's a doctor who's a member at The Lynx who'll be glad to write you your own script."

"I don't think so."

"Well, look, I was just checking on you. I'm going to fix Gabby some breakfast and then I'm going back to bed. I'll talk to you later."

"Okay. Bye." Aisha hung up the phone and walked over to the nightstand. She opened the drawer and reached inside for the vial. Kneading it around in her hand, she stared at the powder inside before throwing the vial in her bedroom trash can.

# 18

Aisha danced at The Lynx two nights a week. Averaging a grand, sometimes almost two grand, each time she performed, Aisha had already saved almost half of what she needed to make the full down payment on the property, and she'd only been dancing at The Lynx a little less than a month. At the rate she was going, she would have enough cash in another month or less if Jason had agreed to let her work more hours.

Aisha had asked Elisa to talk to Jason on her behalf about dancing a few extra nights, but he refused, telling Elisa that Aisha had to get some seniority under her belt before he would agree to it. What Elisa had managed to do was persuade Jason to let Aisha do a private dance for a new client that was supposed to be coming to The Lynx in a day or two. Jason wanted the girls to have at least three to four months of experience working at The Lynx before he promoted them to private dancer status. Somehow, Elisa convinced him to do otherwise. Aisha had her suspicions as to what Elisa did to convince Jason to make an exception, but she pushed her suspicions aside, shrugged her shoulders, and repeated what she'd heard Elisa tell some of the dancers from time to time: "Sometimes a girl's gotta do what a girl's gotta do."

*Ring, ring, ring.* It was Tameria.

"Hey, Tameria."

"Girl, what have you been up too? It's been God knows how long since I've heard from you. Every time I call you, that answering machine of yours pops on. And you don't need a cell phone either 'cuz you never have it turned on."

"I've been out hustling, girl, trying to get investors for the studio and working a part-time job too. Plus, I know your schedule is so screwed up with school that I haven't bothered to call you. I knew you would get in touch with me when you had a chance. So there," Aisha declared.

"Did you say you found a part-time job?" Tameria interjected. "A part-time job? Doing what?"

Aisha had to think fast. What lie could she tell her best friend?

"Uh, I've been teaching lyrical dance at a studio in Collierville."

"Oh, that's great. How are things going?" Tameria was truly concerned about the studio. She knew how much it meant to Aisha.

"I think everything is going to work out. I'm saving the money I make from this night job. And I've lined up some potential investors who've shown an interest in the studio." With each sentence, Aisha found it easier to lie.

"That's a blessing. Well, do you have to work tonight? Or are you going to be able to come to Bible study?"

"Yeah, I'll be there. I don't have to work tonight. So I'll meet you there around 6:45." After hanging up the phone, Aisha started getting ready for Bible study. She changed from the sweats she had on to a skirt and blouse.

It was amazing how in a few short weeks Aisha had

transformed from a quiet, demure Christian girl who lived and breathed for her dance studio, to a lying stripper who snorted drugs like she'd been doing it her entire life. She was glad she had agreed to let Elisa introduce her to the doctor at The Lynx with the hook up. He didn't mind writing her a prescription for her own supply of Valium.

Before leaving her apartment and going to Bible study, Aisha took a hit of what she had come to call *baby girl*. Only this time, the vial contained something stronger and deadlier than Valium. The switch had occurred two weeks earlier at The Lynx.

Aisha had been in her dressing room preparing for her first set of the night. As part of what was now a ritual for her before going on stage, she took a hit of the substance inside her vial. However, the numbness she felt when she placed it on her tongue and the exhilarating feeling was quite different from all the times before when she snorted the Valium.

She voiced her concern to Elisa who was lying on the sofa thumbing through a lingerie magazine.

"Elisa, there's something weird going on," she explained.

Elisa noticed the expression on Aisha's face.

"What is it?" Elisa asked.

"I don't know, but this sure doesn't feel like Valium," Elisa said, holding the vial up to her face and peering through it.

"How do you feel?"

"I feel pretty good," Aisha giggled. "Like I have more energy or something. I really can't explain it," Aisha told her.

"Okay, okay," Elisa said, slightly sitting up and raising her arms in the air. "I'm guilty," she chuckled.

"Guilty?" Aisha frowned, clueless.

"Here goes," Elisa started. "The more you used the Valium, the less effective it was, which means you were doing more of it. Am I right?"

Slowly, Aisha nodded.

"So, being the wonderful friend that I am," Elisa remarked jokingly, "I decided to turn you on to something better."

"Like what?" Aisha reached down and moved Elisa's legs off the sofa and sat down. "What is this stuff?" she asked pushing the vial toward Elisa.

"It's only a little *coke*. It won't hurt you. Guaranteed," Elisa told her.

Aisha stared at Elisa as she gently removed the vial from Aisha's hand, opened it and tasted some for herself.

"Yep, that's what it is," she laughed.

"Cocaine! I can't believe you would do such a thing!" Aisha screamed.

Waving Aisha off with her hand, Elisa said nonchalantly, "Chill out, Luscious. You'll thank me later."

Aisha stood up hurriedly, finished dressing for her set, and then let her eyes say what she could not find the courage to say.

Elisa was expressionless.

Aisha stomped out of her dressing room, slamming the door behind her.

Like always, Elisa had been right because by the time Aisha climbed on stage that night, not only was she higher than she'd ever been, but she felt good, real, real good.

Aisha looked at the clock on the dashboard of her car. It was still early when she arrived at church for Bible study. She sat in the parking lot until she saw Tameria driving up. Getting out of the car, she waved in Tameria's direction.

"Hey, girl," Aisha said as they met up. They hugged each other.

Tameria glimpsed at her watch. "We still have a few minutes before Bible study starts. Let's go inside to the members' lounge," she suggested.

"Okay, we can have a chance to talk," Aisha added.

They went into the practically empty members' lounge

and sat down on one of the numerous sofas that filled the student center type room. Tameria wasted no time asking Aisha to tell her what was going on in her life.

"Have you talked to what's his name?" Tameria asked.

"Who? Chandler?"

"Yeah."

"I talked to him earlier this afternoon. Since I have to-night off, I'm going to meet him for coffee after Bible study."

"That's good to hear. At least you haven't shut everyone out of your life."

Ignoring Tameria's remark, Aisha asked her, "And what about you and Chase?"

"Things couldn't be better."

"I heard that, girl," Aisha laughed, her eyes glassy-looking from the drugs.

Talking for a while longer, until they were partially satis-fied that they had caught up on what was happening in each of their lives, the two friends went to the sanctuary for weekly Bible study.

Both girls sat on the padded pews, listening attentively to Pastor Shipley. When it was over, they told each other goodbye and went their separate ways, Aisha to meet Chandler and Tameria to the hospital to start a new rota-tion.

Aisha passed Chandler's car parked on the street in front of the coffee shop. She wondered why he would park in a 'no parking' zone rather than simply using the parking area reserved for coffee shop customers.

She drove onto the coffee shop lot, parked her car at the far end of the parking area and went inside.

"How was Bible study?" Chandler asked, pulling the chair out for Aisha.

"Good as usual. Pastor Shipley is the greatest. The man makes things clear and easy to follow. I love his method of teaching."

"I'll have to come along and hear him some time."

"Okay, I'd like that. So tell me, what's been up with you these past couple of weeks?"

"I've been busy trying to close a couple of deals. Believe it or not, my job can be quite exhausting, not to mention time consuming and stressful. But seeing you tonight eases my tension," he flirted.

Aisha smiled broadly before answering. "It's good to see you too. I've been rather busy myself." She sipped a cup of hot tea and looked out of the restaurant window. A light frost had formed on the window, making it almost impossible to see the trail of people moving quickly up and down the busy sidewalk.

After they finished their coffee and tea, Chandler invited her to his apartment. She had never accepted his invitation to go to his apartment before, but tonight she told him yes. This newly changed Aisha yearned for affection and attention. Night after night men at The Lynx stared lustfully and sometimes propositioned her, but Aisha understood that it was only for her body. She wanted to be wanted for who she was on the inside, not as somebody's sex toy.

"Would you like to leave your car here and ride with me?" Chandler offered.

"No, I'd rather follow you," she told him, opening her purse to get her keys.

Within minutes of arriving at Chandler's apartment, Aisha asked to use his bathroom. She came out of the bathroom glassy eyed and wiping her nose with the back of her hand.

"How do you like my humble abode? I know it's not as nicely decorated as yours, but it is home," Chandler said.

"I like it. It's soothing and comfortable." Aisha walked around, admiring his apartment. "And I think your antique pieces are lovely."

"Thank you. They belonged to my great, great paternal grandmother."

"I see. Well, they're beautiful."

Chandler strolled over to the entertainment center and put on KEM's latest CD before he went to the bar and poured them a glass of white wine.

"Here, pretty lady." He sat down close beside her on the deep high-backed sofa. Aisha relaxed in his colossal arms. They snuggled for several minutes. Chandler inhaled the fruity scent of her hair and then kissed her on the forehead before turning her face to meet his. He kissed her intensely and a flame of passion was ignited between them.

A moan escaped her lips and she pulled back in surprise from his embrace. "Don't you think we're moving too fast?"

"No, I think we're moving according to how we feel about each other," he whispered while planting butterfly kisses along the side of her neck. He pulled her closer to him, tilting her head toward his. His tongue sought desperately to find hers.

"But, Chandler," she spoke between his kisses. "I don't think we should." She couldn't hold back any longer. His kisses were too demanding and the touch of his hands moving expertly over the contours of her body set a fire ablaze inside of her. She had to make him stop before there was no turning back. Her mind suddenly thought about the very advice she'd given Tameria. *Don't put yourself in a situation where you're alone with Chase. If you do, you're setting yourself up for things to get way out of hand.* Now, who was she to talk? She was in Chandler's bachelor pad, with KEM crooning in the background and a fine man doing things to her she'd often dreamed of, not to mention the drugs in her system that momentarily heightened her senses and impaired her judgment.

"Chandler, wait," she pleaded softly. "There's something I have to tell you."

He leaned back and looked longingly into her hazel eyes. "What is it, baby? Talk to me."

Before she could respond, he kissed her again lightly on her lips. His rough but gentle hands moved slowly up and down the length of her thighs.

*Why did I have to wear a skirt tonight of all nights? I should have put on my fuchsia pantsuit like I originally planned.*

"I'm listening. Tell me what's wrong, Aisha. Tell me, baby." The warmth penetrating throughout her body made it difficult for her to speak.

"I've. I've never been. Oooh, Chandler. Please, don't."

"You've never been what?" He stopped caressing her and waited to hear what she had to say. He didn't want to run her off. He liked her too much, way too much.

"I've never, you know, been with a man."

"Did you say never?" He couldn't believe what he just heard. *A twenty five year old virgin. No way. Not in this day and age.*

"Never," Aisha confirmed.

"I see." He didn't know what to say. He was stunned. Here he was sitting next to the most beautiful woman he'd ever seen, a woman who brought out feelings in him that he thought he'd never experience again and she was saying that she was a virgin. "Aisha, this is, man this is something I'm not used to hearing every day. You know?"

"Yeah, I know. But it's true. So you see, that's why we can't let this get out of control. I can't put myself in this position. I think it's time that I leave."

"Look, you don't have to leave. I told you that I like you. I really, really like you," he stressed. "And I can tell that you like me too. Don't you?" He waited to hear what he believed was in her heart.

"Yes, I do, but . . ."

"No buts," he said, placing a finger over her lips. "Let's just take things one day at a time. I promise I won't pressure you to do anything you don't want to do." He had no idea how he was going to keep his hands off her. But he was a man of his word and he wanted to earn her trust and respect. He stood up, walked over to the stereo and turned it off. Then he grabbed the remote and turned on the big screen.

With her eyes, she quietly followed his every move.

Chandler sat back down on the sofa and pulled her in his arms, allowing her to nestle against him. He flipped the remote until they settled on watching a movie on the Showtime Channel. Aisha was relaxed and no longer felt like she was losing control of her emotions.

The ringing of her cell phone disrupted their moment. She looked at the caller ID. It was Elisa. "Sorry, but I have to take this call." Chandler nodded his head and gingerly removed his arm from underneath her head. She answered the call while simultaneously standing up and going out to stand on the apartment balcony. "Hey. What's going on?"

"What are you doing?" Elisa asked.

"I'm with my friend."

"Oh, sorry. But look, how would you like to make a little something extra later tonight?" Aisha leaned her slender dance body against the concrete balcony wall. She spoke low so Chandler wouldn't hear her.

"How much something extra are you talking about?" Aisha asked.

"I can't really say, but probably close to two grand."

"How can I say no to that? But tell me first. What's the catch? What do I have to do?"

"What you do best," Elisa laughed over the phone. "It's a private dance request. I knew if you got this extra job tonight, it would help you out. So whaddaya want to do? Do you wanna go for it?"

"Thanks Elisa. I owe you one."

"Thank me later. Just get your butt here."

"I'll be there in less than an hour." Aisha walked back into the warmth of the living room, looking flustered with cheeks as red as an apple.

"Everything all right?" Chandler asked, his wrinkled brow revealing his concern.

"Sure, it's just that I have to leave. A friend of mine is in trouble."

"I'll come with you," he offered.

"No, please. That won't be necessary. I need to handle this by myself. Plus, I don't think she'd appreciate me bringing a stranger along with me. It's a sensitive situation."

"I see."

"I'm really sorry, Chandler. But I can't let this person down. She's done too much for me." Without giving him a chance to show his obvious disappointment, she gave him a peck on the cheek, grabbed her purse and rushed out the door. "I'll call you tomorrow. Bye now."

Hurrying to get to The Lynx, Aisha put the pedal to the medal on E-way 240. She fussed at herself for almost blowing her cover with Chandler. There was no way he believed her story about going to some friend's rescue at ten thirty at night. But she was still thankful that Elisa happened to call. It helped her out of a situation that could have turned into something she didn't want. No matter how much she shook her tail at The Lynx or used a little nose candy, she was not going to give her body to any man outside of marriage. Surely, that had to count for something with God.

Her tires squealed as she put on the brakes and parked her car in front of the the Lynx. She hurried inside, said hello to the bellman and headed for her dressing room. Her client, she was told, was a cowboy at heart. So Aisha wore her blue tight-fitting, rubber cowgirl mini with blue stilettos. She surveyed herself in the mirror and smiled while pulling her twists in a poof on her head and putting on a pair of blue oversized hoop earrings. Before leaving to meet her client, she said hello to *baby girl* and then proceeded to walk to the private suite elevator.

The morning after her private dance session, Aisha made a phone call. An hour later, Thaddeus arrived at the studio.

"Come in, Thaddeus." Aisha welcomed him into her studio office. Her private dance session the night before provided her with the rest of the money she needed to make the payment on the building. "Could I offer you a cup of coffee, tea or soda?"

"No, I'm fine. Thanks. I'd really like to get down to business. I have another appointment that I must get to and it's all the way on the other side of town." Thaddeus hoped that Aisha hadn't called him over to beg for more time. The owner of the building wanted out and he made it clear to Thaddeus that he wouldn't take any more extensions. Thaddeus had heard that the owner was already in debt up to the ying yang, and worst of all, that he faced big trouble with the IRS. It was necessary for him to liquidate some of his assets as quickly as he could to pay them off or they would take everything he'd worked hard for.

Aisha sat on the edge of her oblong walnut desk and reached over to the side drawer. Unlocking it, she reached inside and pulled out a green envelope and passed it to Thaddeus.

"What do you have for me here?" He eyed the envelope with curiosity, turning it over in his hands before opening it. His eyes appeared large as saucers when he spied the cashier's check for the exact amount of the building. "You do mean business don't you?"

"Yes, I most certainly do."

"I'm impressed. You definitely go after what you want, don't you?"

"Yes, and you make sure the owner of this building knows that."

"Did you say the owner of this building?"

"Yes, I sure did."

"Well, let's take care of that by finalizing this deal and filling out these papers. And the owner of this building will be *you*."

She breathed a welcome sigh of relief. Though she was less than pleased with the fact that she had to become an exotic dancer to get the money, she was glad to be blessed with the talent to make the kind of money she'd always dreamed of making by doing what she always loved. Her life could get back to normal now and The Lynx and all it stood for could be a thing of the past—soon, anyway.

# 19

"Every time I come to church, I get a free workout." Tameria burst into laughter. "This place is way too huge. I see why people are starting to call it a mega church," she said as they walked inside the building.

"That just lets us know that we're reaching people, Tameria," Aisha replied. "If a church isn't growing, then something's drastically wrong. That's the purpose of the pastor and the different ministries—to reach the lost."

"Yea, I know that. But I still miss that small, cozy family type atmosphere that you find in small churches."

"Me too, but we can't have it all. Is Chase coming tonight? He's tagged along with you the last few times you came to church."

"He's on call tonight. And I have to report to the hospital at midnight myself. How's everything coming along with raising the money for the down payment?"

"God is blessing me, Tameria. I found some investors so I should have enough money to close the deal on the property real soon." No way was Aisha going to tell Tameria how she really got the money.

Tameria clapped her hands together and starting jumping. "Oh my God, that's shouting news! When were you going to tell me?"

"I planned on telling you once I signed the final papers. I should have known that would be impossible with you," Aisha laughed and then joined in Tameria's praise jump. "Can you believe it?" Aisha squealed and turned around and around.

"Don't tell me what God can't do," Tameria said as church goers filed pass the two of them.

Sitting in church on the padded pews, Aisha felt a bit of guilt at the lie and the undercover life she was leading. She wasn't still dancing at The Lynx because she wanted to. She was there because she still had debts that she needed to pay off. She didn't want to find herself in the frightening situation she'd just come out of ever again. She was just going to work long enough to pay off the rest of her bills and build up her savings account. After that, she would quit The Lynx and never look back. God understood and if she was wrong for doing what she believed she had to do in order to get ahead, He would forgive her. That she believed for sure, so she opened her Bible and began listening to Pastor Shipley.

"God desires for His children to have a personal relationship with Him. He wants us to be holy and pure. We all have sinned and fallen short of the glory of God. That much is true. But we don't have a right to freely sin and go against God's commandments," he taught. "People, God has a plan for our lives. Let's begin to listen to His voice. Take heed to His message and live a life of holiness dedicated to loving and living for Him."

Aisha squirmed in her chair as she listened to Pastor Shipley's every word. She felt uneasy about her secret life but she had no choice. She had to do what she had to do in order to keep the studio. Anyway, she had convinced herself that God had opened the door for her to receive her blessing. And so what if it was at the Lynx. It was no strip joint. It was a private upscale club; hers was just another job. And as for the cocaine, she only did it every now and then. She needed a boost of energy after leaving her studio every evening. She wasn't hooked on it or anything. Because when she searched for information about cocaine on the internet she found out it was not addictive anyway. She just liked the way it made her feel. Aisha refocused on Pastor Shipley's closing remarks.

"Remember, if sin didn't feel good, look good, and taste good, there would be nothing for you to worry about. You see sin is a great disguiser. Merriam Webster's defines it as an offense against God, a weakened state of human nature in which the self is estranged from God. Then there's the word insatiable. Insatiable is when you have a craving for something but you can never get satisfied or full of it. No matter what you do, you can never get enough of it. Sin is like that. It feels so good and looks so good sometimes that you find yourself craving it more and more. You want more money. More sex. More cars. More houses. More men. More women. More things of this world. All the time, you're being deceived, trapped by the devil. I call it, *sinsatiable*. But there's something false about these sinsatiable desires and feelings. They're fleeting, and only for a moment does it feel good. So be wise my brothas and sistas. Resist the schemes of the devil as if your very life depended on it. Because it does."

After speaking to several of the church members after Bible study, Aisha said goodbye to Tameria, rushed out of the sanctuary, and dashed to her car. She was infuriated when the screeching set of tires against the wet blacktop pulled in front of her. The oncoming car barely missed her steel gray Acura as she pulled out of the church parking lot. Thoughts of Pastor Shipley's remarks were easily replaced with a string of expletives flowing from her mouth. She sped off down the winding street until she reached I-240. The digital clock on the console read 8:45. She had less than an hour to get to The Lynx, shower and change. She had a client who thrived on promptness so being late wasn't an option. She reached over in her purse, fumbled for the rectangular pill box instead of her brown vial. When she found it, she popped open its latch and pulled out a tiny round blue pill with a cut out V design. "*Ahhh*, nothing like a little Valium to relax one's nerves," she said and sped off.

Aisha made it to the Lynx in seventeen minutes flat. She rushed inside and ran past the armed doorman. "Good evening, Miss C."

"Hello, Thomas," she responded in an exasperated voice. She walked briskly to the elevator, pressed the button and without bothering to wait, raced to the stairwell and walked up to the second floor.

The first person Aisha ran into was Elisa. She looked radiant as usual. Every time Aisha saw her, Elisa was perfectly dressed from head to toe. Tonight she had on a revealing black flared mini and the front of the dress had a plunging V like neck line that stopped at her belly button. The sleeveless dress sparkled with tiny sequins. The black king-toed stilettos she wore and sheer black hose added an extra dose of sex appeal to Elisa's already flawless body. Elisa greeted Aisha as she walked into the lounge.

"Slow down, girl. You aren't late you know," Elisa told her.

"I know but if I don't hurry up and get changed, I will be."

"Who's the lucky man tonight?" a well dressed Jason asked as he walked up to her and Elisa.

"Jason, you know we can't divulge who our private clients are," Elisa responded before Aisha could answer.

Of course Jason knew all of the members already. He was

fully aware that the names of their high-paying, exclusive clientele were never to be mentioned unless it was behind closed doors. He continued to tease the two of them, especially flirting with Aisha. He found her exceptionally beautiful and her innocent persona made him desire her that much more.

"Aisha, whoever he is, I envy him."

With much attitude, Aisha retorted, "From what I've heard, you have a wife and four kids at home so I suppose you're getting enough action already. Don't you think you need to lay low?"

Elisa laughed when Jason turned beet red before stomping off.

"Girl, why you dog that man like that? You know he just wants to get a little something on the side."

"Please. Jason needs to be at home spending time with his family instead of leading a double life. And you said he has a gorgeous wife. I don't understand men like him."

"You still have a lot to learn. Take a look around. Most of these men have families at home, gorgeous wives, mistresses and lots of money. Some are even preachers, elders and deacons at churches, so wake up and smell the roses my friend. This is life and no matter how you think it ought to be, it is what it is."

"I know, but I'm just saying. I don't understand, that's all."

"Look, we'll talk later. But for now, you better go and get ready. You don't want to disappoint your new client."

"You're right. I'll see you later on," Aisha told her and proceeded to leave.

The more she hung around the open area, the more Aisha began to sense that The Lynx was not all it portrayed itself to be. It was as if she'd been seeing through rose-colored glasses. When she began to mix and mingle with some of the other girls she started to get the impression from their conversation and looks that they were awfully young. She tried discussing it with Elisa but she nonchalantly shrugged her off by explaining that every girl at The Lynx was at least eighteen years old. Aisha dismissed her weird feelings and told herself that if there *was* any illegal business going on, then it wasn't any of her business. She was there to make money.

After showering, Aisha stood in front of the full length mirror and surveyed herself. All of her life she had been raised to be a "good girl." She was taught to carry herself like a lady at all times. Her father often emphasized to her while she was growing up the importance of respecting her own body and that she should demand that any man who called himself a men who was interested in her should respect her as well. To Aisha, her father represented all that she wanted to have in a man. Being raised by Christian parents, she spent more than half her life in and out of church. Every morning before she went off to school, her father prayed with her and every single Wednesday night and Sunday evening they attended Bible study. She basically knew the Bible like the back of her hand.

As she studied herself in the mirror, she felt somewhat ashamed of where she had allowed herself to be in life. Here she was being critical of Jason and the other men who led a double life, but she was doing the very same thing. No matter how she tried to justify her actions, she felt that she was no better than the girls who danced around a pole in the strip clubs lining Brooks Road and Lamar Avenue. Maybe she hadn't slept with anyone, but she was still no better than a common whore, at least that's what the face in the mirror called her. Aisha looked around the dressing room until she saw the brown vial on the round table. She walked over and picked it up. Again, doing what she never thought she would do, she opened the top and inhaled.

When she stood in front of the mirror a second time, the

shame she'd felt a few minutes earlier had disappeared. She felt relaxed, without a care in the world. She inhaled another hit then smiled at the image in the mirror.

Aisha wore a strapless white halter top along with a sheer sarong that revealed her white thong underneath. Her twists were gathered up and held together by a white and silver band. The large silver diamond-cut hoops glistened as they dangled from her ears. She lightly squirted Gucci Rush on each wrist and added a squirt at the base of her throat. Lastly, she placed her freshly pedicured feet into her white leather Minolo stilettos then placed her top coat over her outfit and proceeded down the back hallway that lead to the private elevator. After pulling out her elevator key and placing it in the key hole, she then pushed the button next to the word Private Suites.

By the time she made it to the Private Suites floor, she was relaxed and confident in her talents. She wasn't going to allow the devil to make her feel inadequate. Not tonight. As she walked along the corridor, she convinced herself that what she was doing wasn't wrong. She wasn't fornicating. She wasn't stealing, robbing or hurting anyone. She was merely doing a job, using her talents to satisfy other people. She proudly strode to room 1066 and lightly tapped on the door. The voice on the other end invited her to come in. Aisha removed her topcoat and stepped inside. *Another day and many more dollars.*

# 20

Chandler was relieved when his Chief informed him that he wouldn't have to go out of town for his next undercover assignment. This would give him more time, he hoped, to get closer to Aisha. It was hard trying to establish a relationship when he had to keep his unexplained whereabouts a secret and when he had to lie about the type of work he did. In the past, it hadn't really mattered with the girls he had dated, but Aisha was different. For some reason, he didn't want to lie to her. But right now, he had no choice. He had a dangerous job at that. And if he wanted to maintain a sense of safety he had to keep everything he did confidential.

The well-dressed older gentleman walked into the exclusive Cordova men's store in Cordova. He went straight to the top-of-the-line clothing area. He settled on two pairs of Sean John slacks with coordinating shirts and blazers, three Armani suits and one Gucci linen slack set with shoes to match each outfit. Before leaving, he picked out a pair of three hundred and fifty dollar Versace sunglasses. He climbed into a black onyx Lexus LS 430 and sped off toward his destination—3289 Riverside. He entered the destination address into the navigation system on the console and listened as the mechanical voice gave him step-by-step directions.

As he pulled up in front of the gated residence, he exhaled loudly as he looked at the tri-level mansion that resembled a medieval castle. The steps leading up to the house were marble and the porch stretched the length of the house. He turned the key and entered the 7,500 square foot dwelling. The 20-foot foyer was elegant and led to a winding double staircase with intricate wrought iron railings. On the main level to the left were the living room, dining room, gourmet kitchen and family room. To the right of the foyer he walked into a huge master bedroom suite with vaulted ceilings and windows that extended from the floor to the ceiling. The master bath included a gigantic walk-in closet, stand-alone steam shower, sauna and a Jacuzzi. A separate whirlpool tub sat in the middle of the slate floor.

The man checked out the other two levels of the house before he went outside and brought in his recent purchases. The home was furnished like an HGTV dream house and the landscaped grounds added even more class to the already dramatic home. After searching through the fully stocked black and chrome refrigerator, he pulled out all the fixings for a fresh deli-style turkey and ham sandwich.

He toured the remaining rooms while munching on his sandwich. Once he was satisfied that he'd visited every room in his new abode, he retrieved his briefcase and settled into the library.

He pulled out a blue folder and began to read, "The Lynx, a privately-owned gentleman's association is located on the outskirts of Memphis in the secluded Southwind area. Owner suspected of drug trafficking, money laundering and human trafficking of under-age girls."

The contents of the folder described, in detail, the various forms of abuse the girls experienced. Many had been enticed with promises of modeling careers or food and shelter if they were runaways, only to be lured into a web so strong, it was impossible to escape.

Kyle's jaw muscles tightened. He stopped reading and pushed the folder aside, hoping the sick feeling in the pit of his stomach would soon pass.

# 21

"Welcome to The Lynx, Mr. Taylor." Jason extended his chubby hand to the newest member of their circle.

"Thank you, Jason. And now that we're comrades, call me Kyle.

"Of course, Kyle," Jason responded, pushing his black designer eyeglasses off the bridge of his equally chubby nose.

"From the looks of this establishment, I believe I've made the right decision to become a member. But as you know, I can't be totally sure until I see what this place has to offer other than elegance of structure, if you know what I mean?"

Kyle was smooth talking, with charisma that drew people to him.

"Now that you've toured your new home away from home, let me show you some of the perks that come along with being a V.I.P. member of The Lynx. After that, I'll show you to your suite. You must be tired after such a long flight.

Kyle nodded, "Yes I am. But I'm about business, so let's see what you have to show me."

"Of course." Jason led him into the lounge area. It was close to midnight, and the ambiance of the lounge was impressive. Kyle's eyes lingered on the host of stunning scantily clad women sitting and standing around. From the cocktail waitresses to the voluptuous blonde and brunette dancers that moved back and forth over the raised floor, they were hot. Their assets moved invitingly along with them as they kept up with the beat of the hip hop song playing. Their attire left little to the imagination.

Rubbing his hands together as he walked next to Kyle, Jason asked, "What do you think, Kyle? Do you like what you see so far?"

"I do, I do. But I've seen even better where I've just come from."

"Is that right? Where might that be? If I might ask."

"St. Thomas."

"I've made several trips to St. Thomas myself. They have some fine women there but they can't compete with the ladies you'll find here at The Lynx. I believe you're well aware of that already. Successful brothers like us don't pay for services that we aren't one hundred percent sure about," Jason laughed.

"Well said, Jason. And, oh so true. Show me more," Kyle prodded. "I want to make sure I did the right thing when I purchased a home in Memphis."

"Come, I'll take you to your suite." Kyle allowed Jason to lead him down the same corridor Aisha had taken earlier that led to the private elevator.

"I believe you'll find that the key to the elevator is already in your possession."

"Is that so?" Kyle asked, rather curious.

"Just push the black square on the elevator and hold it there for ten seconds."

Kyle did as he was instructed and the elevator door opened. "Ah, another plus. You've already programmed my fingerprints, huh. How clever."

"The men at The Lynx are not your typical run of the mill men. We have the best of the best in every field. That includes the best technology that you could ever imagine." They stepped on to the elevator and Jason guided Kyle again. This time he told him to push the blue square button that read 11. Kyle did as he was told and when the elevator reached the eleventh floor they stepped out, turned right and walked down the wide hallway until the two of them stood in front of Suite 1177. The two-bedroom Presidential suite occupied the entire eleventh floor. When Kyle walked inside, he stepped on to black marble floors. The first bathroom had mahogany ceilings. To his right was the sitting room, which featured unique glazed faux finished walls, an entertainment center, and Victorian antiques. Through another entrance leading from the sitting area was a study that had a mahogany and leather desk with matching leather, both from the *Ernest Hemingway* collection. Another area of the study was equipped with a state of the art computer. Each room of the suite was lavishly decorated and furnished. Kyle turned and looked at Jason when they walked out on to a private balcony. Kyle looked out over the Memphis skyline. *Aaahh*, Kyle said to himself. *Winter has given way to Spring.*

"Your clothes have already been brought up to your room. Someone will be up shortly to unpack them for you."

"Okay. But give me a few minutes to relax and make some business calls, then you can send the person up."

"Sure, and we'll talk tomorrow. You'll get a chance to meet some of the other members at that time. Goodnight."

"Goodnight." Kyle went back into the master suite and looked around. Next to the walnut California king-size bed was an antique side table. A key rested on top of it in a solid gold tray. Kyle tried to see if it was the key to the locked drawer on the table, and it was. He pulled out the drawer and saw a black octagon-shaped box. He opened it and couldn't believe what he was seeing. The white powder stung his tongue when he tasted it. Pure cocaine. "Well, I'll be . . . ," he swore before replacing the box inside the drawer and locking it.

Talking out loud, he said, "I'm going to take a bath and then I'll call . . ." but a knock on the door halted his conversation with himself.

"Who's there?" he asked.

"I'm here to unpack your things sir," the demure voice said from the other side of the door.

Kyle opened the door and was shocked to see a young girl standing before him with hair the color of onyx. She looked to be about the same age as his fourteen year old niece. Her dark eyes displayed a look of utter fear. Kyle resisted the urge to pull the terrified looking girl inside his suite and tell her that everything would be all right. The frightened look on her face pushed him to his limit. But he had to play his part well if he was to be successful in nabbing these oversexed, drug dealing, perverted men he was about to encounter at The Lynx.

"Come in, young lady," Kyle directed in a polite tone.

"Sir, are you ready for me to unpack your things?" He could barely hear her, as she spoke just above a whisper. She shied away looking directly at him as she moved deeper inside the suite.

"Yes, I'd like that. What's your name?"

"Hallie," she answered quickly.

"Hallie. That's a pretty name. My name is Kyle"

He wanted to make her feel somewhat at ease, hoping he would be able to gain her trust over the next few days and then get her to confide in him. He wondered if she was at The Lynx against her will. From the drugs he'd discovered in his room already, he guessed The Lynx probably had a lot of illegal activity to be unveiled, and he was just the man to do it.

He focused his attention back on Hallie. He watched as she carefully removed each piece of clothing from his suitcase and hung them on the wooden hangers in the closet or placed them in the drawers. When she finished, she slowly turned toward him and began to peel off each layer of her own clothing. She slid the delicate sleeves of her lavender dress down off her shoulders and was about to push the one-piece dress down over her hips when Kyle ordered her to stop. He didn't mean to frighten her with his fatherly tone, but at that moment he saw a child standing before him, not a woman.

"What are you doing?" he said in an angry voice.

"I'm here to please you, sir."

He rushed over to her side and pulled her dress back up over her shoulders. The girl cowered in fear. "Please me? What are you talking about, please me?"

"I'm here for you, to serve your needs, Mr. Kyle. What would you like me to do? How can I show you how much I want to satisfy you?"

"You're just a child. Tell me something, Hallie?"

"Yes, what is it sir?" she asked, eager to respond to his request.

"How old are you?"

Hallie's face turned ashen. She didn't know what to say. Why would he ask her such a thing? She had been brought to The Lynx three months ago and she was still new to what was expected of her. She longed to be back home in St. Thomas with her three younger brothers and two little sisters. When her father woke her up that terrible night, she didn't know that her life was about to change. Some of her friends on the island had suddenly disappeared over the past two years without a trace, and she'd heard frightening stories about what happened to them. But she didn't want to believe the horrid things she heard about them being kidnapped, raped, sold as sex slaves and child laborers.

*"Hallie, wake up," her father had ordered that horrible night. He shook her hard and yanked her out of the bed. "Hallie," he screamed again. "Hurry, they're waiting on you."*

*"Who, Father?" she asked. "Who's waiting on me? Is everything okay?"*

*"You have to go. It's time for you to do something to help the family. I can't do it alone anymore. You're thirteen years old now. It's time you start fulfilling your responsibilities as a woman." He pushed her toward the front door. She saw her mother and siblings hovering inside the dingy hut they called home. A look of helplessness and despair lay openly over her mother's face. Her brothers and sisters watched as her father continued to pull her toward the bamboo door. When he opened it, she saw three men she'd seen before on the island. She'd heard terrible rumors about the reason the men scaled the island. Tonight it seemed as if the rumors weren't rumors at all. They really were who people said they were—men looking to buy young girls, and sometimes boys, from the poorest inhabitants on the island.*

*"Daddy, please. Please don't do this." She felt fear rise up inside and envelop her newly developing body.*

*"Come on, Hallie. Everything will be all right."*

*While kicking and screaming against the darkness, the men laughed at her. One of them remarked, "She's a feisty little thing isn't she?" Another one of the men passed a wad of money over to Hallie's father. She met the empty gaze of her father just before he turned and walked back in the house, pushing the door closed behind him.*

"Hallie, I asked you a question," Kyle repeated. "How old are you?"

"Thirteen and a half," she responded, sounding even more like the little girl she was.

"Get out of here, Hallie," he demanded.

"What did I do wrong, Mr. Kyle? Please, I'll do whatever you want. Just tell me. I don't want any trouble," she begged.

"Trouble? What kind of trouble?" he asked the terrified child.

"I, I don't want them to hurt me. I'll do whatever you want," she began to cry.

"Then what I want is for you to leave. I'm tired and I don't want to be bothered," he insisted.

Hallie hurried toward the door. A look of relief washed over her innocent face.

"I'll be here early tomorrow with your breakfast," she said and ran out the door before the stranger changed his mind.

After she left, Kyle gritted his teeth before slamming his fist against the wall. He couldn't suppress the thoughts of the vile acts that Hallie may have been subjected to, not to mention other girls who might be at The Lynx against their will. Hoping to clear his mind of any more such thoughts, he ran himself a hot bath. After soaking for close to forty-five minutes, he climbed out, dried off and checked the time.

"Dang, it's almost two in the morning," he said out loud. "Too late to call her or anybody else now." Kyle turned back the thick covers on the bed. He climbed between the white Egyptian cotton sheets and was asleep almost as soon as his head hit the pillow.

There was much to uncover at The Lynx. Hallie was just the tip of the iceberg.

# 22

Taking the liberty to go and knock on Aisha's closed dressing room door, Elisa patiently stood with one hand on her hip and waited until she heard Aisha respond, "Come in."

"Hey. What's up?" Aisha stood aside so Elisa could come all the way inside the small dressing room.

"Nothing. I just thought I'd come by before my next set so you could tell me how it went with your first private dance. How did he look?" Elisa asked, closing the door behind her and sitting down. "Did he try to get freaky with you?"

"Nope. You know I'm not going to stand for anything other than doing what I do and getting out of there. He looked okay but there was something about him. He looked familiar, like somebody I've seen before.

"You may very well run into somebody you know every blue moon, but that's highly unlikely, girl. These men pay too much for their privacy and we don't see men like them walking the Average Joe streets of Memphis, you know."

"Anyway, I would guess him to be in his late thirties,

medium build but dark and rugged looking. The brother was dressed to the nines and smelled even better. He wanted me to slow dance with him. At first I was like, no way," Aisha laughed. "But a one-on-one with my *baby girl* helped change my mind in a hurry.".

The two ladies gave each other a high five. "Jason says he's the head of his father's million dollar technology company," Elisa told her.

"He didn't bother telling me his profession and I didn't bother asking. I wanted to get the show on the road, make some money and scoot on out of there."

"So you said that you slow danced with him? You are getting bold aren't you?" Elisa remarked curtly.

"I couldn't help it, really. He was rather charming, plus when I saw that Presidential Rolex dripping from his arm," Aisha chuckled again, "suddenly slow dancing sounded like child's play."

"Do I detect a change here, girlfriend? I thought a Christian girl like you wouldn't want a man rubbing up against her. Especially since you say that you're a virgin. Unless the virgin tale is just that, a tale," Elisa questioned, raising her arched eyebrows.

Aisha stared at her, and her ebony complexion appeared to change to a tinted red hue. She was totally embarrassed and became defensive. "I don't have to lie to you or anyone else about being a virgin."

"No, you don't have to lie to me. That's exactly my point. I'm just saying that you Christian folks kill me. I don't see how you call yourself a Christian anyway," Elisa said with a smirk on her face.

"I *am* a Christian and don't you forget it, Elisa," Aisha angrily responded. "Maybe I *have* gotten on the wrong track, but I'm going to stop. I'm going to stop using and I'm going to stop stripping. You'll see." Aisha had become so angry, that she stood up from the sofa, pointed her finger toward Elisa and blurted out, "As a matter of fact, I'm quitting The Lynx at the end of the month."

Silence.

"What? You can't be serious."

"Well, I am," Aisha said, still angry that Elisa had questioned her faith and religion.

"When did you decide this? A second ago?" Elisa asked sarcastically.

"I don't see why it's any concern of yours, *when* I decided," Aisha shouted. "The point is, I have and so I am!"

"Girl, calm down. Can't you take a joke? I wasn't trying to make you feel bad. I swear. You take life way too serious sometimes."

Pausing, then sitting down trying to regain her composure, Aisha replied slowly, "I'm sorry I went off on you like that. It's just that it's time that I quit. I got what I wanted which was to save my studio, pay my credit cards off, not to mention the perk of finally having a nice size bank account. Anyway, look at me. I'm a mess. I do drugs, for God's sake," Aisha cried, looking at herself with total dissatisfaction and shame. "Me, of all people."

"What do you mean by *you of all people*? You're human just like the rest of us. You think that just because you call yourself all into God and stuff that you're supposed to be little Miss Perfect, better than the rest of us or something?" Elisa tried to refrain from becoming angry herself. But she wasn't about to let Aisha get away with her holier-than-thou gibberish.

"I didn't say that, you did," Aisha fired back, both of them angry now.

"You're no better than me or the rest of the girls. Look at yourself, honey. What separates us from you?"

Aisha's face turned crimson and Elisa continued reading her. "That's why I can't get into the God thing. 'Cause there are a lot of so-called Christians right here at The Lynx."

Flinging her hands, Elisa kept talking. "Rich men parading around night after night, lusting after me, then they take their hypocritical behinds home to their wives and their children like they're so godly and all. Going to church Sunday after Sunday, wanting people to believe they're so holy and righteous. None of it's for real, if you ask me. And I don't mean any harm, but no one can tell by looking at *you* or listening to *you*," Elisa emphasized, "that you're a so-called Christian. But still, I ain't mad at you."

Elisa quieted down long enough to take a couple of snorts from her personal stash.

"I didn't say I was better than you or anybody else," Aisha shot back. "And you're right. I'm on the wrong road right now. I know that things in my life have gotten out of control and I shouldn't be doing what I'm doing. I should have trusted God in the beginning. But *noooo* I had to take matters into my own hands. Now here I am dancing for men, letting them ease up on me, and snorting drugs. God, forgive me!" Aisha bowed her head in shame.

"Well, you better hope God really is the forgiving kind, sweetheart, because you have a lot of forgiveness to ask for. But don't worry, you're still a good girl, Aisha. I'm not trying to down you," Elisa said in a much calmer tone. "I only wanted you to see that we're all the same and nobody, I mean nobody is perfect. Right?"

Aisha held her head back up and sighed deeply. "You're right."

"Now, come on. Let's get out of here. I'm beat and I promised Gabby that I would be home early tonight."

Aisha became more consumed with guilt. What happened and how had she turned into the person she was now? Where had her faith failed her? Everything Elisa said to her was on target. She was no better than the unsaved people she encountered everyday. As a matter of fact, she was worse. Because at least they weren't pretending to be something other than what they really were. Tears crested in the corners of her eyes and she took one hand to wipe them away. It was time for her to make a change before things got any worse. Her cell phone rang, pulling her away from the condemning thoughts that invaded her mind.

"Hello," she spoke softly into the razor thin cell phone after hearing her parents' distinctive ring tone.

"Aisha. Where are you? I called you at home but you didn't answer," her mother said.

"Mom, I'm on my way home. Remember I told you that I have a part-time night job."

"I know what you told me, but it seems more like a full-time job to me. You're never home anymore and we can barely reach you on your cell."

"I know, and I'm sorry. But I have some things I'm trying to do and in order to do them, I need this job." Aisha was trying to hide the irritation she felt at her mother's inquisition.

"Well, still, you shouldn't be working so much. Remember Sister Beverly?"

Aisha rolled her eyes up in her head. She suspected where her mother's conversation was leading. Beverly was one of her mother's church friends who resided in a retirement community owned and operated by the church.

"Yes, ma'am. I remember Sister Beverly," Aisha dragged. "What about her?"

"She told me that she hasn't seen you at church or Bible study lately. Nothing should come before God and church, Aisha. Your father tells you that all the time. 'Always, *always* put God first,' is what he tells you," her mother scolded.

Her mother's words stung and added to the guilt she already felt. "Mom, I know I haven't been to church lately, but Daddy also taught me that it's not the number of times a person does or doesn't attend church. It's what's in your heart that matters. And Jesus is in my heart," Aisha declared.

"Don't try to use your father's words against me, Aisha Denise Carlisle!" her mother shouted over the phone receiver. "When you get through justifying putting God, not to mention me and your daddy, on the back burner, you're still wrong. If we didn't call you, then we don't know when we would hear from you. And you know that your daddy hasn't been feeling the best lately."

"What's wrong with Daddy?"

"If you would check on him more, then you'd know that I took him to the doctor a couple of days ago. They had to run some tests and x-rays."

Attributing everything to Benjamin was something Sandra Carlisle did often. Aisha rarely heard her mother telling her anything on her own. It was always, *'your father said,'* or she'd say something like, *'Why don't you come see your father.'* Aisha had grown accustomed to it, but tonight she was irritated with her mother.

"What kind of tests?" Aisha stomped on the brakes when she saw that she was about to run the traffic light. "Mom, look, I should be home in about fifteen minutes. Let me call you when I make it to the apartment. I want to know what's going on."

"Okay, call me as soon as you get home," her mother said, then hung up the phone.

Aisha would never be able to forgive herself if something serious was wrong with her daddy and she hadn't been around to see about him. She rushed inside the empty apartment and kicked off her shoes at the same time the auto lights popped on. She dropped her duffel bag full of her costumes, threw her purse on the table and headed straight to the den to call her mom.

"Mom, I'm home," Aisha said into the receiver.

"You made it home that quick? You better stop driving so fast. I know it hasn't been five minutes since we hung up."

"Mom, please. Tell me what's going on with Daddy," Aisha asked, ignoring her mother's sharp criticism. Sometimes she felt there was nothing she could do well enough in her mother's eyes.

Sandra Carlisle had been the disciplinarian in the family. Growing up, Aisha felt her mother's wrath more than a few times. She wasn't abusive, but she could cut Aisha with her words. And the look in her eyes when she was angry could stop a train in its tracks. There were times when Aisha was young that she preferred an outright whipping rather than listen to her mother's scathing verbal slashing.

"The doctors think he has some kind of respiratory problem. We won't know for sure until the tests come back."

"Where is Daddy now?"

"Asleep," she answered.

"What made him go to the doctor?"

"He's been laying around the house a lot for the past couple of weeks complaining about being tired. It's just not like him."

Aisha put one hand to her forehead while pacing back and forth across the living room floor.

"I don't understand. I just spoke to him a few days ago and he sounded fine."

"That's because he knows you're too busy working your two jobs," Sandra told her in an accusatory tone.

Aisha was livid but she bit her tongue and remained quiet as her mother kept talking.

"He said his muscles ached and his head hurt too. I thought maybe he had the flu or a really bad cough, but after it persisted I told him he needed to see a doctor."

Why hadn't her mother called and told her any of this? Sandra Carlisle could be quite vindictive, but Aisha hated to think that this was her mother's way of punishing her for not being around or calling them as much. Ever since she started working at The Lynx, Aisha had found it more difficult to find time to visit as much as she used to. She mostly relied on phone communication to keep her abreast of what was going on, but of course her mother didn't see things the same way. The two women were stubborn and often butted heads.

"Mother, I can't believe you haven't said anything about this to me. I know I've been working non-stop and I haven't been over there lately. But I'm still entitled to know what's going on with you and Daddy." Aisha ranted on the cordless phone while she walked through the house.

"If you really wanted to see your father, you'd make the time to do it. Maybe if you slowed down a little and took a look around at the things that are, or *should* be important to you," she emphasized, "other than making money and more money, you would know what's going on."

Aisha knew by her mother's last remarks that she was definitely punishing her. She began to cry, but managed to keep her mother from hearing it in her voice. "I'll be over there first thing tomorrow morning. I'll talk to you then," Aisha remarked without responding to her mother's cutting words. She said goodbye and went into her bedroom. Plopping down across the bed, Aisha allowed the heavy flow of tears to have their way. She was too tired and too upset to hold them back. She buried her face in her pillow to muffle the sound. Without flinching, she reached over on the nightstand next to her king-sized bed and pulled out *baby girl.*

# 23

"Aisha, pick up the phone," Tameria screamed into the answering machine. "Aisha, if you're there, please pick up the phone. It's an emergency!" Aisha shifted her body in the bed as she slowly awakened to the screaming woman who interrupted dreams of her and Chandler walking hand in hand along the river walk.

Still half asleep, she clumsily felt around on the bed for her cordless phone. "Hello, whuzzup Tameria? What time is it?" Aisha asked, too sleepy to be angry.

"Wake up. You need to get to the hospital right away."

As if someone had suddenly prodded her with a hot poker, Aisha jumped upright in the bed. "What's wrong? Tell me, Tameria, what's wrong?" she screamed frantically.

"It's Mr. Carlisle. He came through the emergency room about an hour ago. You need to get here as soon as you can." Tameria hated to be the one to have to call her best friend with such horrific news, but better her than some other doctor or nurse who didn't know anything about Aisha or the Carlisle family.

"My daddy? Oh my God. Tameria, is he all right?" She

moved across the cold hardwood floor with the swiftness of a jaguar, grabbing a pair of sweats off the back of the door.

"Just try to take it easy and get here as soon as you can. Come to the first floor Critical Care Unit."

"Oh, Jesus have mercy," Aisha cried. Her hands shook and big tears rolled down her round face. She dropped the phone and slammed the door behind her.

"Oh, Lord, I need you to hear me. I need you to answer me. Please make my father be okay," she pleaded as she sped to St. Francis Hospital. Her tears almost blinded her and thoughts of her father possibly dying flooded her mind. He was always in her corner. She was daddy's little girl. Whenever her mother criticized, ridiculed or punished her, she would run to the safety of her daddy's arms. Though short in stature, his love for Aisha was mammoth. No one ever meant more to him than his daughter. Sometimes Aisha believed that her mother was jealous of her relationship with her father. Maybe that's why she acted as if Aisha could never do anything right.

Aisha used one hand to steer the car and the other to rifle through her purse for her cell phone. After several seconds of holding down the speed dial button, the phone dialed her mother's cell number. The phone immediately went to voice mail.

"Dang, Momma, why haven't you called me?" Fifteen minutes later, she turned off the Poplar-Germantown exit toward Ridgeway Boulevard. Her heart pounded as she saw the lights of the hospital. She talked to herself. *Daddy you're all right. You've just got a virus, nothing serious.* She turned swiftly into the full emergency room parking lot, barely missing the bumper of a parked car. She frantically drove around the parking lot in search of a parking space. *Lord, come on. Don't allow this to happen. I've got to find a place to park. I've got to get to my daddy.* After circling the lot a few times, she decided to park in a handicapped space. She couldn't worry about a ticket or being towed. All her thoughts were on her father. She jumped out of the car and raced to the information desk and asked for directions to Critical Care.

"I need to know about my father, Benjamin Carlisle," she hurriedly spoke to the clerk sitting at the CCU window. Exceptionally nice, the middle aged redhead pointed in the direction of the far right corner of the comfortably furnished CCU waiting area. Aisha saw her mother with her head in her hands, looking like she'd aged ten years over night.

She rushed over to her and sat in the pearl gray leather chair next to her. "Mother, what happened?"

"He's had what the doctors call a hemorrhagic stroke on the brain. He's unconscious. They don't know if he's going to make it," she cried.

"I've got to see him." She immediately ran back to the window clerk. "Tell me where I can go to see my father!"

"Sweetie, the doctors are working on Mr. Carlisle right now. I'll let the floor nurse know you're here. Are you his daughter?"

"Yes, yes I am and I need to talk to the doctor about seeing my father." Aisha couldn't contain her fear.

Her mother walked up beside her and wrapped her arms around her shoulders. "Aisha, they're doing all they can. We have to pray and believe in God for healing. Let the doctors do what needs to be done."

"Honey," the clerk added, "your mother is right. The nurse or doctor will call as soon as they can. I'll call you up here when they do and then I want you to go right around that corner." The clerk pointed to a corridor next to her reception area. "There are several phones lined up on the walls with a number over each one. I'll tell you which phone to answer. I promise, as soon as I hear something, you'll be the first to know."

Aisha's face was pallid and she began to feel sick. Sweat formed on her brow.

"Are you okay?" The clerk stood quickly and came out of her enclosed glass booth. "Come on. Why don't you sit down?" She and Sandra led Aisha over to a chair close by the reception area. "Sit here. I'll go get her some water," she told Sandra. "I'll be right back."

"Aisha, get yourself together," her mother said in a scolding voice. "This is no time for your dramatics. Your father needs us and he needs us to be strong. This is not about you. What you need to be doing is praying not weeping. And my God, when was the last time you ate? You look anorexic."

Aisha looked at her mother with a coldness in her eyes. All the years her mother had professed to be such a saint. If only the people at church knew how she treated her own daughter. Aisha felt like she was always in competition with her mother, always trying to prove to her mother that she was a good girl. But Sandra Carlisle shielded her emotions like Fort Knox protected its gold. She wouldn't let anyone get too close to her. Her mother had been the same way. She often told Sandra that showing affection was a sign of weakness. True Christians should be strong, not weak is what Sandra had been taught. Sandra looked at Aisha again. The compassion she wanted to feel toward her only child just wasn't there. Instead, she reached into the pocket of her jacket and pulled out her purse-sized Bible. Turning to the twenty third psalm she started to read the Bible verses she already knew so well.

"Tameria, thank God." Aisha said, getting up and rushing to the arms of her best friend. Tameria could barely contain the terrible taste that formed in the base of her throat when she saw how terribly thin Aisha was. It had been several weeks since the last time they'd actually been in each other's presence. Between Tameria's medical rotation shifts and Aisha's full and part-time jobs, they rarely had the chance to spend time with each other. Needless to say, Tameria didn't know what was up with Aisha. She could only hope that Aisha wasn't sick.

"Hello, Mrs. Carlisle," Tameria said, walking over and sitting down next to her.

"Tameria, I'm so glad to see you." Sandra twisted her shaking hands together.

Tameria held Aisha's hands. "I would have come down here earlier, but things are hectic in CCU and I couldn't get a break. I only have a few minutes now."

"How's my father, Tameria?" Aisha asked her.

Tameria could barely look at either of the women. Benjamin Carlisle was hanging on by a thread. After emergency surgery, he'd lapsed into a coma and his prognosis wasn't good. Tameria was not about to share this heartbreaking news with them. She would leave that up to Chase.

"Tameria, I want to see Benjamin. I want to see my husband," Sandra begged.

"Mrs. Carlisle, I'm going to take you up to CCU now. Come with me." Tameria stopped at the window clerk's desk to inform her that she was taking the family to see Mr. Carlisle.

On the way to CCU, the elevator ride seemed to move in slow motion. "Tameria, you never told us. How is my father?" Aisha asked her again.

"Aisha, I'm sorry to say, but he's not doing so well. The surgery was performed in an effort to reduce the risk of rebleeding. Chase is up there too. He can tell you more since he's a neurosurgery resident."

"Thanks, Tameria. We thank God for you," Sandra said in a humble voice.

When she walked into CCU and saw her father lying on the cold white pristine sheet, with tubes in his arms and down his throat, Aisha almost collapsed. The same feeling of weakness and nausea she felt earlier revisited her. Her mother ignored Aisha and walked over to the side of her husband's bed and grabbed his hand. The gentleness she displayed toward him was seldom shown toward Aisha.

Speaking softly close to his ear, Sandra said, "Benjamin, Benjamin, I'm here darling. You're going to be all right. I know you are. Just hang on and have faith. God is with you."

The only sound that pushed from Benjamin's lips was the sound of the breathing tube. His eyes were swollen and his head was wrapped in white gauze.

Aisha couldn't hold back her tears any longer. She moved in on the other side of her father's hospital bed. "Daddy. Daddy, I'm so sorry I haven't been around like I should. But I love you, Daddy. I love you so much," she whispered softly to him.

Tameria moved closer to Aisha and placed her arm around her bony shoulder to hold her up. When her arm rested on her skinny frame, she thought Aisha would break. Tameria began to mentally diagnose Aisha while she stood next to her for support. *Maybe she's working too hard and not eating enough. I know she's not anorexic or bulimic, at least I hope that's not the case. What could it be?* She continued her thoughts as she cast a side-long glance at Aisha.

"Daddy, can you hear me? Please say something, Daddy." Aisha stared at her father intensely and guilt consumed her. If only she had been around more for her father instead of doing obscene dancing for perverted men. She felt the sudden urge to find relief in her vial of *baby girl* that was tucked safely inside the zip pouch of her handbag. Before she could leave his side to find a bathroom, a mild-mannered voice invaded her thoughts. She looked up and spied the hefty doctor standing next to her mother.

"Mrs. Carlisle, I'm Dr. Johnston," the neurosurgeon said, extending his hand as a way of introducing himself to Sandra. "Why don't we go to the consultation area and I'll explain what's going on with your husband."

"Okay," she replied, following the doctor to the consultation room with Aisha scurrying behind the two of them.

"I'm going to go and check on my patients and I'll be back soon," Tameria reassured them.

"Okay, I'll see you later." Aisha kept pace with the doctor and her mother.

"Mrs. Carlisle and Miss?" he paused.

"Aisha," she said. "Benjamin Carlisle is my father. Doctor, is my father going to be all right?" Before the doctor could explain Benjamin's condition, Chase walked in and joined them. His look revealed what Aisha denied in her heart.

"Aisha, hello. Mrs. Carlisle," Chase nodded.

Aisha couldn't find the words to respond. Her mind was saturated with thoughts about her father's condition.

"Mr. Carlisle has bleeding in the brain," Dr. Johnston began explaining. "It's called cerebral arteriovenous malformation or AVM."

"What *is* that?" Sandra clinched her hands tightly around both sides of the chair and waited on the dreaded answer. "Is he going to be alright?"

"I'll try to explain his condition." Dr. Johnston rested on the edge of the chair. "AVM are abnormal connections between the arteries and blood vessels that carry blood from the brain back to the heart. The blood from the arteries normally flows into the capillaries, but instead it is forced into the veins, often at a high velocity. The pressure in the veins

increases and the blood vessel ruptures, causing a hemorrhagic stroke. Now, so far, we've managed to clamp off the
area and stop the hemorrhaging, but there's always the
possibility that the bleeding will start again."

He shifted his eyes and focused directly on Mrs. Carlisle.
The two ladies were obviously distraught. This was one
part of his job he hated. It never became easier, no matter
how many times he'd experienced less than favorable prog-
noses of patients. This was such a time, but it was still not a
time to mince words and give them false hope either.

"Why did this happen?" Aisha asked Dr. Johnston, then
looked directly at Chase. "What caused it?" Aisha couldn't
bear to come to grips with the thought of losing her father.

Chase spoke up. "The most common cause is a sudden
rise in blood pressure. I'm sorry to tell you this," Chase
added. "But Mr. Carlisle's fate is out of our hands now.
We've done all we can do."

"Nooo," Sandra screamed. "God, I do not accept what
this doctor has said. Satan I rebuke you now, in the name of
Jesus!" she hollered. "Both of you listen to me," Sandra
lashed out at the two sympathetic doctors while ignoring
Aisha's sobs. "God is the one true doctor and I cannot and
will not accept this sentence you've placed over my husband's life. I will not."

"I understand what you're saying, Mrs. Carlisle, and I respect your religion, but I'm a specialist, a neurosurgeon.
I'm telling you what the prognosis is for your husband. I
don't want to deceive you, ma'am."

"The chances for his survival are less than 20%," Chase
interjected while Dr. Johnston stood up with his hands
folded over his chest in total silence.

"Chase please, there has to be something else that can be
done. There just has to be," Aisha intercepted.

Chase, sounding hopeless, replied, "I'm sorry, Aisha. I
wish there was."

Dr. Johnston reiterated to Aisha and Sandra that the team of neurosurgeons would indeed do whatever they could to save Benjamin's life.

The pain that consumed Aisha was far too much for her to bear. The doctor's words ripped at her heart over and over again. She ran out of the room and didn't stop until she saw the sign on the door that read, Exit—Stairs. She pushed open the heavy steel door and sat down on the first step. Without hesitation, she reached inside her handbag and pulled out *baby girl*. She uttered a prayer between each snort, pleading and begging God to save her father, promising him that she would change her life if only he would save him.

"Chase. Something's not right with Aisha," Tameria said with deep concern.

"Something like what? The woman is distraught about her father's critical condition. What's not right about that?" Chase asked.

"You know I haven't seen her for several weeks because of our schedules. She looks bad, Chase. I mean, Aisha has always been one to keep herself in perfect shape. Now she looks like a weekend crack head or something. That's the best way I can describe her."

"You don't think she's doing drugs do you?"

"No. Of course not. Aisha's too smart to get caught up in something like that. She's too into God to get hung up on drugs."

"Well, what do you think her problem is?" The very fact that Aisha was in trouble concerned Tameria, and Chase wanted to do what he could to help her get to the bottom of Aisha's problems. He was willing to do anything he could do to help alleviate any pressure or anxiety Tameria was experiencing.

"Look, why don't you go back to CCU and see if you can

convince Aisha to meet you later on when you go on break. You two can talk a little and maybe you can find out what's got her looking so stressed. But being worried about her father probably has a lot to do with it. Then you told me that she's working two jobs too. That's enough to stress anybody out."

"Everything you've said is true. But Chase, the girl looks like she's lost almost twenty pounds in a matter of weeks." Tameria lowered her head and wrung her hands together. Chase reached over and tilted her face toward his and kissed her lightly on the lips.

"Hey, I don't want my favorite girl to get all worked up about this. Everything will be all right. You'll see. Now go and find Aisha and make those plans to meet her later, okay?" His smile always warmed Tameria's heart. The touch of his lips against hers relaxed her and for a moment, thoughts of Aisha disappeared.

# 24

Aisha and Sandra had been camped out in the CCU
waiting room for the past thirty six hours. They could
only see Benjamin for minutes at a time. Not wanting to
leave in case things took a turn for the worse, they stayed at
the hospital. Both of them were drained but they also were
committed to remaining by Benjamin's side.

While Sandra slept on a nearby sofa seat, Aisha was
curled in a knot in one of the CCU waiting room chairs. She
reached inside her purse and pulled out her ringing cell
phone. A grin enveloped her weary face when she saw the
call was from Chandler.

"Hi, you. Long time no hear from," she said gingerly.

"You know that works both ways. You have my number
and I don't recall seeing your digits flash across my caller
ID either," he responded. "Tell me, what's a man got to do
to get some attention from you?"

"Let me see." She made a humming sound over the
phone pretending like she was in deep thought.

"I'm waiting," he said flirtatiously.

"I'd really like to see you," she confessed. Then taking a more serious tone she explained to him about her father's illness. "I've been spending as much time as I can at the hospital."

"I'm sorry to hear about your dad, Aisha. Why don't I come over later and take you to dinner? Or if you're going to be at the hospital, I can bring you something to eat. Just tell me what you want me to do."

Each time he heard Aisha's voice a tiny piece of him surrendered to his feelings for her.

"Chandler, I don't know about seeing you tonight. It probably isn't such a good idea for you to come to the hospital. It's depressing here and I don't want my mood to rub off on you."

"But I *want* to come, Aisha. What hospital is he in?"

"St. Francis CCU," she told him. "If everything is all right with my father, I can meet you after our next visitation with him ends. That should be in about an hour."

"One hour it is," he said before telling her goodbye.

An hour later, when Chandler walked into the CCU waiting area, Aisha's pale face lit up. His charcoal Girbaud shuttle jeans and printed shirt made him stand out like a fashion model out of *VIBE* magazine.

"Hi," she blushed.

It took several seconds for him to respond. He was taken aback by her ghostly appearance. She'd lost quite a bit of weight since the last time he'd seen her and her face looked sunken and almost hollow. He imagined that she'd been through a tremendous amount of pressure with her father being so ill, along with her trying to operate the studio and work a second job.

In a way, he felt sorry for her. He wanted to whisk her away from all of the problems she faced at this time, but his own career kept him from doing a lot of the things he desired in life. Despite his trust issues since breaking up with Tracye, he was beginning to believe that maybe there was a chance Aisha was different.

*Why is he staring at me like that?* Aisha asked herself. *I know I've lost a few pounds, but dang, he doesn't have to look at me like he's zoned out or something.*

"Hey, don't I get a hello, whuzzup or something?" Aisha spoke up.

"No, you get more than that." He pulled her into his arms and held her against his chest, savoring the fruity scent of her hair.

She relaxed in the safety of his arms and allowed herself to enjoy being held and comforted. When they pulled away from each other, he caressed her face with the back of his hand and then led her to the sofa in the back area of the waiting room. When they sat down, he placed the bag he brought in on the table next to them.

"You didn't tell me what to bring, so I stopped and picked up a couple of subs. I hope you like turkey and ham."

"That's fine. Thanks for doing this."

"No thanks is necessary. I brought enough for your mom too. I didn't know if she'd eaten or not, but I know how it can be when you're in a situation like this. It drains you and you find very little time to do the things you normally do."

"You're right about that. But how do you know?"

"I've been through this same sort of situation before. I had a brother who had muscular dystrophy. We stayed in and out of the hospital with him. He passed away when I was fifteen."

"Oh, I didn't know. I'm sorry to hear that, Chandler."

"Anyway, that's how I know. Now, come on, I want you to eat a little something."

"I will, but not right now. I want to spend some time with you for now. I promise, I'll eat something later."

"Okay. Tell me, how is your father?" A real sound of concern was in his voice.

"He's still in a coma and on a respirator," she told him. "The doctors don't give him much hope, but I know that God is in the healing business. I believe that with all of my heart."

"I know you do. And I hope he makes it through this. You know what?"

"What?" she replied in a soft voice.

"I admire your faith. You're the kind of person who isn't ashamed of her beliefs and that says a lot about you."

Suddenly Aisha felt ashamed. How could she talk about God and faith when her life was so screwed up? Here she was sitting across from a man that had penetrated her shell and she was living a lie. She dropped her head and turned away from Chandler's stare.

"What is it Aisha? Did I say something wrong?"

"No, of course not. It's just that I don't want you putting me up on this high pedestal and all. I'm far from perfect and my faith gets shaky sometimes too."

"I know you're not perfect. I never said that you were. I just said that I admire you and that's what I meant. Anyway, I think you're perfect for me," he confessed. She turned her head quickly to meet his gaze. They stared at each other before he pulled her next to him. She rested her head against his shoulder. Within minutes he heard her labored breathing. He allowed her to sleep in the crest of his arms. Gently rubbing her hair away from her closed eyes, he kissed her forehead, leaned back into the soft leather of the sofa and watched CNN on the waiting room TV.

Chandler soon followed suit and drifted off into a light sleep. He was awakened by the feel of someone moving or shaking next to him. When he opened his eyes, he saw a strikingly beautiful older version of Aisha hovering over them, jabbing Aisha on the arm.

"Aisha, wake up. Wake up," the woman ordered. Both Aisha and Chandler's eyes popped open.

"Mother, is Daddy okay?"

"He's the same, Aisha. I came down here to see if you were still here. I think I'm going to go home and change and check on the house. Can you stay here until I get back? I shouldn't be gone for more than a couple of hours."

"Of course . . . I'll stay."

Sandra turned to Chandler. "And you are?"

Extending his hand out toward her, Chandler responded, "Chandler Larson. I met you a few months ago at the Mayor's Gala. I'm a friend of Aisha's."

"Oh, yes, I think I remember meeting you."

"Mrs. Carlisle, would you like to take something to eat with you? I brought a couple of subs for you and Aisha."

"No," she declined, "I don't have an appetite right now, but thanks for thinking of us."

"Sure. I wanted to tell you that I hate that we had to meet again under these circumstances. I hope everything turns out fine for your husband. And if there's anything I can do, please by all means tell Aisha and I'll be glad to do it."

"Thank you, young man," she responded without feeling.

"Aisha, we won't be able to go up to see your father again for another two hours. But I'll be back before then," she told her.

"If you aren't back, you know that I'll be here and I won't miss the visit. It's bad enough that we can only see him for a few minutes at a time every few hours," Aisha said sadly.

"Yes, I know," Sandra responded. She thanked Chandler again for his thoughtfulness then walked away.

"That was nice of you, Chandler," Aisha said.

"I just said what I meant. I told you, I'm here for you, Aisha."

Aisha's cell phone began to ring the familiar tone that let her know it was Elisa calling.

"Excuse me, Chandler, I have to get this."

"Sure, go right ahead. I'm going to stretch my legs for a minute. I'll be back." He stood up and headed into the outer hospital area.

"How's your father?" Elisa asked after Aisha answered the call.

"Not so good I'm afraid."

"I'm sorry to hear that," Elisa replied with sincerity.

Aisha changed the unpleasant topic of their conversation. "What's up with you?"

"I was just calling to check on you. You haven't been here in a couple of days and I haven't heard from you. Jason said he hadn't either. I wanted to make sure you were all right."

"Yeah, I'll be okay. My friend is here. You know the one I've been seeing."

"Uh, Chandler, isn't it?"

"That's right. What's going on? Anything I should know about?"

"Well, I wanted to tell you that you left a favorable impression when you did your private dance, you know." Elisa spoke in a sing-song voice. "Word is, Jason is quite pleased with you too. He's talking about giving you an opportunity to make some real cheese."

Aisha knew that tone in Elisa's voice all too well. She wasn't just calling to check up on her, she wanted something. She hoped Elisa wasn't about to ask her to come to work. She had no time to think about dancing. She hadn't even been to her own dance studio in two days. Her mind was on her father and nothing else.

Aisha quickly cut in on Elisa's conversation. "I already know where this is headed, Elisa. I know you, remember? So if you're thinking about asking me what I think you're about to ask me, then you must be crazy. I'm not leaving my father's bedside to go off and dance for some, some." Aisha hesitated and Elisa intercepted.

"His name is Kyle Taylor. From what I've managed to learn about him, he has it going on. Money out the *wang wang*, girl." Elisa chuckled over the phone.

While Elisa laughed, Aisha was fuming. "I said I'm not doing it. Not until my father is well," she ended. The irritation in Aisha's voice was apparent, but Elisa didn't back down.

"Hey, I know you're going through some tough things right now. But listen, we all are. That's life. You have to learn how to roll with the punches. This man is very important to The Lynx. Jason wants you to work him."

"Roll with the punches?" Aisha shouted. Eyes from some of the others in the waiting room targeted her like a radar screen. She placed her hand over her mouth and the miniature cell phone and continued talking. "Look, this is more than 'rolling with the punches' as you put it. My father is in Critical Care. I don't know if he's going to get better and you want me to come in and shake my tail because some Kyle what's-his-name wants me to?" Inhaling heavily through her nose, Aisha sucked in her breath once more before lashing out at Elisa. "Girl, puhleeze. You must be doing more than coke."

"Jason insists that you come."

"Or what?" Aisha retorted.

"I don't think you want me to answer that." Elisa lightened up her tone but the inflection in her voice revealed the seriousness of her words. "Look, all you have to do is entertain the man for an hour or two and then you're out of here. He's a new client and we really need to make a good impression. I would think you would be flattered to know that Jason thinks you're the one for the job. Even I'm a little jealous. You know, it used to be me that he called on when we had a new client join The Lynx."

Aisha listened as Elisa continued her spiel.

"There's a huge bonus in it for you too. Plus, you don't

have to be here until around eleven tonight. That gives you a few more hours to spend at the hospital. You can come here, do your thing, and go right back to the hospital."

Aisha spotted Chandler walking back into the CCU Waiting Area. "Look, I'll call you back. Let me think about it."

"Don't bother calling back, just come. Like I said, it'll be well worth your time."

"I said," Aisha emphasized through clenched teeth, "that I would think about it, now goodbye." Aisha pushed the end button on her cell and sighed.

Chandler stood in front of her. "Don't hang up on my account."

"No, it's nothing like that. The conversation was over anyway."

He sat down beside her again and held her hand. "What time can you go see your father?"

Aisha glanced at her watch before answering. "Visiting hours are for fifteen minutes every two hours. I still have about a half hour before I can go upstairs to see him."

"Well, that gives you time to taste some of this food you promised me you'd eat. I won't leave here until you do," he smiled.

"If you insist," Aisha answered him dryly.

"I insist." He placed the sandwich in her hand.

Aisha took several small bites of the turkey and ham sandwich before folding the remainder inside the crinkled wrapping. "Satisfied?"

"Not really," he said flatly. "I was hoping you would have eaten a little more, but I won't nag this time around."

"Good." She laughed and kissed him lightly on his full lips.

"*Ummm*. I like that," he crooned sexily in her ear.

"Now you go on and get out of here. Didn't you say you had a client to meet later?"

"Yeah, I do. But I'll sit here with you until you get ready to visit your dad, then I'll be on my way. I'll still have plenty of time to make it to my appointment."

"If you don't mind my asking, what kind of land deal is it? I mean, it's really late and I'm just wondering why someone would want to meet you at this time of night."

Chandler didn't stutter at all when the lie dripped from his lips. He was used to fudging the truth with family, friends and the criminals he found himself working around. "It's a deal for an apartment unit. I've been working with this guy for a couple of weeks now and I think we're going to seal the deal tonight. You know how these big shot guys are. Their work day never ends," Chandler explained, continuing to expound on the lie. "If I want this deal, I have to meet him on his time, not mine,"

"We'll have to celebrate after you close the deal," Aisha told him.

"We will. But for now, you have to concentrate on your family. So, I'm going to get ready to get out of here."

"Thanks for understanding." Aisha gazed into his bright eyes.

Chandler grabbed hold of Aisha's hand and she stood next to him. "Come on, I think it's time for you to head upstairs." Leading her by the hand, they walked out of the CCU waiting area.

Chandler walked her to the elevator. "I'll call you, okay? See you."

"See you," she responded with the same reply. He leaned down, drew her into his arms and kissed her with passion, oblivious to any one standing around them. The *ding* sound of the elevator startled them. Chandler pulled away from Aisha, and speaking in their own silent language, they went their separate ways.

## 25

Sandra had freshened up, packed some snacks to have during her long waits in the CCU and arrived back at the hospital in time for CCU visitation. She walked into the CCU and stood next to Aisha. "How is he?"

"There's been no change. When I first came in, I called his name. I thought he tried to answer me, but the nurse said that they don't think he can hear us."

Sandra grabbed hold of the hospital bed rail and watched her husband's motionless body.

Aisha placed her hand on top of Sandra's. "Daddy, please wake up." Aisha cried softly, her salty tears landing one by one on her father's bed sheets.

Aisha went with her mother back downstairs to the CCU waiting area after her father's attending CCU nurse told them it was time for them to leave. She called Angie and let her know she would be by the studio the next day. Because of her ever-growing bank account, she had hired two part-time dance instructors. That way she was able to keep the studio open while she spent time at the hospital. Working at The Lynx had its perks and whenever her spirit nudged her to give it up, she somehow managed to find a reason not to. This time she convinced herself that all of the extra money she was making helped provide things like dance equipment, costumes and even financial aid assistance for the girls who wouldn't be able to participate otherwise. All of what she said was true, but she still felt dirty and hypocritical. Yet, it wasn't enough to make her quit.

"Mother, I have to leave for a couple of hours," Aisha explained.

Sandra sat in the chair, emotionless. "Do what you have to do."

"Mother, I won't be gone long. Just like you, I have things to do too." Aisha felt her temper rising. She had to settle down. There was no need to let her mother make her go off. Not tonight, anyway. "I have to check on some things at the apartment and I want to take a shower and change clothes."

"I said, go. I'm not stopping you." Sandra flipped her hand off and then stared blankly at the giant-sized flat screen hanging on the waiting room wall.

"I'll see you in a couple of hours." Aisha jumped up, grabbed her knapsack and stormed off. Sandra didn't bother to acknowledge her.

Aisha turned into her personal parking space at The Lynx and stepped out of the car into the warm muggy night. It was almost Easter and normally she would be fasting for Lent but no such thoughts had entered her mind this time. This year she wasn't willing to give up anything for 40 days. "Lord, I promise you that I'm going to stop this," she mumbled under her breath as she took long strides toward the entrance.

"Elisa, what did Aisha say? Is she going to show up or not?" Jason didn't want to disappoint Kyle Taylor. If Aisha didn't show up, Jason already knew there would be serious consequences for him to pay. If that happened, he would make sure that Aisha would pay even more.

"I haven't talked to her again. But if I know Aisha like I think I know Aisha, she'll be walking through that door any second now. She's hooked on making this money."

"I hope you know what you're talking about. We have a lot at stake. I told you in the beginning that I didn't like to recruit girls like her. We should stick to the ones we traffick in instead of women like Aisha. This establishment has managed to maintain its status and stay out of the Fed limelight. Girls like her can bring trouble."

"Jason, stop bugging won't you?" Elisa threw her hand up in the air. "You're being way too paranoid. Not only is Aisha one of our best dancers, she's totally clueless about what's going on around here. And now that she has a nice nose habit, I don't think we have anything to worry about."

Jason cast a strange look at Elisa.

"What's up with that look you're giving me?" She placed a hand on her hip. The tangerine dress she wore barely covered her luscious thighs and her butt reminded him of Jennifer Lopez's luscious booty.

"I remember when *you* first came to The Lynx. You were a scared, frightened fifteen year old runaway. When I saw you standing alone at the entrance of the mall in Maryland, you looked like you were starving to death. When I walked up to you, your eyes grew big as Bo dollars." Jason grinned.

"That was a long time ago. I've learned a lot since then. I've learned how to survive. I've learned that this world won't give you anything. You have to go out and get it for yourself any way you can."

"And you've done just that, my precious. Look at you now. You're basically running this whole operation and doing a fantastic job of it too. That's why you get paid the top dollars. And Gabby will never have to worry about a thing."

Elisa's face turned ghastly at the mention of her daughter. "Don't even go there, Jason."

"What did I say? Gabby's a beautiful girl but you don't have to worry about her being brought into this business." Jason paused. "Unless of course, you decide differently," he remarked in a threatening tone that Elisa knew all too well.

What Jason said was true. She did make plenty of money. But if she ever thought about leaving the business, she had been subtly warned about what would happen to Gabby. She helped bring in young girls all the time, traveling from city to city to snatch homeless, starry-eyed teens and runaways. She'd even gone to some of the islands as well and organized the transport of girls, not to mention a few boys to satisfy the perverted taste of some of The Lynx clientele.

Elisa leaned in to Jason and whispered. "Look who's coming through the door. Do I know what I'm talking about or not?"

"Well, I'll be . . ." Jason shook his head from side to side. "You *are* good, Elisa." He walked over to meet Aisha. Feigning concern, he asked, "Aisha, sweetheart, how's your father?"

"If you really gave a crap, you wouldn't have insisted that I be here tonight," she huffed at him.

Throwing his hand to the side and dragging his words, Jason replied, "Dahling, you're stressed. Take it easy. I promise, tonight will be a breeze. A couple of hours will be gone before you know it. Now, go on and get dressed up real nice for me. We're going to meet him at his place."

Aisha shot back, "Why are we going to his place? I thought we only did that for a very small number of our members. What makes this one so special?"

"Don't you worry yourself about such minor details."

Without so much as flinching, Jason followed up with, "Just go get dolled up."

Aisha swiftly jerked her body around without responding to Jason. The last thing she wanted to do was go to some client's house, but she also thought, the sooner she did this, the sooner she could get back to the hospital.

Aisha showered and changed into a violet slip-style mini dress in stretch lace with a V-neck that rested closer to her thighs than her knees. Her extra drug-thin frame was supported by a pair of matching strappy Giuseppe sandals with a five-inch heel. She resembled one of America's Next Top Models.

The drive to the mysterious Kyle Taylor's Memphis residence led along a stretch of dark roads with twists and curves. She was amazed that there were still areas of Memphis she was unfamiliar with and this was one of them. The long drive led them to a gated community on the bluffs. Aisha's eyes widened as they approached the large estate. They followed the circular drive until the limo pulled up in front of the massive stained glass doors leading to the front entrance.

Aisha reminded Jason one final time about the night's event. "I'm telling you, I'm not going to be here all night. I don't care how important this client is supposed to be. Two hours tops and I'm out of here, even if I have to leave here walking." Aisha glared at Jason like a starving, rabid dog.

"I hear you. Just come on."

Jason rang the doorbell and an older, stocky Asian woman dressed in a traditional maid's uniform opened the door.

"We're here to see Mr. Taylor. He's expecting us," Jason remarked. Without responding, the woman directed them inside the foyer with the wave of her hand. She glared at Aisha with a look of distaste.

As they followed her lead, the maid spoke for the first

time. With a thick accent she said, "Have a seat in here please. Mr. Taylor will be with you momentarily." They walked into an elegant living room richly painted in textured butter cream and accented with oversized printed furniture that was lined with traces of butter cream and splashes of red. The massive stone fireplace curved along the soaring ceilings radiated an aura of peace and tranquility. After waiting several minutes, the maid re-entered the living room with a tray of hors d'oeuvres. She placed them on the table in front of them. "May I get you something to drink?"

"A shot of grey goose with cranberry," Jason quickly answered. He turned his attention toward Aisha.

Aisha rolled her eyes at Jason. "A martini for me, please."

"Yes, ma'am. I'll be back shortly with both of your drinks."

Waiting until the maid was out of sight, Aisha reached inside her tiny string purse and pulled out her *baby girl*. After taking a snort up each nostril she offered the vial to Jason.

"None for me tonight." He motioned the vial away with his hand. Aisha took another hit and immediately felt a sense of relaxation. She didn't notice the gentleman who had quietly entered the room.

Kyle Taylor watched the mysterious woman put what he thought to be coke in each nostril. Her back was to him, but he could make out the side profile of her despite her flowing black twists.

"Uhmm," he said, pretending to clear his throat. "I'm sorry to have kept you waiting." He walked further into the living room. "Hello Jason," Kyle spoke and extended his hand.

Aisha turned and looked in his direction. Kyle found it hard to shield the faint feeling that suddenly washed over him. *Oh my God, no. This can't be*, he thought to himself.

Slightly hesitating, he extended his hand out toward hers and she released a captivating smile, not recognizing the well-disguised Chandler Larson.

Maintaining his composure was harder than it ever had been since becoming an undercover 5-0. "Hello, I'm Kyle."

"It's nice to meet you, Kyle. I'm Luscious." He hoped she couldn't see him reeling with disbelief. The Asian maid walked in with their drinks. The minor distraction gave Chandler time to regain his focus. Aisha and Jason took their drinks.

"Mr. Taylor, unless you need something else, I'm going to leave now. I'll return for Luscious when I receive your call."

"That'll be fine. I'll talk to you later." He turned to the maid and asked her to escort Jason to the door.

Kyle sat in the high back chair across from Aisha. Clasping his hands and placing them on his tailored slacks he watched her for a few seconds before speaking. "Luscious, ahhh. A befitting name, for a beguiling woman."

"Thank you." Aisha toyed with her martini glass before slowly bringing it up to her lips, in an enticing manner. Kyle continued watching her. She was nowhere near the Aisha he'd come to know.

Realizing she had no idea at all who he really was, he relaxed and continued playing his role. He couldn't chance his cover being blown, not when he was so close to unveiling the inside operation going on at The Lynx. He had discovered that Jason and Elisa were the two who worked directly for the illusive mastermind behind the whole trafficking operations at The Lynx. But what part did Aisha play in this sordid game? Did she know what she was involved in and who she was involved with? He thought he knew her so well. From all indications, she had fooled him into believing she was a good Christian girl. Adding insult to injury, she tried to come off like she was so shy and reserved. But looking at her tempting attire and remembering her lies about her second job, he couldn't see her being a part of anybody's church or religion.

How could she have deceived him like she had? He began to second guess everything she had told him. *Another Tracye*—Chandler's mind retraced the pain she'd caused him. He wasn't going to let that happen again. Not now, not ever. At that moment, whatever feelings he thought he had for Aisha, Chandler erased them out of his mind and off of his heart. *Game time*, he said to himself. Standing up, he walked over to where she sat. Reaching out for her hand he commanded, "Come with me."

Aisha did as she was told, allowing the dashing silver-haired man to take her hand inside of his own. Leading her into the master suite, Aisha stepped into a room of dimmed lights and seductive music playing softly on the surround sound system. As he strolled over to the taupe wrap around chaise, he dropped Aisha's hand before sitting down. No matter how much he felt like she had deceived him, he was still sucked in by her beauty. His eyes burned with lust for her, and the rest of his body became aroused at the sight of her.

Aisha began to sway seductively back and forth, becoming one with the sensuous music. She knew what her clients liked and she had no problem giving them what they wanted. Any thoughts she may have had of her father, friends, or God were replaced with what she was doing at that very moment. She flung her head back, allowing the thick locks of her hair to blanket over and past the back of her shoulders. With each pulsating beat of the music, she moved rhythmically, masterfully luring Kyle into her web of femininity. As if reading his mind, she moved her lithe body in closer to him. The tantalizing aroma of her cologne underneath his nostrils, the thought of making love to her, of touching her and holding her, sent Chandler into a world where he *was* Kyle Taylor, a wealthy executive with an insatiable sexual desire. For the next few minutes, he totally forgot that the woman dancing before him, enticing him, luring him was Aisha.

While dancing, Aisha was drawn to Kyle like a moth to a flame. *He is one sexy senior*, she thought to herself about the older, suave and handsome Kyle Taylor. Her attraction to him was mounting as she stared into his dark eyes. With feathery strokes, she used the back of her hand to caress his tense jawline, watching his eyes close, as he slowly relaxed his body against the back of the chaise lounge.

Chandler couldn't resist her. His eyes closed, Chandler envisioned the Aisha he thought he knew, the Aisha he'd longed to touch and caress. His heartbeat quickened. Reaching for her, his hands became familiar with the contours of her slender body. Opening his eyes and raising up slightly, he grabbed her around her tiny waist. He pulled her down on the chaise next to him and covered her round mouth with his. "No wonder they call you Luscious," his voice deepening from the fever pitch of desire.

Aisha was caught in a grip of passion. Her desire for Kyle was paramount as he filled her with kisses and touched her all over. The faint smell of liquor on his breath and the roughness of his mustache aroused her that much more. She had never allowed a client to get this close and personal with her but something about him ignited a flame within her. Weakened by desire, she moaned and he sucked in her breath as if it was part of his own. His kisses engulfed her and he became rough and more demanding. His hands briskly explored her freely. When she heard his heavy breathing and felt his hands touch places she'd never let any man visit, she yanked away from his tight grasp.

Her heart pounding and flesh tingling, Aisha reluctantly pushed herself away from him. "Hold on, Kyle. This is not what I'm about. You're, you're out of line," she said, breathing heavily while trying desperately to muster up control over her body and emotions.

The sound of her voice jarred him from his lust-filled state of mind. Sitting upright on the chaise, he began pressing the wrinkles out of his shirt with his sweaty hands. Though he was physically attracted to her, at the same time he was sickened at the thought of her profession. Whatever he once hoped and thought they could have together was gone. It took every fiber of his being not to do to her what, in his mind, he'd been forced to do to Tracye. The longer he looked at her, the more infuriated he became. He abruptly stood up and looked down on her. The music continued to play as silence filled the space between them.

*Aisha, why? How could you do this?* His thoughts twirled round and round inside his mind. *Tracye, you betrayed me. I hate you*, he screamed inside. *I hate you both.*

Fear rose in the base of Aisha's throat. *What's going on inside his mind?* she thought. *I hope he understands that when a woman says no, she means no. He may be fine but I'm not going to give up my virginity unless it's my choice, certainly not by force. And there's not enough money he can pay to make me either.*

Aisha watched as his face reddened and his jaw quivered. His eyes reminded her of burning embers and her desire changed to fear.

Chandler watched her. He read the fear on her face. He'd seen it on the face of Tracye that fateful day. And just like with Tracye, seeing Aisha's fear became Chandler's pleasure.

Jumping up from the chaise, he locked on to her wrist, squeezing it until she thought he was going to break it. Chandler was enraged. "You really don't know do you?"

"Know what? Please, you're hurting me, Kyle." Aisha twisted and turned her arm as much as she could, trying to escape from his vice-like grip. Fighting back tears, she asked, "What are you talking about?"

As quickly as he'd grabbed her, he let go of her now bruised wrist.

"Call your pimp and tell him I'm finished with you," he ordered and stormed out of the bedroom.

Aisha couldn't stop her tears. Frantic, she scanned the room for her purse. *Where is it? Did I leave it in the living room?* Pounding footsteps halted her thoughts.

"I want you out of my house, now," he demanded. "You can go wait for your ride outside. You're no better than she was. A two bit . . ." Stopping in mid sentence, he huffed and the feeling he had for her was swallowed up in the all too fresh thoughts of the pain of betrayal. He was fast approaching the breaking point of self-control. There was no telling what he would do if she didn't leave his house pronto. "Get out!" he roared.

Aisha moved away from the chaise and dashed madly out of the house. She felt the wind of the door close behind her then open again as Kyle threw her purse out on the porch. Bending down, almost falling from fear, she picked it up and nervously removed her cell phone so she could call Jason. Standing outside of Kyle's mansion, trembling in fear, and hoping he wouldn't come outside and do something terrible to her, she came to the conclusion that it was time for her to make a change. Time to turn her life around. When she saw the limo pulling up some twenty-five minutes later, Aisha lunged toward it, grabbing hold of the door before it came to a full stop.

Jason opened the limo door, and sprung out. "What happened? What did you do?" All he could think about was what Aisha could have done to be standing outside. If word got back to his boss that one of the girls had disrespected a client, he'd be in manure up to his waist.

"What did *I* do?" Aisha's fury mounted. Jason had automatically assumed that she had done something wrong.

"Aren't you going to ask me why I'm standing outside? Aren't you going to ask me if I'm okay?"

"Don't tell me you acted like some uptight religious prude. Don't even go there. Because if you did, you're going to pay dearly." Jason was incensed. "Now tell me what happened."

"Why don't you go inside and ask that fool. I guess he thought he had himself more than a private dancer tonight. But *babyyy*, I'm not the one and I've told you that before." Aisha screamed and climbed inside the limo. She slammed the door before Jason had a chance to say another word. Jason knocked on Kyle's door. Aisha peered through the tinted windows of the limo and watched as Kyle yanked the door open and Jason walked inside. After waiting in the limo impatiently for him to return, Aisha was irate. She watched as Kyle stood in the doorway while Jason exited the house.

Instead of Jason taking her side, he chose to totally ignore her. On the way back to The Lynx, he didn't utter a word. She suddenly became sick of the whole thing with The Lynx. For the first time she understood that Jason and probably Elisa and any of the rest of them, didn't care the least bit about her or her well-being. They were all about self-gratification. The past couple of months she had started to consider Elisa her friend. Not friends like her and Tameria, but friends, nonetheless. After tonight, Aisha wasn't so sure.

*God, I'm tired of this*, she prayed within. *I'm sick of living a lie. I've gotten myself in way too deep and I don't know how to get out of it.* When the limo pulled up in front of The Lynx, Jason hopped out of it so fast it was like a whirlwind had come and swooped him up. Aisha grabbed her purse and yelled at him.

"You wait just a minute," she yelled. "I don't know what just happened back there and why you have a major attitude with me." Aisha's hands flailed and her voice cracked. Jason had no right to treat her the way he had. "I did what you wanted me to do, so give me my money and I'll be out of here," she said in a raised voice.

Without so much as looking back, Jason remarked coolly, "Every penny you deserve is in the limo." With that, he walked inside The Lynx.

Aisha whirled around and opened the door to the limo. A brown envelope was lying on the seat next to where Jason had been sitting moments before. The driver sat motionless as if nothing had occurred. Aisha opened the envelope and counted thirty, one dollar bills instead of the thirty, one hundred dollar bills she was supposed to have been paid. Slamming the door with all of her force, she mouthed a string of expletives while each step led her closer to the main entrance of The Lynx. Just as she was about to open the door, she stopped and then turned around. She was no match for Jason or anyone else at The Lynx; that much was certain. And if she had gone inside, she would be stepping into God knows what. She went straight to her car, jumped in and sped off.

As she neared her apartment, her cell phone rang. She looked down and saw an unfamiliar number. "Hello. Helloooo," she said again, but still no one answered. "Look, whoever you are, I don't have time for games," she yelled into the receiver and then pushed the end button as forcefully as she could. It was almost three o'clock in the morning and she needed to change and get back to the hospital. She thought about calling Elisa to tell her what had happened but decided to wait until later in the morning. Her cell rang again. "Hello," she screamed. "Didn't I tell you I don't have time for this crap?" Then Aisha heard someone. A whimpering sound like that of a child crying caused Aisha to keep the phone up to her ear. Aisha listened closer. "Who is this?"

"Aisha."

Aisha pulled over on the shoulder of the road and screamed. She didn't need to hear anything else her mother had to say. The sound of her mother's grief stricken voice on the other end told her everything she dreaded to hear. Her father was dead.

Aisha slammed the brakes as she pulled into the tight parking space. After popping the trunk lever and simultaneously kicking off her stilettos, Aisha jumped out of the car and searched inside the cluttered trunk for what she called her *just in case* duffel bag. She kept a duffel bag with a change of clothes for those times she was too tired to go home from the studio. Aisha pushed things aside until she saw a pair of sneakers, sweats and a tank top. She stood next to the car, not caring if anyone saw her, and put them on over the skimpy outfit. She ran through the hospital corridors. The doors of the elevator opened almost as soon as she lifted her finger off of the button.

Aisha ran down the hall until she reached CCU. One of the CCU nurse's recognized her and mashed the buzzer that opened the door and Aisha dashed inside.

Aisha refused to believe that she was really looking down on her father's lifeless body. He looked so peaceful, and rested, like he was simply asleep. Tears streamed down her face, leaving streaks. Aisha prayed to change places with him. Aisha, lost in her own pain, didn't notice her mother sitting in a chair on the other side of her father's bed. But she heard her because without warning, Sandra Carlisle bolted out in a tirade of seething, vicious words.

"Get her out of here; get her out of here now!" There was no stopping Sandra's rampage.

The nurse rushed over and tried to calm her down but Sandra was practically out of control. The words spewing from her mouth dripped vile and vicious accusations against her only daughter.

"Why couldn't it be *you* lying there instead of my Ben? You're too late!"

The nurse pushed the panic button and more nurses rushed into the room, grabbing hold of Sandra. "You're too late!" she sobbed. "You weren't here. It should have been you."

Aisha's tears erupted like a volcano. She placed her hands over her ears to drown out the condemning words coming from her mother. But no matter how she tried, she couldn't shut them off.

"You are so selfish. You always have been," her mother said pointing and reaching for Aisha like she wanted to tear her apart. "He was asking for you, Aisha. He took his last breath with your name on his lips. You were always his favorite. I had to compete with you. Selena had to compete with you. But you always won. Didn't you? And in the end, you were the one who let him down!" The nurses struggled to get her out of the room.

"Miss, please just go. Get out of here. Can't you see your mother is distraught?" one of the nurses shouted at Aisha.

The sight of her dead father and the words of hate rolling off of her mother's lips made it impossible for Aisha to comprehend the nurse's command.

"Momma, please, please," Aisha begged mercifully. "Please don't say that. I don't know what I'm going to do without my daddy. Mother," she kept repeating.

It took two male nurses to carry Sandra out of the room. The doctor ordered a sedative for Sandra and then returned to check on Aisha. Aisha stood in the room frozen, watching as they prepared to take her father to the morgue. She held on to the side of the bedrails, screaming.

One of the nurses paged Tameria and informed her about what was going on. She and Chase rushed to CCU. The sight of Aisha ripped at Tameria's heart and she couldn't control her own tears of pain. She ran up to Aisha to try to settle her down but there was no consoling her.

"Aisha, come on honey. Come on now," Tameria repeated while she and Chase led her out the room.

"Noooo, Tameria. I can't leave my daddy. I can't."

"Shhh, it's going to be okay," Tameria cried. "It's going to be okay." Tameria leaned over to tell Chase that she was going to take Aisha home as soon as her shift ended, which would be in about half an hour. "Aisha, come on, I want you to sit down for just a little while." Tameria led her to the nurse's lounge. I'm going to take you home in just a few minutes, okay?"

"Chase, will you ask one of the nurses to go and check on Mrs. Carlisle? I want to know where they took her."

"Okay, and I'll be back with something that will help to calm her down." Chase ran out of the room.

"Dr. Matthews, you wanted to know where Mrs. Carlisle was taken to?" the nurse asked with his hands in both pockets.

"Yes, where did they take her?" Tameria confirmed her request.

"She's down the hall. We had to administer a tranquilizer. She was inconsolable. Some people are here from the CCU waiting room area. I think they're friends or church members. They said they would make sure she gets home or she'll spend the night with some of them."

"Okay, that's good. Will you stay here with her daughter? I'm going to go and check on her. I won't be long."

Tameria was relieved to walk in the room and see the faces of several of Mr. and Mrs. Carlisle's friends and church members. She walked over and hugged the distraught woman and kissed her on the cheek. "Momma Carlisle, I'm so sorry." Tameria hugged her again. "I'll call and check on you a little later. I'm going to take Aisha home, okay? If you need anything, you just call me or my mom and dad. You know we're here for you."

Grief stricken and in shock, Sandra spoke without feeling or emotion. "I don't have a daughter anymore, Tameria. I don't."

A man dressed in a dark suit with a white Nehru-collared shirt approached Sandra and Tameria. Tameria assumed it was the minister from Mr. and Mrs. Carlisle's church. Kneeling beside the grieving widow, he took her shaking hands inside of his, and then looked over and nodded at Tameria.

"Sister Carlisle, everything is going to be all right. Brother Carlisle is resting in the bosom of Abraham. He's with God now. One day you're going to see him again." Sandra fell against his chest. This time quiet tears of pain trickled from her eyes.

# 26

Aisha hadn't heard from Chandler since the night her father died. She dialed his cell phone for the fifth day in a row. She heard the same automated message before the phone rolled over to his voice mail. The last time they'd seen each other, things were great. She reminisced about the kindness and compassion he'd shown when he came to the hospital to sit with her. What could have happened? She hoped he was all right. She became agitated and worried. It wasn't like Chandler not to call. Was he sick? Maybe he had gone out of town and forgot to mention it to her.

When Chandler didn't attend her father's funeral, send a card, flowers or anything that acknowledged he had heard the message she left about his death, Aisha worried that much more.

Aisha's pain was unbearable which only made her want to see Chandler even more. If only she had his shoulder to cry on, his strength to carry her, maybe she could somehow make it through this nightmare.

She picked up her purse and cranberry parka, stepped outside of her apartment and met a zesty summer breeze.

She pulled her parka closer to her, shrugging up her shoulders like it was a winter day instead of a pleasant 73 degrees. She then jogged the short distance to her car.

Aisha drove the next few blocks with the radio playing a rap song by Kanye. There was a time not long ago when you couldn't pay her a million dollars to listen to rap, but here she was now, moving in rhythm to the beats.

Aisha guided her car to the parking space right in front of Chandler's apartment. Searching around to see if his car was in view before she stepped out of the car, she spotted one that looked similar to his, parked a few spaces down from his apartment. Aisha couldn't be sure that it was. She climbed the flight of stairs leading to his apartment and knocked on the door. No answer. Knocked again. No answer. After knocking on the door several more times without hearing anything on the other side of the door, Aisha gave up and left.

Chandler was about to leave his apartment when he heard someone knocking on the door. He waited inside until the knocking stopped before peaking through the side of the closed blind. He saw Aisha return to her car. He never would have taken Aisha for the *popping up unannounced kind*, but then again, he never in his wildest imagination thought Aisha would turn out to be another glorified whore just like Tracye.

A prick of sympathy had tugged at his heart when one of her voice messages told him about her father's death. But Chandler's sympathy didn't last for long. He remembered saying to himself before erasing the call, "What goes around comes around, Aisha Carlisle."

He peeked out of the window one last time to make sure Aisha had left, then locked up his apartment and walked down the flight of stairs.

On the drive, Chandler thought about Aisha. Everything about her had been based on a lie, and at that moment, he felt nothing toward her. How could she be connected with drugs and the trafficking of young girls? How could she live her life knowing that men were raping and abusing these girls and still call herself a Christian? Chandler couldn't think about it without becoming angrier. He wondered about the girls whose parents were at their homes crying their hearts out because they didn't know what had happened to their daughters. How could she be so heartless?

The information Chandler had gathered about The Lynx since his short time as Kyle Taylor made him even more determined to shut it down for good. Women like Aisha, lining the pews Sunday after Sunday, pretending, faking it, they all could burn in hell for all Chandler cared.

Everything was about to come to an end anyway, thanks partly to Kyle Taylor gaining young Hallie's trust. Hallie had told him everything she knew about The Lynx, including the name of the owner, Ronald Shipley. Chandler thought it more than odd that when asked, no one at The Lynx other than Hallie, admitted to knowing the illusive owner. Instead, Chandler was referred back to Jason for answers. Needless to say, Jason wasn't singing; he kept his mouth closed like a deaf mute.

The name Ronald Shipley didn't register for Chandler. He ran his name through NCI and it came back clean as a whistle. But thanks to Sunday morning televangelism, Chandler's luck began to change. The name clicked loud and clear when early on Sunday morning, Chandler landed on the worship services of none other than the church Aisha attended, Faithside Temple, whose Senior Pastor was one Donald Shipley. *Shipley?* Bells and whistles sounded off in Chandler's head. Without hearing what the Sunday morning message was about, Chandler unplugged his cell phone from its charger, rushed from his apartment and sped to police headquarters. With his desk mate, Jay's help,

Chandler pulled up everything and anything he could
about Reverend Don. Hours into the background check,
Chandler yelled, "Jackpot."

"What's wrong with you, man?" Jay whipped around in
his chair to see what Chandler's yelling was all about.

"I found it. I found a connection. Reverend Donald Shipley is clean as Gabriel's long white robe."

Jay folded his arms over his protruding belly. "So?"

"So, *he's* clean, but guess who isn't? Ronald!" Chandler
pounded his fist on top of the pile of papers on his desk.

"Well, I'll be a monkey's uncle. You're telling me that the
righteous Reverend has a not so righteous dirty brother?
Man, isn't that something?" Jay rocked back and forth in
the wobbly office chair, chuckling.

Chandler sat back down, massaging his hairless chin
with his thumb and forefinger. "Yeah, but he's more than a
brother, he's the Reverend's fraternal twin brother. After
learning about Ronald's connection, Chandler quickly surmised that busting The Lynx was going to be more than a
local bust. It was going to make national news, of that
Chandler was certain.

Over the course of his investigation, Kyle had arranged
with Jason for Hallie to come to his suite on a regular basis,
whenever he stayed at The Lynx. He informed Jason that he
wanted exclusive rights to the girl to do as he pleased, and
that no one, absolutely no one was to touch her. Willing to
make up for the fiasco with Aisha, Jason was eager to
oblige Kyle.

Hallie tapped on the door of Kyle's suite.

Kyle opened the door and smiled when he saw her.
When she smiled back at him, he could swear that the sadness that was in her eyes the first time he saw her, had been
replaced with a glimmer of hope. For that he felt good.

Soon he would be able to reveal who he really was to her, but for now he couldn't chance telling Hallie anything. It would be far too dangerous for her.

Kyle made sure whenever Hallie came to his suite that she relaxed, watched TV and ate. He allowed her to be the young girl that she was. For a short time she didn't have to think about the prison she was being held in against her will. Hallie believed that Kyle would get her out of The Lynx and reunite her with her mother and sisters. He was going to make sure her father was prosecuted to the fullest extent for selling his own daughter.

Today, Kyle was taking Hallie to his house on the bluffs to spend a few days. Once there, Hallie would have the run of the house, with dolls, clothes, toys, DVD's and a refrigerator full of food. With the help of a department store sales clerk, Chandler brought practically everything a teenage girl would want in her room.

Hallie had managed to find out more than Kyle could have hoped. His undercover investigation of The Lynx had netted him enough evidence on Shipley, Jason and Elisa to put them away for years, not to mention the men who were members.

At his bluff side home, Kyle and Hallie watched a movie starring her favorite teenage actress, Raven Symone. Hallie opened up to Kyle, feeling safe and secure for the first time since being taken away from her mother and siblings.

Hallie pleaded with Kyle not to send Elisa to jail. She told him that Elisa was the one who looked out for all the girls, especially the younger ones like her. But Kyle made her understand that Elisa was in this for her own selfish reasons and keeping the girls safe wasn't one of those reasons. He further explained that if Elisa really was on their side, then she would never have been part of manipulating and kidnapping innocent girls and bringing them to The Lynx in the first place.

Hallie's sea green eyes mimicked Rockwell figurines. Tears formed in each corner when she realized that Elisa was going down with the rest of them.

As for Aisha, so far he hadn't found any evidence linking her to Shipley, Jason and Elisa. Like some of the other girls who were of age, Aisha stupidly thought that what she was doing was perfectly legit. However much Chandler wanted to believe that Aisha didn't know anything, he couldn't be sure. How could Aisha work for a place like that without clearly seeing that some of the girls at The Lynx looked no older than her dance students? She couldn't be that blind, or could she? He was definitely going to find out for sure, which is why he had to cut all ties with her as Chandler Larson. He couldn't and wouldn't take any chances of his cover being blown.

Sandra hadn't spoken to Aisha since Benjamin's funeral. She was swallowed up in her grief and still blamed Aisha for not being at her father's side when he died. She believed Aisha had placed her own selfish desires before everything, including her dying father, so Sandra refused to have anything to do with her daughter.

One week after Benjamin's death, Sandra packed her bags, closed up the house until she could think of what she was going to do with it, and moved back to her hometown of Little Rock, Arkansas. In Little Rock, she would be surrounded by people she'd known all of her life. Though she had just as many friends in Memphis, in Little Rock she hoped she would find her journey through grief somewhat easier to travel. She wanted to be as far away as she could from the painful memories, not to mention the daughter she believed had betrayed Benjamin.

# 27

Three and a half weeks had gone by since her father's death and Aisha had retreated into an impenetrable shell. She hadn't been to her dance studio or to The Lynx. She refused to answer her phone calls or listen to messages. Not even the sound of Elisa and Jason pressing down on her doorbell almost everyday, or Angie's incessant calling, could bring her out of her self-induced reclusiveness. Only Tameria was able to get inside the apartment, and that's because the two of them kept a key to each other's apartments for emergencies.

Tameria unlocked the door like she'd done over the past few weeks, whenever she wasn't at the hospital. She entered the smelly apartment, calling Aisha's name but like all the times before, Aisha didn't answer. Garbage overflowed from the trash can. The bathroom had a stench that had begun to percolate out in the hallway. The bedroom made Tameria think of a militarized war zone.

Aisha was sprawled across the bed with her head face down and her arms dangling over the side.

"Aisha, come on girl, get up. You need to take a bath. It'll make you feel better. Please don't make me call Chase to help get you in the tub," Tameria threatened her. To Aisha, the words coming from Tameria sounded like the glob, glob, glob of the cartoon character Charlie Brown's parents.

After much poking and prodding, Tameria managed to convince Aisha to take a hot shower. While Aisha was in the bathroom, Tameria started cleaning Aisha's room. She started by pulling the dingy covers from Aisha's bed. Her eyes became glued to the brown glass vial lying underneath Aisha's pillow. She looked over her shoulder to see if there was any sign of Aisha before she opened the vial and poured a sprinkle of the white powder. After placing some of it on her tongue, within seconds the tip of her tongue started to become numb.

"Oh God, no, not Aisha," she whispered to herself when her suspicions were confirmed. "No wonder she's lost so much weight. She's using drugs."

Tameria fell back on the bed and cried into her hands. She hurt at the thought of what Aisha had gotten herself involved in. Losing her father had been tough on Aisha. The two of them had been thick as thieves. But why had she turned to drugs? Tameria couldn't understand any part of this nightmare she'd stumbled on to. Aisha had always been the strong-minded one. Her Christian convictions were rigid and she used to put nothing before God. But Tameria began to look back over the past few months. There had been a serious change in Aisha. They used to talk all the time but when Aisha had to get another job, their conversations became sparse and with Tameria's medical rotations, the two of them just couldn't spend time together like they used to. She didn't want to believe that Aisha could be on drugs. Now she was faced with the truth. Things were worse than she had imagined. Tameria went to the door of the bathroom and knocked lightly.

"Aisha, are you okay in there?" she asked in a soft-like whisper.

Aisha answered as the water showered her face. "Yes, I'm fine. I'll be out in a minute."

When Aisha came out of the bathroom, Tameria was seated in the bedroom chair next to Aisha's bedroom window.

"You want some soup or something?"

"No, I'm not hungry." Aisha picked up the printed pajamas that Tameria had laid out on her bed. She paused before putting on the pajamas. "Tameria?"

"Yes?"

"Thanks for coming over here and being the friend that you are. I feel like my whole life has spun out of control. The funny thing is, I don't remember how it happened."

"Why didn't you tell me you were in trouble?"

In a confused voice, Aisha responded, "I'm not in trouble. Unless being in trouble means missing my father and feeling guilty for not being there when he died." Aisha's voice raised a pitch. "Or maybe you're talking about the fact that my mother hates me now and I feel so alone. I can't even pray right now, Tameria." Aisha started to cry, something she hadn't done since the day they buried her father. She felt like she didn't deserve to shed tears of grief because she had let her father down.

"I'm talking about *this*." Tameria held up the vial. "Why didn't you tell me you were on drugs? Why?" Tameria pleaded.

A stunned look spread over Aisha's face. "Who are you supposed to be? A private eye? You had no right to search through my things. No right at all," Aisha screamed.

"No, see that's where you're wrong. I have every right. I'm your best friend. You can try to avoid the issue if you want too. You can try to blame me for being a snoop. Whatever you want to say is fine, but when you get finished I still want to know why you, of all people, Aisha, would do something like this."

Aisha felt like nothing. Tameria had always admired her, looked up to her and respected her for her Christian values. Now here she was standing before Tameria feeling like the lowest of the low. *Is this what hitting rock bottom means?* she questioned herself.

The anger in Aisha's voice turned to a shallow whisper. "I, I didn't know how to tell you. It happened so fast. I went from abhorring the very thought of drugs to needing a hit every day all day. I can't explain it. It, it just happened. That's all I know how to say."

"Well, that's not good enough. Because first of all, it just didn't *happen*. Nothing just happens, Aisha. I'm sorry if I sound harsh. But I won't let you give me some lame old excuse."

Aisha slowly fastened each button on her shirt, then leaned against the wall and slid down to the floor. Sitting with her legs up to her face, and her head bowed and resting on her knees, Aisha heard the hurt in Tameria's voice.

"When was the last time you really looked in the mirror? You look like a walking skeleton. I thought it was because you were stressed about the studio. Since you eat like a rabbit anyway, I didn't think too much of it when I saw you at the hospital. But drugs? Oh my God. Talk to me. Tell me if any of this has to do with this part time job you have. Because it seems like that's when you began to change."

Aisha started thinking about whether she should confide in Tameria. There was nothing the two of them hadn't been able to share. But this time things were different. They were both adults now and some things, no matter how close two people were, just couldn't be shared. She slowly lifted her head and looked over at Tameria. Tameria's gaze remained fixed on her.

"I'm waiting," Tameria spoke up, sitting in the chair with folded arms, and patting her left foot.

"All I can tell you is that I'm in way over my head. You

know I needed money desperately to keep my studio going."

"Go on," Tameria encouraged her.

"I couldn't let the studio go under. If I lost that building, you and I both know it wouldn't have been long before everything would have started to fall apart. I couldn't allow that to happen."

"What happened to having faith and trusting God, Aisha? All the things you used to tell me about? When that man first told you about buying the building you really didn't seek God's will about it. You know that and I know that. Instead you panicked and started making things work the way you thought they should work."

Aisha didn't open her mouth. "Remember, when my parents wanted me to become a teacher because the both of them were teachers? What did you tell me, Aisha?" Aisha didn't budge. The natural air in the room slowly dried her hair. "That was different," Aisha said under her breath.

"No, that's where you're wrong. Because it wasn't different. You told me to pray and seek God's will and purpose for my life. You're the one who reminded me that all of my young life I had believed that it was God's will for me to become a doctor. You're the one who told me that I had to do what God wanted me to do, and that I had to become what God ordained me to become. *You* prayed for me and with me, Aisha. *You* prayed for my parents and for my future."

"I know." Aisha was barely audible.

"And God showed me, and my parents, what He wanted for me when I got a full four year scholarship to attend college. Then remember when I got a stipend for room, board, books, meals and transportation when I entered medical school? All because I sought God and waited for Him to do what He willed in my life." Crocodile sized tears began streaming from Tameria's eyes with each word she spoke.

"Aisha, I don't know what you've gotten yourself involved in and honestly I don't care. But what I do care about is you finding your way back to God, back to the only one who can deliver you from this evil. He's the only way out of this, and you know it." Tameria stood up and ambled over to Aisha. Tameria held the vial in front of Aisha. Aisha wanted to snatch her *baby girl* from Tameria's hand, but chose instead to look away and proceeded to get up from off the floor.

"I've been so stupid. I feel dirty and disgusting. You don't know the half of what's been going on in my life these last few months." Aisha sat down on the edge of her bed.

Tameria nudged her to move over so she could sit down too. "I'm listening."

Aisha sighed before she started talking. She twisted her hands and her nervousness was apparent. "When I found out about the building going up for sale, I told you that I had to increase my fees, but it still wasn't going to generate enough money for me to pay down on the building." Aisha wiped tears away from her eyes.

"Keep talking," Tameria insisted.

"Remember that day a few months ago, when I told you about the offer of help I received from one of the parents? What I didn't tell you is *how* she offered to help me."

"You're talking about Gabby's mother, right?"

"Yes, Elisa."

"Ohhkay, just how did she propose to help you?" Tameria scooted around to get more comfortable on the bed.

"She offered me a part-time job where she worked. She said the pay was excellent and that I could have the money I needed in a matter of weeks."

"Let me get this straight. Miss Elise or Lisa, whatever her name, told you that you could make over $20 grand in a few weeks? I don't see how that's possible. I don't know of any job, and part-time too, where you can make that kind of money. Even a stripper, as much as they can make some nights, can't make that much." Tameria watched Aisha's face as it changed to a weird tone, like she was ill. "Hey, are you alright?" Tameria didn't know if Aisha was sick from the drugs or if something else was wrong.

"I'm fine. Anyway, where was I?" Aisha rubbed her hand over her damp head of hair.

"Uh, oh I know. You were about to tell me what line of work Gabby's mother does that can pay you twenty thousand bucks in a few weeks time. I need to hear this because I might need to switch from the medical field to doing what she's doing," Tameria answered, jokingly but noticed that Aisha failed to see the humor.

"Loosen up. I want to help you, Aisha. I'm your friend." Tameria reached over and rubbed the back of Aisha's hand.

Aisha blurted out. "I'm an exotic dancer at a private men's club called The Lynx."

Tameria's head fell. "Are you telling me that you're a stripper?" Tameria tried to hide the deep disappointment she felt. She didn't want to pass judgment on Aisha, but at the same time she couldn't believe that Aisha could stoop so low as to defile her body by displaying it to God knows who.

"I know you probably think badly of me. But at the time, I thought I would work there until I made enough money to buy the building, and that would be the end of it."

Tameria stared at Aisha, her eyes large as quarters. "You're a stripper?" Tameria waited to hear Aisha tell her that what she told her was a big joke.

"I am *not* a stripper. I'm a private dancer. I dance for a select group of wealthy clients who are members at The Lynx." Aisha fidgeted nervously on the bed. She tucked one leg underneath her.

"Please tell me I'm not hearing this. Please, Aisha. Tell me this isn't true."

"Believe me. I wish I could. But I can't. That's where I was the night Daddy died. Elisa called and told me a huge bonus was in it for me if I could dance for one of the new members. I left the hospital, went to the association and got dressed. I had only planned to be away from the hospital for a couple of hours. My employer took me to the client's house. I started dancing for him but he wanted more and I wasn't about to give him what he wanted.

"You mean he wanted to have sex with you?"

"Yes. But believe me, Tameria, I have never given my virginity to any one. I made that vow to God and to you. I would never give my body to anyone but my husband. You know that."

"Do you know how ridiculous you sound?" Tameria rose from the bed and planted herself directly in front of Aisha. Her voice escalated and she pointed her fingers in anger at Aisha. "Well, let me tell you how you sound. You sound like a fool, a hypocrite, Aisha." Tameria shouted. "On one hand you're telling me that you haven't given your body to any of these tricks. And yes I said tricks because that's what these men are. And you may as well have given it to them because you had them lusting over you. Maybe you didn't go all the way, but you still gave your body to who knows how many men, just in a different kind of way. And don't you tell me there was no other way to come up with the money. You could have put in for a grant or something. Or better still, you should have just moved the studio to some other place, any place. Regardless, you didn't have to do what you did! You had a choice. You always have a choice and you definitely made yours," Tameria screamed. "Now you want to sit here and sound all sorry and pitiful and try to make me believe that you're still little Miss Church Lady? Well, I don't think so."

Aisha's face had turned beet red. She'd never seen Tameria so angry. Not in all the years of their friendship had Tameria lashed out at her like that. But Tameria was right. How could she even try to justify her actions?

"I'm so sorry. I really am. But think of how I feel about *myself*. I gave in to something that was totally against my Christian morals, and then the drugs. Oh my, God, let's not even talk about the drugs. The first night I was supposed to dance I was so uptight, so afraid, Tameria. Elisa offered me a Valium to relax my nerves and that was the beginning of my addiction. I went from using Valium to cocaine. Little by little I began to want *baby girl* more and more." Aisha cried and looked at the vial of cocaine peeking out from Tameria's closed hand.

Tameria held the vial up in front of Aisha's nose. "'*Baby girl*'? Is that what you call this stuff?"

"Yes." Aisha hung her head down and turned away. "I can't do this anymore. I've said too much already. Please, just go. I have to be alone right now."

Tameria hated to admit it, but she was glad Aisha wanted her to leave. She couldn't digest all she had just confessed to her. She needed time away from her to think and pray. Tameria drew in a deep breath before she spoke again. Maybe she had been too harsh. Aisha was human. She was subject to the same mistakes as anybody else. Tameria thought about the sin she'd committed with Chase that she hadn't told Aisha about. Only God, Chase and she knew that she was no longer a virgin. So how could she condemn Aisha? Aisha got up from the side of the bed and began walking toward the hallway. She wanted Tameria to leave right away. The shame she felt was too great.

"Sure, I'll leave. But before I go, let me say this. I know I sound like I'm condemning you for the choices you've made. I'm sorry for that. Regardless of what you've done, you're still my best friend, and when you hurt, I hurt. I love you. I just wish I could have been there for you and that you would have come to me before things escalated out of control the way they did. But just like you've always told me, God forgives. When He died, He died for our past sins, the sins we commit now and the sins we will commit in the future. We will sin every day of our lives for the rest of our lives, so please, please don't sit in this apartment and beat up on yourself, Aisha. God doesn't condemn us, so don't condemn yourself." Tameria hugged her and left.

Bright and early the next morning, the piercing sun poked through Aisha's window shades. She rose and sat upright in the bed and began to pray.

"Lord, please forgive me. I need your help. I can't fight this battle by myself any longer." When she finished, peace had filled her body. For the first time in months she felt a heaviness leaving her. She climbed out of bed, took a bubble bath and prepared herself for the eleven o'clock church service. It had been weeks since she'd graced the doors of Faithside, but she was determined to go, no matter what kind of thoughts were going through her mind. She leafed through her walk-in closet. After several minutes, she settled on wearing a dusty rose cascading dress and a pair of black Astor pumps. After finishing up with light touches of makeup, she grabbed her cell phone and purse then headed out to church.

Her cell phone rang minutes before she turned down Elvis Presley Boulevard. This time she decided to answer when she heard Elisa's ring tone. "Hello, Elisa" she said in a voice that lacked enthusiasm.

"I can't believe you finally decided to answer the phone. I've been worried sick about you. How are you? I've called the studio and Angie wouldn't give me any information. She just said you were taking some time off because of your father's death."

"No need to worry. I'm fine. I just need some time alone, that's all."

"I understand. And I feel really bad about your father, Aisha." Elisa sounded genuine and Aisha accepted her sentiments.

"Thanks. And look, I know you and Jason have been calling and leaving messages, but I just haven't been able to talk to anyone."

"I understand. Believe me I do. I just wanted to hear your voice and believe it or not, Jason is concerned about you too. He really is. We've been by your apartment several times as well."

"Like I said, I'm sorry. Look, I'm about to turn into the church parking lot so I have to go right now. I'll call you later. You take care."

"Sure, I will. Bye now."

"Oh, wait, Elisa."

"What is it?"

"How is Gabby?"

"Gabby's fine. She asks about you all the time. I don't know if you know it or not, but the studio isn't holding many classes since you took time off."

"Yes, I know. Anyway, I'm thinking about closing it for a while. I need time to get my life in order. You know what I mean?"

"I think I do. But you go on to church. Say a prayer for me, okay?"

Aisha responded with a grim look on her face. "Yeah, I'll do that. I just hope God still wants to hear from me."

# 28

Aisha shuffled inside Faithside Temple with the rest of the crowd. The church was filled to overflowing. This was the eleven-thirty service, the third and final service of the morning. She scanned the crowd for familiar faces. Several members spoke to her as she made her way down to the middle section of the church.

"Girl, where have you been?" asked a woman named Paulette who Aisha used to sit next to at the nine o'clock service. Aisha turned, looked at her and smiled. "I've been working a second job. How have you been?"

"Oh fine. I can't complain. Like they say, it won't do any good anyway."

"I know that's right," Aisha agreed.

"Do you still have your dance studio?"

"Well, yes and no. I mean right now I've closed it for a while. Since my father passed, I just haven't been in the frame of mind to do too much of anything."

"Oh, that's right. I heard that Mr. Carlisle passed. I'm sorry about that," Paulette said and laid her hand over Aisha's in a sympathetic gesture before leaving. "It's good to see you Aisha. You take care of yourself and remember that nothing is too hard for God."

"Sure will. See you, Paulette." Aisha hoped that no one else would say anything to her. She wanted the service to start to avoid any more uncomfortable encounters. When she was active in church, she had done the same thing Paulette did when she ran into someone she hadn't seen at church for a while. Now she knew how those people felt and decided that if that ever happened again, she would just say hello and keep on stepping. She skimmed through the church bulletin at the order of service and the weekly announcements.

The sound of a man's voice interrupted her reading by calling her name. "Aisha, Aisha Carlisle is that you?" Aisha jerked her head up to meet the sound of the gentleman's voice. She barely recognized him. It had been several years since she'd seen Leland Parker. After graduating from high school he had joined the Peace Corps and that was the last she'd seen or heard from him. It wasn't like they were ever close friends, but like Paulette they had been members of Faithside Temple since they were youngsters. They used to be active in youth functions around the church and participated in almost everything that had to do with the youth. But when they became adults, they went their separate ways.

"Leland, right?"

"Yeah, in the flesh," he grinned and his glistening uneven teeth seemed to sparkle. He sat down next to her and immediately began talking. "How've you been?"

"Pretty good. Are you still in the Peace Corps?"

"No. I've finished with that. I just made it home a few months ago. What are you up to these days?"

"I own a dance studio in South Memphis," she remarked without much excitement.

"You got it going on, don't you? How's your friend, Tameria? You two still thick as thieves?"

"Yeah, we are. She's doing fine. She's in her second year of medical residency."

"Gosh, I sure would like to see her. You know I always had a crush on her," he added. "I haven't seen her at church since I came back, but of course I guess with the growth of this church, it's easy to do. Take you for instance, I've been here just about every Sunday and Wednesday evening since I made it back to town but this is the first time I've run into you."

Aisha was now getting bored with Leland's conversation. She looked at her watch to see how much longer it would be before the service started. Leland must have taken a hint because he stood up and said, "Look I'm going to move up closer. I usually don't sit this far back."

"Sure, Leland. It was really good to see you again." To erase some of the guilt she felt for brushing him off she said, "Like you said, since the church is so big we don't get a chance to see each other as often as we used to and then we have three services on top of that. But I'm really glad you're home."

"Thanks, and remember to tell Tameria I asked about her." He turned and walked down the aisle until he made it to the second row.

Aisha's eyes focused on the handsome man walking up the steps leading to the pulpit. She hadn't seen him before but ministers joined Faithside regularly so she wasn't surprised. She listened intently when he stood at the pulpit and began to speak.

"Good morning," his voice boomed throughout the sanctuary. "I said good morning. It's good to be in the house of the Lord." The congregation responded with rounds of praise and waving of hands.

Aisha studied the gentleman who spoke so articulately. He was attractive, spoke like he was highly educated and he moved with an aura of self confidence. He led the congregation in praise and worship. Not only was his voice magnetizing, his swagger added a slice of charm that sucked Aisha in like a vacuum. When he started singing, "Lord we lift your name on high," Aisha couldn't resist the urge to stand up along with the rest of the congregation and sing. The people standing on both sides of her raised their hands in praise, but Aisha felt unworthy. On one hand she wanted to clap and wave her hands too. But the voice in her head told her she was nothing more than a charlatan, one of those folks Jesus talked about in the Bible who shout Lord, Lord, but God says they're none of His true children. She used to believe that she couldn't lose her salvation. That's what she'd been taught since she was a small child in Sunday School. But now she wasn't so sure anymore. She felt like she'd betrayed God. Would he forgive her for turning her back on Him? She continued to stand and sing, "You came from heaven to earth, to show the way . . ."

The man in the pulpit prayed and then motioned for everyone to be seated.

"Who is he?" Aisha couldn't resist asking the lady sitting to the right of her.

The lady whispered. "Are you talking about the minister?"

"Oh. Yes, I'm sorry."

"He's one of the associate ministers. He's been here for about a month. We love him."

"What's his name?" Aisha asked, leaning in closer to the woman so as not to disturb anyone.

The lady responded in a friendly voice, "Minister Jackson Williams. He's over Pastoral Care. He does counseling too."

"Thanks." Aisha sat upright and listened to the choir sing. By the time Pastor Shipley made it to the podium to deliver his sermon, Aisha was ready to receive his message.

\* \* \*

"That was a powerful message wasn't it?" the woman who Aisha had talked to earlier remarked.

Aisha responded, "Yes it was. Pastor's messages are always prolific. And I needed to hear it too."

"I did too. Well, I guess I'll get out of here. It was nice talking to you. You have a blessed day."

"You too," Aisha said and walked down the corridor in the opposite direction of the woman. She weaved through the crowd that had formed a line for tapes of today's sermon. She paused, contemplating whether or not she wanted to purchase a copy. She turned around and walked until she reached the end of the line. That's when she spied him. It was Chandler and he was headed in her direction. Before she could move away from his line of view, their eyes locked.

"Hi," Aisha said, trying to shield her surprise at seeing him.

Chandler was equally surprised. He recalled this being the church she told him she belonged to, but given her double life, he didn't know if that remained true.

"Hello, Aisha."

She stepped out of the slow moving line and stood in the middle of the floor. People passed by, excusing themselves and going around the two of them.

Aisha's temper began to rise at the thought of how he had dropped her like a hot skillet.

"What are you doing here?"

"I have the right to worship too," Chandler answered her dryly.

"True."

Chandler wasn't totally heartless. He took the opportunity given to express his condolences to Aisha. "I was sorry to hear about your father."

"Sure." Aisha wasn't the least bit moved by his better-late-than-never condolences. Seconds later, Aisha told him. "Well, I have to go. Good seeing you."

Aisha watched him squirm uncomfortably.

With a transparent lack of emotion, Chandler said flatly, "Goodbye."

Aisha speed dialed Tameria as she pulled out of the church lot.

Tameria answered the phone. "Hey, what's up?"

"Just leaving church. Guess who I just saw?"

"Who?"

"Chandler. Can you believe it?" Aisha remarked.

"Girl, no. Did he see you? Did the two of you talk?" Tameria asked.

"Yeah, we talked for a minute. Nothing special. He told me he was sorry about my father. I wasn't trying to hear his fake self, so I told him I had to go, and I did," Aisha added, then jumped in the middle lane of traffic.

Tameria agreed with Aisha. "Good. That's what he deserved. How was church?" Tameria inquired.

"It was pretty good. Do you remember goof ball Leland Parker?" Aisha mashed her brakes as she approached the red traffic light.

"Yeah, is he back in town?"

"Uh huh, and the brother looks pretty good too. He still has that crush on you. Wanted me to tell you, hello." Aisha grinned.

"Girl, puhleeze. I have who I want." Tameria rested against the wall in the doctor's lounge. "Tell me what Pastor preached about because I sure don't want to spend my precious minutes talking about Leland Parker."

"He preached about accepting yourself as you are instead of trying to live your life for others. Definitely something I needed to hear." Aisha accelerated as soon as the light switched to green. "He said we should stop being something other than what God has purposed us to be."

"I think we all need to be reminded of that every now and then. Anyway," Tameria drawled. "I'm going to have to hang up in a second. You know, we're not supposed to use our cell phones unless we have to answer a page."

"No problem. I was just calling to let you know that I took your advice and went to church. I didn't know we had a new minister over Pastoral Care."

"I didn't know that either. That's one reason I really miss church. I'm losing out on what's going on by having to work these long rotations. But listen, I'll call you later tonight when I get a break. That is if it's not too late. Hang in there."

"Yeah, I will. Bye." Aisha turned the volume up on her radio, and then changed it from 103.5 to Hallelujah FM.

Tameria was elated when Aisha told her she'd gone to church. Maybe she was on the road to getting her life back on track. She'd been praying for both Aisha and Mrs. Carlisle. The other thing she hoped to do was encourage Aisha to get counseling. Tameria believed things would begin to turn around for Aisha if she did that.

Chase appeared from out of nowhere and grabbed Tameria around her waist and twirled her in the air. It was a blessing to have someone in his life who shared his same dreams, goals and aspirations. And like Chase, Tameria possessed compassion, concern and a gentle spirit for others. That's why the two of them fit perfectly in the medical field.

Chase heard his name being blared over the intercom. "Sorry baby, duty calls," he said apologetically.

"I'm going to the nurses' station and grab me a donut and some coffee. I'll see you later on." She smiled and kissed him on the cheek as they exited the doctors' lounge.

Aisha felt pretty good. The sermon had inspired her to think differently about herself.

Her phone rang. The hip-hop ring tone identified the caller on her cell as Elisa. Aisha hadn't gotten the word 'hello' fully past her lips when Elisa started talking.

"How was church? Did you remember to say a prayer for me?" Elisa asked.

Aisha laughed over the phone. "Dang, girl, can't you at least say hello first?"

"No, I can't. We already said hello before you went to church," Elisa responded in a carefree voice.

"Whatever. Anyway, to answer your questions, church was good and second, yes, I did remember to say a prayer for you and Gabby. So there. Anything else?"

"Yea, what are your plans for the rest of the day? I don't have to work and we haven't hung out in a while. You game?"

"I don't see why not. We can meet up at Ruby Tuesday on Winchester," Aisha suggested. "I haven't had a thing to eat and I'm starving."

"Okay, let me get ready and I'll be there around 2:30."

"Okay, see you then because even though it's over, I still wanted to tell you my version of what happened that night with Kyle Taylor."

"My ears are itching to hear it too. I'll see you in a little while."

Since Aisha was already dressed, she had time to go by her dance studio, something she hadn't done in a couple of weeks. There was a time when no one or nothing could pull her away from her studio.

She drove to the location, unlocked the door and stood in the vast space. She inhaled while outstretching her arms and closing her eyes. Aisha pictured the room full of students, each of them dancing gracefully around the studio. She opened her eyes, then felt a tear traveling along the contours of her cheek.

Being back at the studio reminded her of how much she missed doing the one thing she used to live and breathe for. It wasn't dancing at The Lynx because that wasn't the same. It was about teaching the girls the art of dancing, how to feel the music within, and show passion in every move-ment. Aisha eased down in her office chair. Her desk was piled high with messages and other paper work that Angie had left for her to go over. *Angie*, she thought. *Lord, thank you for her. Angie has kept things going virtually on her own, like this is her studio.*

Aisha wrote a note to remind herself to do something extra special for Angie, like giving her a nice bonus. She dialed her voicemail and listened as the Audix said that her mailbox was full. She listened to the messages, deleting unimportant ones and saving the ones that required her attention. When she heard Kyle Taylor's message, she shivered at the sound of his voice. He sounded exceptionally charming. For a moment she forgot about the way he had treated her. Then she became somewhat uneasy. He had called her studio and he knew her real name. How could he have discovered who she really was? She trembled at the thought of how he'd talked to her the last time she'd seen him. Now here he was, sounding so charming and sensi-tive. She'd have to ask Elisa what was going on. *Maybe Jason's sorry behind told him*. Her nostrils flared at the thought of how low down Jason could really be. She replayed Kyle's message.

"Aisha, Kyle Taylor here. First let me say how sorry I am about your father. I also want to apologize for my totally senseless and cruel behavior when you came to my home. Will you forgive me and allow me to make it up to you by taking you to dinner? Please call me at The Lynx. I'll be waiting."

*You sure will be waiting, and you'll be waiting a long time too if you think I'm going to call you*, she exhaled a heavy sigh of disgust at his unmitigated gall and proceeded to delete his message. She listened to the last two messages, erased them and stood up to leave. Before locking up, she turned and surveyed her turf one more time.

Dressed in a gold-colored parchment silk tube skirt and a black tailored blazer, Elisa waltzed into Ruby Tuesday like she was a runway model, turning the heads of several gentlemen with each long stride she took. Her soft patent and linen sling backs added height to her already gazelle-like frame. She asked the hostess to seat her in the back of the restaurant near the window so she and Aisha could enjoy the breathtaking view of the mighty Mississippi while they dined.

Aisha scanned the restaurant until she saw Elisa's hand waving back and forth in the air motioning for her.

"It's about time. It's after three. I was beginning to think you weren't going to show," was Elisa's response as she stood up and hugged Aisha.

"Now you know I would have called if I had a change of plans. I stopped by the dance studio and just lost track of time, that's all. Have you ordered yet?"

"No, just this Cosmopolitan. I wanted to wait on you before I ordered."

"Well, let's check out the menu because I'm starving." After placing their orders the two of them laughed and talked endlessly about Gabby. Aisha laughed when Elisa told her that she had taken Gabby to the school parking lot and let her practice driving. Elisa said she thought she was going to pee in her pants when it looked like her daughter was about to run into the side of the school. Aisha hadn't laughed like this in a long time, and it felt good.

The waiter brought Aisha's gold margarita and a glass of water with lemon. Another server came up behind the waiter with their orders. They allowed the server to place their orders on the table.

Between bites, Elisa started talking again. "Enough said about Gabby's driving techniques. Let's get to the juicy stuff. Tell me about this Kyle Taylor and what happened with him," Elisa goaded.

"Every time I think about that night, I almost lose it. If it wasn't for him, maybe I would have been there when my father died. But let me tell you what happened."

"Look, if it's too painful for you to talk about, then don't tell me. We haven't been out in a relaxing atmosphere for a while now, and I sure don't want to ruin it by asking you to relive something that's obviously still hurting you quite a bit."

The look on Elisa's face expressed her genuine empathy for Aisha. By choice, she didn't have any women friends, but Aisha was the exception to the rule. Aisha possessed the kind of personality that drew people to her and Elisa was one of those people. Forming friendships with any of the girls she and Jason brought in to The Lynx was definitely taboo, plus most of them were way too young. Knowing that Aisha, more than likely, didn't think of them as friends like she did, Elisa refused to dwell on it. In her hurried, sometimes harsh life, Elisa had learned to take things in stride, friendships, or the lack thereof, included.

The one girl who had tugged at Elisa's heart was Hallie. Hallie reminded her so much of herself when she was a teenager. Shy, frightened and afraid to trust anyone. Elisa managed to gain Hallie's trust a few months after the girl was brought to The Lynx. Slowly, Hallie opened up to her about how scared she was. Elisa promised her that she would never let any of the men at The Lynx hurt her and so far, she had kept her word. Whenever Ronald Shipley asked for one of the girls, Elisa made sure it was one of the older girls and never Hallie. When the new member, Kyle Taylor, joined The Lynx, Jason assigned Hallie to him before she could intercept. So far, Hallie told her that Kyle Taylor was a nice man. That's why she couldn't believe it when Aisha told him how mean he was to her. She was even more surprised to hear about how he had put her out of his house and made her wait outside until the company limo came to pick her up. There was another side to him and Elisa wanted to know what made him tick.

"So when he put me out of his house," Aisha continued with her story, "I called Jason and told him to high tail it to that fool's place and get me."

"What did Jason say, girl?" Elisa bent in closer so she wouldn't miss a word.

"I don't know what he and Kyle talked about. All I know is that Jason went inside the house and stayed in there about five or ten minutes. When he came back to the limo, he didn't say one word to me. The dog didn't even ask me if I was okay or anything. He acted like I was some hooker on the street or something. All the way back to The Lynx he refused to say one word to me. I hate him for that."

"Jason can be low down when he wants to be, Aisha. But that was a bit much, even for him, especially when it wasn't your fault.

"I guess he expected me to sleep with Kyle but I'm not about to lose my virginity to some oversexed executive. I don't care how much paper he has," Aisha insisted.

"I can't believe that he acted like that. But I'm proud of you for standing up for your beliefs. So I say, hats off to you." Elisa raised her glass up in the air toward Aisha and took a sip of her second Cosmopolitan. "Did you get paid or did the lowlife hold back the three grand he promised you for meeting that chump?"

"I wasn't about to let him mess me out of my money. No way. So since he was playing the silent treatment with me in the limo, when we made it back to The Lynx I asked him where my money was. He turned around like he was the exorcist or somebody and said it was in the car. I looked back inside the limo and saw the envelope lying next to where he had been sitting.

"Shoot, as long as you got your money, then I say forget him."

"Oh, let me tell you about that! Instead of the three grand

I was supposed to be paid, Jason gave me 30 one dollar bills. I was so mad I could have killed him. Forgive me, Lord, but that's the way I felt. Then I grabbed hold of my senses and I let it go. I told myself he wasn't worth it. I didn't even go inside The Lynx. I would have lost it. Jason will get his. You can bank on that. Anyway, it was my intent to go home and change clothes but before I could do that, I got the call from my mother." The two ladies became suddenly quiet. Aisha drank some of her water and Elisa stirred her plate of Carolina Chicken Salad around with her fork.

Aisha broke their momentary silence. "I stopped by the studio before coming here." Elisa shook her head in response. Aisha continued. "Can you believe that I had a message on my Audix from one Kyle Taylor?"

"Are you kidding me?"

"I wish. But I'm not. Jason had to tell him how to contact me, unless you did." Aisha waited on Elisa's answer.

"Twasn't I. I don't play that."

"Good, then it was Jason. Do you know that he even called me by my real name? He offered his condolences over my father's death. If Jason did that, he's stooped to an all time low! He doesn't know what Kyle Taylor is up to."

"You're right. I think you should confront Jason about it. I know I would."

"I'm thinking about it. But one thing I don't have to think about is calling Kyle back. He said he wanted to have dinner with me."

"Girl, he must be on something more potent than either of us." Elisa laughed and took another sip of her drink.

"Seriously though. Elisa, it's over for me. I'm not going back to The Lynx. I have to get my life together in more ways than one. I'm a wreck. I'm no better than the crack heads that walk up and down the streets doing any and everything for a hit of that pipe."

"No you're not, Aisha. That's not true at all. So what if you snort a little coke every once in a while? I've been doing coke and Valium for years and I'm fine. If I wanted to stop, I could. But I don't want to. It relaxes me like a person who smokes cigarettes or drinks a glass of wine every night before bed. So we do our thing—we snort coke. What's so terrible about that?"

"For one, it's illegal. Two, it's addictive. And three, it fries your brain, which is obviously true if you think that what we're doing is okay. I am a drug addict. That's what's so terrible about this. I even have a name for the coke—*baby girl*. I have to have it. I don't care if I'm in church, at The Lynx or the dance studio. I take it with me wherever I go. It's like that commercial that says American Express—never leave home without it. Except I say *baby girl*, never leave home without it. Before I got out of the car and came in here I took a hit. And you tell me there's nothing wrong with that?"

"There isn't. But have it your way because somehow you always manage to make insignificant things into huge mountains. Everybody has a vice of some kind, Aisha. None of us are perfect. At least that's what you've told me. And if you quit The Lynx then your brain is fried. The kind of money you make! And you're ready to kiss it goodbye because you're feeling guilty because of what happened to your dad?" Elisa took another swig of her drink.

"Don't you dare bring my father into this! Don't you dare." Aisha raised her voice in hurt and anger. "If I had been where I was supposed to be, I could have been there to tell my father goodbye."

"I don't mean to sound insensitive, but when it's your time to go, there's nothing anyone can do about it. Who's to say that you would have been there to tell him goodbye if you hadn't been with Kyle? You could have easily been doing something else. It could have been something as simple as having been in the hospital bathroom and before you made it back to his side your father could have died."

For the second time, they both remained silent. Aisha was lost in her thoughts and Elisa in hers. Both of their lives had connected along the pathway of life but they had started on two entirely different roads. Aisha's faith and convictions were what used to hold her up and keep her going whenever trials and tribulations entered her life.

Elisa grew up living a hard knock life where her parents constantly fought each other verbally and physically. When she was about the same age as Hallie, Elisa ran away from her home in Kansas City. The day she ran away, she was supposed to be at school. But she had made other plans. Plans that included a life of living on her own and becoming a famous model. All of the cussing, fighting and threats at home had escalated to a point where she had begun to fear for not only her mother's life but her life and the lives of her two younger brothers. She vowed to make a life for herself and then go back to Kansas City to rescue her brothers. She had saved up enough money from babysitting and her after school job at McDonald's to purchase an airline ticket. She had been saving her money for almost a year and a half. She arrived in Houston, Texas with high hopes and fast dreams so when the well dressed man and woman approached her while she was eating alone inside the mall, she was thrilled. They both told her how pretty she was and how they were searching for models for some of the top magazines like Seventeen, Vibe and Essence.

Appealing to the naïve Elisa, they convinced her that they operated an exclusive modeling agency located in Memphis, Tennessee. They wanted to sign her for the opportunity of a life time and were willing to take her to Memphis and introduce her to the owner of the agency. Something within told her not to go, but what if what they told her was true? She couldn't pass up this chance. If things turned out differently than what they said, she still had enough money to last a couple of weeks for her to get a room and some food. Within two hours of climbing in the car with them, Elisa was on a flight from Houston to Memphis. She couldn't believe the stroke of luck that had come her way and she'd only been gone from home for a little over two days. It wasn't until a few days after her recruitment she realized something was wrong.

One day after arriving at The Lynx, Elisa was introduced to the owner. For Elisa, it was love at first sight. His charm was magnetic and he treated her like a queen. He lavished her with gifts, clothes, jewelry, took her on trips with him and gave her lots of money. So when he told her he wanted to seal their love for one another, Elisa, though scared, gave in to him. But six months later when she told him she was pregnant, he flipped. He accused her of sleeping with the other members without protection. Soon after that, his demeanor toward her did a 360 degree turn. He became physically and verbally abusive just like she remembered her father being toward her mother. She wasn't allowed to leave her room until after she gave birth.

The doctor who delivered her baby was a member at The Lynx and knew better to say anything about Elisa. Elisa, seeing her tiny daughter for the first time, finally understood what love was all about. She named her little girl, Gabby. The baby's daddy, notorious Ronald Shipley, wanted nothing to do with her. Life for Elisa became a living nightmare. What she had seen and endured at home was nothing compared to the way she was used as a sex slave by Ronald and some of the other men at The Lynx.

After Gabby was born, Elisa wanted to take her baby girl and run away to California, but she was kept secluded on a locked floor along with several other girls. The only time she was allowed off the floor was when she was forced to perform sexual acts and illicit dancing for the men. Eventually, money started flowing in by way of tips from the men. By the time Gabby had turned one year old, Elisa was raking in over $750 a week. That was a heck of a lot of cash for a sixteen year old teenager. When Gabby turned two years old, Ronald allowed Elisa to move into a place of her own with the understanding that he owned her. He couldn't have a child, especially his, running around The Lynx. Elisa was relieved to have her own space. She was willing to do whatever it took to keep Gabby from the clutches of her pedophile father and his sick buddies. In exchange for her freedom and Gabby's safety, Elisa understood that she was forever bound to do whatever she was told.

Gabby was fifteen years old now. To protect her from the horrid life she'd led, Elisa made it her business to keep her end of the bargain with Ronald over the years. That meant going out with Jason to recruit new girls. Whatever Ronald wanted from her, she gave it to him. She couldn't understand how totally opposite Ronald Shipley was from his twin brother. Ronald had no problem with carrying out his threats. Elisa had witnessed his anger unleashed on many of the girls. Through the years, she had been the recipient of it. Though she couldn't prove it, she knew that he had committed murder as well. It was like Ronald was Jekyll and Pastor Shipley was Mr. Hyde. They were as different as night and day.

Aisha and Elisa finished the last of their food, paid the check and left.

"What are you going to do about Kyle?" Elisa asked her as they exited Ruby Tuesday. "Are you going to call him back and accept his apology?"

"You really think I'm that stupid? I told you, Elisa. It's over. I'm never going to The Lynx again. And I'm certainly not going to call that scumbag, Kyle Taylor."

"All I can say then is, good luck. You're a better woman than I am."

"Why don't you quit too? You can come and help me at the studio. I can use a good director. You're talented, smart and good with the students. You're a great dancer too. What do you say?"

Elisa's face beamed at the thought of being able to get away from The Lynx. She could have a new start and a real job. For once, things could be normal for her and Gabby. *Gabby*, she thought to herself. *If I leave, he'll take Gabby.*

"Aisha, I wish I could, but I've been at The Lynx for a long time and you can't begin to pay me the kind of money I make there. I'm sorry." Elisa explained reluctantly without telling her the real truth about why she couldn't leave The Lynx.

"Suit yourself. But still, at least think about it," Aisha pleaded.

"Okay, I'll give it some thought. Now come on. I've got to get home. I promised Gabby that I'd take her to the mall. She's going to a spring fling at school, so you know that she insists on having a new outfit." Elisa hugged Aisha tightly before walking to her car.

Elisa watched as Aisha got in her car and drove off. For a few moments, she sat in her car, allowing her mind to usher in a flurry of thoughts. Elisa began telling herself that she was to blame for Aisha's involvement with The Lynx, drugs, and an out of control life. After learning of Aisha's desperation to save her studio, Elisa set out to entice Aisha to work at The Lynx. Initially, Elisa felt no sense of betrayal. Since there was no escaping The Lynx or Ronald, Elisa's mission in life revolved around anything or anyone who could take Ronald's attention away from her and Gabby. There was nothing she wouldn't do to make that happen. Seeing Aisha's tremendous talent, like a lion laying low waiting for its prey, Elisa pounced on the opportunity after learning about

Aisha's problems. Developing a soft spot for Aisha was not part of Elisa's plans. Yet the more she hung around Aisha, the more she liked and respected her for the morals and values she possessed.

Elisa wasn't totally at fault for doing what she did and being where she was. It was years of having to live with being abused, of being treated like nothing more than a piece of meat, that drove Elisa to develop a hard core shell that led her to think: *better her than me.* It was the only way for Elisa to live with herself, the only way to protect Gabby. Determined not to ever let him hurt Gabby, Elisa jumped aboard Ronald's bandwagon. Elisa was now doing to other young girls what was done to her; stripping them of their hopes and dreams. *I'm no better than him,* Elisa told herself.

Elisa dreamed of another way of living. She would give anything to have a simple life for herself and Gabby. But she was trapped, trapped in Ronald's prison, serving a life sentence. She sat in her car, and for the first time, she took a long, hard look at the life she was living. Elisa understood that she could never, ever be free. Would the God Aisha professed to know, help an evil person like her? Would God forgive her after all the terrible things she'd done to so many people? Was she worth saving? Question after question flooded her mind and spirit. Feeling it was too much to bear any longer, Elisa rested her head in the palms of her hands and then did something she hadn't allowed herself to do in years—she cried.

# 29

Chandler sat in his suite at The Lynx thinking about the night at the mansion when he recognized Aisha. All the years he'd worked undercover, his cover had never been blown. That said a lot about him. But he came awfully close when he recognized the dancer that called herself, Luscious. He thought back on that night and remembered the sexiness she exuded as she danced to the music. Watching her move back and forth with her hair swaying against the flow of her agile body aroused him and he wanted her. When she brushed off his advances, his ego was severely wounded and without warning, he went into Chandler Larson mode, lashing out at her before forcing her out of his house.

The knock on the door jarred him from his thoughts of Aisha and the indictments that were about to go down in the next few days. Having located the files of Shipley and the members of The Lynx, Chandler had discovered the method used to ship drugs into the city and to traffic in girls. He had taped conversations, videos and a reliable inside informant, not to mention Hallie. All Chandler had to do was give the final word to his Chief and his back up team was ready to spring into action. Every facet of Operation Lynx was in place. The back up team was prepared just in case there was any trouble when they delivered the indictments to Shipley, Jason and Elisa. But first Chandler had a few loose ends to tie up. One of those loose ends was Hallie.

"Who is it?" Kyle asked.

"It's Hallie, Mr. Taylor," the familiar sound of the child's voice responded. He opened the door and ushered her inside.

"Hi, sweetie. Everything all right?" he asked her.

He had everything arranged so he could get her out of The Lynx first thing tomorrow morning. The plan was for his maid to pick her up from The Lynx and carry her to his estate, where she was to remain until he arrived.

"Hallie, I want you to do everything I've told you to do tomorrow morning. Do you understand me?" he asked the anxious girl.

"Yes. I understand."

"You're going to be picked up around nine thirty. I want you up and ready. Don't take anything along with you. Absolutely nothing. Do you hear me?"

Her eyes brightened at the thought of leaving The Lynx forever. "Yes, I know. I promise I won't take a thing."

"Honey, things are about to change for you." Chandler placed both hands on her shoulder. "You'll never have to worry about being hurt ever again. You hear me?"

Without any advance warning, she reached around his waist and hugged him as tightly as she could. Tears flowed freely from her child's eyes. He stroked her hair gently like a loving father would his child. He fought back his own tears at the thought of all Hallie had experienced in her yo life. But anger mounted in the base of his throat wh thought of Aisha again. Taking a step back, he lo

Hallie then began to wipe away her tears with his finger-tips.

"Hey, I have your favorite. Chocolate chip cookies and vanilla ice cream," he smiled at her.

"Yum, yum," Hallie answered, rubbing her hand over her flat belly in a circular motion. A smile had quickly exchanged places with her tears as she took off for the kitchen.

While Hallie was in the kitchen, Chandler went into the study to go over the final plans for the downfall of The Lynx and Ronald Shipley. He looked at the pictures he'd taken when he was at Faithside and searched for any evidence that the Revered Donald Shipley knew about The Lynx operation. For the past few weeks the Feds had kept a close eye on Donald too. So far neither Chandler nor his police partners had evidence or proof that the illustrious Pastor Shipley was part of his twin brother's scandalous, illegal lifestyle. From all indications, Donald Shipley was everything he portrayed himself to be, which was a man highly spoken of, with integrity, upstanding Christian morals, and who displayed a love for God that appeared to be sincere. His twin, Ronald, on the other hand was a bad seed. Whether the Reverend knew about his brother's lifestyle was yet to be determined, but Chandler was confident that what had been going on in the dark was about to come to light.

# 30

Sandra sat in the living room of her Little Rock home staring blankly out the picture window on to the sidewalk. The move to Little Rock proved to be good for her, but nothing could keep her from thinking about Benjamin's hearty laughter, and the way he used to shuffle around the house. Getting used to living alone was hard for her. Though much smaller than the one she and Benjamin had in Memphis, the Little Rock house echoed a silence that Sandra was not accustomed to. Maybe she would go to Springfield and visit her brother and his wife for a few weeks. The church she joined after moving to Little Rock was supportive. Members frequently called or came by to check on her. But things weren't the same and never would be without Benjamin. There was no running away from her pain.

Since his death, and her move to Little Rock, Sandra hadn't seen or heard from Aisha for weeks. Initially that was the way she had wanted it. Benjamin loved Aisha and for her to be out in the streets somewhere while he was dying was unforgivable. How could she have even thought about going to some job when her father was on his death bed? Sandra thought her daughter was insensitive and selfish. Benjamin's last request to see Aisha went unfulfilled. Sandra cried until the doorbell rang and invaded her loneliness. She hurriedly wiped away her tears. As she pressed the wrinkles out of her cotton dress with both of her hands, she moved closer to the side entrance. Her mouth dropped open wide when she saw Aisha standing on the other side. At first, she felt anger and rage toward her child. Unable to make her words come out, Sandra stood in the doorway staring at her. She eyed Aisha's car parked in the side driveway.

"Mother, may I come in?" Aisha asked in a sorrowful voice. Without waiting on her mother to respond, Aisha eased past her and stepped inside the kitchen. "How are you, Mother?"

Sandra followed Aisha with her eyes. "I'm, I'm okay. What are you doing here?"

"I came to check on you. To see if you were okay. You won't accept or return my calls."

"And you wonder why I won't? Aisha, please. Why don't you think of somebody else other than yourself for a change?" her mother retorted.

"That's why I'm here. I care about you. My God, I love you, Mother. Don't you know that for the rest of my life I'm going to remember that I wasn't there when Daddy needed me the most? I wasn't there to hold him and tell him I loved him for the last time. Mother, knowing that Daddy died asking for me is tearing me apart. But if I lose you too, I don't know what I'll do."

Sandra's heart began to soften somewhat as she listened to her daughter. The hurt Aisha felt was evident as she expressed her sorrow for what she had done. "I know you're sorry, but sometimes sorry just doesn't cut it. Some things can't be fixed no matter what you do."

"And I know not being there for Daddy is one of those things. Believe me, if I could turn back the hands of time and do things differently, I would. But I can't. What I can do is let you know that I love you and ask you to forgive me. I want us to have a real mother-daughter relationship. I know things between us have always been strained, but it's just you and me now. Can't we be there for each other?"

"I don't know." Sandra clasped her hands together. "I need time to think. I miss your father so much. It's lonely here without him. But right now I can't allow anyone in my life."

"What you mean is that you can't allow *me* into your life." The stab of hurt at hearing her mother's words punctured Aisha's heart. "I'm your daughter, *Mother*. Your only child."

Sandra walked toward the living room. At the entrance to the hallway, she looked back over her shoulder and said, "Lock the door when you leave."

Aisha, blinded by tears, ran out to her car. Dark clouds formed in the sky. Aisha knew it was about to rain. But she didn't care because it was already raining inside her heart.

The two hour drive back to Memphis from Little Rock forced Aisha to spend time with herself and with God. Driving along the highway, Aisha committed her life back to God. Asking for his forgiveness and guidance again was difficult but she knew that God was the only one who's mercy and grace was limitless. There was so much that needed to be done to get her life back on track but she had to make a start. *One foot, then another*, Aisha thought as the rain began to come down hard against her car. Maybe one day her mother would forgive her. Until that day came, Aisha vowed to forgive herself and try to move ahead to sort out her twisted life. Transferring her thoughts over to her father, she cried as hard as the rain that pelted against the car. She missed her father terribly. It was almost unbearable for her to think that she didn't get the chance to say goodbye to him. Her life had to change. Somehow, someway, she had to make it.

On her way from Little Rock, Aisha made a couple of stops before going to the studio. By the time she arrived at the studio, she had settled some things in her mind.

Aisha walked toward Angie.

"Hi, Aisha. You made it back from Little Rock already?"

"Yes. My visit turned out to be shorter than I had expected." Aisha didn't explain much more than that, and Angie, taking the cue, didn't ask anything else.

Aisha rested her elbows on the reception counter. "Angie, thank you for all of your help."

Looking surprised Angie countered, "You're welcome, Aisha. This is my job, you know." Reaching over and covering Aisha's hand with hers. Angie smiled.

"That's not all I want to say."

Angie removed her hand, and gazed at Aisha, hoping she wasn't about to tell her that she was closing the studio. "I'm listening, Aisha."

"I know I haven't been around much lately. I've all but let the studio run itself. If it wasn't for you, everything would have fallen apart." Aisha reached in the pocket of her pants and pulled out an envelope. "This is for you."

"For me?" Angie studied the envelope, looked up at Aisha, and then proceeded to open it. Her astonishment was evident when she pulled out the tidy-sized bonus check. "Oh Aisha, you shouldn't have." She jumped up and ran from behind the receptionist area and hugged Aisha. "Thank you, thank you, thank you."

"I owe all the thanks to you, Angie. And that's just something to show how much I appreciate your loyalty and dedication. I haven't been the best person to get along with lately or to get in touch with for that matter," Aisha grinned.

"Maybe we can get things back to normal, huh, Aisha?"

"I hope so. I'm going to take things one day at a time. I have a lot of healing to do mentally, emotionally and physically before I can give my all to anything else."

"Well, listen. You do what you need to do to take care of you. The studio will be here. The part-time instructors you hired are really good with the girls, and as long as you want me here, I'll be here."

"Oh, I'm glad you mentioned that. That brings me to something else I need to tell you."

Slightly holding her breath, Angie didn't budge from where she stood.

"I don't just want you at the studio, Angie. I want to offer you a job as Assistant Director. Of course there'll be a raise in it for you. Really, if you think about it, you're already doing the job anyway. Whaddaya say?"

"Oh my God," she yelled, while jumping up and down like a bunny rabbit. "Are you serious?" she squealed.

Placing her hand over her heart, Aisha remarked, "As a heart attack."

"Then the answer is yes. I'll be glad to accept the position. I have to call my husband. He's going to be ecstatic. Thank you. I don't know what else to say." Angie's hands fluttered up and down like a baby bird trying to fly for the first time.

"There's nothing for you to say. Just continue to do the outstanding job that you're doing. That's thanks enough for me. I'm going to go in my office now. I need to try to dwindle down some of the mountain of paperwork on my desk. We'll talk later about your salary increase if that's okay with you. But I'm sure you'll be pleased."

Angie squealed again. "Of course. Let me know if you need me. I'm going to call Kevin and tell him the good news now."

Aisha clicked on Yahoo Yellow Pages and entered the name Faithside Temple. When the number came up, she dialed it nervously.

"Good afternoon, Faithside Temple. How may I help you?" a female voice asked through the phone receiver.

Her voice slightly quivering, Aisha slowly spoke into the phone receiver, "I, I'd like to make an appointment to talk to someone in Pastoral Care." .

"I'll transfer you to Pastoral Care. Please hold."

This was the first step toward reclaiming her life. Aisha hoped she could keep her voice from trembling. The thought of a hit of *baby girl* weighed heavily on her mind. Having gone without the drug for almost a week, Aisha craved it. Thoughts ran rampant. *All I need is just a taste then I won't do it anymore.*

At night more than any other times, the sense of hopelessness and depression that consumed her proved almost unbearable. There were nights filled with paranoia and insomnia. Irritable and anxious, her thoughts about her life and where she would go from here were inconceivable to think about. Aisha burst out, "I can't do this. Who do I think I'm fooling?"

Just as she was about to change her mind and hang up the phone, she heard another pleasant, calming voice over the phone.

"Hello, Pastoral Care, Natalie speaking."

"Uh, Natalie, I need to make an appointment for counseling please," Aisha stammered.

"Sure, I just need you to answer a couple of questions, if that's okay."

"Yes, I guess so."

"Are you a member of Faithside, ma'am?"

Though curious, Aisha answered. "Yes, is that a requirement?"

"No, ma'am. We ask that because we want to see if our members are utilizing the ministry, that's all."

"I see. What else do you need to know?"

"I need your name please and your membership number."

"Aisha, Aisha Carlisle. My membership number is 72054."

"Miss Carlisle, I have a couple of more questions then we can schedule your appointment."

After giving Natalie the information she requested, her appointment was scheduled for Thursday morning. *Two days. I hope I can hold out until then.* "Could you tell me who I'll be meeting with?"

"Minister Jackson Williams. You'll love him. He's really good and he'll make you feel comfortable. Everyone who talks to him leaves the office praising him," she babbled.

"Okay, thanks. I'll be there Thursday at ten." Aisha interjected, cutting off Natalie's spiel. She rested her chin on the back of her propped up hand and reflected on the handsome minister and how she was drawn in by his presence when she initially saw him in the pulpit. If Jackson Williams was everything Natalie made him out to be, then maybe, just maybe, he was the one who could help her. Thursday would tell.

# 31

Aisha kicked her legs up on the purple futon in the break room. She flipped the remote while sipping on a cup of warm green tea. Earlier, she had thought about going home to her apartment but in times such as this, she seemed to find more solitude by staying at the studio. Another reason she preferred the studio over the apartment was because she'd noticed that being at the studio helped ease her drug craving. Reflecting on the past few months she quickly zoomed past the red background on the TV with the words *Breaking News Alert* flashing across the screen. She turned back just in time to catch the Memphis Police Chief talking to Tony Williams, anchorman for Channel 24 News.

"Tell me, Chief, what led to the indictments of some of this city's most notable and well known constituents, especially Ronald Shipley, the brother of Reverend Donald Shipley."

"Let me say this, Tony. Our department has worked diligently with the Feds in Operation Lynx for over a year. Ronald Shipley may be the twin brother of Reverend Shipley, one of the most well known and respected preachers in the South, but I can tell you that he is certainly not at all like him."

Placing the microphone close to his lips, Tony asked, "What has Shipley been indicted on?"

"Ronald Shipley is suspected of being the mastermind behind trafficking in underage girls, against their will, for the sole purpose of turning them into sex slaves for members of The Lynx Association. He's also been indicted for drug trafficking. Ronald Shipley is suspected of being responsible for three fourths of the cocaine and crack distributed on the streets of Memphis."

"Chief, is there anything else you'd like to say?"

"Only that we want to keep scumbags and lowlifes like Shipley off the streets. There are mothers and fathers out there who've been searching for their children, not knowing if they're dead or alive."

Aisha rolled off of the futon, on to the hardwood dance floor. Folding her legs Indian style underneath her body, she sat directly in front of the television.

Her eyes glued to the screen, focused again on the newsflash, she listened as the reporter recapped what had happened.

"And there you have it. Just moments ago, News Channel 24, learned that five people, using the exclusive men's association, The Lynx, as their headquarters, were indicted for human trafficking and drug trafficking. The suspected mastermind is, Ronald Shipley, the twin brother of Pastor Donald Shipley of Faithside Temple Church. Faithside, with over 8,000 members, is said to be one of the largest Baptist churches in the mid-south. Join us tonight at ten for more about Operation Lynx. I'm Tony Williams, News Channel 24; good evening."

A knot formed in Aisha's chest and rose through her

throat, as she thought about Elisa. *Is she one of the five that was indicted? And what about me? Could I be brought into this mess? God please say it isn't so.*

Aisha jumped up and ran over to retrieve the cordless phone from its cradle and dialed Elisa's cell phone. The phone rolled over into Elisa's voice mail on the first ring. "Her phone isn't on. Gabby, where is Gabby?" Aisha became increasingly frantic at the thought of Elisa being carted off to prison.

Aisha dashed to her office to get her purse so she could look up Gabby's cell phone number. After retrieving her phone, she scrolled through her contacts until she landed on the name, *Gabby Cell.* She pushed the green call button to dial Gabby's number. Beads of sweat formed on Aisha's brow when Gabby's phone rolled straight to voice mail too. She started to pray. *"Please don't let Elisa be involved in this. Let her just be out of reach right now. And I pray that both of them are safe wherever they are. Amen.* After she finished her prayer, she went back into the break room, turned off the television and prepared to leave the studio.

Hoping she wouldn't get pulled over for speeding, she got on I-240 heading in the direction of Elisa's house.

Chandler twiddled his thumbs. Being the kind of cop that he was, observant with a keen sense of knowing when to make a move and bring down a crook, he was sure that if Aisha had heard about The Lynx she would be running scared. Now was the time to get the truth out of her.

He dialed her home number and her voice mail message instructed those who knew her cell phone number to try calling her on it. He did.

Aisha picked up her ringing cell phone and almost dropped it when she saw Chandler's number pop up on the display screen. Fumbling to answer it, she pushed the button.

"What do you want?"

Chandler didn't beat around the bush. "Have you seen the news?"

"What kind of question is that? Why are you calling me asking me whether I've seen the news?" Aisha didn't have time for Chandler's mind games. Too much was already going on and whatever his reason for calling and asking some stupid question about the news, Aisha had no intention of entertaining it.

Chandler's voice loomed over the phone. Smiling wickedly, he had already begun to enjoy hearing the uneasiness in Aisha's voice.

"You heard me. Have you seen the news?"

"Chandler, I don't have time for this. I don't know what this is all about, but I don't want you to call me ever again." Aisha pushed the end button. Her phone rang again.

"You haven't answered my question," Chandler told her.

"What do you want?" Aisha screamed into the phone receiver.

Before she could end the call a second time, the words that poured from Chandler's mouth into the phone almost caused her to lose control of her vehicle.

"If you want to know about your friends Ronald, Jason and Elisa, you'll meet me in fifteen minutes at Java, Juice and Jazz." This time, he was the one who ended the call. Part of him was relieved when there was no evidence that tied her to the illegal operations at The Lynx. But her friend, Elisa, was a horse of a different color. He turned his unmarked police car in the direction of Bellevue Boulevard and Java, Juice and Jazz Cafe.

Trembling, Aisha could barely concentrate on her driving. *How does Chandler know about Jason and Elisa? How did he connect me to them?* Aisha felt a stabbing pain in her temples. Her stomach knotted up. Something was wrong. She felt it. But what did Chandler have to do with it?

Almost missing her exit on to Norris Road, Aisha accelerated and moved from the right lane all the way over to the left lane, narrowly escaping the bumper of the car that was in her blind spot. She arrived at Java, Juice and Jazz, known for hosting spoken word and literary events. She fidgeted with her purse and phone. Grabbing hold of the door handle, Aisha stopped when she saw Chandler. She sat in her car for a few seconds and watched his Denzel swagger and his Brad Pitt butt before she climbed out.

Aisha strode inside the dimly lit restaurant and instantly felt the tug on her arm.

"This way," Chandler ordered.

"Well, hello to you too," she said in a gruff voice. She was just about sick of his disrespectful treatment of her lately. He had no reason to treat her like this and before she left she was going to tell him exactly how she felt.

"You want something to eat or drink?" he asked.

"I'm not hungry," she told him. "But I'll take an iced tea." He went to the bar and came back with a beer for himself and her requested tea.

"Okay, let's have it. What is this all about?"

"I believe I should be the one asking *you* the questions."

Aisha's eyebrows raised and she flung her twists back off of her face which was a sure way to determine that she was nervous.

"I'm a police detective."

The stabbing pain raced through her temple again when she heard Chandler say that he was a policeman.

"A policeman?" She hoped she'd heard him wrong but she knew she hadn't. *Was he about to arrest her? But she'd done nothing wrong.* "As I recall, you told me you were some big shot land developer. Now you're telling me that you're a cop?"

Chandler took a swig of his beer and listened to Aisha.

There was a time he thought she could be the one for him, but again he had misjudged a woman's feelings for him. Maybe he should give up the pursuit of finding that special girl and concentrate on his career. Or he could become the playa he used to be and start lovin 'em and leavin 'em.

"Let's see, Mizz Carlisle of Carlisle Dance Studio. Or no, no. On second thought, perhaps you're not that Mizz Carlisle. Maybe you're Mizz Carlisle behind door number two." His words were sarcastic and confusing.

"What are you talking about?" Aisha looked at him like he was crazy. It was times like these when she missed *baby girl* the most. She could have shrugged his weird antics off if she had a snort of coke, but she didn't, so she couldn't. She sat across the table twitching and searched the faces of people coming into the Jazz Cafe.

"I guess you don't hear me now, huh?"

"Chandler, I don't have time for your games. I really don't care who you are. I want to know what this has to do with me."

"Only if you'll tell me how long you've been stripping and having sex with men at The Lynx." He cursed and looked at her like she was nothing.

"I, I don't know what you're talking about," she stuttered. *Surely he doesn't know that I was one of the dancers at The Lynx. Did Elisa tell him or Jason? Oh my God, no wonder he all of a sudden didn't want to have anything else to do with me."*

"What? Cat got your tongue now? You see, I know all about you. How long you've been working at your so-called part-time dance instructor job. I know about the men you danced for as a private dancer. I even know about you and Kyle Taylor. So, who's the liar, Aisha? You want to sit up here so self righteous and all, and go off on me for not telling you something I obviously wasn't at liberty to tell you. But tell me something. What's your excuse for being a ho!"

Aisha rose up from the chair like a lion about to pounce on its prey. Her petite hand curled up in a fist in striking mode.

"Don't you dare or I'll lock you up so fast, it'll be tomorrow already when you walk outside to my police car. Now sit down." he ordered.

Aisha did as she was told. How could she not have recognized that Chandler was no good? She should have seen through his façade. "What do you want from me?"

"I don't want anything from you anymore. I thought you were a classy lady but you're nothing. You're no more than a high priced hooker. Just like your friend, Elisa."

Defensively, Aisha said. "Elisa?" What about Elisa? Where is she?"

"She's exactly where she needs to be. Like all the rest of them. She's like that song that goes something like this. Chandler mimicked the song. "Locked up, they won't let me out."

Ignoring his mockery through song, she continued her line of questioning. "How long have you been involved in this, Chandler? Will you at least tell me that much?"

"No, I won't tell you anything." Chandler leaned across the table until his face almost touched hers. "You tell me what you know about The Lynx operation. That's what you do," he demanded.

"I don't know anything about it except what I heard on the news earlier," Aisha told him.

With eyes blazing with rage, Chandler pointed his finger in her face, and threatened her. "I know you'll never tell me the part you played in all of this. But believe me, I swear if I ever find out you were mixed up in this, you'll be teaching dykes in a jail cell how to dance instead of young girls. For all I know, maybe you planned on pawning off some of the girls at your studio to Shipley and his group. After all, didn't you say you'd do anything to save your studio?"

Aisha felt her blood pressure rising. The words spewing from Chandler's mouth stung her repeatedly. How could he even form his lips to say the things he was saying to her? It became impossible for her to hold back her tears. She sat at the table and cried. Pellets of tears landed in her glass of tea.

"You really don't know me at all do you? If you think for one minute," she spoke between crying, "that I would allow harm to come to any of the girls at my studio or anywhere else, then you're the psycho. Okay, I admit it. I *was* a dancer at The Lynx. But I didn't know anything about the illegal side of that place. I was there to make some money to save my dance studio and that's it."

"Don't put on the sad little girl act now," Chandler's voice escalated. "You were there to support your drug habit. That's the reason you were there." His tone was evil and his words were wounding and full of sarcasm.

Stunned again, Aisha hated Chandler at that very moment. How could he have known that she had a drug habit? She never thought it was possible to feel hate toward another human being. She had always been taught to love others and have compassion for other people. But Chandler made her life's teachings null and void. The sound of his cruel words wafted in and out of her mind. Aisha's mind suddenly went into overdrive. There was something about Chandler. *But what?* she thought. *Think, Aisha, think.* Aisha listened closely to him and watched him even closer. He continued his verbal onslaught. Like a photographer focusing and zooming in with his camera, her mind zoomed in on Chandler. Then it clicked. She pointed an accusatory finger at him.

"It's you. *You're* him. You're Kyle Taylor." Aisha gasped at her discovery. "I recognize you now. Your voice, your build, everything. You were in a disguise. But it was you all along."

Aisha envisioned Chandler then she switched her mind to see him as Kyle. She was one hundred percent sure they were one in the same. Why couldn't she see it before? "When Jason brought me to your house, which probably isn't *your* house, after all," she said sarcastically. "I had a weird feeling about you. There was something familiar, but I pushed it aside. All the time you were pretending to be someone you're not. How could you?" Aisha was enraged at the thought of being deceived by Chandler. "How could you? I hate you!" Aisha jumped up and ran out of the cafe. Just as she made it to her car, Chandler was beside her.

"Sorry to bust your bubble, *Luscious*. But like the good book teaches, my sista," he mocked, "What's done in the dark surely will come to the light."

Looking at him with evil blazing in her eyes she asked, "Where is Elisa? Is she in jail? At least tell me that much."

"Don't you worry your pretty little head about Elisa," Chandler grabbed her by the waist and began twirling his fingers through Aisha's twists.

Aisha fought against his hold but she was no match against Chandler.

He turned her loose and pushed her away from him then he tilted his head back and released a hateful laugh.

"I want to know where she is!" People were beginning to stop and stare at them.

Chandler whirled around and flashed his police badge and they scattered. "I told you all you need to know. And don't bother trying to find her or her daughter," he commanded. "Now you go and have yourself a good night. That's an order." With that said, he turned and walked away, leaving Aisha standing next to her car, shocked and hurt.

# 32

Thursday, and time for her counseling session. Aisha called in to the studio to remind the receptionist she wouldn't be in until early afternoon. Usually she went to the studio first to check her messages or return calls up until it was time to leave for her counseling session with Minister Williams. But this morning she just wasn't feeling it.

Since starting the counseling sessions three weeks ago, Aisha had opened up very little to Minister Williams. Most of what she'd shared with him centered on her love of dance, how she started the studio and about the close relationship she had with her father before his death. Minister Williams hadn't forced her to talk about anything more, until last Thursday. That's when he explained to Aisha that at their next session, he wanted her to tell him her real reasons for seeking counseling. Aisha lounged around the apartment feeling unsure how she would tell him about her sordid past and drug addiction and contemplating if she should even go to today's session. To help calm her nerves, Aisha went to the kitchen and fixed herself a cup of hot decaf tea with lemon. She glanced at the clock on the kitchen counter—*7:45. Plenty of time to decide if I'm going to my session.* Aisha sipped her tea and turned on the 19 inch TV that she kept in the kitchen and began listening to the morning news.

The reporter talked about a murder that happened on the East side last night that was thought to be the result of a botched robbery. Then the reporter followed up with something more pleasant. "Urban Knowledge bookstore, at Southland Mall, is hosting a book signing event for New York Times Bestselling author, Carl Weber, Tuesday at 6 p.m," the red-haired reporter announced.

Next, Aisha listened to the meteorologist talk about the weather. The same red-haired reporter came on again after a commercial break.

Aisha got up from her favorite tomato red chair. She halted when she heard the reporter mention The Lynx.

"Ronald Shipley, former owner of The Lynx Association indicted last November on charges of capital kidnapping, drug trafficking and human trafficking, was sentenced to thirty five years to life. The remaining three people indicted in the sting will stand trial in the next few weeks. It has been reported that a fifth accomplice, Elisa Santana, the prosecution's star witness, has not been seen since the reading of the verdict. Speculation has it that she's been placed in the witness protection program. Stay tuned to the five o'clock edition of News Channel 24, giving you up to the minute news."

"So that explains Elisa's sudden disappearance," Aisha said out loud. "It all makes sense to me now. Maybe now she'll be able to make a decent life for her and Gabby without fear of Ronald's revenge. Take care of her, God. Take care of them both wherever they are," Aisha prayed.

Aisha turned off the television. In its place she turned on the radio. Yolanda Adams was singing *In The Midst Of It*

*All.* Aisha listened like she was hearing the song for the first time. "I've come through many hard trials . . . not because I've been so faithful . . ."

"God you *have* kept me in the midst of it all," she said. She listened to the rest of the song before getting dressed for her meeting with Jackson.

Aisha waved dryly when she passed the receptionist and continued to her morning session. She felt exceptionally down today and dreaded her meeting with Jackson Williams. If only she could have one hit of *baby girl*, she'd be fine. Most of her nights were spent tossing and turning and dreaming about the drug. When The Lynx was raided, her supply line was cut off. There were times when she considered going to some of the same drug infested neighborhoods where she once used to knock on doors and witness to people. Only she wouldn't be witnessing about the Lord. She'd be searching high and low for her drug of choice. So far she'd resisted the strong urge to do it. If Elisa were here, she'd know where to get some without having to resort to a street dealer. *Dang, I miss her. What am I thinking? I've got to get a grip*, Aisha thought.

She hurried along the familiar corridor leading to Jackson's office. With each step the tug of desire for *baby girl* intensified. She stopped, turned around and went back outside to her car in desperate search for even a crumb of coke. She rambled through her glove compartment, under the seat cushions and floor mats. There had to be some coke somewhere. She was growing more and more frantic by the minute. When she caught a reflection of herself in her rear view mirror, she sat upright in the seat and then leaned back. She pounded her fists against the dashboard, jumped out of the car and strode back inside the church.

Chandler spied from across the street until she disappeared inside Faithside Temple. For the past several weeks he'd been following her. Now that the trial had ended and

Ronald Shipley would never walk the streets of Memphis or anywhere again, he could concentrate on finding out if Aisha had anymore secrets he should know about. He didn't really want to see her go to prison, but if he discovered that she knew anything about The Lynx operation, he had no choice. He wouldn't rest until she was prosecuted to the fullest extent of the law. He looked at his cell phone to check the time, wondering what she could possibly be doing at the church every week. Like clockwork, he watched her arrive at Faithside between 9:30 and 9:45 a.m. every Thursday. *Whatever your reason, you better believe I'm going to find out sooner or later,* Chandler thought to himself as he sat in his car, waiting on her next move.

The session with Jackson helped Aisha feel somewhat invigorated. Almost as soon as she heard his voice, she dispelled any thoughts of her drug craving.

"Aisha, remember that I told you last week that at today's session, I want to delve deeper into some personal issues going on in your life." Jackson tapped his pen on his desk. "Are you willing to do that today?"

"I think so. But I don't know if you're going to like what I have to say," she answered nervously and rotated her fingers in a circular motion.

"Like I told you, I'm not here to judge you, Aisha. Quite the contrary. I'm here to listen and give you Godly counsel. Now why don't you start from the beginning," he urged.

He clasped his hands together and placed them underneath his chin. He didn't want to stare at her and make her feel uncomfortable, but she was ravishing. He could tell that whatever her real problem was, it was weighing heavy on her because while she was indeed beautiful, he often detected dark circles underneath her eyes. She was jittery too, like she had a lot on her mind. Out of all of his past rela-

tionships, none of them had been as lovely as Aisha
Carlisle.

During college and seminary, he could have had his
choice of women, but remaining true to his faith, Jackson
refused to be a player. He dated for the sole purpose of
finding a life long mate instead of physical gratification.
Being celibate was indeed hard, especially since he wasn't a
virgin. He'd had his share of sexual encounters, but since
entering ministry full time, he tried to present his body as a
living sacrifice. To Jackson, this meant that subjecting his
body to activities that were outside of the will of God was
unacceptable. Some of his friends were ministers too. One
of them smoked cigarettes, another one was still sexually
active, and yet another one, maybe two, had an occasional
drink and smoked. But Jackson didn't have the desire to do
any of it and he refused to judge or condemn them because
of their habits because he believed that every person had a
shortcoming. *"It's all about the heart,"* Jackson's father would
often say. *"If you believe and accept Jesus Christ as your Lord
and Savior. That's what matters."* Jackson fidgeted in his wide-
backed chair and leaned back to listen to Aisha.

It took several minutes of talking, about nothing in particular, before Aisha began to open up to Jackson. He watched
the way she moved her lips in a pouting manner and resisted the urge to tell her how pretty she was to him. The
more she talked, the more he wanted to hear.

"The studio was my dream, my answered prayer," she
told him.

"So tell me, when did things take a turn for you, Aisha?"
Jackson asked.

"When the studio turned from a dream into a nightmare.
You see, the owner of my building decided to sell it. But I
didn't have enough cash or assets to buy it. I couldn't bor-
row enough money, which I wasn't supposed to do any-

way. And I didn't have anyone who could loan me
$35,000."

"So why didn't you just move to another location?" he
asked in a sincere voice.

"Because moving was not an option for me. My students
are mostly inner city students. They already have enough
trouble getting to practice as it is. Moving the studio would
have meant that I would lose a considerable number of talented students. For some it was all they had to look forward to. The other thing was my credit. It stunk. I had student
loans, rent, car note, bank notes, credit cards, and anything
else you can think of. When the leasing agent contacted me
and told me the owner was going to sell the building, I
went into action."

"What did you do?"

"I petitioned for investors, put in for another loan at my
bank but I still came up short. So I did what I thought was
best for me at the time."

"And what was that?"

Listening to him, Aisha thought of how genuine he
sounded. His voice echoed with compassion and understanding. She hoped her intuition was right because she
was about to confess to him the double life she had been
living. Taking a deep breath, she looked down at her shaking hands.


"I'd like to go into the sanctuary to pray. I won't be
long." Chandler spoke, low and reserved.

"Sure, go right ahead," the receptionist said. "You do
know where to go, don't you?"

"Yes, ma'am. I think I know every square inch of this
church," he quickly lied.

"Go on then," she prompted.

"Thank you." He tipped his hat toward her. Chandler
saw that there were only a handful of people. An elderly

man sat on the front pew with his head bowed and eyes closed. A young couple was on bended knee at the altar holding hands. While perusing the rest of the sanctuary and balcony he saw five or six more people, but none came close to fitting Aisha's description. Just to be certain none of them were her, he quietly walked along the sanctuary and glanced at each person he passed. He did the same thing when he went upstairs to the balcony. Next, he walked to the other side of the church where the sign read, "Staff Offices" with an arrow pointing straight ahead.

"Aisha, there's nothing you can tell me that will make me think differently of you. So just relax and start talking," Jackson coaxed.

"The mother of one of my students made me an offer I couldn't possibly refuse," is how Aisha began. "She said that she knew how I could not only make a lot of money, but that I could make it quick. I didn't have to do a lot for it," she told me. She couldn't bring herself to look at Jackson's handsome face.

"Don't be afraid, Aisha. Let it out," Jackson told her in that same calm, soothing voice.

Still unable to look him in the face because of what she was about to divulge, Aisha kept her head bowed and continued to talk.

"I'm a private dancer at an exclusive men's club. No, wait. Let me rephrase that. I *was* a private dancer until the club was shut down by the Feds. I had special clients who were extremely wealthy, I must say. They paid me a lot of money to dance for them."

Jackson stared at her. His thoughts were scrambled but his attraction to her was still in place. "Would you like to take a break before going on?" Jackson offered. "I can get you a soda or coffee."

"No, I want to continue while I can. Anyway, I accepted

the job and my friend was right. The money was good. I made enough to buy the building, pay off my debts and then some. But that's not all. I don't know if I can tell you the rest," she said in shame.

"Don't stop now. The only way to confront what's attacking you is by talking about it and praying about it. I've been praying every day about you and your situation. But you've got to have faith for yourself and hope for your problems."

"Okay. I'll try." Aisha lifted her head slightly. "I'd never done anything like that before. I believed that a woman's body should be reserved for her husband. As for being physically intimate with them, I didn't engage in anything like that," she explained, raising her head. "I've preserved my virginity but what I have done is to showcase my body in an undesirable manner that I know God is not pleased with. I was no more than a stripper. The only difference in what I did and what a stripper does is that I happened to work for extremely wealthy clientele. And while I'm confessing, I guess I'll tell you the other part."

"What is it?" Jackson sat upright in his chair trying to prepare himself for what she was about to reveal.

"I have a cocaine addiction."

As many confessions and stories as he'd heard, Jackson Williams couldn't believe that the woman sitting before him was an addict. Had she not told him, he never would have suspected it. She was quite slender, almost frail, but to be on drugs, he never would have guessed that. He definitely would have to pray for God to deliver her from such a powerful stronghold.

"Do you snort it, use a pipe, a needle? What?" Jackson had to know. He had to find a way to help her.

"I snorted it. I haven't done it in a while now. Not because I haven't wanted to, but because they shut down The Lynx. But anyway, I lost my connection when they were busted. I didn't mean for it to get out of control. I only meant to use it to help me relax before I danced for my clients. It kept me energized, less shy and reserved. Before I realized it, I was using it all day every day. I had an endless supply available to me at no charge at my place of work. The more I became addicted, the less I turned to God and the church. It got so, I couldn't even pray." Aisha started to cry. "Before I came in here this morning, I wanted a hit so bad that I searched around in my car like a car thief.

Jackson opened his side desk drawer and pulled out a box of tissue and passed it over to Aisha. He wanted to sit beside her and hold her, to reassure her that everything would be all right, but she was in a fragile state and he was too attracted to her to do such a thing.

"Aisha, please don't cry," he begged. "I tell you what. Let's stop right here. You've shared a lot today and by confiding in me, you've shown that you trust me. What I want you to do when you finish your day is to read some scriptures. Begin with Romans chapter 7, verses 14 through 25." Jackson used his note pad to write down the passages of scripture he wanted Aisha to read. She looked so hopeless and helpless sitting across from him. "I also want you to read Romans 8 verses 1 through 4. Don't just read the scriptures. Meditate on them. Pray for spiritual understanding. It's well and fine for others to pray for you, Aisha, but you have to learn how to pray for yourself too. You're just as much a child of God as I am. And yes, you've made some mistakes and you've walked outside of God's will, but it doesn't change who you are."

Aisha cried even harder. "I'm sorry, but I can't help it. I hear what you're saying but it doesn't make me feel better about the decisions that I've made for my life. It doesn't change what I've done."

"Please stop crying." This time he walked over to where she was sitting and knelt down beside her. She could smell the scent of his cologne and the minty freshness of his breath as he spoke. He reached for her hands and gently held the tips of her fingers. Jackson looked her into her eyes. "I promise you right here and right now that everything will be all right. Just don't give up. Don't throw in the towel. Allow God to create something new in you. It may not happen over night, but you have my word. No, I take that back. You have God's promise that He is forever by your side, loving you just as much as He did before all of this." Without thinking, he reached up and pushed aside one of her fallen twists from her face. He grabbed a tissue and patted her cheeks until they were dry. Aisha stopped crying and began to watch the caring man kneeling before her. Her heart fluttered.

With compassion, Jackson asked her, "Will you read the scriptures?"

Aisha didn't respond immediately. But after several seconds of silence, she told him that she would do as he asked.

"There's one last thing I'd like you to do before you leave this morning. And that is to pray with me. Do you mind?"

How could she turn him down? Between sniffles she answered, "Okay."

Jackson prayed and asked God to guide Aisha's thoughts, her actions and her body. He prayed for deliverance from her addiction and for the guilt and condemnation she felt to be moved out of her life. When he finished his prayer, he got off his knees and sat next to her. "Feel better?" he asked.

"Yes. Thank you, Jackson. Thank you very much."

"I'm just doing God's will. Just doing God's will." He took hold of her smooth hands and gently helped her out of the chair. "Are you going to be all right?"

"Yes, sure. I'll see you next Thursday," she told him as she walked out of his office.

"Next Thursday? What about Sunday? You've come the

last few Sundays and I expect to see you again this Sunday."

A slight smile filled her face. "Sunday it is."

As Chandler made his way along the winding hallway, several office doors were open. He saw several staff members busily working. He had never thought about the inside operations of a church, but today he was getting a lesson in the behind the scene functions of a mega church. He walked to the other end of the hall, but no sign of Aisha. He was about to give up his search. *Where could she have gone?* he pondered.

The sound of the woman's voice caused him to pause. "You have a good day too, Natalie," the woman said.

As she made her way closer to him, Chandler recognized her clothing and her walk and knew that it was indeed Aisha. As she approached him, he saw her. Without looking in his direction, she turned down the opposite hallway. Chandler walked to the office where Aisha had just come out of. Though the door was still open, he could see the sign on it—Pastoral Care Offices. Chandler peeked inside at the woman sitting at her desk working on something at the computer. "Excuse me, miss," Chandler said politely.

Startled at the unannounced intruder, she jerked her head around quickly. "Yes, do you have an appointment?" she asked.

"No, no, ma'am. But my, my sister did and I was supposed to meet her after her session."

"Oh, well what's your sister's name?" Natalie asked, knowing that it had to be Aisha he was talking about since she had been the first appointment of the morning.

"Her name is Aisha. Aisha Carlisle. He smiled charmingly.

"Oh my, you just missed her. Her session ended a few minutes ago."

"Is that right? Oh well, let me see if I can catch her. She's probably out in the parking lot waiting for me. Thanks for your help." *So she must be running scared and now she's trying to make things right with God,* Chandler thought. *Poor baby, guilt must be eating her up,* he snickered and proceeded down the corridor leading to the outside. By the time he made it to the front of the church entrance, Aisha had disappeared.

After saying goodbye to Natalie, Aisha had proceeded to walk down the winding hallway. She hadn't noticed the gentleman at the opposite end of the hallway. She looked at her watch, glad that she had made plans to spend time with Tameria. After today's session, she was in desperate need of some girlfriend time.

# 33

Aisha maneuvered her car in and out of the mid-morning traffic. She called Angie. Kaye, the geeky receptionist, picked up and answered in an overly happy voice. "Good morning, Miss Carlisle. Are you on your way to the studio?"

"No, as a matter of fact I'm not. I forgot to let you know that I won't be in until around three. The girls should be coming in around that time. Is Angie near by?"

"Yes, hold on just a minute. I'll get her." Kaye paged Angie over the intercom. "Angie, Aisha on line three. Angie, Aisha on line three, please."

Angie heard the page and went to her office to retrieve the call. "Good morning, Aisha. How did your appointment go?" Angie didn't know the details of Aisha's weekly sessions, but she assumed they had to do with her father's death. Angie waited on Aisha's slow response.

"Everything went okay, I guess. But what I wanted to tell you was that I won't be in until later this afternoon. Tameria called last night and told me that her schedule is free today so we're going to hang out," Aisha explained.

"Oh, good. I know you two don't get the chance to see each other often. I tell you, when you get involved in the medical field, it's a big sacrifice isn't it?"

"Yes it is. But you know Tameria loves it. That's why I know she's doing exactly what she's supposed to be doing. I'm about to turn down her street now, so I'll talk to you later. I just wanted to let you know that you can reach me on my cell if anything comes up."

"Sure. See you later." Angie was about to hang up but stopped when she saw Kaye standing inside of her door, and waving her hands.

"Aisha, hold up. I think Kaye is trying to tell me something."

"Yes, what is it?"

"I need to talk to Miss Carlisle when you finish."

"Alright."

Kaye turned and proceeded to go back to her desk.

"Kaye needs to talk to you. I'll talk to you later. And you and Tameria have enough fun for me," Angie chuckled before placing Aisha on hold.

Angie buzzed Kaye.

"What is it, Kaye?" Aisha asked as soon as she heard the girl breathing over the phone.

"I almost forgot to tell you that someone called for you earlier. A guy, but he didn't want to leave his name."

"Is that right? Did he say what he wanted?" Aisha asked with a puzzled look on her face. She turned into Tameria's driveway and opened the car door.

"He wanted to know if you had made it back in the office."

"*Back* in the office?"

"Yes, that's what he said," Kaye assured her.

"And he didn't say who he was?"

"Nope. When I asked him his name, he hung up. I looked

on the office caller ID and it said unknown name—unknown number."

"It was probably some salesman wanting to sell me some more equipment or something. If anyone else calls, just put them into my Audix. I'll check it later." Aisha ended the call but wondered who the caller could have been. She pushed Tameria's doorbell.

*Who was it that knew I was out of the office? Who could it have been?* She thought about Chase, but why would Chase call her? *Maybe it was Minister Williams. No, I just left him. Plus he would have left a message.* Tameria opened the door and halted the guessing game playing in Aisha's mind.

"Good morning," Tameria said happily.

"Hey, Tameria," she replied and stepped inside her cluttered apartment. Aisha walked over to Tameria's favorite chair she had owned since high school. She rested her butt on the arm of it. Tameria used to be the kind of person who kept everything in order, but since med school she was hardly ever home and her free time was spent at Chase's place. Aisha looked around at the medical books spread out over the sofa and floor.

"I know. Don't even say it. The place is a disaster but I'm off tomorrow too and I've already made plans to clean up from top to bottom. Tameria looked around the room. "I can't stand all of this clutter."

"I know that's right. What's on the agenda for us today? If you want, we can stay here and I'll help you tidy things up."

"No way! Off days from the hospital come far and few. I do not want to spend it cooped up in this apartment cleaning. I thought we'd go shopping and then have lunch. Whaddaya say?"

"That'll work. Let's get out of here then." Aisha pounced off the arm of the chair.

* * *

The two friends shopped until they dropped. Aisha bought a tangerine jogging suit, a diamond print DKNY mermaid skirt and two pairs of sling backs. Tameria couldn't resist going into Victoria's Secret. Aisha couldn't believe it. Tameria was never shy or inhibited but she'd never guess that she'd want to get something out of Victoria's Secret.

"Tameria, I know you aren't going to get anything in here," Aisha leaned over and whispered.

Tameria continued to browse through the undergarment section until she chose two pair of no-show panties and a fire red thong and bra set. Aisha was speechless but she refused to comment.

"Don't start your criticizing, Aisha. I know you don't want me to go there with you again."

"I wasn't criticizing you. I was just going to say that you're really flaunting your stuff aren't you." She managed to release a fake laugh.

"How is buying panties flaunting my stuff, Aisha? You can never have enough bras and panties. That's what my mother always said and working in a hospital emergency room, you better believe I've seen the worst when it comes to undergarments." Tameria turned her upper lip until it covered her nostrils. Without missing a beat she pulled out a couple more bras for her size DD breasts and happily went to the counter with her garments tucked safely in her hands.

Aisha chose not to respond. While Tameria paid for her items, Aisha browsed through some of the lotions and oils.

"Okay, on to the next store." Tameria scooped up her bag.

"Hey, let's go inside that new store over there," Aisha suggested, and pointed across the way.

Quickly putting aside their near confrontation, the two of them giggled when they saw a guy and girl pass in front of them holding hands, both with pink and blue hair.

"Can you believe that?" Tameria turned her head and followed the odd looking couple with her eyes. "Love truly is blind."

"I just can't believe they're black. If they were white, I wouldn't think anything of it 'cause white people will die their hair green, orange and any other color without thinking. But us? No way."

"Yea, but wait a minute," Tameria added and kept on laughing. "You know we can be ghetto fabulous ourselves. We'll dye ours kool-aid burgundy and peroxide blonde in a minute." They were still laughing and chattering as they made their way over to the store. They searched through the sale items until they each found a pair of jeans they liked and shirts to match.

With almost an armful of shopping bags, their next stop was the food court. While munching on chicken nuggets and waffle fries, they people-watched between bites. "So you're telling me that you still haven't heard from Chandler?"

"That's right. And I don't want to either. Chandler said some cruel, disrespectful things to me the last time we talked. I refuse to go through that with him or any other man. Not to mention he lied about his profession. All the time I thought Mr. Right had come along and he turns out to be a liar and a skeezer. I guess he was using me all along so he could make himself look good. I think he thought he was going to catch me mixed up with those terrible men at The Lynx. But thank God, I didn't know anything about it."

"You got that right. Instead of sitting here eating in the mall, you could have been serving time. You see why you need to get your life back on track? God has been far too good to you for you to keep on doing what you were doing. You need some help."

"Puhleeze, Tameria, don't ruin the day. I don't need to be preached to." Aisha shrugged her shoulders and held her head down.

"Preaching is *exactly* what you need. Are you still using drugs? And tell me the truth too," Tameria insisted. "I'm your friend, but I'm also a doctor, and doing drugs can be not only addictive, but deadly."

"I've started going to Cocaine Anonymous meetings at the church. Minister Williams convinced me to try it. I've been a couple of times. To be honest, once I got over the initial shame of walking into my first meeting, I've been doing okay. I haven't had a hit of coke for four weeks and a day."

Tameria stood up and went over to hug Aisha. "I knew you could do it. You just have to take it one day at a time. I'm proud of you," she said as she went back to her seat. "Sounds like Minister Williams has some influence, huh."

"You can say that. I think it's the way he listens without making me feel worse than I already feel. He doesn't look at me like I'm a terrible person. I feel comfortable talking to him. To be honest, I look forward to our sessions on Thursdays. I really do." Aisha looked as if she were in a daze as she talked about Jackson Williams. Tameria noticed the sparkle in her eyes and the manner in which Aisha spoke about him. Maybe Aisha wasn't aware of it, but Tameria could tell that Aisha liked Jackson Williams a lot.

Tameria changed the subject. "Have you heard from your mother?"

"I've tried talking to her but she's so cold toward me. I don't know what else to say or do. I love my mother and I'm sorry for so many things, Tameria." Aisha's voice dropped and Tameria detected her sadness.

"Just give her time. She has her own burdens to bear too."

"That's what Jackson, I mean Minister Williams said."

Tameria raised her eyebrows when Aisha called Minister Williams by his first name. *So things are on a more personal level*, Tameria thought to herself but acted like she hadn't noticed Aisha's slip of the tongue.

"He told me to give her time to come around because she's still grieving. I just don't know how much more time she needs though. I wish I could help her in some way. If we pulled together instead of apart, maybe Daddy's death wouldn't be so hard to deal with."

"Everything will work out. You'll see." Tameria reached over and grabbed Aisha's hand and squeezed it. "Come on, let's get out of here." Tameria looked at her watch. "Didn't you say you wanted to be at the studio by three?"

"Yeah," looking at her watch Aisha added, "It's one forty now. By the time you take me to your place to get my car and I drop off my clothes at the apartment, it'll be close to three. So you're right. Let's go."

The drive to Tameria's afforded the two friends more time to talk and enjoy each other's company. Tameria told Aisha that she'd met Chase's parents and they loved her. Tameria said she couldn't see herself spending her life with anyone else but him. Her cell phone rang and she looked down to pick it up and almost rear ended the car in front of her. Aisha tightly gripped the door handle. Tameria giggled and made smooching sounds in the phone. She was still talking to Chase when she turned off the I-240 exit on to Bill Morris Parkway.

Aisha used her time to dial her Audix and retrieve her messages. She didn't want to keep listening to their lovey-dovey conversation. Especially when she had no one to love.

# 34

Jackson positioned himself on his extra long blumarine sofa. He fluffed its pillows, stretched out, and then crossed his legs one over the other. He turned his big screen to channel 633 and he began watching the Memphis Grizzlies' basketball game. Tonight they were playing against the Cleveland Cavaliers. He wanted to see if the Grizzlies could do a repeat of their last win against the Rockets. Normally he would be putting his season tickets to use by rooting for the Grizzlies in person at the FedEx Forum but the day had been a long, tiring one, so he had made a hard decision to stay at home.

He had counseled twelve church members today plus attended the weekly youth meeting. He awarded two young men with his tickets for tonight's game. They deserved it and Jackson wanted to show them how much he thought of them. Living in one of the worst areas of the city, the two young men had been involved heavily in drugs and gang activity. Both of them were high school dropouts who lacked parental influence and supervision. The Youth Program turned out to be their saving grace. During the past year, they had managed to make a 360 degree turn by giving up drug dealing and gang involvement. It hadn't been an easy road for either of them. There often were deadly consequences when a gang member wanted out, but it was God's grace that had kept them both safe. It was a small-time neighborhood gang claiming to be as bad and as dangerous as some of the more notorious ones. Their bark, thank God, was far worse than their bite.

The two youths had recently accepted Jesus Christ into their hearts. The difference in their personalities was remarkable. They attended the GED classes offered at Faithside and the Human Resources manager hired them at the church to work along with the sound engineer. When Jackson gave them the tickets, they were ecstatic and humbled at their blessing. Jackson felt just as good, knowing he had brightened the life, if only for a moment, of the two young men.

"Oooohhhh!" He screamed when Gasol made a three pointer. At half time, he went into his modern kitchen and fixed himself a turkey burger on his George Foreman grill and added ice to his all time favorite drink, root beer.

The past week's events flashed through his mind. When he thought of Aisha, he put his mind on pause and gave himself permission to reflect on the woman who pricked his heart each time he was in her presence. She had no idea that he understood her hurt and pain. The relationship with his mother had been a strained one as well, which is why he understood Aisha when she told him about her mother's attitude toward her.

Jackson never had the desire to become an attorney like his mother. His mind was always focused on Jesus. Every time his father made a step toward their front door, Jackson was at his heels determined to go along. Unlike most children, any time the church doors opened, he wanted to walk through them. Any and everything that had to do with God and church, Jackson yearned to be part of it.

His father was thankful that his youngest son loved the Lord as much as he did. Jackson's father and mother often argued about all the time Jackson's father spent away from home preaching, counseling, visiting the sick and doing anything he could to help save someone else's soul from going to hell. She disliked it even more when he started taking Jackson along with him. The friction intensified in the couple's relationship, and after fifteen years of marriage, Jackson's mother left.

Jackson refused to move with her and his two brothers. Once it was made apparent how much he wanted to stay with his father, she relented and allowed him to remain with his dad. She had very little to do with Jackson and his father after that. It took years for Jackson to let go of the anger he felt toward his mother for walking out on him and his daddy. But once he did, he began to slowly allow her back into his life. She told him she felt like he chose his father over her. But Jackson wanted her to know that it wasn't his father he chose over her, it was God, and that choice was something he would never be sorry for. How could anyone be jealous of a man that was called to do God's work? Jackson decided he would stop trying to answer that question and instead, he did like God wanted him to do, which was to love his mother unconditionally and to forgive her.

He took small bites from his sandwich and decided that at the next session he would share his story with Aisha. He wanted her to know that he truly understood some of her pain. She seemed to be doing better physically and mentally since she started attending Cocaine Anonymous. For that he was grateful.

He noticed that the last time she came to his office, she

appeared much healthier. In the beginning, he suspected she was fighting hard not to let him know she was on drugs. But he'd seen enough people on drugs to recognize that she was one of them. One of his close friends from high school was on crack back in Ohio. From what Jackson had heard from some of his other buddies back home, the guy was basically living on the streets and walked around begging for money to buy his next rock. Jackson had him on his long prayer list. Every day he called out the man's name. He did the same when it came to Aisha. He believed with all his heart that God had great things in store for her. Now he had to get her to believe it as well.

Of all the people he had counseled, Aisha was rather special. She possessed some of the qualities that he wanted in a wife. She was kind and humble with a spirit that radiated love and sincerity. Sure she had a lot of healing to do, but he saw past her imperfections and focused on the Godly woman he knew was inside of her. He thought about her smile, the way she threw her head back when she laughed and how it broke his heart each time he witnessed her tears and pain. Out loud he made his requests for her healing to God then assumed his previous position and started watching the ballgame again.

Aisha climbed out of the bath tub, dried off and curled up in her favorite chair. She was exhausted after coming home yet again from another Cocaine Anonymous meeting. When she initially joined the group she made a pledge to attend ninety meetings in ninety days. It was tough, but she was determined to beat her drug addiction and make things right in her life.

This time when she opened the nightstand drawer, she wasn't searching for a hit, she was looking for the white sheet of typing paper with the twelve steps of Cocaine

Anonymous printed on it. She picked up the paper, went over to her chair and began to recite out loud the twelve steps.

## The Twelve Steps of Recovery—Cocaine Anonymous

- I admit I am powerless over cocaine and all other mind-altering substances—that my life had become unmanageable.
- I believe that a Power greater than myself can restore me to sanity.
- I made a decision to turn my will and my life over to the care of God as I understand Him.
- I made a searching and fearless moral inventory of myself.
- I admitted to God, to myself, and to another human being the exact nature of my wrongs.
- I am entirely ready to have God remove all these defects of character.
- I humbly ask Him to remove my shortcomings.
- I made a list of all persons I have harmed, and I am willing to make amends to them all.
- I made direct amends to such people wherever possible, except when to do so would injure them or others.
- I take personal inventory and when I am wrong promptly admit it.
- I seek through prayer and meditation to improve my conscious contact with God, praying only for knowledge of His will for me and the power to carry that out.
- Having had a spiritual awakening as the result of these steps, I try to carry this message to addicts, and to practice these principles in all my affairs.

She made it a daily ritual to recite the steps after she prayed every morning and before she prayed at night. Her sponsor, a recovering addict named Beverly, had been clean and sober going on three years. Whenever Aisha felt the pressure of the drug tugging at her, she picked up the phone and called Beverly for support. The program was her lifeline to a drug-free life. She prayed that she would not go down the destructive path of using drugs again.

The ringing of the phone startled her. Her first thought was to let it ring. Whoever was on the other end could leave a message if it was important. Her decision was quickly changed when an unfamiliar Little Rock number appeared on the Caller ID.

Curious, Aisha answered. "Hello."

"Aisha?" the woman said.

"Yes, who is this?"

"Mrs. Simmons. Your mother's next door neighbor." Aisha didn't know if she could take what she believed Mrs. Simmons was about to tell her. Her heart started pounding against her chest and her hands shook.

"Is my mother all right?" Aisha asked in a panic.

"She didn't want me to call you, but I did anyway. My husband and I had to take her to the emergency room. She kept complaining about being short of breath. She was sweating and could barely talk."

"Mrs. Simmons, is my mother okay?" Aisha asked again in a loud voice.

"Darling, calm down. She's going to be fine. They kept her in the hospital though because they suspect she has a mild case of pneumonia. We just left there, me and my husband and some of the other church members."

"What hospital did you take her to, Mrs. Simmons?"

"She's at St. Vincent, baby. Now you be careful driving over here. You need to get somebody to come with you because you're too upset."

"Thank you for calling me, Mrs. Simmons." Aisha didn't take Mrs. Simmons advice. She hung up the phone, hurriedly threw on some clothes and dashed out the door.

Two hours later, not only had Aisha made it to Little Rock, but she was at the hospital, and on her way to her mother's room.

Aisha tapped on the closed door before pushing it open and going inside. She saw her mother in the bed with an oxygen tent over her. "Mother, how do you feel?" Aisha's voice was tender as she spoke to her mother and stroked her forehead. "I came as soon as I heard."

Sandra Carlisle removed the oxygen mask from over her nose and mouth. "You didn't have to do that. I'm fine. I bet Mattie Simmons called you, didn't she?"

"Mother, it doesn't matter who called because it was the right thing to do."

"I told her not to call anybody but my church members and the pastor. There was no need for you to come all the way over here."

"Well, I'm here and I'm not going anywhere until you're better. Now you just close your eyes and get some sleep." Aisha kissed her mother's sweaty forehead and pushed back the loose strands of gray hair away from her mother's face. Within a few minutes, Mrs. Carlisle was asleep. Aisha sat down in the chair next to her mother's bed and watched her while she slept. Her own eyes became heavy and she succumbed to the call of her body to rest.

"Mrs. Carlisle, how are you feeling, hon?" a short white chubby nurse asked her. Aisha's eyes flew open and she sat upright in the chair, rubbing her eyes.

"I'm feeling better. My breathing is better too," Sandra said in a weak voice.

"Good. Who is this young lady here with you?"

Sandra looked over at Aisha. Her voice was weak and she sounded like she was struggling to talk. "My daughter."

"Hi, daughter," the nurse teased.

Aisha nodded and smiled. "Hello. My name is Aisha. Nurse, is my mother going to be okay?"

"Yes, but she does have pneumonia and it can be rough on our older patients. The doctor will be able to tell you more when he makes his rounds first thing in the morning. Will you still be here?"

"Yes, I'll be here. And thank you."

"No problem. Mrs. Carlisle, I want you to take this pill for me, hon. It'll help you rest easier tonight." She gave her a glass of water with the pill and without any protest, Sandra swallowed it. "Good girl," she said like Mrs. Carlisle was a child instead of a seventy-two year old woman. The nurse patted Sandra on the legs and said, "Press the button on the side of the bed if you need anything, hon."

Aisha pulled open each drawer in the room until she found a hospital blanket. Sitting back down, she proceeded to make herself comfortable in the oversized leather recliner that would serve as her bed for the night.

The following morning, when Sandra's doctor came, he didn't waste any time assuring Aisha that her mother would be fine. He explained that he was going to keep her in the hospital for at least another few days just to make sure the fluid on her lungs was clearing up.

"Aisha," her mother called out soon after the doctor left. Aisha leaped up from the chair and rushed to her mother's bedside.

"What is it, Mother?" Aisha asked.

"Shouldn't you be at work? I told you I'm fine and you heard what the doctor said."

"Mother, I'm not going anywhere. I already called Angie and told her where I was. She knows how to reach me if she needs me. Anyway, I'm not worried about the studio right now. I'm going to be here for you as long as I have to." Aisha became upset when she witnessed the tears falling from her mother's eyes.

"Momma, what's wrong? Are you in pain? Do you want me to get the nurse?"

"No, no. I was just thinking."

"Thinking about what, Mother?"

"Never mind, I'd just like to rest now." Sandra Carlisle turned over away from the glares of her daughter.

Irritated, Aisha responded, "I wish you wouldn't do that."

"Do what? What have I done now?"

Aisha felt her temper rising against her mother but managed to keep it in check. Now was not the time to explode. But this was her mother's typical way of getting Aisha on edge and she was sick of it. But there was nothing she felt she could do about it because disrespecting her mother was the last thing she wanted to do.

"Mother, look you go on and rest. I'm going downstairs to the cafeteria to grab a bite to eat. I'll be back shortly."

Without turning to look at Aisha, her mother responded curtly, "No need to hurry. I told you anyway that I would be fine. You should go back to Memphis and see about your dance studio."

Ignoring her mother's comments, Aisha proceeded to walk out of the room. *Not tonight. I am not going there with her tonight,* she repeated to herself. She went outside and sat on the veranda. Inhaling the fresh air and feeling the night air against her body sent a shiver up and down her spine. Why did she let her mother get under her skin? It was time she learned to do like her father told her—"let it roll off you like water rolls off of oil," is what he would often tell her. But through all these years, she'd not yet learned how not to let her mother's harsh reprimands and stinging comments affect her.

Reaching on the side of her jeans, she removed her cell phone from its clip and turned it on. Aisha phoned Beverly and told her where she was. Beverly searched on the internet for Cocaine Anonymous meeting places, in or surrounding St Vincent Hospital, while Aisha waited on the other end of the phone. The two of them were elated to discover that a nearby community center held a nightly meeting seven days a week. It was remarkable—God had opened another door for her to walk through, and she was going to take it.

# 35

Aisha met up with the doctor at the entrance to her mother's hospital room. As he opened the door for her, she anxiously stepped ahead of him to hear his latest report concerning her mother.

"Mrs. Carlisle, how are you feeling today?" the doctor asked her.

"I'm feeling fine, doctor. I want to go home. I've been lying in this bed for God knows how many days," she complained.

"Well, the last series of tests we performed late yesterday show significant fluid decrease. I'm pleased with your rate of recovery."

"Thank you, God. Doctor, you have made my day. Now tell me, when can I get out of here?" Sandra eased upright in the hospital bed and waited on his response.

"You can be discharged this afternoon if you promise to follow my instructions."

Sandra raised her left eyebrow and slowly folded her arms.

"You are not completely over this. Until you've regained

some of your strength, I want someone with you around the clock. If that's not possible, I'll have to insist that you remain in the hospital for a few more days." He shifted his piercing green eyes in Aisha's direction.

"Doctor, there's no need to look at her. She has her own life to lead in Memphis. I have good neighbors and church members who won't mind watching out for me."

Aisha managed to hold back her embarrassment over her mother's thoughtless comments. *Just who does she think she is? Acting as if I don't have time for her?* For now, she held her tongue so the wrong words wouldn't spill out. *Lord have mercy.*

"I understand that your daughter has her own life. And I'm certainly not one to tell you who should or shouldn't take care of you over these next couple of weeks. My main concern is that you have someone with you. You're still weak and you still have some healing to do. Is that clear?" The doctor was stern and refused to leave until Mrs. Carlisle promised to follow his directions.

"I understand, doctor. Like I told you. I have plenty of people, thank God, to help me."

"That's fine, Mrs. Carlisle. He studied her chart like he was searching for anything he may have forgotten to cover. "I want to see you in my office in one week." Any questions before I leave?" he asked Mrs. Carlisle and Aisha.

Both of them shook their heads. "No I don't have any," was Aisha's response.

"I think you've answered all of my questions," was Sandra's response. "But I know how to call your office if I think of anything. No need to worry about that because you know I will."

"Yes, how well I do know," the doctor laughed. Sandra Carlisle was not one to mince words. Whenever she came to his office for any reason she commanded the full attention of his staff.

Aisha reached out and shook his hand and thanked him for taking such good care of her mother.

"Aisha, I meant what I told that doctor. There's no need for you to keep staying over here. You haven't been home in God knows when. Mattie will help look out for me. She told me that yesterday when she came up here to see me. And my church has some of the sweetest members. Pastor already made it clear that it's the church's responsibility to take care of the elderly and the widows. I don't want to stop you from living your life. I'll be just fine."

"Why do you do that?"

"What on earth are you talking about now?" her mother sighed, eased down in her bed and pulled the dingy white hospital covers up to her shoulders.

"Mother, please. You know full well what I'm talking about. Telling the doctor that I needed to get back home to Memphis. I've been here for you ever since Mrs. Simmons called and told me you were sick," Aisha fussed.

"Exactly. And that's what I'm talking about. You need to get back to a sense of normalcy. If you keep on, you're going to let that studio of yours go down the drain. You can't keep putting all of your responsibility on poor Angie."

"Will you let me handle my own business? Angie is totally capable of running things while I'm away. Plus, I talk to her every day. Sometimes three or four times a day."

"Look, I don't want to argue with you. I'm trying to get well. You're just like your father—stubborn and strong-willed. He never wanted to listen to what anybody else had to say. And you're a carbon copy."

"I *do* listen to you. But I also listened to the person who knows what you need better than you right now—your doctor. So I don't want to hear about what I can do or should be doing. Or hear you talk about daddy like it's so terrible for me to be like him. The only thing I'm going to be doing is taking care of you. And that's that."

Aisha walked over to the huge picture window and looked out over the city. She looked back and realized her mother had fallen asleep. Aisha stole the opportunity to begin gathering the small wardrobe and the mini florist's shop her mother had managed to collect during her hospital stay. One thing was for sure, her mother had many friends at the church she'd joined when she moved to Little Rock. The small congregation of Holiness Tabernacle of Praises was the perfect size. It offered Sandra the attention she always craved from others. The people adored her. Regardless of this, Aisha felt it was her responsibility and no one else's to take care of her mother. Sure, she wouldn't deny any one from helping out, but ultimately she wanted to be her mother's caregiver. It took almost an hour for her to finish packing everything. Next she went to the Nurse's Station to check on the discharge papers and the medications the doctor wanted her mother to take. Once she finished doing that, she called and talked to Angie and updated her on her mother's condition.

"Angie, I haven't received any more strange calls have I?" Aisha inquired.

"No. Not that I know of. Kaye hasn't said anything to me. The calls she passes my way have all been regarding something legit pertaining to the studio. Is everything okay?"

"Yeah, sure. I was just checking that's all. You know where to find me if you need me. And again, thanks for handling everything at the studio."

"Girl, please you're not only my boss, you're my friend Aisha. And friends help each other out during times like this."

"Well, I certainly couldn't do this without your support. I'm going to let you go before I start boo hooing. Just put me in my Audix so I can check my messages. I'll call you later. Bye bye," Angie said and transferred her.

Aisha quickly bypassed the automated instructions. A couple of calls were from people checking to see if she had any available slots for new students. She forwarded the message to Angie's Audix. The next call totally caught Aisha by surprise. It was from Minister Williams. As soon as she heard his voice, she flipped out. She had totally forgotten about their Thursday meetings. When was the last time she had attended a counseling session? "Oh my, God! I can *not* believe this, and I haven't even bothered to call him. He must think I'm an idiot."

An hour later, Jackson informed Natalie that he was leaving the building and offered to bring her back a sandwich.

"No thanks, Minister Williams. I'm going to the cafeteria to get a salad and a sandwich a little later. Thanks anyway."

"No problem."

"Are you going to be away long? Because if you are, I want to remind you that tonight is the Ministers' Meeting."

"I know. I have it in my BlackBerry. I shouldn't be gone more than a couple of hours. You know how to reach me if something comes up."

"Yes, sir." Natalie made a thumbs-up sign and smiled. She loved being Minister Williams' Admin. He was easy to work for, considerate and thoughtful too. *If I wasn't close to being a senior citizen, I'd give these young women at the church a run for their money. And that Aisha Carlisle doesn't seem to be aware that he has a special attraction for her. I can see it and I'm blind as a bat.* She laughed out loud then turned around in her swivel chair to resume working on the quarterly Pastoral Care report.

Jackson floored the accelerator of his pearl blue Chrysler Crossfire on to the interstate. There was hardly any traffic, which was unusual for a Friday. But it was to his benefit because he felt like he had the road to himself. For some reason, driving relaxed him. He drove until he read the green sign that said Bailey Station exit. He took it and continued his drive through Collierville. The town was growing rapidly and the hustle and bustle of traffic was more than he expected. Nevertheless, it worked in his favor because it forced him to slow down and take in the beauty of God's world. He could no longer ignore the rumbling sounds of his stomach so he stopped at his favorite restaurant for a bite to eat.

After placing his order for Cajun chicken pasta, Jackson took his phone out of its side clip and dialed Aisha's office again. This time, instead of a live person answering, Aisha's phone automatically rolled over into voicemail.

"Aisha, Minister Williams here. I hope you're all right. I haven't heard from you. Natalie said you haven't called to cancel any of your appointments. Give me a call when you can to let me know how you're doing." The next two messages were also from Jackson. "Aisha, it's me again. Jackson Williams. Are you okay?" I'm really worried now. Please call me. And remember, God is everywhere you are, call on Him."

Aisha could tell by his somewhat pleading voice that he was genuinely worried about her. He probably thought she was back on drugs which she thanked God was far from the truth. His last message made her smile. His concern for her was touching.

"Guess what? Me again." Jackson thought to add a bit of humor to this message. Jackson didn't want to come off like he was overly concerned about her, although he was. "Aisha, I know what you're probably thinking; this minister has flipped his wig." Jackson chuckled over the phone at his own corny remark. "But not to worry, I'm not the wig wearing type," Jackson laughed again. "Seriously, though, if you've decided not to attend any more counseling sessions, then call me, or Natalie, and let one of us know. I promise I won't be mad at you. God Bless you, goodbye."

*He sounds so sweet.* Aisha saved the message. I really do owe him an explanation as to why I haven't been coming to my sessions. He must *really* think I'm crazy now. She picked up her cell phone and scrolled through her contacts. The receptionist forwarded her to Pastoral Care. Natalie answered the phone.

"Natalie, is Minister Williams available?" Aisha asked politely.

"May I tell him whose calling?"

"Yes. This is Aisha Carlisle."

"Aisha. I mean Miss Carlisle."

"No, you were right the first time. Please call me Aisha."

"Well, Aisha, Pastor Williams and I have been really concerned about you. It's like you just dropped off the face of the earth. And Minister Williams said he hasn't seen you at any of the services lately.

"Thank you, Natalie. Did you say Minister Williams was in his office?"

"Oh, no I didn't say. I'm sorry. I get carried away sometimes you know. Anyway, he's out of the building right now. I can take your number and have him call you when he returns if you'd like."

"Yes, yes that would be fine. By the way, Natalie, let me give you my cell phone number. The member form doesn't ask for one. It's easier to reach me there," Aisha remarked.

"I keep telling the church secretary that form needs to be revised. Just about everybody has a cell phone these days," Natalie chuckled, while Aisha rattled off the number.

"Thanks, Natalie. Be sure to let him know I called."

"I sure will. You take care and have a blessed day." Natalie hung up the phone and started typing an email to the church secretary about updating the member forms again.

# 36

"I'm ready to go home." Sandra woke up from her two hour nap. "Have they finished writing up my discharge papers?" she asked groggily.

"Mother, everything is fine." Aisha rubbed her mother's shoulder, hoping to calm her down. "By the time you get dressed, we should be able to call for a wheelchair. Then I'll take you home. Come on, let me help you out of the bed so you can get dressed. And please, take your time. You may think you're okay, but you still have a long way to go before you get your energy level back up.

"I hear you. And I know what the doctor said. I was here, remember?" Mrs. Carlisle retorted.

In addition to taking care of her mother, Aisha took the time to clean out her mother's cupboards and closets. When Sandra moved to Little Rock, she moved many of Benjamin's belongings right along with her. There were still plenty of clothes of her father's that needed to be given to someone who could use them. Before she washed them, she breathed in for the last time, his scent. Folding and packing the freshly washed clothes, she placed them in several large bags before carrying them out to her car. After her CA meeting, she planned to stop by her mother's church and donate the remaining clothes to the Clothes Closet.

Sandra reclined in her bedside chair and reached for her Bible lying on the TV tray next to it. Before she contracted pneumonia, her Sunday School class at church had committed to reading the Bible in one year. They had made it to the book of Psalms, chapter 89. Sandra turned to the chapter, read it and finished it. For the purpose of catching up with the rest of her class, she started on the next chapter. As she read chapter 90, Sandra began to sense that God was speaking to her through the scriptures. Each verse she read seemed to jump off the page at her. "For a thousand years in thy sight are but as yesterday when it is past, and as a watch in the night." Sandra read. ". . . For we are consumed by thine anger, and by thy wrath are we troubled . . . For all our days are passed away in thy wrath: we spend our years as a tale that is told." Sandra placed one hand over her heart. Her face became flushed and tears landed on her satin nightgown, as she started to think about her relationship with Aisha. Why couldn't she let go of the bitterness she felt toward her child? Benjamin was gone now, and no one, or nothing, could ever change that. All she had left *was* Aisha, Benjamin's princess. Within her spirit, Sandra heard a voice saying, *It's time to make things right with your daughter. Tomorrow is promised to no one, my child. Go to your daughter.* Sandra sighed heavily. Through her tears, she continued reading. "Who knoweth the power of thine anger? Even according to thy fear, so is thy wrath. So teach us to number our days, that we may apply our hearts unto wisdom." Closing her Bible, Sandra bowed her head and prayed to God for the strength to let go of anything that would keep a wedge between her and Aisha.

Sandra heard Aisha shuffling about the house doing

things that she'd wanted done but hadn't been able to do. "Mother, I'll be back," Aisha yelled from the front room. "I'm going to drop the last of Daddy's things off at your church for their Clothes Closet."

Aisha walked up the hall to her mother's room just to make sure she had heard her. Standing in the entrance to the master bedroom, Aisha said it again, "I'm going to drop the rest of Daddy's things off at your church. I'll bring us some Chinese food back for dinner. That is unless you want something else." When her mother still didn't acknowledge her, Aisha walked over to her bedside. "Mother, are you all right?"

Sandra slowly looked up at her.

"Mother, what's wrong? You look like you've been crying." Aisha rested her hand on her mother's shoulder. "Are you in pain?" Aisha sat on the bed in front of her mother and felt her forehead to see if she was warm.

Sandra gently removed Aisha's hand from off of her forehead. "I'm fine. Go ahead and take care of your daddy's things," Sandra told her daughter. "I had planned on taking them, but I could never bring myself to do it. I'm glad you're doing it for me."

"Well, I tried to do it several times before now, but you wouldn't let me."

"I know, but I just couldn't at the time."

"I know, Mother. I understand. It was difficult for me too. Somehow even though I know he isn't coming back, when I was packing his things, it hit me again and I began to miss him terribly." Aisha blinked repeatedly in an effort to keep her own tears from falling. "The last thing she wanted to do was make her mother more upset than she already was.

"You go on before it gets dark out there. And Chinese is fine with me. You know what I like."

"Okay, I'll be back as soon as I can. I've already talked to Mrs. Simmons and she's going to come over and sit with you until I make it back."

"I wish you wouldn't worry Mattie. I told you that I'll be fine."

"Well, I won't be fine if I know you're here alone." Aisha kissed her mother's forehead and turned to leave. Just as she made it to the back door, Mrs. Simmons ambled up the concrete path.

"Hello, Mrs. Simmons. Thanks again for coming over."

"Honey, please, I don't mind at all. Me and Sandra are close like that. There's nothing I wouldn't do for that woman and I know she'd do the same for me. So you go on. Take your time too."

"Yes, ma'am. I'm going to stop and get some Chinese. Do you want me to bring you something back?"

"No, young lady. Me and Chinese don't see eye to eye. Plus I just ate not too long ago." She reared back and laughed.

Aisha closed the back door behind her, got in her car and drove off. Along the way, she thought about a gamut of things that had transpired during the year, most of them unpleasant. The death of her father, Chandler, who turned out to be a policeman, The Lynx, Elisa, her drug addiction and of course, Jackson. It was when she thought about Jackson that she smiled.

The Clothes Closet at her mother's church was glad to take her father's things. The woman overseeing the Clothes Closet told Aisha there was always a shortage of men's clothing, so her mother's donation of the clothes was much needed. *Mother will be glad to know that.*

On her way out of the church, the Pastor saw Aisha and stopped her so he could ask how her mother was doing. They talked for a few minutes then Aisha left and drove to the Chinese restaurant which was about twenty minutes away from where her mother lived.

Two hours after leaving to run her errands, she was turning her car back on to her mother's street. Aisha got out, grabbed the bag of food and proceeded to walk up to the house. A calico cat ran up beside her and began meowing. Not really an animal lover, Aisha shooed it off and kept on walking until she got to the back door.

"I'm back," she called out, as she stepped inside the house.

Mrs. Simmons shuffled down the hall. "You're back already? That didn't take long."

"No, not really," Aisha agreed, while removing the Chinese containers from the bag, and sitting them on the cabinet. "How is mother?"

"Honey, your mother is just fine. She and I have been talking up a storm. I'm glad she moved back here. I like having a neighbor that I can talk to, and do things with," Mrs. Simmons commented.

"My mother is blessed to have someone like you, too, Mrs. Simmons."

Sandra slowly walked into the kitchen. "Did you get everything taken care of?" she asked Aisha.

"Yes, ma'am. Pastor told me to tell you that he's been praying for you. He said that he and the First Lady would be over tomorrow to sit and pray with you."

"Oh, that man is such a blessing to me. And his wife, that woman knows she stands by her man," Sandra remarked.

"He *is* a good man," Mrs. Simmons agreed, while walking in the direction of the back door. "Well, I'm heading back to the house. You know you can call me anytime, Aisha. And I do mean *any time*," Mrs. Simmons emphasized to Aisha.

"Mattie, I'll see you tomorrow," Sandra told her.

"Okay, bye now. And y'all have a good night."

"You too, Mrs. Simmons," Aisha said, walking behind her and closing the door as she left.

"Mother, are you ready to eat?"

"Yes, my stomach has been growling," she said while

laughing. Aisha placed some of the food from each of the containers onto their plates. The two of them sat at the table and ate.

"Aisha, I want to talk to you about something," Sandra said, after they finished eating. "Let's go in the living room."

"Mother, please. I already told you. I have everything under control with the studio and my apartment. I have enough clothes here and Tameria and Angie both check on the apartment. So there. Now, can we talk about something else?" Aisha pleaded.

"Actually, that's not what I wanted to talk to you about." Sandra walked over and sat down on the sectional.

"It's not?" Aisha wrinkled her brow and appeared puzzled. "What is it then?"

"Sit down," Sandra ordered, patting her hand for Aisha to sit down next to her. "Aisha, God has been dealing with me about some things lately." Her mother began.

"What kinds of things?"

"Things pertaining to me and you." Sandra spoke slowly, choosing her words carefully. "Aisha, honey, I made a lot of mistakes when it came to you. And I want you to know that, I'm sorry."

"Sorry for what? There's nothing to be sorry about," Aisha tried to convince her.

"There's plenty for me to be sorry about. I said some terrible, hurtful things to you when your father died. And I am so sorry, Aisha. So very, very sorry." She looked over at Aisha and witnessed the pain on Aisha's face. Sandra gently stroked Aisha's face with the back of her hand, as though she could stroke away the pain she'd caused her daughter.

Aisha sat still and silent and listened as her mother continued talking.

"When Benjamin was alive, I felt neglected by him. Don't

get me wrong. I know that he loved me. But it was just that sometimes I thought he loved me only because I gave him you. You see, it was you, not me, who was the center of Benjamin's universe. You were his princess and everything centered on you. It was you, not me, he showered with attention and gifts. It was *you* he wanted to spend his time with. I'm not saying that I was the easiest to get along with, either. I was always so critical of him. Nothing he ever did was ever good enough for me. But you, you were so easy to please. He adored you."

"Mother, please, this isn't necessary." Aisha thought her heart was about to give out, it was beating against her chest so hard. To hear her mother expressing her feelings about her and her father's relationship was always too much for Aisha. She wanted to put her hands over her ears and drown her out but she couldn't.

"Mother, don't say anything else. Why don't you go lie down and rest? We'll talk about this later."

"No, I have to say this, Aisha. You see, you had the kind of relationship I always wanted to have with my father when I was a little girl. I wanted to have all of his love and attention, but he was too busy working all the time, trying to make a decent living for us. He worked hard too, Aisha. But instead of being thankful for him, I despised him for being away from home so much. When I became older, I barely even spoke to him. No matter how he tried to reach out to me, I wouldn't accept him. I wanted to hurt him as much as he had hurt me. Then when I met your father, he was attentive and romantic. He wanted to spend all of his time with me. There was nothing that Benjamin James Carlisle wouldn't do for me."

For the first time since she'd been talking, Aisha saw a smile spread on her mother's aging face. "And I loved him. I loved him with everything I had," she said with eyes all aglow. "Now they're all gone. Daddy, Mother *and* Benjamin. And I've been left behind to think about all of the years I wasted. Aisha, I don't want to waste any more years." Tears glistened in Sandra's eyes. "I love you, sweetheart. I want you to know that and I always have."

Aisha laid her head on the side of her mother's shoulder. Wrapping her arm around her mother, Aisha wept. Between sobs, she said, "I love you too. You have no idea how much you mean to me, Mother."

Sandra stroked the top of her daughter's head and brushed Aisha's hair with her hands. At that moment, Aisha felt the weight of the heavy burden she had carried during her life being lifted from her.

After a long and tiring day, Aisha retired to her bedroom. Aisha curled up in a knot. She went over everything her mother had told her, Aisha felt like she'd been spiritually and emotionally rejuvenated. *Jackson was right*, she thought. *"When the time is right, things will work out. Each day is an opportunity for a new beginning,"* was what he had told her. Aisha was starting to believe that Jackson was right.

She pondered over whether or not she should call Jackson. The clock radio displayed 9:00 p.m. *Jackson left his cell number. And he did say call him whenever I got his message.* She placed her hand on the receiver, picked it up, then abruptly placed it back on the hook. *Naw. It's too late. The man didn't mean for me to call him this time of night. I'll call him tomorrow.* To keep her mind off of him, she took a long bath, then got back in the bed and started reading an old J. California Cooper novel, *Some Love Some Pain*, until sleep overtook her.

For the next several days Aisha remained at her mother's side almost constantly. They talked and went on short walks along the sidewalk to help her mother regain her strength. They laughed and had a good time watching Sandra's favorite daytime show, *Judge Mathis*. It was as if they were getting to know each other for the first time.

# 37

"It's good to have you back, Aisha. Things haven't been the same since you've been gone."

"Angie, thank you. I've missed this place." Aisha looked around the studio, noticing every detail around her. It felt good to be back at home. Her mother was doing fine and their relationship had improved dramatically. Every now and then, Sandra had snapped at Aisha or said something that the *old Sandra* would say, but Aisha had come to understand that there were some things that would never change. Finally, she had been able to let her mother's sometimes insensitive, thoughtless remarks roll off of her like water rolled off of oil.

"Come on, girls. Let's get with it! Just because I've been away doesn't mean you should be unprepared. You've had some great instructors and I want you to show me what you've been doing in my absence. Now, come on. Get with it." She clapped her hands and yelled out her instructions.

"Rock forward on the right. Recover weight back on to left, three and four. Step right foot. Half turn to the right.

Step slightly forward onto the left. Now facing the six o'clock wall, shuffle forward. Right, left and right. Step left. Forward and pivot half turn. Right foot. Weight onto the right and step to the left. Bend slightly forward. Now facing the twelve o'clock wall I want you to . . ."

Being back at the studio watching the girls perform energized Aisha. Her body seldom harassed her now about doing drugs, thanks to the support she received at her weekly CA meeting. The seven and a half pounds she'd gained had given her a healthier glow. For now, things for her couldn't be better.

Aisha, Tameria and Angie danced around Aisha's spacious living room while Beyonce's latest chart topper blared on the stereo. *"Ohh, Boy you looking like you like what you see,"* the three women sang in unison and laughed wildly. It had been such a long time since the three of them had gotten together for a girl's night out. Aisha felt good having her friends around. Having been off of drugs and alcohol for close to six months, her outlook on life was upbeat again.

"Aisha, I thought you said you were going to mix some more daiquiris and margaritas," Tameria asked while sipping the last bit of her peach margarita.

"Hold up, girl. Don't you see I've got my dance on," Aisha yelled over the music.

"She doesn't need any more anyway. You know she can't hold water, let alone a third *virgin* margarita. No telling what she'd be doing if alcohol was really in our drinks," Angie teased before breaking out in the Beyonce booty dance.

After the song ended, the three of them fell on the sofa and chair, exhausted.

"Tameria, what's up with you and Chase?" Angie asked while Aisha got up to go and mix the other drinks.

"We're going strong. I tell you, I love me some Chase." Tameria tilted her head back, laughing loudly again.

From the kitchen Aisha added, "Tell us something we don't know already. We already know he has your nose wide open."

"Angie, I don't recall hearing you ask Miss Know It All anything," Tameria shot back.

Aisha appeared from the kitchen with two pitchers. "Okay girls, settle down," Angie remarked and jokingly raised her hands like she was trying to part them.

Aisha placed the pitchers, filled with non-alcoholic peach daiquiris and margaritas, on the living room table and then stood in front of Tameria with her hands positioned on her hips.

"And? What are you supposed to be doing?" Tameria asked.

"I'm about to get my groove on again. That's what." Aisha pranced over to the stereo and turned on another song. This time it was *Unpredictable* by Jamie Foxx. After putting on the CD, she looked at the girls and said, "You know, I'm unpredictable myself," and started laughing and clapping her hands together.

"Yeah right, I think it's Minister Jackson Williams that's unpredictable." Tameria answered and swayed to the beat of the music.

"I know you didn't go there. Jackson and I, I mean Minister Williams and I, are just friends. He's been a great counselor," Aisha remarked.

"What?" Angie put her weight on her right hip, folded her arms and looked over at Tameria with a knowing smile on her face. "Tameria? Naw she didn't just play us for crazy."

"I don't know what y'all mean," Aisha said, pretending to hide the blushing. "There's nothing going on between me and Minister Williams."

"Go on, call the man Jackson," Tameria insisted. "No sense in pretending to be all professional now. It's too late for that." Tameria and Angie laughed again while Aisha looked at them like she had no idea what they meant.

Aisha was still somewhat uncertain about her feelings for Jackson Williams. He was a minister and she couldn't see herself becoming caught up with a man of the cloth. Her life had been far too complicated for her to start living the life of a preacher's lady.

"Okay, okay, I admit it. I do like him, but that's about it," Aisha said, trying to convince her two friends. "The man is a preacher for God's sake. What kind of relationship can we have?"

"A real one, just like anybody else," Angie answered. "He's a man who happens to preach for a living. He's no different from any other fine brother out there."

"Except if you cross him, he has the power to report you directly to his *Father*," Tameria joked. Aisha picked up the fluffy sofa pillow and threw it at Tameria. In return, Tameria grabbed one and threw it back at Aisha.

"Angie, don't think you're getting away," Aisha yelled between laughing and dodging pillows. "We know you and your hubby are going strong."

"I'm not like you," Angie said as she ducked the flying pillow. Almost out of breath she responded, "I'm not ashamed about anything. I do what I do," she breathed heavily, "and I do it good. My baby, Kevin and I, aren't trying to hide a thing."

"Oh, that we know. Don't we, Aisha? When you have a husband things are different," Tameria answered.

"That's for sure. Especially when you have a good man like Kevin." Aisha giggled and plopped down on the sofa, tired from the pillow fight. "I like it when we get together like this."

"Yeah, me too," Tameria replied, breathing heavily.

"We just don't do it often enough," Angie added. "Maybe

when you finish your residency we'll have more time to hang out."

"I don't know about that," Aisha commented. "By that time she'll be doing her full time doctor thing, you know. And she and Chase will be tying the knot."

"Tying the knot?" Angie sat up right and glanced over at Tameria in surprise. "You and Chase are getting married? When?"

"Girl, puhleeze." Tameria flapped her hand. "Don't listen to Aisha. Chase and I haven't talked about marriage, well not lately anyway. We have to get our careers going first. I'm not saying that I don't want to marry him, but first things first. Shoot, Aisha will probably be married before Chase and I get hitched. Isn't that right, Aisha?"

"Yeah, *right*," Aisha answered sarcastically.

"I'm hungry." Angie got up and went into the kitchen. "If you're going to invite your friends over you're at least supposed to have something for us to munch on," she called out.

"You know I don't cook. The best I can offer is Pizza Hut," Aisha answered.

"Pizza Hut sounds good to me. Tameria, are you going to order? You always know how to talk them into giving us something free."

"All right, as if I have a choice." Aisha passed the phone to her. "What would you two do without me?" Tameria asked, and then called and ordered the pizza.

When the pizzas arrived, they practically gulped them down, along with the order of hot wings and cheese breadsticks Tameria ordered with it. Once their bellies were filled, Aisha got up and exchanged hip-hop music for gospel. The ladies quieted down and each found a spot in the living room to lie down. Aisha curled up on the floor near the stereo, Angie on the loveseat, and Tameria in the chair. Except for a word or comment here and there, they were silent. Caught up in their own thoughts, the soothing lyrics touched each of them in its own special way—just like God intended.

It was almost two o'clock in the morning when Tameria and Angie left Aisha's and went home. After they left, Aisha reflected on the evening's events. It was times like these when she was reminded of how valuable it was to have true friends in her life. Her mother had taught her never to trust other women. "Other women," her mother said, "are easy to become jealous over another woman's relationships, good fortune, success or whatever." But Angie and Tameria had never displayed a jealous or envious bone in their bodies.

Aisha and Tameria had been friends since childhood. Angie joined their circle a few years ago. The one thing different about Aisha and Angie's friendship was that Aisha didn't confide in Angie like she did with Tameria. Aisha believed in degrees of friendship. Some friendships were meant to be deep, totally giving and last forever. Others were the kind of friendships that, perhaps, filled a void in a person's life, but yet, were not meant to be as deep as the best friend kind of relationship. Angie fell into the latter category. Nevertheless, Aisha felt truly blessed by both of the ladies. Before she settled down for the night, she thanked God for her friends.

During her sleep, Aisha dreamed about her and Jackson. The two of them were standing in front of Pastor Shipley. She couldn't tell what they were saying in the dream, but Pastor Shipley was smiling. She and Jackson were holding something in their hands. Jackson pulled her underneath his arm and held her close to him while they continued to stand before Pastor Shipley. A glowing bluish light suddenly appeared and she and Jackson smiled as they looked toward the light. Jackson turned to face her and then his lips met hers. Just as Aisha was about to wrap her arms around Jackson, the alarm clock jarred her from her sleep. She stretched in the bed. She smiled when she remembered that she'd dreamed about the exceptionally charming, Minister Jackson Williams. She envisioned him standing at the foot of the bed smiling at her with arms outstretched, waiting to hold her. *Don't go there, Aisha. Don't you even go there.*

# 38

Aisha forced herself to get out of bed and into the shower. The warm rushing water helped to revive her and when she stepped out of the shower she felt rejuvenated. The weekend had been fun and relaxing, especially Saturday night when Angie and Tameria came over. Sunday morning was nice too. She'd driven over to Little Rock, gone to church with her mother, and afterwards she took her out to eat at a fancy restaurant, which Sandra thoroughly enjoyed. But now it was good ole Monday morning, time to get back to the daily grind.

Humming a gospel tune, Aisha searched around in her closet for something to wear. The weather was supposed to be clear, sunny and a little on the warm side. Aisha chose a pair of pink leggings and an oversized pink and white shirt. After sliding into a pair of white open-toed slides, Aisha packed her duffel bag with an extra set of clothes and replaced the toiletries with some fresh items. *I think I'll stop at the coffee house on my way to the studio. And this will go along with it just fine,* Aisha thought to herself, as she removed a blueberry bagel out of a bag.

As usual, this time of morning the specialty coffee shop was crowded. Finally, after waiting in a slow-moving line for ten minutes, she made it up to the counter and placed her order. The server returned with a fresh steaming cup of caramel apple cider. Aisha couldn't resist bringing the cup up to her nose and inhaling its sweet aroma. With steaming brew in hand, she raised her arm over her head, to lessen the chance of someone bumping into her and causing her to drop her cider. She'd seen it happen too many times to other people. Through the maze of caffeine heads she went until she reached the exit. The brightness of the sun when she walked out of the coffee shop temporarily impaired her sight. That's when she realized she'd forgotten to grab her sunglasses off of her dresser. *Oh well,* she thought, and turned the corner in the direction she'd parked.

"Hello, Miss Carlisle."

The voice startled her, and she jerked, almost losing the hold she had on her drink. The man grabbed her by her arms and steadied her. "It's good to see you too," he mocked.

Aisha's face reddened. Her mouth flew open but no words came out.

"Don't you have something to say to me? Or is it that you don't speak to your clients outside of your former place of employment, The Lynx?"

"What do you want, Chandler?" she asked nastily. She hadn't seen or heard from him since her unpleasant meeting with him at Java, Juice and Jazz. And she did not miss him one bit after she found out what kind of guy he really was, a lying snake.

"Now that's no way to treat me, is it?" Chandler said in a creepish type of voice that made Aisha uneasy. "If it wasn't for me, you would be locked up along with Shipley, Jason and the rest of them."

"Chandler, I don't know what you're talking about. I did nothing wrong. And anyway, that's over with. That part of my *life* is over with," Aisha yelled. "The Lynx has been permanently closed for months and everyone who *was* involved in illegal activities has been prosecuted. And I'm not one of them. So there. . . . Now get out of my face and leave . . . me . . . alone!" Aisha turned from him and briskly walked away but he wasn't about to let this opportunity pass him by. He'd been waiting for this time. He'd called her office several times but never left a message. His anger against her was still raw since he felt like she had tricked him into believing she was something other than the stripper she really was.

"Hey, what's your hurry?" he snarled.

Aisha didn't bother to turn around. She wanted to get to her car as quickly as she could. The strong hand grabbed hold of her arm, pulling her back with such force that this time she did drop her cup of cider. She was furious and frightened at the same time.

"Let go of me, Chandler," she demanded, twisting and jerking to escape from his hold. He proceeded to pull her into the alley on the right of them.

"Where are you taking me? I swear, if you don't let me go I'm going to scream."

"Go on. Scream. I'm a cop, remember? And you're a what? Oh yeah, you're a whore. So who's going to help you?" He flashed an evil grin at her that made her stomach turn.

Hidden from view, in the filthy, smelly alley, Chandler slammed her backwards against the brick wall. The pain that traveled up her back was excruciating and she couldn't stop the wave of tears that formed in her eyes. *This fool is crazy,* she thought. *Lord, help me,* she prayed to herself.

"What do you want?" she cried again.

"Oh, let's put it this way. You're just like your friend, Elisa."

At the mention of Elisa, Aisha jerked her head up and glared at him. "Where is Elisa? Is she all right? Tell me, Chandler!" she demanded.

"Unlike you, Elisa is long gone. You'll never see *her* again. I guess you'll just have to find yourself another whore to help you with your tricks. Maybe I can do you a favor and turn you on to some of the girls at the Platinum Plus."

"How dare you talk to me like this. Let go of me, or I'll report you to Internal Affairs."

"Don't you threaten me!" He tightened his already vice grip on her. "If you do, I'll make sure you're locked up for a long time. You see this?" He pulled out a package of white powder. "How'd you like to go down for *this*? This little package can easily get you, oh say, twenty years at the least." He laughed wickedly. "Better yet, wouldn't you like a little hit of this, Luscious. Huh?"

Chandler opened the package of cocaine and began moving it back and forth underneath her nose. Aisha jerked her head from side to side in an effort to keep the drug from going up her nostrils. Seeing the drug for the first time in months was tempting to Aisha, but Chandler would never know it.

Aisha kept trying to fight against him but his grip on her was way too tight. "Why are you doing this?" Her tears were flowing heavily and she didn't know what to do.

"Because you're walking around thinking you got away with something. You should have gone down with the rest of them. Do you know they were using little girls as young as thirteen and fourteen years old to satisfy their sick sexual desires? You know that, Miss Luscious? Do you?" He stood so close to her she could smell his mint breath. His chest was against hers, and she was pinned between him and the wall.

"I didn't know anything about that. I told you that. If I *had* known anything or suspected anything illegal was going on, I would have gone straight to the police."

"You're lying and you know it. You fooled me once, but you won't fool me again. You're not going to tell me that you didn't notice that some of those girls looked like little teenyboppers. And you sure can't make me believe that you thought the cocaine they were giving you was legal. Whore, puhleeze."

"Stop calling me a whore. I'm *not* a whore!" she finally yelled back.

"Let me tell you this, then I'll bid you farewell. If I ever, and I do mean ever, catch you doing so much as pausing at a stop sign instead of coming to a complete stop or jay walking, whatever it is, I'll lock you up so fast you won't know what day it is. You better watch your back every step of the way, Aisha because you never know just when I might be watching." Without warning, he shouted, "Boo!"

Aisha jumped. Chandler laughed loudly and walked off.

"Now you go and have yourself a good day," Chandler called out.

Aisha was shaken. By the time she made it to the studio, she was still a mess and barely spoke to Kaye. She closed the door to her office and sat down until she calmed down. When her breathing began to feel more normal, she called Jackson.

"Good morning, Natalie." Her voice was shaking as she spoke. "This is Aisha."

"Good morning, Aisha. Are you all right? You sound a little strange."

"No, I'm fine. I wanted to know if I could schedule an appointment with Minister Williams. I really need to see him. I know it's short notice but if you'll ask him and get back with me, I'd really appreciate it."

"Hold on. He just walked in. I'll let him talk to you."

"Minister Williams, Aisha Carlisle is on, uh," Natalie looked down at the multi-line phone, "line 4," she said.

"Thank you, Natalie. I'll take it in my office. Oh, and, good morning," he told her.

Smiling, Natalie replied, "Good morning, Minister Williams."

Jackson laid his briefcase on his desk and walked around to answer Aisha's call.

"Good morning, Aisha. What a pleasant surprise. How are you?" He was surprised that she was calling him. Their sessions had ended several weeks ago and since then he'd seen her at church a few times but he never had a chance to talk to her.

"I, I need to talk to you." Her voice trembled.

"Sure." Immediately he sensed that something was wrong. His initial delight in hearing from her gave way to concern. "How soon can you get here? Or would you prefer that I come to you?"

"Would you do that?"

"Of course. I don't usually make house calls, but since you're high on my list, I'll make an exception," he said, hoping to hear her laugh. When she didn't, Jackson really became worried.

She was still trembling from her traumatizing encounter with Chandler.

"Look, tell me where and when," Jackson said.

"My, my studio . . . now, if you can."

"I'm leaving the church now."

"Jackson?"

"Yes," he answered.

"Thank you. You don't know how much this means to me."

"I think I do. I'll see you shortly."

In less than twenty minutes, Jackson was walking through the studio doors.

Kaye admired the handsome man coming toward her. *Mercy, mercy*, she thought to herself. "Good morning, how may I help you, sir?" she asked in her usual polite manner.

"Good morning. I'm here to see Aisha. She's expecting me," he answered pleasantly.

"Your name?"

"Jackson. Jackson Williams."

Kaye immediately recognized his name from the times he had called the studio. She dialed Aisha's intercom and informed her of his arrival.

"Mr. Williams, you can go on back. Just go down that hallway." Kaye pointed to the hallway on the right of her. "Her office is the first door on the left."

"Thank you. Uhh," he paused and read her name plate, "Kaye," he said and proceeded to walk away.

*Knock, knock.*

"Come in," Aisha called out, after hearing the knock on her office door.

As soon as he stepped inside her office he saw her puffy face and red eyes. She'd obviously been crying. He wondered what could have her so upset. He walked over to her and knelt down beside her.

"Hey, what's wrong? Tell me what happened," Jackson urged, taking her hands in his.

"It's awful. I'm scared, Jackson. I'm really scared," Aisha said, shaking. She grabbed the center of his arm in a tight grip.

"I'm getting you out of here. You're no good to anyone in this shape. Come on," he ordered. Gently taking hold of her arms, he pulled her up from the chair. He led her out of the office.

Without looking directly at Kaye, Aisha said, "Kaye, I'm going out. Please send all my calls to voicemail. Tell Angie when she comes in that I'm with Minister Williams."

Surprised, Kaye had no idea he was a minister. "Okay sure. I'll tell her."

Jackson opened the passenger door of his Crossfire and waited for Aisha to get in. He ran to the driver's side and jumped in. "My place or yours?"

"Mine, I guess." Aisha suddenly thought about Chandler and changed her mind. She didn't know what else Chandler was capable of and she didn't want to find out. "On second thought, I'd rather go to your place. If that's okay with you."

"Sure."

They rode the twenty minute drive to Jackson's place in total silence. There would be time for talking soon enough. Pulling up in front of Riverfront Condominiums, he keyed in his security code and the massive iron gates slowly opened. Aisha lifted her head slightly to survey her surroundings.

After parking his car, he led her into his domain. Upon entering his split level condo, Aisha immediately noticed it was immaculate beyond belief.

"Your condo is very nice," she commented.

"Thank you. Why don't we go in here?" Jackson led her to the den. "Have a seat." He motioned with his hand for her to sit on the plush melon couch. "Can I get you something to drink or eat?" he offered.

She nodded and said, "A cup of decaf if you have it."

"Give me a minute and I'll check. I'll be right back."

"How's instant?" he called out from the kitchen.

"Instant is fine," she answered flatly.

"How do you take it?"

"One sugar, two creams."

"Alright, one cup of instant decaf coming right up," Jackson said.

"Okay." Her eyes zeroed in on the mantel over the fireplace to the right of her. She walked over to the fireplace and started looking at the pictures. She picked up a picture of Jackson standing in a pulpit in a burgundy robe. Aisha smiled. Another picture was of him graduating from somewhere. There were pictures of his family members, Aisha assumed. Aisha became lost in her thoughts as she started thinking about her own family, rather, about her father. He loved taking pictures of *his princess. Why couldn't he still . . .*

"That's my family," he said, startling her. He placed the coffee mug in her hands. "That portrait there is of my father." He pointed to the oil painting on the wall above all of the smaller pictures. "He's a minister in Ohio."

"Oh. I didn't know that." Aisha tasted the coffee. "Umm, good," she commented.

"I'm glad you like it," Jackson countered. "There's a lot you don't know about me."

"I'm beginning to see that."

Jackson smiled. "These are my cousins." Jackson picked up some more pictures and explained who each person in the photo was. He could see that she was still trembling. He hoped this minor distraction would help her to calm down. "This here's my best friend, Jeremy, with his wife and kids."

"Nice family," Aisha answered, trying to sound as normal as possible.

Jackson determined that it was time to find out what had happened to her. "Look, enough of that. Let's sit down so we can talk. I want to know what has you so upset this morning."

He walked back with her and sat down on the couch beside her. "What is it Aisha? You know you can talk to me."

"I know. That's why I'm here. You remember the policeman I told you about?"

"The undercover guy who you ran into at church?"

She nodded.

Jackson eased in closer to her and held her hand. "What

about him?" The look on her face was one of utter fear. *What could have happened?* His mind traveled round and round with thoughts.

"I, I stopped at the coffee shop this morning. On my way out, I ran into him."

"Okay," he wanted to be as patient as he could but he also wanted her to go on and tell him what he'd done to make her this upset.

"Remember, I told you that he had disguised himself and pretended to be a man named Kyle Taylor."

"Yes, but what did he want this morning?"

"He always thought I knew about the illegal operations going on at The Lynx, but I didn't and you know I told you that, Jackson. But this guy, Chandler, he seems to think I was involved in the whole thing. But I honestly had no idea what was going on at that place." Aisha's face turned red again. He saw the tears swell up in her eyes once more. He reached behind him and took the box of tissues off the sofa table and passed it to her.

"Are you okay?" he asked her.

"Yea, I think so. Anyway, this morning he was outside of the coffee shop and he started talking crazy. I told him to leave me alone but he wouldn't. I tried to get to my car and get away from him but I couldn't. He forced me into an alley."

Jackson's jaw tightened. The fury he felt was hard to keep under control.

"He called me names and pinned me against the wall in the alley." Aisha wouldn't look at Jackson. With her head hung low, her twists shielded the sides of her face. H . . . he pulled out some cocaine and told me he could easily plant it on me if he wanted to, and that I would go to jail for years. Then he tried to make me snort it, but I didn't." This time Aisha jerked her head up and stole a look at Jackson. Her eyes loomed large. "I didn't do it, Jackson."

"I believe you and I'm proud of you," he said and squeezed her hand.

He told me I'd better watch my back." She stopped talking and started to cry in the tissue. "After that, he left and that's when I went to the studio and called you."

"I'm glad that you did. But that good for nothing, crooked . . ." Jackson stopped himself before he said something he would later regret. He wanted to go out and find this chump and beat him to a pulp but he knew that he had to exercise restraint. He was a minister, for God's sake. But at this moment, his thoughts were far from being Godly. But he didn't dare let Aisha know how angry he was. "Aisha, there's nothing to be scared of. This guy is trying to control you by putting you in a state of panic and fear." A soft spot formed in his heart for her.

She looked up at him. "He's succeeded, Jackson because I *am* in a state of panic and fear. I can't live like this. Looking over my shoulder, wondering if he's watching me, or if he's going to plant drugs in my car or at my studio."

"*Shhh*, he's not going to hurt you. I promise I won't let him," he assured her and pulled her trembling body next to his and held her. She smelled like jasmine. He slowly leaned back against the sofa, her head resting against his chest. Cautiously, he lifted her chin up until her lips were almost even with his. His heart raced as he resisted his emotions. "Aisha, I want you to listen to me," he told her. "God is greater than anything you're facing. Chandler has no control over you. He wants you to walk around scared and frightened, but God has not given us a spirit of fear, Aisha. But you have to trust Him. He won't let you down."

Aisha looked into Jackson's eyes. She began to feel calm and peaceful. He was such a gentle, compassionate man. His words penetrated her heart and she believed him. She listened as he continued to reassure her that everything would turn out just fine.

"As for the name calling, you know who you are in Christ. No man can take that away from you. You're God's child, fearfully and wonderfully made. You hear me?"

"Yes, I hear you. I, I was just so scared when he came at me like that. I had no idea that he was such an evil man. And to think that I really did like him at one time."

Jackson hoped she didn't detect the look of surprise on his face. During their sessions she had never divulged that she had been involved with Chandler.

"Let it go, Aisha. You can't let him do you like this. He's manipulating you. God wants you to live your life free. Chandler wants to make you miserable. But what he's try-ing to do is a lie from the pit of hell and we are coming against that right now." Jackson squeezed her hand tighter and whispered a prayer. When he finished praying, he stood up and looked down at her.

"What?" she said, looking confused.

"I'm going to fix you some brunch. I did tell you that I'm an excellent cook, didn't I?" he laughed.

The heaviness was lifted from her heart and she smiled. "I'm not sure you did." She stood up and followed him into the kitchen. "I'm going to hang around. Then I'll be the judge of that."

The remainder of the morning, the two of them laughed, talked and enjoyed the delicious French toast, sausages and grits Jackson prepared. Their time together ended when Jackson's cell phone rang.

Jackson removed his phone from the holder and looked at it. "Excuse me."

"Go ahead," she said.

"Hello. Yes. Uh huh."

Aisha moved away from the breakfast table and walked back into the living room so Jackson could talk in private. She sat in the bay window and looked out over the Muddy Mississippi River. Being here had a peaceful effect on her.

Looking out on the water, she felt safe and secure. She watched as the waves brushed up against the shore. People were walking along the river walk, some hand in hand. Others walked alone or with their pets. Some were jogging.

"Earth to Aisha," Jackson's voice boomed. She jerked her head around swiftly. "It's beautiful isn't it?" he asked as he moved in closer to her.

"Yes it is. I could sit here forever. Your condo really is beautiful," Aisha complimented.

"Why, thank you. That was Natalie on the phone. I'm needed back at the church. But come on," he reached for her thin hand. "Let me give you the full tour before I take you back to the studio. That is unless you want to stay here until I return."

"Are you kidding me?" she responded with a look of awe on her face.

"No, I'm not. You can get you some rest and there's plenty of food in the fridge. Plus we have excellent security here. So at least for a while your mind can be at ease. He led her through each room while he continued his spiel.

Aisha followed him around and was continually impressed with his style of decorating. "I don't know if I should stay here while you're gone, Jackson," she finally confessed.

He stopped at the top of the curving stairway and turned to face her. "Look, if I didn't want you here, I would tell you. I'm going to a staff meeting which usually lasts a couple of hours. I have two counseling sessions after that. In the meantime, you can take a nap, eat, watch satellite, read or whatever. I should be back around four. Then I'll take you to get your car. How does that sound?"

"Well . . ."

"Okay. It's done," he said before she could finish her sentence. "You can finish looking around while I grab my briefcase and a couple of other items I'm going to need for the staff meeting."

When he finished gathering his things he turned and without thinking, kissed her on the cheek. Immediately after doing so, he stepped back. "I'm sorry. Really I am. I didn't mean anything by that."

She was reeling from the touch of his soft, thick lips pressed against her cheek. Electric sparks tingled throughout her body. "Jackson, please. There's no need to apologize. Now go before you're late for your meeting."

"I'll see you later," he said with a sheepish look on his face.

When he closed the tall oak door behind him, Aisha leaned against it and breathed in slowly. Her heart still fluttered from the kiss. Smiling, she skipped over to the bay window, sat down and pulled her legs up to her chest.

Jackson buckled his seatbelt, placed both hands on the steering wheel, and began to pray. "Father God. You know my heart. And you know that I like Aisha. Father, I need you to guide me every step of the way. Help me to do things in the way you see fit and not succumb to my own fleshly desires. Amen."

# 39

Jackson left the church as soon as the staff meeting ended and went back to check on Aisha. He called out her name. "Aisha." The apartment met his call with silence. He laid his briefcase and keys on the granite kitchen countertop and slowly maneuvered his lean, physically fit body throughout the lower level but there was no sign of her. *Maybe she had decided to leave and called one of her friends to pick her up.* He climbed the stairs and peeped in the guest bedroom. No Aisha. He checked in his office. No Aisha. He spied the petite frame in his master bedroom. The pace of his heart settled when he spotted her laying on his bed sound asleep. He stood in the entrance of the bedroom and watched her. She reminded him of a fragile child in need of love and affection. *Sleep, my angel.*

Jackson retreated back downstairs. He opened the door to one of the hall closets and pulled out a pair of casual slacks and a shirt before going into the bathroom to take a shower. The piping hot streams of water pounding against his creamy-colored skin released some of the tension of the day. Afterwards, he dressed and went to the kitchen to prepare something to eat. He searched through the freezer and finally settled on preparing a vegetable casserole with grilled chicken slices.

Aisha turned lazily in the supple king-sized bed and opened her eyes. It took her a few seconds to remember that she was still at Jackson's condo. She hadn't meant to fall asleep in his bed. Aisha jumped up and sat on the edge of the bed and listened to the noise coming from downstairs. Her instincts told her to sit quietly and gather her thoughts. *Could Chandler have broken into Jackson's apartment? Oh God, please no, don't let it be him.* Frightened, she tightened her grip on the edge of the bed. Her fear was replaced with a smile when she smelled the tantalizing aroma of food that filtered threw her nostrils. She ran barefoot down the stairs to greet Jackson.

"Hello, there. Did you sleep comfortably?" Jackson asked her as she made her way into the kitchen.

Aisha blushed and lowered her head. "I'm sorry for falling asleep in your bed. Believe me when I tell you that I don't go around sleeping in strangers' beds," she said with an embarrassed look.

"Did you just call me a stranger? And here I thought we were friends. When did I lose my status?" he smiled and closed the door to the convection oven.

"No, we *are* friends. I, I didn't mean strangers as in strangers, I meant . . ."

"I think I know what you meant. I was just teasing anyway. I'm actually glad that you felt comfortable enough to go to sleep. Why don't you sit down and after I feed you, I'll take you to get your car. Unless you want to crash here for the rest of the night."

Aisha was surprised at Jackson's offer. It must have shown on her face because Jackson immediately clarified his statement. He didn't want her to get the wrong idea about him. "Hold up. I didn't mean anything by that,"

Jackson explained. "I only thought that you might like to lay low for the night, no funny business. Before I go to the office in the morning, I can take you to get your car."

"Jackson," Aisha paused. "I really appreciate the offer. I'm tempted to accept it."

"Then do it."

"Not this time. I think I'd better go and get my car this evening. I don't want to invade your privacy. You've already done more than enough for me today by rushing to my rescue and allowing me to stay here. Gosh, I can't thank you enough. And on top of all of that, you're feeding me too."

The smile on her face when she spoke resurfaced emotions he'd suppressed for the past several years. The more he was around her, the more his desire grew. His vow of celibacy was being tested but he was determined not to allow his flesh to make him forget that he was a man of God. His father often reminded him that if there was ever a time that he started to feel weak to his fleshly desires, he should find a wife.

"Son, it's better to find a wife than to burn," his father would tell him. "The Word of God says, the man that finds a wife, finds a good thing. Just make sure she's a Godly woman and that her beliefs and convictions are just as strong as yours. You know not every woman can handle being a preacher's wife."

"Jackson, what's that you're cooking?" Aisha asked in the middle of his thoughts. "It smells heavenly."

"Vegetable casserole with grilled chicken, madam. I'm almost done. I hope you enjoy it."

"I'm sure I will. Tell me. Where did you learn to cook, and clean too, for that matter? Your place is immaculate."

"I wish I could say that I'm responsible for the cleanliness of my apartment. But I have a confession to make."

"Okay, I'm listening." Aisha placed her head in her hands and leaned on the table.

"Some of the senior women at church do a great job of taking care of me. Two times a week they come over and clean my apartment. As for the cooking, they taught me how to do that as well, but I did have some experience already from living with my father growing up. We had to learn how to fend for ourselves unless some of the church ladies brought food over to our house. I also have plenty of prepared foods that the mothers of the church have cooked and frozen for me. All I have to do is come home, pop a meal in the microwave or the oven and *voila*!

"Well, aren't you special."

"I guess you can say that. Not having my mother around when I was growing up makes me enjoy the attention showered on me. The church has been good to me. God has shown me favor. I can't thank Him enough."

Aisha gazed at Jackson. Listening to him, watching him move around the kitchen, and his kindness and gentle spirit touched her deeply. The more she talked to this man and spent time around him, the more she felt safe and secure.

They ate the meal he prepared and just like he promised, when they finished eating, he drove her back to the studio to get her car. He waited patiently for her to go to her office and grab some paperwork that she wanted to take home with her, then he followed her home to make sure she arrived safely.

"Let me check everything out before I go." Jackson gently removed the keys from Aisha's hand and opened the door to her apartment. He walked in ahead of her, clicking on lights and checking every closet and room. She followed closely behind him. After making a full search of the apartment, he walked to the door and turned to tell her goodnight.

"Jackson, thank you," Aisha said. "Thank you so much."

"If you need me, I want you to promise me that you'll call. Or better yet, if you get frightened, just jump in your car and come back to my place. You hear me?"

"Yes, I hear you. And . . ."

He placed two fingers against her lips. "Please, don't say thank you again. Just accept the fact that I'm here for you. Now lock up. I'll talk to you tomorrow."

Chandler watched from across the street as Jackson walked to his car. With a smirk on his face, Chandler drove off just as Jackson opened the door to his Crossfire.

# 40

Aisha had been *Chandler-free*, as Tameria started calling it, for the past four and a half months. Since the terrible morning outside the coffee shop, Aisha hadn't seen or heard anything else from him. After the first month passed without so much as a peep out of Chandler, Tameria made up the name hoping to lighten things up for Aisha. It didn't take long for Aisha to catch on to the phrase. Sometimes when she and Tameria hung out, Aisha would go around saying, "Thank God, I'm Chandler-free." Everything seemed to be going good for Aisha. God had smiled on her. For the first time in a long while, Aisha allowed herself to accept what God had already done in her life. She had made peace within and had forgiven herself.

The friendship between Aisha and Jackson bloomed as haunting memories of Chandler faded. Aisha had told her mother about him, which was something she would never have done when her relationship with Sandra was rocky.

Sandra's birthday was in one week and the Seniors Ministry had planned a birthday celebration for her at the church. Aisha invited Jackson to go with her and he gladly accepted. The day of the party, Jackson insisted on driving Aisha. The two and a half hour drive seemed like only minutes with Jackson. Around him, Aisha was happy and always smiling.

Jackson's charm and thoughtfulness lured Sandra in too. At her birthday party, he was attentive and catered to her sometimes diva-like personality. Of course, Sandra soaked it all in. She loved to be in the spotlight and Jackson had no problem making her feel like a queen.

After the party, there was never a time that Sandra didn't ask about Jackson when Aisha talked to her. Aisha felt like a miracle occurred when her mother began doting over Jackson like he was the best thing since ice cream. He had a way about him that brought out the best in Sandra. The fact that he was a minister made Sandra like him even more. She bragged to her friends, her church family and anyone who would listen, telling them that her daughter was seriously dating a minister at Faithside Temple in Memphis. Aisha hadn't seen her mother this excited in a long time. Jackson began going with Aisha to Little Rock as often as possible. His visits sparked a change in Sandra's whole demeanor. Being considerate as he was, Jackson even took the initiative to call and check on Sandra at least once a week. The more Aisha was around him, the more she was pulled in by his generosity and caring spirit.

Jackson reciprocated his feelings for Aisha by inviting Aisha to go with him to Dayton, Ohio and she was eager to accept. Jackson's father wanted him to come to his church in Dayton and preach for his Pastor's Anniversary.

In Dayton, Aisha met the man who mirrored Jackson in mannerisms, looks and spiritual strength. In some ways, Jackson's father reminded Aisha of her own father. Just like Benjamin, Pastor Williams was easy to talk to and he made Aisha feel comfortable during her stay. The trip brought the two of them closer than ever. They hadn't discussed the depth of their feelings for one another, but Aisha believed that she was falling in love with Jackson.

Aisha stayed behind at Jackson's condo while he went to visit some of the sick and elderly members who were unable to attend church. His condo was a sanctuary for Aisha. It provoked an inexplicable sense of peace, calmness and security. Whether he was there with her or whether she was alone, her spirit felt at home. She had a dance competition to attend later that evening and Jackson was going with her. He asked Aisha if she'd like to wait for him at his place and they could leave from there. Aisha eagerly accepted.

Aisha strolled over to the bay window and sat down, folded her legs up on the window seat and began daydreaming about becoming Jackson's wife. Could she fulfill the role that was expected of a minister's wife? Would she be jealous of the late night phone calls from distressed women? Could she handle the times he'd have to be away from her and their family? Would she be able to attend numerous church services? Being Jackson's wife surely wouldn't be an easy task. As if someone suddenly poked her with a pin, Aisha snapped out of her daydream. It wasn't like Jackson had proposed. He hadn't come close to talking about marriage. Things were going too good and she wasn't about to blow it with her thoughts of anything as serious as marriage.

Jackson had a long day. He had visited several church members at Baptist East Hospital, Methodist University and Methodist South Hospitals. In addition to the hospital visits, he made a couple of stops at nursing homes as well as homebound members. After he finished, he stopped off at the church then rushed home to the love of his life.

He had promised Aisha he would go to the dance competition with her. His emotions were hard to contain whenever he saw her dancing. Dancing was her calling, a God-given talent that continued to flourish and blossom in her life and the lives of the kids she taught.

Driving along the BMP expressway, he admitted to himself that Aisha was the woman for him. He loved her and it was time to let her know. He already knew that he wanted to spend the rest of his life with her. But the timing had to be right. He wasn't going to ask her to be his wife until he was sure about her feelings for him. Their level of intimacy was another obstacle in his way. If he didn't make a serious move soon, his desire for her would be even harder to suppress. He flipped the radio from 95.7 to 103.5 solid gold just in time to hear Stevie Wonder singing one of his favorites, *"Everyone has got a certain weakness in life, your love just happens to be mine . . ."* He smiled and sang along with the song.

Jackson parked his car and rushed to his condo. Knowing Aisha was inside waiting on him made his heart flutter. It felt perfect for her to be at his place. The more time he spent with her, the more time he wanted to spend with her.

He turned the lock and went inside. The apartment was relatively quiet except for the sound of some reggae music playing on the stereo.

"Boo," Aisha yelled and pounced from behind the hallway door onto Jackson's back.

Grabbing her by the waist, he brought her around to face him. Without saying a word, he kissed her with fervor and passion. In response, she caressed his face and shoulders with her delicate hands. His lips traveled to her ear lobes and he gingerly kissed them before moving to her cheeks, her forehead and her eyelids. Jackson was consumed by the taste of her lips and the feel of her softness pressing against his taut chest. The sounds of desire escaped and pushed their way up and out of her mouth.

"Jackson," she whispered before he pulled away from

her. Each time he held her in his arms, pulling away from her became more difficult.

"Come on, Aisha. We can't do this. Not until—Not until it's right."

She slowly shook her head in agreement and stepped aside. She exhaled before changing the subject, "How did visitation go?" she asked with her face still flushed.

He forced himself to answer, though his body was still begging for something else.

"Everything went well. I managed to visit fifteen of our members. I know that may not seem like a lot, especially when we have a church roll of what? Six to eight thousand? That means every week we have a growing list of sick and shut-in members reported to the church office. Think of the ones we don't know about. But hey, thank God for the different ministries we have that address the needs of our sick and elderly. They do an excellent job too, which makes the jobs of the pastor and the ministers somewhat easier. There's no way our ministry staff, even though we have a huge group, can cover all of the members who are sick or unable to get to church."

Talking about church relaxed Jackson, and soon his flesh had quieted down. Jackson could count on his love of God and the church to help him regain his focus whenever his flesh tried to dictate to him.

Aisha, as much as she wanted him, accepted that there could be nothing sexual between them unless they said those three words, I love you, followed by those two words, I do.

The dance competition was the third one this month for *A. Carlisle Studio.* The girls looked forward to it and so did Aisha. They were competing against several other top dance groups from the tri-state area. It was during competitions like this when Aisha thought of Gabby and wondered how she was doing. Wherever she was, Aisha hoped that Elisa had found a place that would recognize Gabby's exceptional talent and love of dance.

Aisha waved both hands in the air when she spotted Tameria and Chase, along with Angie and her husband, sitting in the bleachers. Tameria was excited that she and Chase's schedules had made it possible for them to attend the competition. It was a huge event for Aisha, and Tameria wanted to be there to show her support. If *A. Carlisle* won, they would move on to the national competition which would be a dream come true for Aisha.

The competition lasted for almost three hours. At the end, *A. Carlisle Studio of Dance and Choreography* went home with the first place trophy in lyrical dance and second place in the hip-hop category. Aisha screamed and jumped up and down when they announced their first and second place wins. Afterwards, she pushed through the crowd to find Jackson. When she reached him, his embrace sealed the exhilarating triumph of the night.

Chandler stood undetected on the other side of the gym watching the couple who obviously were in love. It was apparent that Minister Jackson Williams had stepped up his game. Chandler turned and walked out of the gym. He'd been silent far too long. It was time to make his move.

Aisha was still on a natural high from winning when she opened the door to her empty apartment. After a warm bubble bath, she curled up in her bed and pulled out her Bible. Turning to one of her favorite passages, Psalms 30, Aisha read the words that brought her to tears. *"I give you all the credit, God; you got me out of that mess, you didn't let my foes gloat. God, my God, I yelled for help and you put me together. God, you pulled me out of the grave, gave me another chance at life when I was down and out."*

The phone rang and disrupted her quiet time. She looked

at her caller ID. *Private name, private number* flashed across the caller ID screen. Must be some telemarketer or something. She hesitated before answering.

"Hello."

"Aisha. Please don't hang up." Chandler's voice sounded almost child-like and innocent.

She recognized his voice instantly. "Chandler, I thought you were out of my life and had moved on to torment some other woman." Aisha mocked in anger. Everything had been going well. Today had been totally one of the best days of her life. Now Chandler had to pop up and ruin what was left of a perfect day.

"Okay, I deserved that. But if you'd just wait and listen to me. I don't want to start any trouble with you. I promise if you'll see me tonight, I won't bother you again. But I need to talk to you, Aisha."

"Sounds like a personal problem to me," she rebuffed. "Whatever it is you have to say, you'd better say it in the next thirty seconds or I'm hanging up this phone."

"I need to see you face to face," he insisted.

"Why? So you can set me up for the kill? I don't think so." She slammed down the phone. *The nerve of that man. Why won't he leave me alone?* She got out of bed and began to pace back and forth for several minutes before glancing down at the phone. She dialed Jackson's number. When he answered, she immediately relaxed. They talked for almost two hours. By the time she hung up, she had forgotten all about Chandler's pathetic pleas.

The next morning Aisha met Jackson for breakfast which was becoming a weekly ritual. At least twice a week they'd meet up for breakfast at The Kettle before Jackson went to the church office and before she went to the studio. The relationship she had with him was what she'd envisioned in her dreams. The time they spent together was always fun.

He was easy going and his Christian convictions were real. There was no pressure to engage in sexual intimacy. That alone made Aisha comfortable around him. They could sit at each other's apartments for hours, listening to music, watching movies or television or doing nothing and the both of them would be content. She had thought about telling Jackson about Chandler's call, but decided to put it off. They were having too good of a time, and she wasn't about to ruin it by talking about Chandler. After all, like Tameria said, she was Chandler-free.

Aisha walked into the studio, and just as she turned the knob to walk inside, she was met by a man with the most beautiful bouquet of mixed flowers she'd ever seen. There were roses, carnations and lilies in the oversized arrangement.

"Are you coming here?" Aisha asked him.

"Yes, ma'am," he replied.

"Follow me then." Aisha proceeded to walk inside the studio. "Good morning, Kaye."

"Good morning, Aisha. Who are those for?" Kaye asked when she saw the flowers.

"Angie," Aisha answered. She turned and looked at the delivery man. "Oh, I'm sorry. I know that vase of flowers must be heavy. You can sit them right over there on that round table. Angie's husband is something else," Aisha said to Kaye. He's always so thoughtful when it comes to his wife. "Has she made it in yet, Kaye?"

"Not yet."

"Ma'am," the man said. "I need one of you to sign here please?" The delivery man passed the paper to Aisha. She glanced at it and saw her name instead of Angie's on the yellow slip.

"Wait. I thought you said these were for Angie Walker."

"No, ma'am. I didn't say who they were for. But uh, let's see. Okay, they're for . . ." He turned the slip of paper around so he could read it. "Miss Aisha Carlisle. Is she here?"

Kaye jumped from behind the receptionist's counter so she wouldn't miss a word of the conversation.

"I'm Aisha Carlisle," she stated.

"Good, then have a great day. Enjoy your flowers too," he said before turning to leave.

"Who are they from?" Kaye inquired.

"Oh my, they must be from Jackson," Aisha said excitedly. She rushed over to the bouquet and pulled out the card tucked on the side. *"Won't you giv'a brother another chance. Everyone deserves to be forgiven, including me. Chandler."*

"Who is it?" Kaye continued to press her for an answer.

"No one. I mean the card doesn't say," Aisha lied. She refused to air her dirty laundry with Kaye. She placed the card in the pocket of her sweat pants then turned and walked to her office. The light on her Audix was on. She dialed into it to listen to her morning messages.

"Aisha, I hope you'll accept my peace offering. I know flowers can't begin to convey how sorry I am for being so foolish, but people can change. I should know because I'm one of them. I know I've frightened you. I've said some horrible things about you. But that was a long time ago. It's in the past. Let me talk to you, Aisha. I want to ask for your forgiveness in person. Call me and tell me that you'll see me."

Aisha listened to his pleading. He sounded like the Chandler she'd first met. The one who had been sensitive, kind and attentive. *Maybe I should consider his request.* She paused before pushing the button to move on to the next message. The last message was from her mother telling her that she might go to Dallas to visit one of her friends who'd recently retired and relocated there. "Call me back, Aisha. I'm thinking about flying out Wednesday."

Aisha returned her mother's call, assuring her that she thought it was a good idea for her to go. Sandra agreed and told Aisha she would call her back to let her know when she would be leaving.

Aisha sat behind her desk and leaned back in the chair. Reminiscing about her and Jackson made her giddy inside. She soon came from behind the desk and went into one of the practice rooms. For the next two hours she worked on a series of new dance moves that she'd planned to teach her students. The national competition was four weeks away and their routines had to be the best ever. It was almost noon by the time she walked out of the room.

"Hey, those new routines looked great," Angie remarked when she saw Aisha coming down the hall in a sweat.

"Thanks, girl. I've got to keep working on 'em until they're perfect. I'm not planning to come home from the nationals without a trophy."

"With what I saw when I peeped in on you, the girls will be hard to beat if you can teach them to do what you were doing in there."

"*If* I can teach them? Now you know me better than that. *If* is not in my vocabulary when it comes to dancing. They will learn this routine plus two more. Before long, we're going to be the national champions." Aisha used the towel around her neck to wipe the sweat from the side of her face.

"I saw the flowers. Kaye told me they were for you but that you didn't know who they were from."

Aisha motioned for Angie to join her in the break area. She opened the fridge and pulled out a cold blue Powerade before sitting on the bench in the room. When she finished telling Angie about Chandler and his sudden change of heart, Angie appeared just as dumbfounded as Aisha. She didn't trust Chandler Larson as far as she could throw him. But listening to what Aisha said about him, she almost felt a tinge of pity for the guy. Still, she told Aisha to keep a clear head when it came to Chandler and not to let him force her to do anything she didn't want to do.

Angie reminded her friend that the relationship between her and Jackson was going too well to allow someone like Chandler to come in and mess it up. Aisha agreed to some point. But on the other hand, if Chandler was serious, then it was her Christian duty to accept his apology by forgiving him. *Even the Bible says that we should forgive seventy times seventy*, she reminded herself. She hadn't forgiven Chandler one time yet. She so wanted to believe that he had recognized the vast error of his ways. If he was willing to ask for her forgiveness, she had to at least afford him that chance.

Kaye's voice blasted over the intercom. "Aisha, line two. Aisha, line two please."

Aisha pushed the button on the phone in the break room. Angie gestured that she was leaving the break room and then disappeared.

"Hello, this is Aisha."

"Hi, beautiful," the male caller said through the phone receiver.

"Hi, Jackson. How's your day going?"

"It's been busy. I can say that much. But hearing your voice makes me feel better already. How's that new routine you've come up with coming along?" he asked. She'd told him over breakfast about the new choreography she'd planned to teach the girls for the nationals.

"I've been practicing my butt off all morning. I feel pretty certain that once I perfect all the moves, we'll have a winning routine." Her confidence was obvious with every word she spoke. "I'll probably be here late this evening. Once the girls come in and leave, I'm going to stick around for a while. So it's unlikely that I'll see you tonight."

"I understand. But I don't like it."

Aisha could hear the smile in his voice. Having someone who understood her was such a wonderful gift.

"You're too good to me. You know that," she said.

"Yeah, I do." He laughed. "I'll call you later."

"Okay."

"Line three, Aisha. Aisha, line three," Kaye said the minute she'd hung up from talking to Jackson.

*It must be Jackson calling back. He must've forgotten to tell me something*, Aisha thought as she got the phone. "Hello, · Aisha speaking."

"Aisha, hi. It's Chandler."

"I know. You have one of those distinguishable voices. I've told you that before, haven't I?"

"Yeah you have. Did you get my message?"

"Yes," Aisha answered without acknowledging the beautiful flowers he'd sent.

"I just want the chance to make things right with you. I don't want to come off as pushy or like the stalker I once was. So this time if you tell me not to call you again and that you won't see me, then I'll accept that. But seriously, all I want is a chance to talk to you face to face."

"I, I don't know, Chandler. You've done some crazy things that gave me a totally different view of you. You've scared the mess out of me. You've had me constantly looking over my shoulder wondering if you were lurking around somewhere to hurt me. It hasn't been a good feeling either. Now you're calling me and telling me that you need to see me. How do I know if you're telling the truth or not? I just can't do it."

"Look Aisha, I'll meet you in a public place. That way you won't have to be afraid. We can talk, or rather I can talk. All you have to do is listen to what I have to say." He waited on the other end of the phone. Her silence let him know that she was considering his offer. If he could get her to meet up with him, he felt certain he could convince her of his feelings. She finally gave in.

"Okay, I'll do it. But I'll pick the place."

"Wherever you say, I'll be there," he answered. A big smile covered his face. He'd made it over the first hurdle.

"Interstate Barbeque on Third Street, this evening at seven thirty." Aisha didn't allow him time to reply. She hung up the phone and quickly returned to working on her choreography.

The waitress seated her at a booth near the middle of the restaurant. Chandler walked in just as the waitress was bringing Aisha's order of tea.

"Thank you for seeing me," Chandler said and leaned over so he could kiss Aisha on the cheek. Aisha quickly moved her head before his lips met its intended target. He chose not to comment. He gave the waitress his drink order and proceeded to sit down.

Before walking away, the waitress asked if they were ready to place their orders. Aisha nodded and smiled. After scanning the menu, they ordered their food.

Aisha studied his profile. He was a handsome man, always had been. He looked more chiseled, like he'd been hitting the gym around the clock. His crystal white teeth and mustached lips enhanced his already good looks.

"What do you want to talk to me about? If you're going to start stalking me again and trying to set me up, I'm telling you that I'm not going to put up with it anymore. I'll go to Internal Affairs, the newspaper, whatever I have to do. But I won't live in fear of you any more."

Chandler watched her as she demanded that he leave her alone. He had to make things right with her. He wanted to convince her that he wasn't out to harm her. He reached across the table to grab hold of her hand. She quickly removed it before he could grasp it. Anger formed inside of him but he couldn't let her know that she was pissing him off. *Who does she think she is?*

"Aisha, I know I've done some questionable things. I understand why you feel the way you do about me. But the fact is, I didn't know how to deal with my feelings when I found out you were working at The Lynx. Imagine how I felt when I saw you walk into that house as my private dancer. I almost blew my cover right then and there. I was devastated. I loved you, Aisha. I know I never told you but I was planning to tell you as soon as my assignment ended. But seeing you that night reminded me of Tracye. I felt like I was being betrayed all over again."

Listening to his confession, Aisha's heart began to soften as she witnessed the hurt look on his face. She remembered the night she stood before Chandler, the man who she thought was Kyle Taylor at the time. Putting herself in his shoes, she imagined how she would have reacted had the situation been reversed. She admitted that their relationship was ruined because of her actions. For that she was sorry.

"I'm sorry, but I can't do anything to change that. All I can tell you is that I didn't mean to hurt you," Aisha told him. "I didn't mean to destroy what we had together. Things in my life plummeted out of control so fast I got caught up in the game of making fast money. Along with the fast money, came drugs to help me keep making the fast money. With the drugs came a downward spiral of my life. But I never meant to hurt you or anyone."

"Aisha, you don't know what it means to hear you say that. I know I said some atrocious things to you. That's why I wanted to see you face to face. I'm asking if you can find it in your heart to forgive me. I didn't know how to react, or how to express to you what I was feeling, so I retaliated by calling you names and stalking you." Tears crested in the corner of Chandler's eyes. "Aisha, I still care about you. I want the chance to make things work for us. But if you say that they can't, then at least please tell me that we can be friends."

The waitress brought their orders and placed them on the table. Aisha glanced at her barbequed salad. Chandler didn't bother looking at his jumbo shoulder sandwich and onion rings. He concentrated on Aisha, afraid if he looked away that she would be gone from his life forever.

Aisha picked up her fork and picked over her salad. She was taken aback by Chandler's outpouring of love for her. She didn't know what to say or how to counter what he'd said. There was a time she had believed that Chandler was the man of her dreams, but it hadn't worked out that way. Yes, she blamed herself for hurting him, but she also believed there was a reason for everything. She believed that Chandler was basically a good man with a lot of love to give. But time brings about a change and now her heart belonged to Jackson.

"What are you thinking?" Chandler asked sullenly.

"I'm thinking of how much I hurt you, Chandler. I don't want to hurt you ever again. That's why I have to be honest with you. First, let me say that I do forgive you. I really do. I hope you can find it in your heart to forgive me as well. I once cared deeply for you. I think I can even say that I was starting to fall in love with you. But that was then and this is now. I can't change the series of events that took place. Neither can you. And now I'm in love with someone else."

"Is it that minister? Jackson Williams?"

Aisha reared back in her chair. "Yes," she answered, confessing to Chandler something she hadn't yet admitted to Jackson. She loved Jackson. Sitting across from Chandler confirmed her feelings. "But how do you know about Jackson?"

"I'm not going to lie to you. I promised you I wouldn't. I've seen the two of you together. It really doesn't matter where," he told her. "But needless to say, I'm a cop, Aisha.

I'm observant. And from what I observed when I saw the two of you together, I knew there was something between you. That's it. That's the God's honest truth." Chandler threw up his hands in surrender.

This time it was her turn to reach out and console Chandler. She held his hand and tenderly squeezed it. Reaching across the table she used the back of her hand to wipe away his falling tears.

Jackson dialed Aisha's cell for the fifth time and for the fifth time it went straight into her voice mail. He hung up and dialed her apartment number again, still no answer. He scanned his memory to see if he could remember whether or not Aisha had told him she was going somewhere after leaving the studio. It was almost ten thirty and she wasn't at the studio. He knew because after he couldn't reach her, he had driven by there to see if her car was still there. The lot was empty and all of the lights were off. He sat at his kitchen table and ran both hands through his hair, a sure indication that he was worried about her. He grabbed his keys and stormed out the door.

While Jackson worried himself sick, Aisha and Chandler left the restaurant.

"I'll follow you home to make sure you get there safely," Chandler offered. "If that's okay with you."

"That's not necessary," Aisha assured him.

"Please, let me do something. I can at least make sure you get home safely."

Aisha relented. "Okay. But I'm tired, Chandler. I just want to get home. I've had a long day and will have an even longer day tomorrow."

"Sure, no problem. I'll just follow you and then go on about my way." On that note, they each went to their cars and Chandler proceeded to follow Aisha.

They arrived at her apartment. For the first time in

months, they were able to enjoy one another's company. Aisha felt convinced that Chandler had been sincere with his apology.

"Everyone deserves a second chance," he'd told her and she agreed. That was all Chandler had hoped for. Then thoughts of Tracye's betrayal resurfaced in his mind. The more he looked at Aisha, the more she began to look like Tracye. Tracye was a slut. Or was it Aisha? He couldn't think. *Tracye slept with your friend. Aisha is no better*, the voice inside of his head kept toying with him, confusing him. *Aisha betrayed you too.*

"I'll walk you to your door." The two of them stood in front of her door. Without warning, Chandler grabbed her shoulders. He pulled her toward him. His breathing became heavy within seconds.

"What are you doing? Turn me a loose."Aisha tried to yank away from his grip. But his lips crushed hers violently. She twisted her body but his massive hands were unyielding. The force of his teeth against her lips bruised hers.

"Chandler. Stop it. No. Let . . . me . . . go," she tried to yell as her head snapped back. He held her so tightly she could barely speak.

"You know you like it like this. You don't really want that jacked up preacher. You want some roughness in your life. Don't you?"

Aisha was petrified. Chandler was crazy. She realized that now. How could she have allowed Chandler to deceive her again? She should have known better.

He kissed her forcefully again while his hands invaded the most private areas of her body. Her salty tears flowed but her tears only excited him more as he lapped them up with his tongue. He viciously pulled her hair back and sucked on her neck while he squeezed her breasts hard. His legs forcefully parted her thighs and he used his knee and hands to do vile things to her.

Jackson pulled up in front of the complex. He witnessed Aisha and Chandler kissing. Furious, he was about to jump out of the car and attack Chandler. *How could she do this? How?* Jackson's heart skipped a beat when he saw her head tilt backwards. *Is she laughing?* His head rested on the steering wheel. He pounded his fists against the dashboard and put the car in reverse. Unable to watch the two any longer, he sped away.

Chandler slammed Aisha against the door and forced her to unlock it. He pushed it open so hard, it sounded like it was about to pop off the hinges.

"Chandler, please. Please don't do this," she begged him.

Chandler's laugh was that of a deranged person. His eyes narrowed menacingly. He violently pushed her inside her apartment.

Aisha fell on the cold hardwood floor. Aisha realized she was at the mercy of a sick man. One whose mind had been tormented and broken to the point that he must have gone mad. With a glazed look in his eyes, he saw Tracye's face plastered on Aisha's.

Aisha tried to use her feet to push the door close before he could get all the way in but she didn't have the strength.

He bolted inside, reached down and punched her in the gut with brute force, rendering Aisha totally incapacitated. "Did you really think I would want somebody like you?" He jeered. "Well, I don't, Tracye. And I never will! You want forgiveness?" he asked her. "Look in the mirror. That's how I forgive!" With the very next breath, Chandler stopped, kneeling down beside her, he held her in his arms and started weeping. "Aisha, I'm sorry. I didn't mean to hurt you. I'm so sorry," he said. "I'm so sorry." Then he turned around and ran.

She thought she heard him drive off, but she was too scared to move. She didn't know if she *could* move. She was in agony, but still managed to whisper, "Thank you, God for saving me," and she began to weep.

# 41

Aisha lay on the floor for almost forty-five minutes, barely able to move, and if she could she was too afraid that Chandler was still lurking outside. Finally, mustering up the nerve, she slowly crawled over to the door. She locked the dead bolt and slid back down to the floor, bent over and sobbed into her hands. For the next several minutes Aisha lay next to the door trembling in fear. She was traumatized. Should she call 911? What would she tell them? It would be her word against the well respected detective, Chandler Larson. Once he finished telling his chief about her past, no one would believe her.

All of a sudden, she screamed like a wounded animal, followed by a wave of nausea that caused her to retch and heave. It hurt for her to touch her own belly. "Oh God," she continued to sob as inch by inch she dragged herself in pain to the bathroom in the hall. She managed to run a hot tub of water. She climbed inside and began to scrub her violated body until her skin started to tingle from the roughness. It was over an hour before she got out of the tub. Dripping wet, she held on to the wall, like a zombie; stumbling into the bedroom, she fell diagonally across her bed.

Pulling the covers up around her neck she wept until she gave in to the call of sleep. Even in her sleep, Chandler's assault tormented her. She bolted upright in the bed. Glancing over at the clock on her nightstand she saw that it was 3:45 in the morning. *Jackson. Oh my God.* She reached for the phone to call him so she could explain to him what had happened. Just as she was about to dial his number, she looked on the caller ID. He'd already called her several times. *I can't tell him. He won't understand. He'll ask me why I met him in the first place. Why did I?*

She glanced over at her answering machine and saw the message light flashing. *Why didn't he call on my cell?* she asked herself. She got up from the bed and stumbled into the hallway where her purse and keys were still lying on the floor. She shivered again in fear. She quickly grabbed up her purse and raced back into her bedroom, slamming and locking her bedroom door behind her. Frantic, she searched inside her purse until she found the razor thin phone. *Oh, dang, I didn't even turn it on when I left the restaurant last night.*

Throwing the phone down on the floor, she pushed the buttons to listen to the messages on her home phone. With each message, Jackson's concern escalated. She heard the sound of worry in his voice as he spoke into the machine. *"Aisha, if you're there, answer the phone. Beep. Aisha, where are you? Beep. Aisha, are you okay? Call me." Beep. "Aisha, you won't answer your cell." Beep. "Aisha, sweetheart, call me and let me know you're all right."*

After listening to the messages, she picked up the phone to call him. She thought about what she would tell him. *I'll remind him that I worked late. Then I'll tell him that I was worn out so I came home, took a shower and fell asleep. I can't tell him the truth. I just can't.* There was no answer at his apartment.

*He must be asleep himself. Good, maybe he'll believe me when I talk to him later today.* Aisha rocked back and forth on the bed. Her eyes had begun to swell from crying and her body ached from Chandler's attack.

Early the next morning, before the sun came up, Jackson was awakened by Aisha's distinct ring tone on his cell phone. But Jackson ignored her phone calls, the same way she'd obviously ignored his calls last night to be with Chandler. He couldn't believe that she had been lying to him all of this time. She had managed to convince him that Chandler was some kind of crazed maniac cop who was stalking and harassing her to no end. But what he witnessed surely hadn't looked like someone who was afraid of Chandler nor did Chandler look or act like a stalker. Had she been fabricating these tall tales all along? And if so, how many more lies had she been feeding him? For the first time he had serious doubts about Aisha's honesty. If he couldn't trust her, there was certainly no way he could hope to continue a relationship with her, let alone contemplate asking her to become his wife.

His phone began ringing again. He turned it off. He wasn't ready to confront her about what he'd seen, not now. Thoughts tackled his mind about the good times he'd spent with Aisha and the love that had evolved in his heart for her. He had prayed for God's hand of guidance and direction to be upon him throughout this relationship. Dropping down on his knees and clasping his hands together, Jackson lifted his petition up before God. At this point, he believed that God had allowed him to witness Aisha's betrayal so he could realize that she wasn't the one for him. As bad as it hurt, he trusted God and he determined within his spirit that he would get through this painful situation with God's help.

Aisha's body was banged up and awfully sore. She could

hardly move a muscle. Had Chandler broken any of her bones or ribs? *Call Tameria and ask her to come and check you out.* Ignoring her inner voice, Aisha began dialing Angie to tell her that she wouldn't be coming in today. "I feel terrible Angie. I think I might have the flu and I don't want to give it to the girls. I don't want to set off a chain reaction this close to competition," she managed to do a fake grin, but even that felt like Chandler had punched her all over again.

"Do you need anything?" Angie asked her. "I can bring you some soup or something," she offered. "You sound terrible. I can barely hear you?"

*That's because every word that comes out of my mouth makes my body hurt.* "No, that won't be necessary. I'll check back with you later, Angie, bye." She couldn't lie to Angie for much longer. She looked at her cell phone to see if she had any missed calls or voice mails, but there were none. Neither were there any messages on her home phone from Jackson. Her concern mounted even more after she had called him and didn't get an answer. Her cell phone rang and before it went to the second ring, she answered.

"Jackson?"

"No. Your mother."

Aisha's chest sunk. "Good morning, Mother. How are you?"

"I'm fine. But you sound like a Mack truck just ran over you. Is something wrong?" Old habits die hard and Sandra was the perfect example of that. Not waiting on Aisha to give her an answer, she jumped on what was important to her. "I hope you haven't upset Jackson. You know you can be excessive and overly dramatic, Aisha."

"Mother, please, not this morning. Jackson and I are doing fine," Aisha answered, forcing each word out of her mouth as cautiously as possible to reduce the pain. "And, Mother, I don't appreciate your early morning criticism. I don't feel well and I'm not up to hearing it. Just because I assumed you were Jackson on the phone doesn't make me dramatic."

"I know when you're feeling guilty about something, but if you've blown it with that man, that's on you. I'm finished with it," Sandra answered. "I think he's a good catch. And he's a minister too."

Aisha tried to mask her emotions and her pain by changing the subject. "So you're back at home?"

"Yes. I called last night to tell you, but like always, I didn't get an answer."

"Sorry, Mother," Aisha mumbled. *But I was busy being brutally assaulted last night*, she wanted to say but held her tongue. Knowing her mother, if she knew what Chandler had done to her last night, she would somehow manage to blame Aisha for that too. For once, Aisha would have agreed with her mother's conclusion. She ignored her inner voice and continued talking. "I had a lot of things going on yesterday. But I'm glad you made it back home safely."

Sandra didn't like the sound of her daughter's voice. There was something she wasn't telling her. Sandra stood in the kitchen with one hand positioned on her hip. "Have you tried calling Jackson on his cell phone?"

"Duh, of course I have. He doesn't answer. But if he's with a church member at the hospital or sitting with someone who's dying, then you know he isn't going to answer," Aisha explained while trying not to get annoyed with her mother's drill.

"Seems to me like there's something more going on. Certainly Jackson would call and let you know he's okay even if he can only talk a second or two. Let me see, it's almost eight o'clock. The church office opens around eighty thirty doesn't it?"

"Yes. Why?" Aisha responded with her own question.

"Because you need to get on that phone and call his secretary as soon as that clock strikes eight thirty. Do you hear me?" Sandra's voice raised an octave.

"Look, Mother. How many times do I have to remind you that I am *not* a child? Plus, I don't feel well. Jackson can call *me* if he wants to talk to me. Understand this, Mother. I can handle my own affairs and I can certainly handle my relationship with Jackson, which is none of your business anyway," Aisha retorted through clinched teeth.

As if she hadn't heard a word Aisha said, Sandra ordered, "Find out where he is. Do not mess this up. Jackson will be good for you. I'd hate to see you lose out because of your lackadaisical attitude about things. Now follow my advice and call me as soon as you hear something. Goodbye."

Sandra hung up the phone, shook her head and positioned her eyes toward heaven. "Father, help that child of mine. She's just like her daddy; stubborn, naïve and narrow minded." Sandra grabbed her house keys and headed out the door for her daily three-mile walk.

Aisha called the church office twice. Both times Natalie told her that Jackson wasn't available. Natalie offered to transfer her to his voice mail, but Aisha had refused. What she had to say couldn't be left on an answering system. She tried working on the choreography moves, but she hurt all over and she couldn't concentrate. *Did Chandler do something to Jackson too? No, if that were true, Natalie would have had a different response when I called.* Her worry about what was bothering Jackson soon began to transform into anger. Where was he when she needed him? Whenever she reached him, she planned on giving him an earful!

Aisha stayed at home nursing her physical and emotional wounds. She forced herself to take another hot bath, although every bone in her body seemed to hurt. While dragging around the apartment all day, Aisha tried concentrating on writing the steps for a routine she wanted the girls to perform at the competition. Angie called to see how she was feeling, offering to come over and make her something to eat. Aisha turned her down. There was no way she wanted Angie to see her bruised and crippled. She didn't want anyone to know. Aisha ran her hand along her swollen cheek bones. Her neck was bruised. She almost passed out when she saw the black and blue marks that practically covered her from her chest all the way down below her waist. Even when she peed, it hurt.

For the life of her Aisha couldn't understand the sudden change in Jackson. Chandler, well at least with him, Aisha wasn't as surprised. But Jackson, the short time they had been friends, he was attentive, affectionate and kind to her. Every moment they spent together was fun and Aisha's feelings had definitely deepened. Then he has to pull something like this? She didn't understand. Every scenario she could think of concerning his weird behavior did not make sense. *There must be something wrong with me.* Aisha thought. *Maybe he wants more than what I'm willing to give. Or maybe he thought he liked me but found out he didn't. Is he gay? Oh, God say it isn't so.* She grinned when that thought surfaced. *Jackson was far from gay. There is just no explanation that makes sense. I guess I have to let it go and let God handle it.*

During the course of the day, Aisha began to feel slightly better. She even watched *The Young and the Restless,* her favorite soap opera from high school through college. While watching the soap opera, Aisha rubbed herself down with green alcohol with aspirins inside. It was an old remedy her Oma used to relieve aching, sore muscles. Aisha rubbed her body throughout the day. Sure enough, by the afternoon she began to feel some of the soreness and tension easing up.

As another day came to an end, there had still been no word from Jackson. Aisha laid in her bed trying to concentrate on writing out the final dance steps for the nationals.

Each sound she heard in her apartment caused her heart to skip a beat. Before retiring for the night, she checked the locks on the doors and windows for a third time. She exhaled when she didn't see any signs of Chandler. Unable to kneel, Aisha prayed in bed. She prayed for God's protection and thanked him for not letting Chandler rape or kill her. She reached on the nightstand for the Bible her father had given her when she got saved and turned the crinkled pages until she came to Psalms 91. It soothed her spirit and her fear of Chandler returning faded. She placed the Bible next to her on the bed and then tried to go to sleep. Hours later, she was still awake, tossing and turning.

Having had less than three hours of sleep, Aisha got out of bed and called Jackson again. This time she left him a hot message.

"I don't know what kind of game this is that you're playing, *Minister Williams*," she said sarcastically. "But I haven't done a thing for you to treat me like this. If you didn't want us to be friends anymore, you should have just told me that. I thought that ministers were supposed to be so trustworthy. I see that you sure aren't." Aisha didn't say anything else. She ended the call. She hurt too badly. *I should call Tameria*, she thought, as another piercing pain ran from her head to her belly.

# 42

Tameria had been at Chase's apartment making plans for her impending graduation. This was another milestone that moved her closer to reaching her goal to become an internist. The next step would be to complete her medical residency. By the time she completed residency Chase would have three years under his graduation belt and would be either working with a group of doctors or entering into private practice for himself. Tameria looked forward to their careers as doctors. She couldn't have chosen a better field. The hours were long, the work was extremely difficult but the thought of being blessed to help save lives was stupendous.

She and Chase were practically living together and she no longer felt a need to hide the fact that they were. At this point, Aisha had definitely shown her that just because a person behaves one way in front of one group of people, that it surely doesn't mean they're who they say they are. Aisha was still Tameria's best friend and there was nothing she wouldn't try to do for her, but let's face it, when Aisha told her about her double life, Tameria had been absolutely floored by the revelation. *Aisha? Nice, innocent, church lady Aisha?* Every time Tameria thought about Aisha's past, she was still amazed and shocked by the things Aisha had gotten herself into. But now it looked like her friend's life had truly taken a turn for the best. Jackson was not only a good person, but he was good to Aisha. And as far as Tameria knew, Aisha had told Jackson everything about her past.

Chase entered the bedroom and sat down beside Tameria. "Hi there, Dr. Matthews."

"Hello yourself, Dr. Gray," she replied, and smiled in return and kissed him on the lips. "Tired?" she asked him as she noticed his wrinkled brow and the circles forming under his deep brown eyes.

"Yeah. The past thirty-six hours were pure torture. We had eight serious head trauma injuries. This city is becoming more violent as we speak and the increase in the number of African-American teenagers coming into the emergency room is alarming."

Chase had grown up with parents who were avid supporters of groups, agencies, and programs that addressed the plight of youth. The same sense of concern, compassion and the need to help make a positive difference in the lives of teens had been passed down to Chase and his three other brothers, one of whom was an attorney, the second a physician's assistant and the third who was a high school English teacher.

Tameria climbed on the bed and rested on her knees behind Chase. Gently pulling his head back to rest just above her breasts, she massaged his temples in a slow relaxing motion. Chase groaned from pleasure and his body became almost limp as she moved her hands along his neck and on to his shoulders.

"How does this feel?" she whispered in his ear.

"Hmmmm," was his response. His eyes closed and within minutes she heard his labored breathing and light snore.

Carefully moving from underneath the weight of his body, she eased him down on the bed, removed his shoes and pulled the covers up to his chest.

Tameria eased off of the bed and tip-toed in the kitchen. Her medical books were on the table. She opened the fridge and reached for a diet Pepsi, followed by a package of Oreo cookies. She sat down then opened the first book and began studying. Thirty minutes passed and Tameria had a strong urge to call Aisha. She laid her book aside and told herself to take a fifteen minute study break.

"Aisha, 'sup girlfriend?" Tameria said through the receiver.

"Hi, Tameria, nothing's going on. Unless you're talking about the fact that my whole life is in a shambles," Aisha said in a monotone voice which immediately signaled to Tameria that something was bothering her friend.

"What is it? You sound like death?"

"I *feel* like death."

"You and Jackson okay?"

"Not really. But then I don't know."

"What do you mean by you don't know? Either you're doing good or you're not. Which is it?"

"He's acting really strange. I mean, we went from talking two, three four times a day to him not returning any of my calls. It's been like this for the past four days."

"Have you come out and asked him what's bothering him? Maybe he has a lot on his plate. He is a minister and counselor after all."

"Yeah, I know that. But I'm telling you, He *won't* return my calls, so how *can* I ask him?"

"That does sound weird. You need to sit him down and find out what the deal is, Aisha." Tameria suggested. "Run him down at church. Girl, do what you have to do to find out what's wrong with him."

"I thought about that, but I'm not about to chase up behind some man. He might be seeing someone else at that church. Probably has all along. Anyway, this just happened a few days ago, and I didn't go to church or Bible study this week." *I could hardly get out of bed after what Chandler did to me.*

"Don't get all crazy on me. It just might be possible that he's met someone else. But Jackson doesn't strike me as the kind of man that would string a woman along. I would think that before he did that, he would tell you."

"Girl, whatever. A man is a man," Aisha managed to say without hurting as badly as before. "Whether he's a preacher, minister, blue collar worker, a scrub, or a man of the law. It doesn't matter, they're all subject to being liars and deceivers."

"I don't agree with your analysis of our men. That's what's wrong with us women. We're always going around bashing them. No wonder they turn to women outside their race. We still have African-American brothers that are good, decent and know how to treat a lady. But just like us, and anything in life, there's always a bad apple somewhere in the bunch. You just have to find the bad one and remove it from the rest of the bunch."

Aisha wanted to tell Tameria everything but she was too ashamed. Even if Tameria was her best friend, she didn't want her to know how gullible she had been. "Well, I never would have thought Jackson would have turned out to be a bad apple," Aisha rebuffed.

"Who said that he is? The man probably is overextended, that's all. Give him a break. You watch what I tell you. He's going to sit down and talk to you."

"We'll see. Anyway, how are you and Chase? I take it you're at his apartment."

"Things couldn't be better. And yes, I'm at his place. You already knew that before you asked. I've told you before, Chase and I spend as much time together as we can and with the hours we spend at the hospital, every minute is precious to us. If that means I have to camp out at his place or vice versa, then that's what I'm going to do."

"Suit yourself, but it's still shacking up anyway you look at it," Aisha insisted.

"Whatever, but let's not get all self-righteous and judgmental *babee*. I know you aren't even going to try to go there," Tameria shot back.

"I'm not trying to be self-righteous or anything else, Tameria. All I'm saying is if he gets everything you have to offer without marrying you, why would he feel he has to ever marry you?"

"That's something Chase and I have already discussed. You know I'm graduating from med school next month and he'll be finishing his residency shortly thereafter. When he finishes he's more than likely going to go into practice with some other neurosurgeons. Once he starts making enough money to support us both, then we're going to tie the knot and I'm going to continue with school. You may have a hard time believing that, but it's true. We *are* going to get married and we *are* going to spend the rest of our lives together," Tameria said with conviction.

"Okay, okay, no need to get your panties all in a wad. I only want the best for you. You know I have your back," Aisha replied.

"I know. And you'll see. Well, look I've gotta go. I have some studying to do. Why don't you try calling that man of yours again and see if you can get him to open up."

"I might. But I need to tell you something else."

"See, I knew something was wrong with you. What is it?"

"Chandler called me a couple of weeks ago."

"Chandler? You need to report that fool for real. The man is a bonafide stalker. I knew that he had to have something to do with the way you're feeling."

"No, no, wait a minute. Let me tell you what happened. The man begged me to listen to him. At first I told him no, but he kept insisting and he sounded so pitiful and, and . . . " Aisha started to cry. "And so I met him and we sat down and talked. He told me he was sorry for everything he'd done to me."

"Really?"

"Yes, really. And there's more. He told me that he only said and did the things he did because he had a hard time accepting the fact that I was involved with The Lynx."

"That's understandable, but he sure had a scary way of showing it. I thought the guy was an undercover serial murderer instead of an undercover cop," Tameria laughed.

*Tameria has no idea how close she is.* "After listening to him, I really believed he was sincere, Tameria. He told me that he still cared about me and he wanted to start over again."

"What did you say?"

"I told him I loved Jackson. He didn't like what I said, but he accepted it."

"Oh my, there is a God," Tameria teased again. "Anyway, that's good, but I'd still be careful if I were you. Make sure this isn't another one of his games, you know."

*Too late for that. I already fell feet first into the stupid bucket.* "Yea, I know, and I'm going to be cautious."

"If you begin to have any negative vibes about him, promise me that you'll report him without so much as a blink."

*Oops. Already made dumb move number two. My life is a living nightmare and Chandler is the monster in my closet.* "I will," Aisha responded without conviction. "Wait, hold up, Tameria, I can't do this," Aisha said, and exhaled heavily.

"Do what?"

"I haven't told you everything. As a matter of fact, I wasn't going to tell you at all. But I have to tell somebody, and you *are* my best friend."

"Aisha, what happened?" Tameria's voice took on a serious tone. She didn't have a good feeling about whatever it was Aisha was about to tell her.

"Chandler is insane and I mean for real. He assaulted me. Tameria, I thought he was going to kill me," Aisha whispered like someone was eavesdropping on her.

"What!" Tameria screamed under her breath so as not to wake up Chase. "Aisha! When did this happen?"

"Four days ago."

"And you just decided to tell me? I can't believe this," Tameria said, sounding quite upset at Aisha.

"I know, but I didn't tell anybody. I was too ashamed. I mean, I can't believe I trusted him again, after how he did me the first time."

"Forget that. Did you call the police?"

"He *is* the police. Who would believe me?"

"Do you know where he is?"

"No, and I'm scared he might come back. He was calling me his ex-girlfriend's name; he beat me pretty badly. I thought he was going to rape me, or worse, kill me. Tameria it was awful." Aisha trembled in fear at the very thought.

"Have you seen a doctor?" Tameria was livid.

"No, I started to call you, but I just couldn't. I couldn't tell anyone, Tameria. But I'm okay. I feel much better. Just still bruised and sore so I haven't been to the studio this week."

"Oh my God, Aisha. I can't believe this. And Jackson doesn't know about any of this?" Tameria asked, nervously tapping her pencil on the kitchen table.

Aisha's voice escalated. She felt panicky and paranoid. "No, I can't reach him."

"Aisha, I'm so sorry this happened to you." Tameria looked at her watch. "Aisha I hate to have to do this, but I have to get ready for work. But at least come by the hospital and let me check you out."

"I'll think about it. But don't worry about me. I know you have to work."

"But we have to figure something out, Aisha," Tameria said while walking through Chase's apartment in search of a pair scrubs. "If Chandler is crazy like you say he is, then something has to be done. Who knows, he might come back."

"I thought about that too. But then I was thinking that he would have been back by now and he hasn't. I think he's done with me."

"I pray that he is. I'll try to call and check on you later, okay?"

"Thanks, Tameria," Aisha told her, feeling better now that she had confided in her.

"I want you to watch your back. Be careful out there, Aisha. Please be careful. And keep trying to call Jackson. He needs to know what's going on," Tameria urged.

"I will, now go on and get ready for work. Bye."

Aisha thought about Tameria's suggestion to call Jackson. Before she could pick up the phone to call him, her phone rang. It was one of her girl's parents, wanting to know about the competition. After hanging up, Aisha decided that she wasn't going to call him, she was going to see him face to face. Whether he wanted to or not she made up in her mind to find out what was going on with him and why he was taking it out on her. Aisha left to confront Minister Jackson Williams.

On her way to Jackson's condo, Aisha put in her Donnie McClurkin CD. Donnie was one of her favorite gospel artists. His songs could lift her up from the deepest bouts of depression. She needed to hear the words of his song in order to drown out thoughts of Chandler. At the end of the track, she turned off the CD player and flicked on the radio. She turned abruptly into Wal-Mart's parking lot when she heard the reporter. She sat and listened, stunned at what he was saying.

"Memphis Detective, Chandler Larson, pleaded guilty last Friday to stealing money confiscated from the bust at The Lynx. Larson admitted to holding out over $375,000 of the unmarked drug money. Larson is a ten-year veteran police officer with several commendations. He has also admitted to conspiring with Ronald Shipley to transport drugs into the mid-south by arranging clearance of drug runners on I-40. Shipley, brother of Reverend Donald Shipley of Faithside Temple, recently found guilty of human trafficking and drug trafficking, is serving 35 years to life. Shipley was said to be the mastermind behind the plan to distribute over 3.5 million dollars worth of cocaine on the streets of Memphis.

"It has been reported that Larson recently suffered a nervous breakdown, or some type of psychotic episode. He is being held at the Criminal Justice Center in the psychiatric unit of the jail under suicide watch. Larson's attorney has requested a psychiatric evaluation for his client to determine if he is mentally competent to stand trial. Larson faces 35 years to life plus a $475,000 fine. Larson, along with three other officers, has been charged with official corruption in an ongoing investigation labeled Operation Cruise Control. He is being held on a $1,000,000 bond."

*Lord, I don't know whether to be happy or sad.* Aisha sat in the parking lot for fifteen minutes. Her head ached. She pressed the side of her temples hoping it would somehow make it subside. Deciding to take advantage of where she was, she went inside Wal-Mart to purchase something for her headache. With each step the hurt and pain she had experienced slowly evolved into a smile of gratitude when she thought about Chandler's fate. *He won't be able to hurt me any more. He's out of my life for good. Thank you, God.*

# 43

"Northwest flight 5780 departing for Chicago is now boarding at gate 8," the ticket agent spoke into the microphone, repeating the call for passengers to board.

Jackson looked around the area where he had been seated to make sure he wasn't leaving anything. He reached for his carry-on bag and laptop then proceeded to get in line to board his flight.

Pastor Shipley's schedule was already overloaded. So he asked Jackson if he would run revival on his behalf at Faith Missionary Baptist Church in Chicago, whose shepherd was none other than the famous Pastor Curtis J. Black. Jackson jumped at the opportunity to preach his first revival and rejoiced that Pastor Shipley had faith that he could carry it out. It was the perfect occasion for him to get away and clear his head. He would be in Chicago for two weeks and he had made up his mind to be over and done with Aisha Carlisle by the time he returned to Memphis.

Aisha waited at the entrance of Jackson's condo, waiting on someone who had a code to get in so she could rush in behind them. Her wait wasn't long and now she stood at

Jackson's door with her thumb pressing full force against his doorbell. When he didn't answer for the umpteenth time, she curled her hand in a rigid fist and pounded on the heavy steel and oak door. Disgusted and defeated, Aisha turned around in anger and stomped back to her car. "Jackson Williams, I'm through with you," she mumbled underneath her breath before speeding out of the complex.

"I'll call his office one last time. If he doesn't answer, then I'm through." She pushed the speed button on her cell and waited to hear Natalie's always cheerful voice. "Hello, Natalie, this is Aisha. I need to speak to Minister Williams right away please. And will you tell him that it's important," Aisha emphasized.

Natalie had no idea what had happened between Minister Williams and Aisha, but something was going on, that much she was sure about. Over the past couple of weeks Minister Williams had been quiet and elusive, almost with a sad countenance rather than his usually cheerful persona. He always had an excuse for not accepting Aisha's calls. Now Aisha was calling for him again and Natalie wasn't sure what kind of response she'd get from Aisha after she told her that he would be out of town for the next two weeks.

"Aisha, I'm sorry, but Minister Williams is out of town. He's preaching a revival in Chicago and he won't be back for two weeks," Natalie said.

Aisha was stunned. Holding the phone, and biting her bottom lip, she responded, "Oh, is that right? Thank you, Natalie," she said and promptly ended the call.

On the way home, Aisha decided that enough was enough. She couldn't take this anymore. Jackson, like Chandler, was not the man for her. Her life had been far better when God was the head of it and not some good-for-nothing man.

Aisha slung her purse on the sofa and stomped into the kitchen for bottled water. Maybe the ice cold water would somehow soothe her mounting furor towards Jackson. "The nerve of him. He's gone to Chicago for two weeks," she yelled. "Jackson, you will never have to worry about me again. You can bank on that!" The ringing phone snatched her from her anger.

"Aisha, I was just checking on you. How are you?" Tameria asked.

"I'm okay. I just found out that Jackson left town. He's gone to Chicago for two weeks to a revival."

"What are you going to do?" Tameria had no answers this time.

"Go on with my life. I think I can do that now, Tameria. I no longer have to worry if Chandler might be lurking around some corner. As for Jackson, he was a nice friend for a short while and that's that. I just want to move on and that's what I'm going to do."

"I feel you. But I really am sorry things didn't work out with Jackson," Tameria said sympathetically.

"Not to worry. If there's anything I've learned from everything that's happened to me lately, it's that the only man that has my back and that really matters is the man upstairs." Aisha's phone beeped. "Tameria, I have another call coming in. I'll talk to you later."

"Okay, bye,"

She sighed heavily when she saw the name *Mother* on the ID.

Aisha didn't bother with greetings. "What is it now, Mother?"

Sandra jumped right back into her tirade. "Now you may not want to listen and you may not want to hear this, but I *am* your mother. And I'm responsible for telling you what's right, Aisha. If you get an attitude and want to holler, scream and disrespect me, then that's between you and God. You'll have to answer to him for how you treat me. So get mad, or whatever you want to do, but I'm going to say what I have to say."

"I'm sure you are," Aisha said smartly.

"I tell you, sometimes I just don't understand you."

"No, you have it twisted," Aisha immediately retorted. She couldn't hold back any longer. It was like a dam had broken loose and had forced the floodgates to open. "It's *you* I don't understand. I thought you had really changed, Mother. But you're still the same selfish, thoughtless human being you always were. As for Jackson, maybe the two of *you* belong together. He seems to have some of your sense-less, heartless ways." Aisha didn't let up with her assault on Sandra. "It's always me who's at fault, if I let you tell it. Well, I'm tired of always getting the blame for everything. Your precious Minister Jackson Williams is the one who dropped out of sight," she continued yelling.

Sandra Carlisle's jaw fell open as she listened to the tone of her daughter's voice. The more Aisha talked, the angrier Sandra Carlisle became. "Don't you talk to me like that!"

"Don't you come to me with your fault-finding," Aisha shot back. "How can you take someone else's side over your own flesh and blood? You don't even know Jackson like that, Mother, for you to be putting him up on some un-reachable pedestal. So let me enlighten you about the *oh so perfect* Jackson Williams. He's the one who decided he didn't want to have anything to do with me but didn't bother telling me. If he's such the perfect man, Mr. Perfect would have had the decency to tell me when he didn't want to be bothered."

"If what you say is true, he must have a good reason. I may not know him but I do know you. And you are such a stupid child! There's no reaching you," Sandra chided.

"You know what, I'm tired, I'm fed up and I really don't want to continue this conversation, *Mother*, because if I do, I won't be responsible for what I say," Aisha hollered. "Good bye."

Sandra walked through the empty house talking as if Aisha was standing next to her. "You're making a hard bed for yourself. If you want to spend your life alone, so be it. Stupid, stupid girl. Lord, she's in your hands, 'cause she surely doesn't want to listen to her dear mother."

Jackson took a shower and then settled into his hotel room. Revival had been going good. Each night he preached, God used him in a mighty way. He sat down on the side of the bed, picked up his cell phone, and scrolled until he saw Aisha's phone number. *Should I call her? Why am I acting like a two-year old? Just call her. Tell her what you saw and ask for an explanation.* Ignoring the thoughts growing in his mind, Jackson turned on the television. He found a basketball game and began to watch it. During the second quarter, his body told him that it was time to call it a night. He prayed to God like he did every night, then went to bed.

The next morning Jackson awoke, prayed and then got dressed. One of the trustees was picking him up, but that wasn't going to be until noon. *Might as well go downstairs, relax and have a nice, hearty man-sized breakfast,* he thought to himself. The restaurant was serving a buffet. "Right on time," Jackson said to no one. While enjoying his meal of grits, eggs, bacon, toast, and coffee, he started reading the USA Today newspaper the hotel provided every morning as a courtesy to its guests. Jackson went through each section of the paper. He read the articles that appeared to be of some interest to him. There was a headline, not a big one, but large enough for him to notice. *Corruption and Cops: Who Do They Really Protect and Serve?* Jackson chuckled after reading the headline as he thought of Chandler. "I know who one particular cop is protecting, my girl, " Jackson said out loud. He began reading the article. *Police corruption is pervasive. It is not bound by rank. It cannot be attributed to 'just a few bad apples.' Corruption within the nation's police departments is a fast growing problem of epidemic proportions . . . .*The article went on to highlight cities where large scale corruption had recently been uncovered. He was not prepared for what he read. The city was Memphis, the policeman, none other than Chandler Larson.

# 44

Jackson loomed over the pulpit of Faith Missionary Baptist Church and preached his heart out. "I tell you my people, now is the time. Oh yes, now is the time to lay aside every weight that's holding you down. Now is the time to turn your lives over to the one who can give you life. I say, now is the time for you to come to God. Don't wait until things have gotten better. Don't wait until you stop doing the stuff you know you shouldn't be doing. Don't wait until you don't cuss anymore or you don't go to this place or that place anymore. Don't wait until you don't sell this or smoke this anymore. Come now. Jesus wants you to come, just the way you are. If you'll only come, He'll do the fixing up and cleaning up, I tell you. Paul says in Romans chapter one, verse sixteen, *I am not ashamed of the gospel, because it is the power of God for the salvation of everyone who believes. Not just some of us but for everyone who believes.*" Jackson looked out over the sanctuary at the people who had come to hear what God had given him to say.

Every night since he'd been there preaching, God had been moving. At the close of each worship service, Jackson extended an invitation to anyone who wanted to accept Christ in their lives. With his hand outstretched, Jackson welcomed the people to come to Jesus. One by one, people came forward. Jackson lifted up his hands and his head toward the sky and began praising God.

This was Jackson's last night in Chicago and the experience had served its purpose. Pastor Black, like he had done every night, praised Jackson for preaching a powerful revival. After tonight's revival service, Pastor Black and his deacons took Jackson out to dinner and then drove him to his hotel. Not only had he been blessed to minister to lost souls, but he felt like he had been released from a vice grip that had been wrapped around his heart.

Night after night, he'd prayed to God to help him decide about his relationship with Aisha. His sermon the night before had been on forgiveness. In his heart, he knew God had given him that message for himself as well as the congregation. He was the one who had to exercise forgiveness. He lay on the hotel bed and relived the night he saw Aisha and Chandler. Why hadn't he allowed her the chance to explain rather than ignore her? There could be a logical explanation. *But they were kissing for God's sake.* How much more did he need to see? "Everything isn't always as it seems," Jackson thought he heard someone say. Jackson looked around the hotel room. No matter how it had hurt him, within his heart he knew that he had to bring some closure to their relationship. Closure meant that he would have to talk to Aisha and then he could move on with the rest of his life. He dialed her at home. He was about to hang up when he heard her sweet voice.

"Aisha? Hi, it's Jackson." He barely spoke loud enough for her to hear.

"I know. So you finally decided to call," she said with a mixture of anger and confusion. Why was he calling her now?

"Okay, maybe I deserve that, but . . . "

"But *nothing*, Jackson. Just tell me something. What do you want now?" Aisha's anger was apparent with every word she spoke.

"Listen," Jackson answered.

"No, *you* listen. I have tried calling you God only knows how many times. I've been to your house. I've called the church office. I've called and called. And now, you happen to be ready to talk to me and you think I'm supposed to just listen to what you have to say just because you're Minister Jackson Williams? Well, I don't think so. Find yourself another toy 'cuz I'm not the one." She slammed the phone down so hard that the phone and the receiver fell to the floor. She folded her arms in anger and paced back and forth through her apartment. "The nerve of that man. He really has me messed up. Here I am, running, chasing, wondering, thinking about what I could have done wrong. Blaming myself for everything. But no more. Aisha's smarter than Minister Jackson Davis Williams."

Jackson listened to the sound of the dial tone buzzing in his ear. It took several seconds for him to hang up. The initial shock left him dazed and speechless. Should he try to call her back? He thought for several more minutes about his next move. *For now, I'll let her have it her way. But when I get back to Memphis, one way or the other, we're going to resolve this, Miss Carlisle.* He went into the bathroom, turned on the shower and stepped under the rain of hot steaming water. Maybe, just maybe the water would wash away the sense of loss he just felt, but was afraid to own up to.

# 45

It had been three days since Jackson's return to Memphis. He hadn't seen Aisha at any of the Sunday church services or mid-week Bible study. If she was there, it wouldn't be hard for her to blend in with the thousands of members who poured inside the sanctuary week after week. The tables had indeed turned because no matter how many times he called her, went by the studio or her apartment, she managed to make herself unavailable and out of sight.

Jackson wheeled his car into the studio parking garage. He planned on waiting for her for however long it took. The clock in the car assured him that she should be finishing up her last dance class. To pass the time, he pulled out a Bible commentary from his briefcase and began studying passages of Old Testament scriptures. After waiting for almost forty-five minutes, he looked up and saw her familiar silhouette walking toward him. When she was within a few feet, he opened his car door and got out.

Aisha looked at him, and without saying a word proceeded to open the door to her car.

"Aisha, please wait. We need to talk." He blocked her from getting inside her car.

"Move out of my way, Jackson. I have nothing to say to you."

"You have nothing to say to me? Isn't that something," he said in a voice that confirmed his dislike for her attitude.

Her glower let him know that in no uncertain terms, she was angry.

"You can act like you're the victim all you want, Aisha, but let's face it, you're the one who betrayed me."

"What are you talking about? Betrayed you! Let me refresh your memory. You're the one who dropped out of sight without any explanation whatsoever. You're the one who wouldn't return *my* phone calls or answer your door. It was *you*, not me," she huffed and tried to push him out of the way.

"And you're the one who was seeing that crooked, crazy cop behind my back," he yelled back. The look on her face let him know that she was totally caught off guard. Her shoulders slumped and her eyes were like round gleaming balls.

"Are you accusing me of cheating?"

"Like they say, if the shoe fits . . . " The two of them exchanged silent communication. The tension was thick as sorghum syrup.

"I don't know where you came up with these accusations, but to set the record straight, I have not cheated on you with Chandler or anyone else for that matter."

"I guess kissing him in front of your apartment just happened to be your idea of Chandler stalking you, huh?" he mocked, his jaw tightening in anger.

"Is that what this is about? You saw me and Chandler together?" Aisha cocked her head to the side and let out a sarcastic type laugh. "You know something. You men are all alike. Insecure, fault-finding and plain old jerks. Obviously you're no different from that *sicko*. You had to have been watching me. How else would you have seen what you thought you saw?"

"You're right. I did see. I saw more than I bargained for too. I hadn't heard from you, Aisha. I didn't know if something had happened or not, especially after what Chandler had done to you at the coffee shop. You wouldn't answer your cell phone." Jackson held up his hand and began to angrily count off each reason on his fingers. "You weren't at the studio. You didn't answer your home phone."

The more Aisha listened to Jackson, the more she understood that she had been wrong too. In a way she had betrayed his trust. She should have told him about Chandler wanting to meet her. She should have trusted him enough to tell him everything, from the first time Chandler started calling her. But she didn't. Jackson had every right to be upset.

"I was worried, really worried, so I drove to your apartment." Hitting his palm against his forehead and with sarcasm dripping from his lips, "But stupid me. What did I find instead? You and Chandler all lovey-dovey. From what you led me to believe, you were supposed to be so terrified of this guy. Then I drive up and see just the opposite. What was I *supposed* to think, Aisha?"

"You weren't *supposed to think* anything, Jackson. You were *supposed* to trust me. You could have gotten out of your car and approached both of us, especially if you were uncertain about what was going on. But noooo," she said, "It was easier for you to assume that I was a cheater and a betrayer, I guess."

"Don't try to turn this around and put the blame on me. You were the one with him." Jackson screamed. "After telling me how he treated you and the things he said to you." Jackson gestured wildly with his hands. "Then out of the blue, I see you with this dude. So yeah, I didn't know

what to think. I got crazy when I saw you and him together."

"Why didn't you just talk to me then, instead of just writing me off? You didn't *try* to find out what was going on.
You just thought you saw something and then you ran with
it. You and Chandler are two of a kind," she accused him.

"I didn't talk to you because," he paused. "Because I was
afraid, Aisha. I was afraid you would tell me what I didn't
want to hear. That you loved the guy, as crazy as it sounds,
that's what I thought. But I was wrong, Aisha. I know that
now." Jackson tried to explain. He reached out to pull her to
his chest, but Aisha stepped back in haste.

"I thought we had something special. I trusted you with
the sordid details of my past. I trusted you with my hurts
and my deepest emotions. And you, you couldn't trust me
with what you were thinking and feeling?"

"It wasn't that." Jackson's face took on a somber expression. His heart beat wildly. Part of him was relieved to find
out that Aisha hadn't betrayed him. And the other part didn't
know if there was anything she wasn't telling him.

"What was it then? I guess you want to know everything?"

"Yes, I do." Jackson admitted. Aisha couldn't blame him.
She had to tell him the truth about that night, about everything. And so she did. She drew in a deep breath. Tears
formed in her eyes and droplets slid along her face. There
in the parking garage, Aisha relived that dreadful night.

By the time she finished, the both of them were in tears.
Jackson wished he had gotten out of the car that night. He
had been blinded by the very thing he despised—jealousy.
And Aisha, by the very thing she had feared—vulnerability.

Jackson grabbed both of her shoulders and gingerly
turned her to face him.

"Jackson." Aisha called his name softly. "That night, I
told Chandler that my heart belonged to someone else.

That terrible night I tried to call you. I needed you so bad. I needed to tell you what had happened but you didn't answer me. But that's neither here nor there now. Because the man I loved didn't trust me or believe in what I once thought we shared." As hard as it was for her to do, Aisha pushed Jackson to the side and climbed inside her car.

To think that Chandler hurt her and he could have stopped him ripped at Jackson's heart. Although he was a minister, Jackson's flesh overruled his spirit when it came to Chandler Larson.

"Aisha." Jackson cried with her. "I'm so sorry for what happened to you. I'm so sorry I wasn't there to protect you."

"I know you are, Jackson. And I forgive you, and hope that you can forgive me too. But what do we have if we don't have trust? I'll answer that for you. We have nothing." And with that she drove off, leaving Jackson standing alone in the garage with his own supply of fresh tears pouring from his eyes.

She loved him. It was the first time he'd ever heard her admit she loved him. Someway he had to convince her that he loved her too. He had reacted out of jealousy and distrust. Aisha had been right and he had been wrong. As a man of God, he knew she had done the right thing by accepting Chandler's plea to forgive him. She had been the bigger person while he had operated out of his own fleshly thoughts and desires. Standing in the moldy, damp parking garage, Jackson purposed in his heart and his mind that if necessary, he would spend the rest of his earthly life showing Aisha how much she was loved by him. With that being settled, he climbed in his car and sped off to catch up with the woman he'd pray for all of his life.

Aisha stopped at the grocery store to purchase some fruit and the vegetables for a Caesar salad. It had been hard to see Jackson without obeying the urge to fall into his arms.

The thought of seeing him again stirred up emotions she thought she had pushed aside.

She grabbed the plastic grocery bag and headed for her apartment. She was startled by the sound of footsteps rushing towards her. She abruptly turned around to face whoever was behind her. She stopped in her tracks when she saw it was Jackson.

"Jackson, what are you . . . "

He didn't give her a chance to finish her sentence. He walked up to her and placed his finger over her lips. "Aisha, I was wrong. I've been crazy with jealousy over the thought of you loving someone else. I tried to bury my feelings, tried to pretend that what we had wasn't real. But the more I ran, the more my heart pulled me closer to you. I hope you can forgive me. Forgive me for being so stupid. Forgive me for not telling you how much I really do love you."

The callous expression on Aisha's face softened. The look in her eyes exposed what was in her heart. Hearing Jackson confessing his love for her made her weak in the knees.

As if he could read her mind, he removed the grocery bag from her hand, sat it on the porch and pulled her close inside his arms. She allowed herself to relax and breathe in his familiar scent. At last she felt at home. She felt safe and protected. Jackson caressed her and kissed her hair. He ran his hands tenderly up and down the length of her shoulders. She could hear his heavy breathing and feel his excitement. She looked up at him and his lips passionately overpowered hers. The hunger they felt for each other was enhanced as the cool night breeze kissed their bodies. Aisha eased back, and without saying a word, turned the key to unlock the door. Jackson picked up the grocery bag; his other hand gathered around her waist. The two of them walked inside the apartment and closed the door. On the other side they opened the door to a new beginning.

# Epilogue

Tameria walked proudly across the stage of UT Medical Center Auditorium. She felt like a kid in a candy store. It was hard for her to contain her excitement. When she exited on the other side, she spotted Chase standing in the corner near the stage exit. He walked over to her and grabbed her around her full figured waist and nibbled on her neck. "I'm proud of you, girl," he said between nibbles.

"Chase, I made it. And baby," she said, turning around to face him. "I couldn't have done it without you. You've been my rock, the one who believed in me and I love you so much," she said and kissed him on his lips.

Tameria, along with her friends and family, gathered at the dance studio after the commencement exercise. Aisha and Angie had everything decorated. The menu included fresh salads, fruits, baked chicken, salmon and fresh turkey cutlets. There were green beans, turnip greens, fresh corn, broccoli and several deliciously tantalizing desserts.

"Tell me. How does it feel, Dr. Tameria Matthews?" Jackson remarked teasingly.

"Yeah, how *does* it feel?" Angie interjected as she joined the group. "You're a doctor! Wow!"

"Speech, speech, speech! Some of the guests chanted.

Tameria stood up and looked around at the long table of family and friends. At that moment she felt such a tremendous thrill at how much God had blessed her life. Chase eased his hand on top of hers. She looked down at him and smiled, then began to speak.

"I can't begin to put my feelings into words. I'm absolutely in shock," Tameria stated. "I've made it over the first hurdle and I'm looking forward to the next one. And with the support of my loving parents, Chase and his loving parents, all of you, and of course the help of God, I know I'm going to be just fine. I am happier than I ever have been. It's good to know that I have your love and your blessings. Your prayers have sustained me these past years and they will continue to sustain me as I move forward into my residency. I love you all." Tameria walked over to her parents and gave each of them a hug of thanks.

"I say we should drink to that," Angie suggested. "Wait right here. Come on, sweetie," she ordered her husband. Seconds later the two of them returned with a tray of wine glasses filled with sparkling grape juice and passed them around to everyone. Angie lifted her glass in the air. "Aisha, on second thought, why don't you do the toast?

"Of course, I'd be happy to." Aisha stood up and held up her glass. "Today marks a new beginning in the life of my dearest and best friend, Dr. Tameria Shante' Matthews. We've seen some good times and some not so good times. There have been some ups and there have been some downs. But through it all we've persevered. God has watched over you and he has placed his angels charge over you. I'm thankful for your friendship and for your love. So, Tameria, may God's blessings continue to abound in your life. May you forever be happy and may your career be all that you have hoped and dreamed. Cheers," she said and smiled, then turned up her sparkling beverage and drank.

Aisha took her place front and center behind the glass podium. The time had come for her to stand up and allow God to use her in the way He saw fit. She couldn't believe that she wasn't nervous at all. Looking out into the auditorium, Aisha watched as hundreds of youth from area churches filed inside the building for the closing ceremony of Faithside Annual Youth Conference. When Jackson first asked her to share her life's testimony with them, Aisha quickly accepted. If it meant that through sharing her testimony she could possibly help to change one child's life for the better, then she was gung-ho for it.

Jackson had asked her two days ago if she had finished writing her speech but Aisha told him that she didn't have a speech prepared. She was going to speak from her heart.

She faced the diverse group of youth and cleared her throat before she began.

"All of my life, I've had a passion for dancing. My father often told me stories about when I was a toddler, how I would go through the house pretending I was a ballerina. As soon as I was old enough, my parents fed my passion and enrolled me in dance and ballet. I blossomed like a flower. Each waking moment I thought about dancing. There was nothing I wouldn't do if it would afford me the opportunity to fulfill my life long dream." Aisha shifted her weight to one side and continued to speak. "Shortly before my grandparents died, I graduated from college. Their generosity is what enabled me to start my own dance studio called *A. Carlisle Studio of Dance and Choreography*. It was a great blessing in my life because I was doing something I loved. That was a feat in and of itself because so many people leave this earth without ever fulfilling their dreams, goals and aspirations."

The room full of youth sat in the auditorium as if they were hypnotized. The impact of her words was powerful.

"Even though I was able to pass on my love of dance and choreography to young ladies, I still had a business to run. That meant that I had to have financial resources that would keep the studio open.

"Well, unfortunately things changed. I found myself sinking. I didn't know it at the time, but what happened was I began to put dance before God. When I was confronted with some financial difficulties, instead of turning to God for answers and guidance, I looked within. I thought I could handle my problems on my own. I thought I could make my own decisions. But boy was I wrong. I grew desperate. All I could see was if I didn't come up with some money fast, I might lose the studio. I started doing something I never ever imagined I would be doing. I started dancing for money."

Some of the kids gasped, but Aisha continued.

"I was making lots of money, but what I was doing was wrong. I justified what I was doing by telling myself that I wasn't like other women who danced for money. After all, I was a Christian. So I told myself, or rather I allowed the enemy to corrupt my thinking, that what I was doing couldn't be all that bad. I only planned on doing it until I could save up enough money to keep my studio. All along, I was fooling *me*," Aisha said and pointed at herself.

"I took another step in the wrong direction and I became involved with drugs. Taking my clothes off in front of men wasn't easy, so I listened to someone who told me that a bit of Valium would help me to relax. Then I graduated to cocaine. I was on a downward spiral going nowhere fast," Aisha told the room full of spellbound youth.

"It's so important for you to be your own person. Don't let anyone pressure you into doing what you know is not right. Listen to God and those people who will tell you the truth. I learned that the hard way. Anyway, it didn't take long for me to become addicted to the drugs and the money I was making."

The eyes of the teenagers were focused in on every word Aisha spoke.

"It doesn't take long for the enemy to steal what's yours. He knows your weakest point. He tempts us by making what is evil look good. He transforms our selfish desires and our greed into the things we crave in this life like money, material possessions, and he uses those very things to draw us in. For a season, or I should say, for a little while, wrong can seem right and it can feel good and taste good and look good, but in the end, it has to reveal what it really is. I gave it my own definition. I call it, *Sinsatiable*.

"You will be confronted with choices to make as long as you are living. Some will start out looking good and sounding good but ultimately will lead down a path of destruction. Try not to choose that road. In everything, seek God. Ask Him to close the doors that you shouldn't go through and open the doors that you should. But even if you do happen to find yourself in trouble, and you don't think there is a way out, let me remind you that there is. There is always a way out if you trust in God. There is hope for each of you. Don't cling to the mistakes of your past. Don't allow negativity and trouble to hinder and destroy what your divine purpose is in life. The best advice I can give you is to make Jesus the Lord of your life. Keep Him first because no matter what you do or where you go in life, He will forever be by your side if you'll only receive Him into your heart. Then like me, when you don't know where to turn and it feels like the weight of the whole world rests upon your shoulders, He'll be there to uphold you and keep you safe."

Aisha took a deep breath. Fighting back tears, she continued. "Since I came to that realization, my life is much different. I have released the feeling of guilt over past mistakes. Whatever I did yesterday is done and I can't change it. But what I can do is live this day to the best of the ability God has given me. As I prepare to take my seat, I want to tell you that God has restored what Satan stole. I now have two locations for *A. Carlisle Studio of Dance and Choreography*, one of which is located at this very church. I've also been blessed to love and be loved by a wonderful man, Minister Jackson Williams, *and* we're engaged." Aisha laughed and held up her ring finger, displaying a diamond engagement ring. The auditorium full of youth snickered.

"Today, I'm encouraging you to forget what lies behind and look forward to what lies ahead. When I graduated from college my late grandparents gave me this locket." Aisha pulled the locket out from underneath her meloncolored blouse. "The inscription on this locket is Jeremiah 29:11. It is something that I truly believe with all of my heart. 'For I know the plans I have for you,' declares the Lord, 'plans to prosper you and not to harm you, plans to give you hope and a future.'"

Aisha paused, scanned the auditorium, then rested her eyes on Jackson. Her heart flooded with pride and thanksgiving. Her life was now changed. Through the adversities, trials and troubles she experienced, her relationship with God was made stronger. In spite of everything Aisha had done, God forgave her. She gained far more than she lost because she turned her life back over to Him, the only one who could save it. The lesson learned was that God's unconditional love, acceptance and forgiveness was hers for the asking. And because of that she knew that she wouldn't trade her journey for anything.

# Reader's Group Guide

1. In what ways, if any, does Aisha's upbringing affect her as an adult?

2. What kind of influence, if any, does Aisha's father have in her life? Is it positive or negative? Explain.

3. What kind of influence, if any, does Aisha's mother have in her life? Is it positive or negative? Explain.

4. What should Aisha do when Thaddeus tells her about the owner's decision to sell?

5. How can an upright Christian girl like Aisha be persuaded to do the things she did so easily?

6. Do you know any Christians (*including yourself*) who lead double lives? If they do, what is your opinion about their spiritual commitment and beliefs?

7. Are there Aishas in the church today? Why or why not?

8. How can Aisha attend church and Bible study regularly but then go and do the things she did?

9. Will Aisha's relationship with her mother ever change? If yes, why? If no, why not?

10. What is your overall opinion of Aisha's personality?

11. Why does Sandra Carlisle act the way she does with her daughter?

12. Should Aisha have stayed at the hospital with her father? Why or why not?

13. What makes people like Chandler do the things they do when a situation does not turn out they way they expect?

14. Why does Aisha wait to confide in Tameria about what Chandler has done to her?

15. What do you believe contributes to Chandler's odd personality?

16. How can Chandler behave one way with Hallie but entirely differently with Tracye and Aisha?

17. Do you believe God uses evil and/or illegal resources to help Christians? Why? Why not? If you say that God does, give examples or situations that you know about.

18. Does Minister Williams behave correctly when he sees Aisha and Chandler together? Explain.

19. What is your opinion of Minister Williams' personality?

20. What makes Aisha believe Chandler at the restaurant?

21. What is your opinion of Tameria and her relationship with Chase?

22. How does Elisa view God?

23. Was Elisa sincere about helping to make things better for Aisha? Explain.

24. Is/was Elisa a friend to Aisha? Why or why not?

25. Do you believe Elisa will make good use of her second chance? Why or why not?

26. Do you believe Elisa is doing the same thing she was doing in Memphis?

27. Do you believe Pastor Donald Shipley was aware of what his brother was doing? If so, why didn't he turn him in? If not, what makes you believe he didn't know?

28. Do you believe there are establishments similar to The Lynx operating in today's society? Why or why not?

29. How do you rate this book?

30. Should there be a sequel to *Sinsatiable*? If so, which characters should be included and why? Which ones shouldn't be included and why?

# A Personal Invitation from the Author

If you have ever made a decision to accept Jesus Christ as your personal Lord and Savior, God himself extends this invitation to you.

If you have trusted him and believed him to be the giver of eternal life, you can do so right now. We do not know the second, the minute, the hour, the moment or day that God will come to claim us. Will you be ready?

The Word of God says,
*"If you confess with your mouth, Jesus is Lord, and believe in your heart that God raised Jesus from the dead, you will be saved. For it is with your heart that you believe and are justified, and it is with your mouth that you confess and are SAVED." (Romans 10:9-10 NIV)*

To arrange signings, book events, speaking engagements, or to send your comments to the author please contact her at:
Shelia E. Lipsey
www.shelialipsey.com
shelialipsey@yahoo.com
www.myspace.com/shelialipsey